THE NIGHTINGALE WON'T LET YOU SLEEP

BY THE SAME AUTHOR

FICTION

Flight Paths of the Emperor
On earth as it is
The Shadow Boxer
Afterlands
Every Lost Country
The Dead Are More Visible

POETRY

Stalin's Carnival
Foreign Ghosts
The Ecstasy of Skeptics
The Address Book
Patient Frame
The Waking Comes Late

NON-FICTION

The Admen Move on Lhasa
Workbook: memos & dispatches on writing

ANTHOLOGIES

A Discord of Flags: Canadian Poets Write about the Gulf War (1991: with Peter Ormshaw & Michael Redhill)
Musings: An Anthology of Greek-Canadian Literature (2004: with main editor Tess Fragoulis, & Helen Tsiriotakis)

CHAPBOOKS/LETTERPRESS

Paper Lanterns: 25 Postcards from Asia
The Stages of J. Gordon Whitehead

STEVEN HEIGHTON

THE NIGHTINGALE WON'T LET YOU SLEEP

HAMISH HAMILTON

an imprint of Penguin Canada, a division of Penguin Random House Canada Limited

Canada • USA • UK • Ireland • Australia • New Zealand • India • South Africa • China

First published 2017

Pages 6–17, "An Occurrence on the Beach at Varosha,"
appeared in *The Walrus*, January/February 2017.

www.penguinrandomhouse.ca

LIBRARY AND ARCHIVES CANADA CATALOGUING IN PUBLICATION

Heighton, Steven
The nightingale won't let you sleep / Steven Heighton.

ISBN 978-0-7352-3256-3 (paperback)
ISBN 978-0-7352-3257-0 (electronic)

I. Title.

PS8565.E451N54 2017 C813'.54 C2016-904745-8

Cover and interior design by CS Richardson
Cover photo: iStock.com/momcilog

Printed and bound in the United States of America

10 9 8 7 6 5 4 3 2

THIS BOOK IS FOR
SKELETON PARK AND THOSE WHO LIVE HERE:
GRATITUDE FOR INSPIRATION

To leave one's Childhood is to learn to disobey. But that is not Adulthood. Adulthood is to learn again to obey, only something better.

—ROLAND KRÜGER,
"THE POLARIS: ONE VERSION OF A JOURNEY"
(UNFINISHED MANUSCRIPT, CA. 1884)

In July 1974 the Republic of Cyprus—a fragile federation comprising an ethnically Greek majority and Turkish minority—disintegrated in the wake of a CIA-sponsored coup that aimed to bring about *Enosis*, the union of Greece and Cyprus. The ensuing violence provided Turkey with a pretext to invade Cyprus in support of the Turkish Cypriots. By summer's end the United Nations had brokered a truce and established a demilitarized zone. Population exchanges followed, with Turkish Cypriots moving into the northern third of the island—soon to become a puppet state recognized only by Turkey—and Greek Cypriots into the southern part.

On both sides of the Green Line, homes, businesses, even a few small villages were left empty. But on Cyprus's east coast an entire city was abandoned, the Turkish army having pushed south of the initial ceasefire line to seize the island's best beach, seven kilometres long, and the thriving resort quarter beside it, Varosha, whose twenty thousand inhabitants had fled the first Turkish bombs.

Over forty years later, the city remains fenced off, a derelict enclave of eroding structures overgrown with vines, bougainvillea, scrubby palm trees and acacia, teeming with rabbits, rats, snakes and partridges, and reputedly containing at least one car dealership where 1974 Fiats are still on show. Turkish troops continue to patrol the decaying perimeter fence and occasionally they, and the odd U.N. patrol, will enter the "dead zone" and inspect the outer parts.

Neither the U.N. nor Turkish authorities lend any credence to rumours that somewhere in the heart of the ruins a small community has survived for years: refugees, fugitives, deserters, various outcasts and misfits.

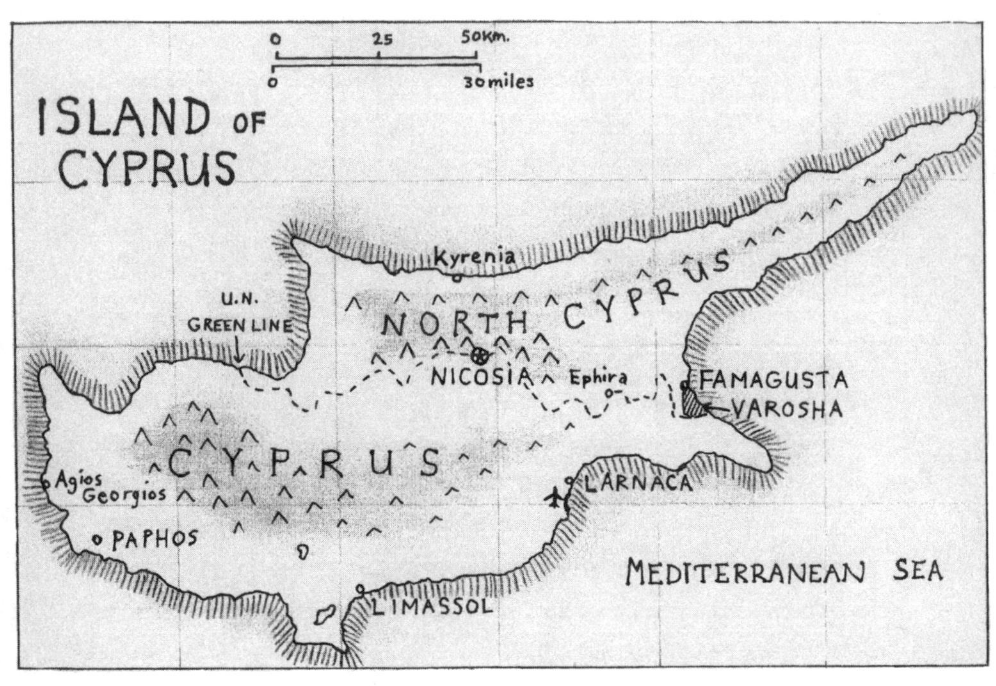
0
25
50Km.
0
30miles
ISLAND OF CYPRUS
Kyrenia
U.N. GREEN LINE
NORTH CYPRUS
NICOSIA
Ephira
FAMAGUSTA
VAROSHA
CYPRUS
Agios Georgios
PAPHOS
LARNACA
LIMASSOL
MEDITERRANEAN SEA

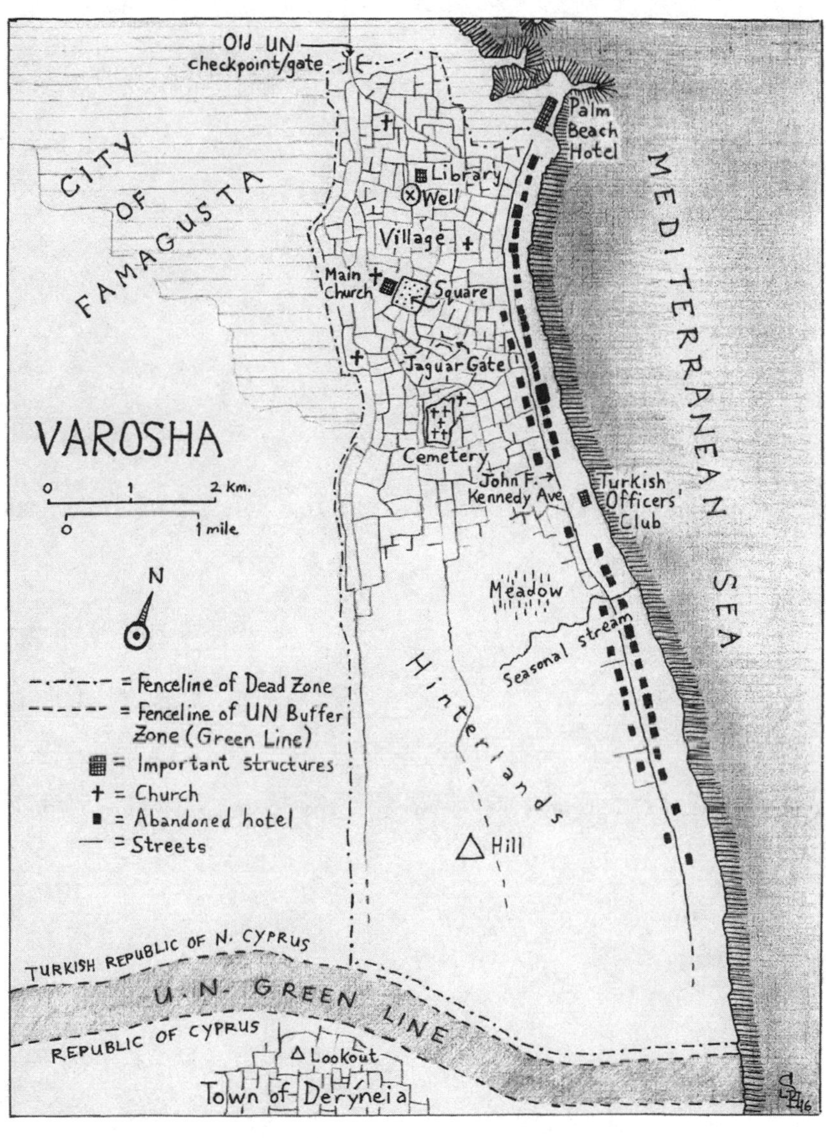
Old UN checkpoint/gate
Palm Beach Hotel
CITY OF FAMAGUSTA
Library
Well
Village
Main Church
Square
Jaguar Gate
Cemetery
John F. Kennedy Ave
Turkish Officers' Club
MEDITERRANEAN SEA
VAROSHA
0 1 2 Km.
0 1 mile
N
Meadow
Seasonal stream
Hinterlands
Hill
-·-·-·- = Fenceline of Dead Zone
- - - - - = Fenceline of UN Buffer Zone (Green Line)
= Important structures
+ = Church
■ = Abandoned hotel
— = Streets
TURKISH REPUBLIC OF N. CYPRUS
U.N. GREEN LINE
REPUBLIC OF CYPRUS
Lookout
Town of Deryneia

CONTENTS

ONE

The Dead Zone

When you have a neighbour, you have God.

—GREEK CYPRIOT PROVERB

PAPHOS, CYPRUS, 26 OCTOBER

"How long is it, then, since you have slept?" the doctor asked.

Elias looked up at the ceiling, trying to recall. The blades of the fan turned listlessly—in fact, they seemed to be slowing, as if the power had just cut out again.

"Surely you've slept a little since we last met?"

"It was yesterday, right?"

"Yesterday morning."

"Okay."

"About thirty hours ago," the doctor said.

"I've passed out a couple of times, for a while. I tried not to."

"So, you did not remain asleep? You had the dream again?"

"Yes."

"You wish to describe it again, or the incident itself?"

"They're almost the same. It's not really a dream. More like a video of an atrocity."

"As I said, this is typical of your condition—diagnostic, actually. However—"

"And, no, I don't."

"Pardon me?"

"Want to describe it again."

Drops of sweat glistened on the raw-looking scalp under the doctor's blond comb-over. Thick glasses magnified his colourless, pink-rimmed eyes, which blinked often. "Avoiding sleep, however," he said. "It's understandable, but I fear that such a—such a practice can only make the matter worse."

"I've never needed much sleep."

"Men of your kind often boast of how little sleep they need."

"You're not meant to mock your patients, are you?"

"You do look tired," the doctor said, as if he hadn't heard, "though in fact you seem somewhat improved today. Still, I apologize—"

"Frankly, I don't feel that bad, I feel relieved, because I'm awake now, not asleep and reliving things. Insomnia is a fucking joy in comparison to that."

"Self-inflicted sleep deprivation—not insomnia."

"What did you mean by men of my kind?"

"Why do you ask?"

"Because I have no idea myself anymore."

"Large men, robust. Metamorphic. Pardon me, *meso*morphic."

Elias Trifannis looked out the window over the doctor's shoulder: a white pebble beach, the calm Mediterranean pixelated with sunlight. The army was using this former student residence on the west coast of Cyprus to treat personnel on stress leave from the war. Last night, while Elias silently performed yet another set of push-ups on the cold cement floor of his room, trying to hold off sleep, the patient in the next room screamed catastrophically. That was helpful: a few extra hours of adrenalized alertness.

"It's funny how people think they can look at your body and know your soul," Elias said.

That magnified blinking again. In a faster, fainter voice the doctor said, "*Ah, mais oui*, you are quite right, one should never assume a correlation between, between . . . how could I put it . . ."

Elias yawned helplessly, gapingly, a pathological yawn that convulsed his whole body. "Sorry, Dr. Boudreau," he said at last. "I really do enjoy talking to you."

"Perhaps you will be able to sleep better on your weekend away? I hope so. You are going across the island, to visit family?"

"Distant relatives."

"How is your Greek now?"

"*Etsi ki etsi*. If you don't mind my saying, you look really tired yourself."

"Yes." The doctor's blinking made it seem he was trying to communicate something in a sort of binary code, words he couldn't bring himself to say. "It's not simply this heat wave. Normally, one grows used to working with the—the traumatized, yet I seem to find it increasingly . . . But what am I saying? I must not say such things!"

The fan still gave the illusion of perpetually slowing without ever stopping.

"In any case, Master Corporal—I wish you a peaceful weekend."

"Don't call me that, okay?"

"And, please, don't speak of what happened in Kandahar."

"I wouldn't know how to speak about it."

"And bear in mind, it was not your fault! Not anyone's fault!" The doctor subdued his twitching by closing his eyes for a second, then opening them wide. "It was simply . . ."

"An accident. I know."

"And don't forget your medication."

"No way. I love my medication."

Dizzy, seeing double, Elias tried to focus his gaze. Out the window in the distance a sunburned figure in a swimsuit—who seemed impossibly to be the doctor—appeared on the shore and walked into the sea.

AN OCCURRENCE ON THE BEACH AT VAROSHA

The evening's last light has drained out of the sky behind the procession of dead hotels lining the beach. Up to fifteen storeys high, they were built so close together that now, their facades darkening, they merge into a single jagged silhouette, like the remains of an immense seawall or ancient coastal fortification. You can barely make out the rusted fence topped with barbed wire that separates the beach from the hotels and the ghost city behind them.

In his current state, Elias can't begin to imagine the optimism and entrepreneurial hustle it must have taken to plan, rapidly construct, and operate this riviera. Somehow people go on doing such things—building cities, waging wars, growing and cutting down forests, organizing international movements, training as bodybuilders or concert violinists. He can only look on in wonder at such committed vim, like the paralyzed casualty of a roadside bombing watching a frantic sprint relay race on television.

The hoteliers' optimism turned out to be misplaced. Elias's aunt and uncle—now living not far from here, in Larnaca, on the Greek Cypriot side of the Green Line—were among the first to build and, they insist, among the last to flee. Their hotel was a small one, just three storeys and twenty-four rooms, the Aphrodite, at least half an hour's walk south of here along the beach. Elias had meant to head down there before sunset, after swallowing his meds and the usual quantity of contraindicated drinks. But in the bar of the Palm Beach—the lone working hotel on the strip, reopened in the late nineties under Turkish management—he met a woman, and now they're walking into the dark along the seafront in the still-warm sand. The lights of the Palm Beach fade behind them. Their fingers brush and link and now their hands clinch and hold firm.

Last night in Larnaca his aunt and uncle asked him to report back on the condition of their hotel. As the holder of a foreign passport, Elias can cross the Green Line without trouble, drive the short distance to the dead city and walk the perimeter, including the palm-lined beach, which is open, though seemingly unused. From the beach side of the fence he meant to grab a few prohibited shots of the Aphrodite with the cellphone now hibernating in his shirt pocket. Technically, his aunt and uncle too can now cross the Green Line, but as exiled Varoshiotes they refuse on principle to go anywhere near the city, not until it is returned to them. They know about the bigger hotels' hopelessly degraded state—in the Greek Cypriot media they have seen furtively snapped photographs in which the beachfront looks as if it just sustained a shelling by Turkish warships—but they still dare to hope that the Aphrodite has fared better. Built with comparative care before the full construction frenzy began, it might still be salvaged, they feel, if peace should ever come to the island, if Varosha, God willing, should ever revert to the Greeks.

His aunt and uncle (they're actually distant cousins but referred to as *theia* and *theios* in the Greek manner) are in their late seventies. Their unshakable hope—at their age, and almost four decades after a violent dispossession that impoverished them for years—strikes him as another example of an optimism he can no longer imagine. He feels as gutted as any of these ruined establishments.

His silences distressed *theia* and *theios*, who did their utmost to distract him with wine, the bittersweet local liqueurs, and *theia*'s ardently oversalted cuisine. Though Elias ate and drank in a dazed, almost catatonic way, he did in fact eat and drink a great deal, which visibly reassured his relatives, as did his promise to check on their property before returning to Paphos on the far side of the island. He called the hospital in Paphos a training centre and said nothing about the military shrinks. He ducked or deflected their questions about the war, sometimes falling back on his rusty Greek to pretend he didn't understand. He assured them he was simply tired—tired in a way he could never have imagined before the army—and this much, at least, was no lie.

The beach is deserted. Neither he nor the woman says a thing, but with the synchronized instinct of two strangers gripped by the same desire they stop and sit down in the fine-grained sand. Tropically tepid shallows lap the beach twenty steps from their feet. She lights a Turkish cigarette. Above the fenceline behind them the ghosts of Varosha—the elite of Europe, playboys and divas, film stars, professional gamblers, trust-fund rogues, crime bosses and heads of state—lounge on their high hotel balconies (the balconies have all collapsed), sipping Campari and soda or whisky sours and watching the constellations fizz up out of the sea like bubbles from sparkling wine.

"Do you recall how you pronounce my name?"

"Eylull?"

"Ey-lool. Over the *u* there is an umlaut."

"Eylül."

"Well done."

"It means December," he says with confidence.

"Already you've forgot—Eylül is September."

"It was loud in there."

"It was *deafening*."

"You were born in September, then?"

"I hope you're not going to ask me how old I am."

He chuckles, a sound lately unfamiliar to him. "You should call me Trif. It's from Trifannis."

"Your family name?"

He nods, not saying that it's pretty much all that remains of his family.

She is a journalist from Istanbul, tall, aristocratically slim, with modish red-framed glasses behind which her dark eyes sometimes flash with startling vehemence—that hair-trigger moodiness he now associates with this part of the world. He likes and somewhat envies the undisguised intelligence of her talk; he himself is in flight from thinking and has been since boyhood. Her bobbed hair is dyed blonde, setting off tanned olive skin and black, solid eyebrows. When she speaks—enunciating with a finishing-school English accent—her hand gestures are lively yet measured. He guesses she's in her mid-thirties, a few years older than he is.

In the bar a small clutch of soldiers and two older Turkish Cypriots monitored them, initially with the frank curiosity of regulars and then—as things progressed, she punctuating a remark with a tap on his wrist; slipping off her glasses; turning off her cellphone—conspicuous disapproval. The place was almost empty, the dance floor a desert. Visibly bored, the young DJ kept turning up the music. He was skinny, had a soul patch and, like the waiter and bartender, wore an oversized fez, which he was trying to hipsterize by tilting at a lazy angle. The bass line's concussive thumping . . . Elias knew it would trigger flashback panic in most of his fellow patients, but lately he welcomed any noise that helped offset his tranquilizers enough to hold off sleep and dreams.

As he and Eylül struggled to speak over the Turkish hip hop, their lips came within inches of each other's ears. Her ear was small, sunburned, surprisingly unpierced. Like her cheek, it gave off heat. The bar was emptying except for the watching men. He felt sure they had decided, more or less correctly, that he was Greek by blood. They would be using that ancient faculty of minute discernment found in any region where ethnic groups collide, where the borders are disputed, where the grievances have grown roots. (Elias knows of that ability but doesn't share it; he thought the glaring men looked pretty much like him.) Certainly they knew she was Turkish—she was ordering the drinks in Turkish—but probably they could deduce a lot more: that she was from Istanbul, educated, modern, a secular sophisticate.

She told Elias she didn't give a toss for such men. At any rate, these soldiers ought not to *be* in Cyprus. The island should reunify and the Greek and Turkish Cypriots share power. She was writing a major article—she smiled, finger-quoting "major," an irony that seemed at odds with the fervent way she was talking about her work—and was impatient to finish her research in this angry, backward outpost and fly back to Istanbul.

A month ago Elias would have been sweatingly conscious of the men, his whole being limbering up for some inevitable friction. Now it seems he can't even acknowledge the possibility of conflict. Conflict exists only in the flow of time, and Elias—sedated and drunk since they flew him into Cyprus two weeks ago—has come to inhabit a blurred, dreamy present, night and day.

She glanced back over her shoulder as they left the bar.

Now, as he takes a drag on one of her cigarettes (there's no sort of drug he would decline right now), she asks, "What would your Larnaca relatives think of you—your fraternizing with a Turkish?"

His ears still throb from the hip hop. The ringing seems to amplify the unearthly silence welling from the dead zone behind where they're sitting.

"I know what my aunt's mother would say. She's almost a hundred. She's got what we call Greek Alzheimer's. You forget everything but the grudges."

"If only," she says, "that were only Greek."

"Anyway, I'm Canadian. And my father was born in New York. My mother was half-Mexican, which means part Spanish, part Indian. My stepmother is Pakistani. I don't even speak Greek properly."

"Canadian men are very polite."

He feels his mouth stretch, as if in a smile. "More so when we're at home, I think. With neighbours around, and cops."

"If only that were only Canadian."

He nods.

"You've been a perfect gentleman," she says, as though to reassure him. "But I know something upsets you."

"Tonight?"

"No. Before."

Taurus is rearing star by star out of the sea. He cranes his head way back. The firmament whirls. Usually it's on standing up that you notice how drunk you are, but now it hits him: he's deeply, comprehensively drunk. All right. He wants to be nowhere now but in his floating body. He wants to do nothing anymore but tender, gentle things, except for those moments when he wants to do nothing but savage things—to lunge and slash at the face of an attacker, an accuser, in a heart-stalling dream.

"At what point can I start being less of a gentleman?"

She pulls her hand free of his and while lifting her bare knees reaches her hands down, slips off her black flats and sets them beside her in the sand—almost the same devastating sequence of motions she might use to peel off underwear. She takes his hand again. His whole arm hums, from the marrow out.

"Now," she says, and her face turns up toward his. Her breath has the pleasant tartness of white wine, the faint scorch of Scotch and tobacco. In her perfume a lemony sweetness, like the scent of water lilies in summer lakes. You would tread water to smell them, or lean over a canoe's cedar gunwale. God, another life! Her lips open for the kiss but she withholds her tongue and for him that absence brings on a sort of vertigo, as if he's tumbling forward into an abyss when he expected solidity, resistance.

A breeze flows up the beach and cools his damp face as the kiss deepens.

Sometime later, he asks if he is too heavy, the sand too hard.

"You could be heavier," she says. "It's very good."

"You mean, heavier would be—"

"Hush."

"I don't want to hurt you."

She laughs. "Like this? So gentle?"

His torpor and sedation do slow him down—he's not very hard, either—so he and Eylül seem to float on and on in a languid, suspended, narcotic rhythm. "Hush," she says again, "it's good." Beneath him she keeps her eyes shut tight, as if striving to remember some crucial thing. She's far quieter than he would have expected. He grates his hips side to side as well as thrusting, very slowly. On and on in this stoned reverie until some impulse makes him speed up, push into her with a new urgency, and finally she tenses and sinks him deeper in, her hands clutching his hips, her sharp-boned ankles and calves gritty with sand. A quiet, mild crescendo of sighs. She lifts her face to his and now he tastes her thrusting tongue.

Her spasms, which he can feel, tip him over at last. His climax is muted and yet oddly prolonged, and when finally it starts to subside, along with his wounded moaning and panting, he's conscious of a faint, dispersed rustling in the sand. He looks up and around. In their density the stars, like bioluminescence in a calm sea, give actual light. Everything wheels around him: somehow the beach is moving, landsliding slowly past them toward the waterline, or else he and Eylül are gliding *up* the beach toward the chain-link fence, the barbed wire and the ruins. It's his head spinning with drink, he guesses—then realizes that hundreds of small creatures, solidly covering the beach to his left, are crawling past. He squints, recoils: tarantulas scuttling seaward like a mass of tiny battle tanks. His eyes adjust. They're sea-turtle hatchlings, the starlight dim on their camouflage-pattern shells, scrabbling flippers, bobbing heads, a mob of them spilling out of the darkness up by the fence. Somehow their arrival triggers in him a surge of tenderness toward Eylül. His throat aches. For some moments he watches them. Again her face looms up. She bites him on his turned cheek. He says, "Look," but she is already looking.

"Goodness!"—he has never heard a woman of her age say this word—"they frightened me."

"Must have just hatched," he says.

"Of course they have."

As he closes her eyes with a kiss, she whispers, "*Arkadash.*"

"What does that mean?"

Faint splashes of light appear among the turtles—some dozen last stragglers with impassive, prehistoric little faces, flippers spastically rowing in the sand. The light shifts. Elias stares stupidly. Heat lightning? He looks over his right shoulder, northward up the beach. A flashlight, sweeping from side to side, is bearing down on them.

"Eylül?"

"I see it. Get off me."

"We'd better—"

She hisses something in Turkish, yet he seems to hear the word in clear English, *Hurry.* Hurrying seems beyond him, but his body, a step ahead, lifts and pulls out of her, the uncoupling even more of a shock than usual. She's muttering in Turkish, sitting up, scrambling in a darkness now strobed by the approaching flashlight. She seems to be crossing herself—a Christian?—then he sees: she's pulling closed and buttoning the lime silk blouse she never fully removed. He is on his feet, hiking up his black jeans, buckling his belt, looking for his shoes, remembering he tossed them under a lamppost hours ago in the sand outside the bar. She stands and slips something into her handbag, smoothes down her skirt. From up the beach a squabble of voices conferring, then a hoarse voice projecting—words cutting out of the dark toward them like shrapnel. The light beam freezes her, blanching her face—her mouth a tight, stricken line—though now, with what seems an almost casual calmness, she fits her stylish glasses back on.

"Should we run?" he asks, and the light swings toward him.

"Don't move. Let me answer them."

The flashlight stops about ten paces away and he senses more than sees the figures bunching up behind it. Four, maybe five. There's something haphazard, unofficial about the party: their lone flashlight, disordered voices, the way they've faltered and stopped short of the couple, who now stand a few metres apart, like two strangers out walking the beach who've been surprised in accidental proximity. The men behind the flashlight are drunk, he hears it in their voices. "It's the guys from the bar," he says, but she's speaking over him, addressing the men in a thin tremolo that sounds scornful, indignant, and scared. A beat of silence, then the men jabber back. Along the edge of the flashlight beam an arm extends, pointing at Elias. He doesn't know whether to move toward Eylül or away from her.

The Cyclopean eye of the flashlight focuses on her but keeps flitting over to Elias's face, as if the men think he means to bolt. He would love to bolt. Despite his sedation he could run full out, he thinks, the blood sluicing inside him, his heart punching up against his palate. These men—off-duty, some of them maybe not even soldiers—might be unarmed. Likely unarmed. He's about to tell Eylül that he and she can run from this posse of drunkards when one of them shouts something and Eylül flinches as if struck—and this flinch, this tiny retreat, is decisive. The men smell blood. The light surges forward, the dim figures bunched behind it. Numbly, Elias steps sideways toward her into the circle of light, trying to make himself look big. He's bigger than these yammering silhouettes. *You are a big guy.* He coaches himself bigger, the way he used to before rugby scrums, nothing serious at stake. A hand shoves the flashlight under their noses and Elias raises a hand to parry it, blocking out the beam. Unblinded momentarily, he makes out four men—three clustered close around the flashlight bearer, who grips a pistol in his other hand, holding it beside his cheek, aiming the barrel straight upward. The men's fatigues show a camouflage motif. Their faces, except for the flashlight man's, look young.

Retreating from them while also moving away from him, Eylül says something that sounds urgently appeasing. Her hands fan open in front of her. A man advances into the circle of light and then clumsily springs forward. Elias sees it in stop-start, a sequence of vivid stills—Eylül stepping back, the man extending his arms and hands toward her like a sleepwalker. "Stop!" Elias orders, the word plosive and louder than any utterance so far, but no one turns toward him. He has become inaudible, invisible; they have forgotten him; he could still escape.

She flails her handbag and it thuds into the side of the first man's head. Two of the men join the attack while the one with the pistol aims the light. Elias grabs the arm holding the flashlight and pushes it up, sending the beam skyward. The man swings the pistol but Elias intercepts the blow and thrusts that hand upward too, then slips his calf behind the man's leg and with his whole body, much larger than the Turk's, topples him backward and pins him. The man keeps the small pistol in his grip but the flashlight falls loose, so now the scene is dimly underlit by the red glow of a lens half-buried in sand. Eylül is down on the beach a few steps away, struggling. For the second time tonight Elias lies on top of a stranger, this one smaller than Eylül but wiry, furiously strong, silent as though holding his breath while he fights.

A flash and sharp popping as the gun in the soldier's pinned hand fires. Butting the man in the face conclusively, Elias lifts and smashes down the hand and the pistol flips loose into the dark. He can't see it. He reels to his feet and moves toward the struggle a few metres off, all in the embering glow of the half-buried flashlight, and brushes past a man hurrying in the other direction—to help the officer Elias just took down? He and this man could be commuters almost colliding on a sidewalk. He drags one soldier off Eylül, she lashing and scratching at the other, who now turns his head up toward Elias, the face a blur in the faint light. Elias shoves the heel of his palm into the face. He reaches down to Eylül but she's already up. She takes his hand and they're running, a slow-motion scramble, feet sinking in, no traction. Every few strides a cry is wrung out of her, as if his body is on top of hers again and pushing down hard and fast.

Suddenly their shadows appear, stretched thin, flailing ahead of them up the beach. "The fence," he says, and they're angling toward it. The light reveals a helix of barbed wire on top of the fence, rusted, sagging. A shot follows the light beam and the sound ricochets off the facades of the hotels.

Somehow he has been transported back to where he was two weeks ago, a place he thought he'd escaped, at least physically. More gunfire. He looks for a breach, wills a breach in the wire or the fence below it. Despite or because of intoxication, the shooter is squeezing off shots with robotic regularity, five, ten. Eylül slows for a moment, seeming to miss a step as if skipping, then runs on beside Elias. No more shots. A small opening appears where the bottom of the fence warps upward, clear of the sand. "Here. Get down." They kneel and he reaches to push her flat but she's already there. He heaves up on the rusted fence, widening the gap. "Go through. Crawl through." In the wavering light, the flashlight juddering toward them, she lies on her front, her face twisted sideways in the sand, looking up at him. "Eylül," he says.

Her glasses are gone, her eyes unblinking. A stain opens at the small of her back. He presses his palm into the side of her neck, his fingers over the ear he spoke into, almost kissed, in the bar a few hours ago. He's not so much checking for a pulse—hauled back into hell, he's sure there will be none—as feeling the warmth of that sunburned ear and cheek. He sags onto his back beside her, as if giving up. Then, both hands pressing upward on the loose chain links, he wriggles through the gap into the dead zone.

BLACK BOX

Three men stand above the woman who lies in the sand by the fence in a circle of light. One of the three, groggy and teetering, leans on a subordinate, who has wrapped an arm around the hurt man's shoulder. In other circumstances this intimacy might seem a slight impertinence, less because of rank (the older man is only a sergeant) than because of the difference in age.

A third man holds both the flashlight and the sergeant's semi-automatic pistol. He was holding neither when he and the others came shambling up the beach, searching for the couple. He would prefer to be empty-handed still—he doesn't want to keep shining the light on the woman's body. He fired the full clip without thinking, partly because in any action film or television drama he has seen, that's what armed men do when people flee from them. He has never shot at anyone before. Firing haphazardly into the night seemed to him, in his drunken excitement, no more consequential an act than shooting off fireworks.

Of all the men, he was the one least angered by the couple in the bar.

While they discuss in loud whispers what to do with the

woman's body, a fourth man stands a short distance away at the waterline, the toes of his boots dimpling down into the wet sand. In either hand he grips a mobile phone. One of them he took from the handbag of the Turkish woman and the other was there on the beach near the handbag; it must have fallen out of the big foreigner's pocket when he attacked the sergeant.

It's this man's job to dispose of the phones.

In the course of their uneventful patrols along the perimeter of the dead zone, the soldiers often compete by trying to pitch stones through gaping second- or third-storey embrasures that were once windows. Small wagers are sometimes involved. This man has by far the best arm. He hauls back and overhands the Turkish woman's mobile out over the sea, toward a horizon softening with the glow of a late moon about to rise. Moments later there's a faint, almost secretive splash. The splash comes too early. The throw was poor. These shallows extend a good distance out, and though few if any people ever swim here . . . In his stupor the man pursues the thought no further, but he does hurl the foreigner's smaller, lighter phone with more follow-through and at a steeper angle. He listens for a splash. His head still thrums from the music in the bar and the gunshots and his own pulse, which clouts louder in his ears now.

As he transferred the phone to his throwing hand he accidentally turned it on, and as it sails through the dark and arcs downward toward the sea, data pings into it from a remote server: a lone voicemail sent several hours ago, while it was turned off. The rim of the phone slices the surface with hardly a splash, but it's enough to alarm the few last turtle hatchlings straggling nearby. The fish-silver thing plunges past them and then, a few feet down—as if noticing the turtles with predatory interest—it slows. The turtles veer in unison, swinging wide around the disturbance and paddling on.

Through thickening black the phone sinks, its angle of entry taking it just beyond the drop-off where the shallows fall away into deeper water. Its circuits go on functioning, like an aircraft's flight data recorder signalling on the drift down among fresh wreckage, though the phone is not watertight and will soon be dead.

Message one was received from 357 594 9744 on Saturday, October 27 at 7:22 P.M. "Corporal—Elias? This is Dr. Boudreau, in Paphos. I do hope you are enjoying yourself with your relations there, and that you—uh—if you would return my call tonight, or tomorrow? Preferably tonight. We do meet on Tuesday, but we must discuss something now. The inquiry into, uh—into the events of which you continue to dream?—I learn now it has been postponed, possibly cancelled, and I wished to advise you before you learn of it, in case it should make you wish to, uh, to speak out. Let me urge again, say nothing, especially now that you are on leave, perhaps relaxing, perhaps drinking. I do hope you can relax! But were you—were you to speak now, the authorities would do their best to discredit you and disgrace. I've spoken again to Colonel McKay. He vows that an inquiry, if it occurs, will be full and impartial and, uh, uh, while you and I might . . . I will explain further when you call. Please. It's unofficial. I should disconnect before the device cuts me off."

From the gap in the fence to the line of buildings was only a few dozen steps. He ran, crouching low, expecting more shots at every moment. Ahead, a solid wall of black. Then the swath of the flashlight beam swept over him and the ruin of a building loomed out of the dark. The beam swung away but at the last moment revealed a gap—an alley opening between the pocked facades of the highrise in front of him and the next one down. He made for the gap, guided by a dim glow seeping out of the mouth of the alley. Sand gave way to shattered concrete stabbing into his bare soles. He ducked into the opening. Starlight carpeted the floor of the alley.

The slap of his steps echoed up between the walls to where the stars trembled in a long strip of sky.

He emerged from the alley onto the remains of a broad avenue that ran parallel to the beach. Above the avenue and the line of lower buildings on the far side, the sky was uncannily brilliant, the Milky Way hemorrhaging light. Weeds and what seemed to be large cacti and small trees grew out of the sidewalk and the avenue. A few cars were parked or stranded along the curb.

He looked behind him, back up the alley. No sounds from the beach. He glanced both ways down the avenue as if about to brave a living street at rush hour, then ran across, dodging shrubs and a reef of prickly pear cacti colonizing a traffic island. On the far side he stopped and considered a side street that ran inland, west off the avenue. Beside a taxi collapsed on its wheel rims, a street-corner signpost tilted way over so that the nameplates were at face level. The name of the side street was illegible but the other, larger plate read JOHN F. KENNEDY AVENUE—a name he knew from the address of the Aphrodite on the discoloured brochures his aunt and uncle kept squared on their telephone table beside a heap of old Varosha phone books. So their hotel had to be a little farther down the strip. For a moment he thought of running in that direction, as if safety must lie in a property to which blood relations still held legal title.

Now he feels his shirt pocket for his cellphone: gone, as expected. At a trot he starts up the nameless side street, picking his way westward into the dead zone, farther from the soldiers. The street is canyoned by solid ranks of two-storey buildings. Here, too, weeds and bushes erupt from the broken pavement, yet in mid-street the going seems easier, less overgrown, like a deer trail in a scrubby field. He has heard that the patrolling Turks never push more than a block or two into the restricted zone, but this faint path is worrisome. Maybe they do go in. He's unsure how badly he hurt the older soldier. Hurting the man was sickening.

His adrenalin spike subsiding, he's reverting to what he was a few hours ago, a drunk, sedated man in a twilight stupor; an intentional insomniac. He was touching the woman just minutes ago, trying to haul her body under the fence, away from the nearing soldiers, yet she and the long evening they shared—her voice and breath in his ear at the bar, breeze cooling their sweat as the hatchlings scuttled past—seem utterly unreal.

Block by block Varosha too seems more unreal, if increasingly visible. The moon has risen behind him, over the sea, and though not yet clear of the beachfront towers, it lends an indirect glow. Where vines and creepers have not engulfed the signage he can read the names of businesses, in Greek, English, or both—a bakery, a steam laundry, a small nightclub, a café whose heavy tables still line the street although the chairs have vanished—and he can tell the makes of the occasional cars melting into the pavement. Some creature flits across his path, rustling through the weeds into an open doorway. He swallows his heart back down. Despite the heat, he's chilled, his shirt drenched. He keeps stopping, hearing footfalls doubling his own, even stumbling and halting when he does—the echo of his own steps, obviously. Yet the hairs on his nape keep hackling and he takes to turning around every half-block, walking backward a few steps, turning frontward again. On one of these pivots he trips over something and crashes, hip and hand first, to the pavement. He mutes his "Fuck off!" to a whisper, yet it seems to detonate back at him off the walls.

A humpback half-moon is lifting out of the roofline back there along the avenue and the beach. He stumps onward, a block deeper, then finds his route barred: two sedans, tires totally flat, form a barricade, their rear fenders almost flush with the walls on either side of the narrow street, while in mid-street their grilles face each other, leaving between them an opening just wide enough to squeeze through. The Mercedes-Benz and Jaguar hood ornaments are intact and still shiny. The effect is of a ritual threshold, though one of a crudely makeshift, post-apocalyptic kind.

This sign of an organizing presence deep in the dead zone—even if the presence must be long vanished—sharpens his sense of being watched. After a look around, he slips through the opening. Beyond it the street seems slightly clearer, as if more often used. A few steps farther and he peers to his left up an alley that connects to a parallel street. Framed in the far mouth of the alley, trotting up the parallel street as if shadowing him, a large, pale, wolflike dog. It glances down the alley toward him. He stops in his tracks, stares up the alley. Nothing.

Lucid dreams, all of it. You could be dying, you could be dead.

Varosha is only a few kilometres across—he must be near the centre, and in fact within a block or so his side street bends north and opens into a moonlit expanse, a wide plaza dominated by a high-domed church on the far side. Entering the plaza he looks left to where the parallel street also enters. No sign of the dog. You saw no dog. He walks on, glancing back and around. The plaza's heavy paving stones are mostly clear of growth—just hanks of weed and a few scrubby trees pushing up through the cracks—but the facades of the surrounding buildings have all but vanished under creepers and vines, so the plaza could be a basin or old quarry walled in by cliffs covered in foliage, just a few slashes of white showing through. In mid-plaza, a raised bed in which a huge shade tree grows, its dense leafage reaching far out over the pavestones. But as he passes it, he sees that it too has been overrun, the tree dead, a swarm of creepers forming a kind of topiary ghost over the frame of the trunk and branches.

In his deepening fatigue he's winded like a sprinter, although he's only walking, his stick-figure shadow preceding him. Above him the upper walls of the church soar out of a murky understorey of what must be bougainvillea. Under the lip of the dome the moonlit surface is pitted with bullet holes. He walks toward the doors of the church, which are framed by the dense growth. Why would the Turks be keeping the doors clear? The flowers in this light look blue instead of purple, and they're as odourless as dried or fake flowers, like the bougainvillea along the mud walls of the village his company was entering two weeks ago.

The door handle is the size and shape of a pomegranate, the brass smooth and clean. It turns easily. He pulls open one side of the double door. A cryptlike odour emerges with a bitter residue of frankincense that for a moment takes him back to boyhood Sundays, the church of the Theotokou in Montreal. He steps inside—a flurry of wingbeats high above. Stained-glass windows admit a dim, diffused light and he begins to make out chairs in the nave on either side of an aisle.

His scalp contracts, his nape freezes; something hard nudges his skull behind the ear. He smells gun oil and masculine sweat. "Enough!" he says, bizarrely, sticking up his hands. Whoever holds the weapon clears his throat importantly, as if about to make an announcement in a crowded room. Elias expects to hear Turkish and is stunned to momentary incomprehension when a deep, scraped-sounding voice speaks in Greek, ending the sentence with a gruff *"Amesos!" At once!* "What?" Elias asks. *"Oriste?"* A ticking of claws outside on the paving stones, then a dog's panting. He senses another human presence behind the armed man—a second track of breathing, faster, higher-pitched. A child? That voice, an older man's, speaks in Greek again but now enunciates carefully, as if over a bad connection: "If you are lost in the ruins and have come in here to pray, then pray as our guest. If you are a spy for the Turks, then simply pray. Now hold still while the woman searches you."

For the second time tonight Elias feels a strange woman's hands moving over his body. They run over his legs and buttocks—slipping his wallet out of his back pocket—then climb his sides and twine around his soaked torso to pat his chest, the empty pocket over his tripping heart. The hands seem tentative, amateur.

"*Dhen eimai hamenos*," Elias says. *I'm not lost*. His male captor laughs and he realizes that what he has just said can also mean "I'm not a loser."

"She will blind you now," the voice tells him in Greek.

"What?"

"With a cloth."

"I mean, I know this is Varosha. Who are you?"

"Hold still," says the woman. She pulls the rough cloth firmly over his eyes and knots it, almost gently, behind his head. Her fingers smell of garlic. He is led outside. Breezes cool the heavy sweat on his forehead, above the blindfold. The woman walks slowly on his left side, holding his arm and guiding him—in fact, partly supporting him—while the man's soft footfalls shadow them, just behind. The dog can be heard trotting ahead. The sounds alter, grow sharper and choppier, the group apparently entering an alley or side street, the air close and hot. Someone is smoking, probably the man. Elias keeps stumbling, groaning. His legs tremble, his teeth chatter.

"You're drunk," the woman says in Greek.

"I *need* a drink."

Repeatedly they turn, left, right, as though his captors are lost as well.

"I need to sit down."

"*Se ligo*," the woman says. *Soon*. She sounds young, her voice soft but husky in the way of Greek women.

"The gun," says the man, behind him. "It was yours?"

"What?"

"We heard shots from the beach."

"Turkish soldiers."

"That's a problem," the man says from deep in his throat; it's as if his larynx is packed with pea gravel. "In the morning you will tell us everything."

They stop and there's a clank and faint creaking, a gate or heavy door. Beyond it the air is cooler, moister, thronged with springlike scents and the insistent chittering of some bird he doesn't know. Another door and he's in a sound-muffled space that smells of dust and mice. The clatter of shutters opening. His blindfold is unknotted. A small dark room, or cabin. Dim light enters through a recessed window covered by a grille. Beneath it there's a bed, and suddenly Elias is finished, his whole body sagging, crutched on his captors (a second man seems to have joined them now). No more able to help or resist them than if he were a paralyzed casualty, he's lowered onto the bare mattress. Someone brings a cup to his lips—it's the woman, her shadow, the smell of garlic from under her fingernails.

Spring-cold water with a chalky taste.

"*Efharisto,*" he mutters.

They leave him. A sound of something being pushed against the door outside. The stars in oddly deformed constellations flare down through the grille and he lies panting up at them while blood shunts behind his eyes. He tells himself he is not hallucinating, though possibly he is, and maybe that would be better. Forget that hope—the worst things are never a dream. Finally he goes still and begins to sink, as though in a warm, enveloping lagoon of opiates; rapture and remission. Then a face rises toward him out of the dark—the bloated features of a drowned woman breaking surface. It shocks him fully awake, arms and legs thrashing.

And yet seconds later he is slipping away again.

* * *

To the ancient Greeks, death meant the loss of everything. What Charon ferried across the river into Hades was no immortal soul, no self-aware survivor enjoying a post-mortem promotion to a better state. At death a person's vital elements—*eros*, bodily desire; *thymos*, a spirited sense of will and worth; and *psyche*, consciousness—dispersed and left only a faint remnant, a shadow with no name, no character, no memory of its former condition. This eidolon existed, if it could be said to exist at all, in a state of perpetual and wandering coma. When the dead appeared to loved ones in dreams it was this shadow that the dreamer saw. *Son of night, brother of sleep*. As for the shades themselves, they didn't dream—as if they were stalled forever in that deepest, delta-wave phase of sleep, when sleepers know no more than the dead.

A local had told her of a maritime abyss off the southwest coast of the island that was the deepest spot in any sea in the world. She seems to be there, at the bottom. Yet now somehow there is light. Another quadrant of her mind realizes: flashlight, its blunt muzzle probing closer, accompanied by the voices of men who, she remembers, mean her harm, her and somebody else, she can't recall whom, a foreigner, big, soft-spoken, very drunk, almost handsome when he smiled. Smiling rarely. (There was a tugging on her shoulders, the foreigner saying her name, September, which must be her name—it comes back to her, her name is September—and he was attempting to drag her somewhere but seemed to give up and disappear as the voices closed in.) Now she is standing among the voices, examining her own body in the sand, prone and with her face skewed sideways, eyes open. She looks down at her own eyes and wills them closed. They close. She sees nothing more. Is she dying? a man asks, and another says, She's dead, the slut. She is not sure which man is correct and she tries to interject, to voice her confusion, but they talk over her. The one with the light in his trembling hand keeps it focused on her and she feels the heat of the light trembling in her wound.

The slut. This time it's said not with venom but with a halting, provisional quality, as if the speaker is testing out a word he might try using in a courtroom, or at a court martial. Now the voices sound less drunk, more frightened. She too: more conscious, more frightened.

One is for leaving her here. One is for heaving her over the fence into the dead zone and hiding or burying her. The one with the light, who sounds kinder or merely less indignant, thinks they ought to call ahead for help, then carry her back to the hotel and say that the Greek killed her. No—the Greek attacked her and we tried to shoot him but we hit her by mistake.

Not we, says the older voice, you. You shot her. The voice is weak and winded, diminished. The Greek attacked her, we tried to help, the Greek attacked me, you tried to shoot him, you hit her. Simple enough? We'll bring her back now. And if she is still alive, she probably won't be by the time we get her back.

MORNING AT THE PALM BEACH OFFICERS' CLUB

Colonel Erkan Kaya reclines in a beach chair of salmon-pink canvas slung on a collapsible wooden frame. Like a solar panel his flat, hairless torso is angled at ninety degrees to the sun. Morning sun: the only sun there is on this otherwise ideal beach. The Varosha Greeks did many things right when they constructed their seafront strip, but uncharacteristically they failed to consider the sun. (Or, perhaps, characteristically; they're an impulsive tribe, argumentative, fickle, anarchic, all traits the colonel finds appealing.) The Greeks built their hotels and apartments high and right on top of the shore, which means that by noon, 1 P.M. at the latest, the sun dips behind the high roofline and leaves the beach in shadow.

Tiny rhinestones of sweat glint on the colonel's brow and clean-shaven upper lip—a touch more sweat than usual, though it's not unusually hot. His laptop computer sits hibernating on a plastic beach table to his left. To his right, on a nicer side table, there's an antique Greek Cypriot tray of buffed copper bearing a thimble cup sludged with coffee grounds, a half-full glass of ice water, an ashtray that needs clearing, and a shot of raki.

Kaya has had no choice but to monitor the Turkish Cypriot news sites all morning. He has had to make some calls. An unusual day. For one thing, it started soon after dawn, when his orderly knocked on his bedroom door on the top floor of the club—the usual four taps, though this time each was progressively louder. Timur Ali knows never to wake Kaya when he's asleep or dozing, except in case of emergency, a state of affairs that has occurred just twice in the past eleven years (holidaying officers; open bar; near-drownings). In some confusion Kaya called Ali in. Ali brought him a cup of coffee, or rather Nescafé—a clear sign of the man's haste. Kaya sat up in bed and sniffed the Nescafé as Ali swung open the shutters and the light of sunrise detonated in the room, formerly a hotel suite where, it was said, the French director Jacques Tati and the British actress Julie Christie would often stay, although never—as Kaya sometimes quips to his guests—at the same time.

In the early '80s this place, a forty-minute walk south of the Palm Beach Hotel, was selected to be an officers' club. It was tidied up, its bar and restaurant refurbished, guest rooms readied for the use of Turkish officers in Cyprus and from bases as far away as the Syrian border, on leave, honeymoon, or family holiday. Guests never took to it. Their laughter echoed hollowly off the rotting towers that backdropped it. At noon every day, when the ruins began eclipsing the deserted beach, their premature shadow seemed a kind of horror-film darkness oozing out of the dead zone. At times, battle tanks would trundle down the shore toward the club and then, just a kilometre short, pivot toward the shallows and sit there monotonously shelling the sea. At night sometimes, the crash of a balcony collapsing. Many found this atmosphere unsuited to a honeymoon or family holiday.

By the early '90s the club was all but abandoned. When Kaya took up his post in 2001, on the death of the mild, quiet colonel who'd presided over Varosha since the occupation began, he set about re-repairing the club, a costly proposition and one that few men, he guessed, could have persuaded the defence ministry to underwrite. Down came the faded dining-room portrait of a presidentially grim Atatürk; up went another in which the great man leered down at the viewer (it was the image from the older ten-lira notes). Today the club remains as underused as ever but Kaya has been able to nudge the figures enough that the defence ministry is not yet concerned. Eventually they will notice; he will deal with the problem then.

In 2002 he moved his quarters down here from Famagusta—the ancient port town just north of Varosha—where his predecessor stayed and where his subordinates prefer to remain. Somehow he found this setting congenial, as if he were a sanguine last Byzantine governor feasting and fucking in the ruins. In a way, the club was his private estate, although now and then there were guests, and a few times a year a horde of visitors would descend for the wedding of a general's son, or a meeting, or some other function. The club cook was superb at fixing the Persian, Italian, and French dishes that Kaya especially loved. Now and then he enjoyed intimate visits from singers or dancers whom Timur Ali drove down the beach from the Palm Beach Hotel. They were not prostitutes. Most of them knew Kaya. He was pretty sure that they would accept his invitations even if he didn't always slip them a gift (one or two hundred lira) in the small hours, before Timur Ali stoically jeeped them back up the beach. But he saw no reason to test his theory; he enjoyed his generosity as much as they did.

He knew that most professional soldiers, hoping to apply their training in war or some comparable crisis, would soon tire of a mission so devoid of challenge. But Kaya had forgotten his training. It never interested him. He enlisted after college because it seemed the simplest, least offensive way to avoid going into business with his father, a successful but invincibly gloomy electronics manufacturer in Üsküdar, exporting to wholesalers in

Eastern Europe. Kaya reckoned rightly that his family would be proud of such a patriotic move and that his younger brother would be drafted into the firm by default.

He rose through the ranks as if by magic. He never much exerted himself, never sought to stand out, never paid court, as such. He never had to. People *liked* him. They couldn't help themselves. And if at first they didn't like him—if they saw him as a rival, some kind of threat—he won them over anyhow with his warm, undefensive nature, his quiet compliments meant not to curry favour but simply to make others feel as good as he did. Since boyhood, things had always gone this way, so that for years he took it all for granted, not realizing how uncommon it was to produce in other people a unanimous affection.

By early adulthood he'd become fully conscious of this . . . this irresistibility, although he was far too lazy to deploy it in any concerted campaign. Yet by thirty-one he was a major. Still, his superiors seemed to grasp that a man like Erkan Kaya was not equipped to rise above a certain level or to take on certain duties. Military ones, for example. So when the Varosha post opened up, they gave him a final promotion and packed him off to north Cyprus. The timing was right, from a domestic point of view; he and his wife had just separated, amicably. The children still live with her in Istanbul, where he visits them at times. Or else they come down here to Cyprus. Both children adore him, especially the girl, fifteen—though come to think of it the boy, a year younger, has seemed a bit distant the last two visits.

Still in bed, squinting at the dawn sun, Kaya listened to his orderly break the news. Timur Ali is a very tall man in his late sixties with a dark, bony little face and a huge grey Ottoman moustache. Stoical brown eyes, the whites discoloured like veiny yolks. He was the first colonel's orderly too. Impassive as ever, he went on briefing Kaya while Kaya sipped the Nescafé, which (he couldn't help but notice) was nicely marbled with sugary condensed milk and, all in all, really tasty. Things right themselves, he reminded himself, still calm, though aware that he had a true crisis on his hands here, one that could blow up as quickly as a March storm over the sea and spill beyond this quiet island, spoiling everything. Well-known liberal journalist Eylül Şahin attacked by a foreign soldier on leave and staying at the Palm Beach Hotel—a man with a very Greek name. Ali had been fielding calls from the hospital in Famagusta where the woman, critically hurt and not expected to survive, was in a medically induced coma, and from the nearby base where the four soldiers involved had been giving drunken, garbled accounts of the event. They had saved the woman from being raped on the beach near the hotel; they had saved the woman *after* she had been raped (the moustache that covers his mouth barely moving, Timur Ali states that the doctors confirm she did have intercourse). They were forced to defend themselves after the man injured their sergeant; they accidentally shot the journalist while shooting at the man; he escaped into Varosha, possibly wounded; no, badly wounded; in fact, he might be dead.

Obviously the story was false. A man with a conveniently Greek name rapes a Turkish woman and then attacks four armed soldiers? Kaya could easily imagine the truth, especially after Ali related the hotel's confirmation that last night the man and woman sat a long time at the bar "courting" (Ali's outdated, faintly reproachful term) and drinking on a shared tab.

Kaya realized his men might well have assaulted and raped the woman themselves, before shooting her. Anatolian goatherds, all of them. Unfortunately their actions were Kaya's responsibility and he would have no choice but to back up their tale, once he'd subjected it to some revision. The alternative was unthinkable. His men shooting, maybe after gang-raping, a well-connected Istanbul journalist critical of the army's "occupation" in Cyprus? And if they really had wounded or killed a foreign national . . .

This was a story that would have to disappear.

Entirely awake now, Kaya gave Ali instructions. The soldiers were to say nothing more; they should sleep and sober up and he would talk to them this afternoon. The full perimeter of Varosha must be kept under surveillance, but for now nobody was to enter. And, pending investigation, local news sources were to refer to the foreigner only as an as-yet-unidentified man.

Ali nodded slowly. His big hands, ropy with veins, hung loose at his sides. He was as unused to crises as Kaya—who was a little pleased to find himself able to rise to an occasion of some urgency, to think and act this fast.

On his way out, Ali stopped, turned stiffly. Should he cancel the colonel's match with Captain Polat before lunch? On Kaya's tongue, the last milky splashes of the Nescafé seemed to curdle. Aydin Polat, his humourless, totally unnecessary new adjutant.

"Thanks, no need to bother. I'll have to talk to him anyway."

Now, on the beach in this inebriating light, Kaya shoots back his raki and savours the solar flaring of the liquor in his chest and gut. He shakes the cigarette pack—empty. He gets up and stretches with a groan of helpless pleasure and then, his step easy and elastic as a leopard's, strolls seaward. Things right themselves. They always do. The sea feels warmer than a sulphur spring. Still wearing his sunglasses, he eases into a lazy backstroke, gliding south along the beach. The crisis nudges and niggles at the pale of his awareness, but Kaya's body, in the innocent complacency of perfect health, keeps forgetting. Many men, facing a crisis, would pray. Not Kaya—though it's not as if he's a disbeliever. Disbelief demands too much mental energy; killing off God takes initiative, not to mention a certain lack of generosity and good manners.

Alas, it's this foreigner who needs to be dead, or perceived as such.

As Kaya swims back up the beach, the club rising out of the platinum sands like a mirage, he makes out two figures by his chair. The sun blazes into his water-specked lenses. The figures are in silhouette. One must be Captain Polat, who for his first weeks here has reliably, annoyingly shown up ten minutes early for everything. Now he's an hour early. The much taller one will be Ali. There's something about how the two men stand stiffly, ceremonially, to either side of Kaya's empty chair . . . it's as though he has seen all of this before. In a dream? Kaya never recalls his dreams. Currents of heat welling up from the sand blur both figures. A queasiness roils through his flawlessly functioning guts, a kind of intestinal vertigo, something he has felt only a few times in his life. *Erkan, this is your father. Your mother is dead.*

In heavy, dripping surfer shorts he saunters toward the men and politely removes his sunglasses. His chair holds the shape of his body like an unmade bed.

Ali steps toward him and hands him a towel.

"You're early," he tells Captain Polat, and his curt tone surprises him.

"Sir, we must hurry—we—I felt I should, uh—that you might . . ." Polat's words stumble and cram up like a file of raw recruits trying to march in close order. He wears clerkish spectacles too small for his unnaturally large head. Long-lashed blue eyes, a snub nose, plump grey cheeks that are faintly pitted. As if to counter his look of boyish softness, he affects a sharpshooter's squint and sports a moustache, though it's threadbare like a worn-out stage prop. He's always in uniform, pistol at his side. When he and Kaya play tennis he simply removes his pistol belt and peaked cap and tunic, revealing a khaki T-shirt sweat-soaked around the armpits.

"Allow me to lead a—sir, I would be honoured to lead a platoon in there—immediately."

"Where, into Varosha? A *platoon*?"

"Of course, sir."

"But, Captain, whatever for?"

"Why—to find the foreigner, sir—of course."

Kaya towels his face and steps closer to Polat, not, he thinks, to intimidate the man, but simply out of habit. He always stands close when conversing. Now Polat—with a glancing frown down at Kaya's drenched shorts and legs—recoils a step. He always keeps his distance, and yet when he speaks, his words loud and surging, he seems to be right on top of you.

"Look, Captain," Kaya says in an indulgent tone, "he's most likely dead anyway, and—"

"But if he's not? We need to capture him! We need to go in now and—"

"Impossible."

Polat's eyebrows draw together. "Impossible? Sir, I . . ."

Ali is tracking the conversation closely, his mournful eyes swivelling, his big moustache fixed. Kaya simply can't be sure how much he can tell Polat this soon. The man is a conundrum. It seems impossible to put him at his ease or to make him laugh, even smile.

" . . . sir, I am not—as for this woman, the journalist, I am not in agreement with any of her—but surely this foreigner will have—should have to face . . ."

"Come, Captain, we both know those men are lying."

"If they're lying, then *they* should go on trial! Let me interrogate them, sir!"

"Interrogate them?" Kaya widens his mouth into a grin. "But I'll be having a word with them myself, after our tennis."

"But, sir . . ."

"Captain, please! This situation is delicate. There are . . . there are certain factors you aren't aware of yet." A hurt, jilted look passes over Polat's face, relegating him instantly to boyhood. Kaya hates disappointing anyone; he feels that he really ought to offer something more, but he's impatient to hear from Ali. He turns to him now: "There's news?" The orderly flicks a look toward Polat, and Kaya thinks, *Ali is right, I should hear this in private*. But then his lifelong inability to fear the worst reasserts itself. His previous two captains were both so easily handled. Still, it's with a slight foreboding—along with a touch of the bettor's fatalistic elation—that he says, "Go ahead, Ali. Captain Polat should hear as well."

"Yes, *efendi*." Ali glances sorrowfully at Kaya, then announces, "News from the docks. A fishing boat came in at 10 A.M. The fishermen found a mobile telephone in one of the nets, among the fish. It seems it was not in the water for long. Judging from the make, it will be the missing man's."

Silence. Sunlight throbbing down. Kaya feels the brine-dry skin of his cheeks stretching in a smile.

"Gentlemen, this is good news."

"But *efendi*," Ali says, "I think the soldiers must simply have thrown the device into the sea. I believe that one of them . . ."

He stops himself, glances alertly at Kaya, who says, "Not at all. Here is what happened. The foreigner tried to swim outward, after assaulting both the woman and our men. Being terribly drunk, he drowned. In fact, articles of his clothing—Ali, take the Jeep now and fetch them from the hotel—will be found later today, on a stretch of beach about, say, a kilometre in that direction." Kaya points vaguely north, the Palm Beach Hotel visible in the distance.

"But, Colonel," says Captain Polat, "the man may well be at large—alive in there! What if he escapes across the Green Line?"

"Good thinking, Captain," Kaya says smoothly, fully himself again. "But naturally I've tightened security around the perimeter. As for bringing him out, if he is still alive, leave that to me. Trust me, for now this is best."

"But . . ."

"I'll see you at the tennis court at noon and we can discuss things further." *If you insist.*

Polat stalks away. If he weren't on a beach, his boot heels would be snapping. He's packed into his uniform, small-boned yet pudgy, his big head with the large officer's cap precariously propped on tiny shoulders. It strikes Kaya that, seen from behind, he resembles a North Korean general or dictator.

Kaya says to Ali, "If the foreigner is still alive, the villagers will have him. Please go to the gate now and signal them. When someone comes, you'll give them a note from me—I'll write it now—to say I would like to meet this afternoon."

In twenty minutes the old orderly, with his lanky stride, is deep inside Varosha, nearing the "gate" where the grilles and headlights of two forty-year-old sedans almost touch in mid-street, like the faces of two snarling old dogs. In a canvas sack with the colonel's note he lugs military-issue parcels of coffee, sugar, lentils, and wheat flour, along with three canisters of propane. These are in trade for the fresh eggs, quail, cucumbers, plums, lemons, and honey he received at the gate two weeks ago.

On arrival now he climbs into the driver's seat of the Mercedes-Benz and squeezes the bulb of the old air horn the villagers have clamped to the side mirror—four even, raucous honks—then tugs the lever at the base of the seat to recline it. On his last visit he oiled the mechanism again; it functions as if the vehicle were new. He lies back. The heat of the sun pulsates down through the roof. The villagers are always prompt. He should be back at the club in time for his noon prayers. Leaving the door ajar—so he can hear the footfalls of whoever comes and be standing, gravely waiting, when they arrive—he lets his eyes close and in moments is adrift.

THE VILLAGE

This small, bare room is filled with light and the trembling shadows of leaves and lemons projected with the pattern of the grille onto a cracked tile floor. It must be near noon, or afternoon. Though barely awake, Elias is already in full sweat, his headache crushing. The foot of the bed—an old mattress on a boxspring—faces an open doorway giving onto a green space frenetic with birdsong.

On a stool beside the doorway sits a man, thin, compact, his trimmed black beard skunked with grey. He is stiffly upright, shoulders back, feet flat on the floor, as if posing for a nineteenth-century photographer. His khakis, like his boots, look old but clean. His faded blue short-sleeved shirt might once have been part of a uniform. On his lap a book with no dust jacket lies open, face down.

"*Kalimera*," he says. It's not the raspy voice of last night. His skin looks Northern European, his hands and forearms sunburned red, his face pale as if he always wears a hat. The forehead is high, heavy-boned, his brows low over embedded blue eyes that pierce like diamond drill-bits. "*Pos eiste, Elia Trifannis?*"

Elias sits up, groans, leans back against the cool wall. "*Kapos kalitera*," he lies: *A little better.*

"We see you're from Montreal," the man says, his Greek confident but curiously accented—maybe Dutch, or German? "We see also that your name is Greek. Would you prefer to speak Greek, French, or English?"

"I grew up in English mostly."

In English the man says, "I can take you to wash before we speak. The privy . . ."

"Where am I?"

"Varosha, as you know."

"I mean . . ." He's too sick to explain.

"Would you take a coffee first? I can ask someone to bring coffee."

Elias nods.

"Water is beside you. Your feet later will need some attention."

A plastic jug on the floor by the bed and a fluted plastic tumbler that must once have been clear but now is scuffed cloudy. Beside it, an empty pail. It seems he's too dehydrated to need the piss-pail and too weary to reach down for the water; or too indifferent.

The man calls out in a voice that strains for volume, almost cracking, "*Kaiti, pedhi mou, fere ena kafe yia ton kseno, parakalo.*" His eyes stay fixed on Elias as he calls. His stillness is a result not only of calm, it seems, but also fatigue. All his energy is confined to those deep-set, discerning eyes. He says, "Turkish Cypriot radio was full of news this morning. I assume this would not surprise you. On the beach late last night, a well-known Turkish journalist was attacked. Several soldiers who came out of the bar of the Palm Beach Hotel—they say they heard her scream for help."

"That's not how it happened."

"*Ja?* Go on."

"They followed us. We were half an hour down the beach. Who are you? What are you doing in here?"

The man folds his thin arms across his chest.

"Look, she wasn't screaming until they attacked us, okay?"

"Tell me your full accounting of events."

Elias leans sideways and grips the jug and lifts it to his lips, spilling water down his bare torso. He spits into the pail, then begins talking in short, stripped-down phrases—all he can manage now—and his terse delivery lends the words a plausibility he himself starts to hear, so that last night's events begin to seem less unreal. Too bad. When he describes butting the soldier, he touches the raw, bruised patch on his forehead and his story is further confirmed. As he finishes, her face surges up again out of the dark and he can't swallow the mouthful of water he needs.

"Ey*lül*," he says, nailing the umlaut.

"Eylül Şahin."

"I can guess what their version is."

"You raped her repeatedly. Then you attacked them when they tried to stop you."

"Did I shoot her in the back as well?"

"They admit that they shot her, but by mischance after you assaulted them in the dark. Naturally, they are emphasizing your heritage. At first on the radio—early this morning I was listening—the announcer said, 'Greek Canadian soldier on trauma leave.' Just once he said this, in the first report. Now you are simply a Greek. Before long, perhaps . . . Greek Cypriot." His mouth is closed but his beard has a faintly smiling look. He uncrosses his arms.

"You believe me," Elias says.

"For several reasons. First, we heard the shots and we know where they came from—a long distance from the hotel. And last night, after Stratis and Kaiti brought you in, he and I went back and saw where, on the beach, the struggle occurred. Also—"

"Wait, what did they do with her body? I thought I—I think I might have dreamed she was underwater."

"But she is alive!"

"What?"

"Yes. It appears they too assumed she was dead, but a medical unit found vital signs. However, she is in a critical state—comatose."

Elias stares through the doorway, seeing nothing, his heart caroming between shame and relief. *You left her behind on the beach*. But no pulse. *You left her.* Her eyes open. *You left her.*

"But you, they do now assume dead. Or so they are saying."

"Fuck me," Elias murmurs. "It's like a trail of bodies now."

"What? You mean, there on the beach?"

"No. Nothing."

The man's clifflike forehead furrows. "They—they were reporting at first that you were badly wounded—that one of the men followed a blood trail for some distance into Varosha, then it vanished. But this account has undergone something of a . . . a sea change." Another faint, rueful smile. "Now they say that your telephone has been fished from the sea and some of your garments found washed up on shore. So you are now missing, most likely drowned."

"If my things were found on shore, they were put there."

"Colonel Kaya will probably confirm that when I meet him."

"A colonel—in the Turkish army? You mean they know you're in here?"

"He knows, *ja*, and his orderly, who can be trusted. It was likewise with Colonel Işik before—though it's truer to say that Işik chose not to know, chose to ignore us. For years we have been here. Decades, in some cases, as with Stratis Kourakis."

Elias parts his lips but can say nothing.

"I hope you will meet them this evening, the villagers."

"But how have you . . ." In the shadows under a tree in the courtyard, two children, delicate as birds, are leaning into his line of sight, peeking in. As he spots them they startle and vanish.

"Ah, are the twins out there again?"

"I thought maybe I was seeing things. I've been doing that."

"No, they are Kaiti's. Aslan is the boy, Lale the girl."

For a moment he considers the possibility that this whole interview is a sort of hallucination; then he asks, "But why would this colonel lie? I could turn up alive any time."

"No one," the man says softly, "would want that to happen, you included. Especially now, with Ms. Şahin alive. The colonel wants no trouble, he never does—he is very attached to his life at the beach club. As for the Turkish army, it too would prefer no contrary version to emerge. So, it will happily accept his word that you drowned. As you might know, most Turkish Cypriots wish the army would go back to Turkey—they want to be reconciled with the Greeks. But Turkey has no desire to leave, especially now, with all the natural gas turning up offshore." Elias nods; his uncle in Larnaca spoke at length on the topic. "The account of those four soldiers makes the army look good, a trusty protector, as in the past, and it stimulates a useful hatred against Greeks. Your version makes the army look brutal and inept—it would bring Turkey an international embarrassment, as if their presence here hasn't brought them enough! So, as of now, you are assumed dead, by all parties. They aren't even announcing your name now. I expect they will try to make an agreement with your embassy to keep things quiet. It might work. Your government will want no more scandal after what happened last year with its—what is the word—its 'decompressing' troops in Paphos . . ."

Elias recalls hearing of a double murder–suicide involving a Polish dancer, her Cypriot boyfriend, and a depressed young private.

"So long as there appears to be a search," the man adds. "Till the story dies down back home."

"I don't really have a home."

"You mean, no country?"

"Wait—isn't she in danger then Eylül? I mean—"

"Because of her injuries, yes, but not otherwise, I think. Consider that if she did recover and told the same story as you, it would be the word of a badly damaged woman against that of four men—servicemen. And how eager would she be to tell her world that she had drunken—pardon me—drunken and public intimacy on a beach with a Greek stranger? If she did believe you were still alive, perhaps she might tell the truth, but if she learns that you're dead . . . well. Even if she is from a liberal family, the truth would disgrace her in Turkey."

"So if I surfaced and spoke up, I could ruin her life. Put her at risk, again."

"So I fear."

"Jesus Christ, as if I . . . and this colonel . . ."

"Kaya, Erkan Kaya. He sent his orderly to us just now with a note. He reckoned we must have you and wants to meet later, to discuss it. I suppose he might ask us to turn you over." Wrinkles multiply again in the man's high brow. Above it, a rumpled ridge of stiff, greying hair. "No. He wouldn't know what to do with you. He is not a violent or stupid man. He's really a kind of . . . a playboy, the kind who would have loved the old Varosha even more. But your existence does pose a problem for him. Likely he will ask that we should keep you here safely, for everyone's behalf, until the story dies down."

"Keep me here."

"*Ja*, and I ought to warn you—"

"No, don't warn me. No warnings, no orders. I'm finished with orders. I'll think about what you've said, but whether or not I leave—that'll be my decision."

The man's beard seems to hide another smile, this time one of discomfort or concern. "Let me just say that Sergeant Kourakis—he who brought you in last night, with Kaiti?—he is not wholly predictable. As you know, he is armed. He was attached to the special forces that flew in from Crete in '74 to help the Greek

Cypriots, and . . . as he himself has never surrendered or been captured, he considers that the war is not yet finished or quite lost. He can be civil, even generous, but he would do anything to protect the village. Then too there is the dog, and then there is Paris. In the old Varosha, this Paris was a—what is the word—one who sleeps in the street, asking tourists for money?"

"I understand."

"He lives as a reclusive, in goatherd huts to the south, beyond the ruins. We hear that he dines on fruits and the roasted meat of snakes. He wanders among the ruins, by the perimeter fence, never letting himself be viewed. Colonel Kaya knows nothing of him. I myself have met him just twice. You will not have seen him last night, but he saw you and came to warn Stratis. This is the first time in some years that he warns of an intruder."

"You mean I'm some kind of prisoner."

"It's not the right word."

"You have a better one?"

"You won't be confined to this room, not at all. And I think, after some time—once the story fades down, and we know we can trust you to say nothing—"

"Everyone wants me to say nothing."

"—maybe then, you could leave us, claiming the amnesia. You *were* here on trauma leave, *ja*?"

"After the therapy they were sending me home or back to the war. No way I was going."

"Home, or back to the war?"

"Maybe both."

"You have found a way not to, it seems."

A shadow in the doorway, a young woman holding a tray. "*Ena kafe yia ton kseno*," she says and enters. From out of the space behind her comes the rich discord of birdsong he'd stopped hearing during the interview, or interrogation. She stands a few inches over five feet, in a black dress like an old Levantine widow, her hair tugged back in a widowlike way, yet the hair is glossy black, she wears sunglasses, and the dress goes only to her knees. Flip-flops on caramel feet. She is slim at the waist and ankles but otherwise rounded, her calves strong. The man sets his book on the floor and takes the tray from the woman, who seems too repulsed, wary, or alarmed to carry it to Elias on his sweaty bed. In his state he feels unthreatening, in fact frail, but he knows the impression he has been making on others since adolescence. He's burly—thick through the waist but not soft—with drastic black eyebrows, the jaw of a bouncer, and thin lips that give him an air of contained combativeness.

The man brings the tray over. Not wanting to be served like a prisoner, Elias tries to get up. "No, please, rest for now, son. Take your coffee and this piece of bread." The word *son* is a complete surprise. The next surprise is how the word locks Elias's throat into a spasm. He lowers his face and brings a hand to his brow, as if the welt there is stinging. Or he's a man overcome at a funeral. The only person officially dead here is him. Three white, pentagonal pills lie on the tray by the coffee—the spare Ativans from his wallet. A cool hand settles on his nape. "Whatever they are, it's doubtful we can fetch any more of them. Please bear this in mind."

Elias nods.

"My name is Roland. This is Ekaterini—Kaiti. You are welcome in the village."

CLEAR-CUT: KANDAHAR, 11 OCTOBER

The briefing took place in a large tent under generator lights bright enough for a film set. 0400 hours. The captain kept referring to good guys and bad guys as if talking to small boys about a combat video game, so more than ever Elias's enlistment looked absurd. Thirty years old and joining up mainly for the sake of a father, albeit a dying one, an ex-soldier, ex-cop, who had always wanted this, or something like it, though when Elias actually went and did it the man sat up in bed and swore torrents in Greek and then, in English, called him a fucking fool. Out of breath, he spoke in half-coherent bursts. "It's not a blue beret now! You can be killed!"

Elias had thought joining up might buoy his father into another remission, maybe buy him an extra year of life, then an easier, less angry death. *I thought you'd be happy, Papa*. But no, it seemed, especially not now with the cancer chewing through him, as if nothing mattered to him anymore but life, the continuity of his own blood and seed. His old hopes for his son had been suspended. Maybe they never were real, never more than a way of focusing frustration because the boy had not become the man he might have been. Oh, he'd developed the proper physique, but not the correct "character," which seemed to involve a kind of adamant certainty, a sensibly impatient scorn for nuances, new ideas, thoughtful distinctions, kindness of the more naive sort (kindness was weakness, weakness a failure of will). The boy had been a tough, talented athlete. He should have graduated to the adult male form of competitive prowess: a career in business, law, finance, or security. Instead he was part-timing in gyms as a personal trainer and playing a few gigs in bars (covering other people's songs). Becalmed. Elias couldn't deny it. He was living with someone but not in love, he was book smart but never touched a book, he was addicted to TV sports and porn, though only mildly, even his addictions lacking real commitment. Another thirty-year-old adolescent adrift in a rich world locked in a coma of complacency.

At his father's soon-to-be deathbed he saw what a mistake he'd made—this rash stab at some parody of adult commitment, this overtime bid for love and family connection—but it was too late, and in fact Papa's shocking insistence that he find some way to withdraw made Elias all the more determined to stay the course, and here he is, months into a second tour of duty, the mission a mess, the regime they're defending despicable, people dying hourly—civilians, soldiers, good guys, bad guys by the ditch-load, some of whom appear to have been recruited from grade schools, impossible, there are no such schools here, that's the whole issue, that's what we've come here to change. And you bought that line (sort of). Made it easier to join up. And for a while, before the deepening desert tedium, the thousandth hand of Texas hold 'em—before any actual violence—it did feel good to belong to something solid; to receive clear orders instead of trying and failing to make decisions; to flow with the simple will of the crowd.

Simply belong.

***

At sunrise the company marched down into a valley along a mud-walled track too narrow for the LAVs. The valley was a terracotta bowl with steep, serrated sides—from down here the encircling horizon was all mountains, sun-baked and sterile. On the other side of the mud wall a stream descended parallel to the track, its melodic trickling a reprieve to the men after so long in the desert. The water, or just the sound of it, seemed to cool and soften the air.

Down below in the valley a small Eden nestled, or so it seemed now compared to the desert above. In fact there were only a few patches of lush green down there among the brown, flat roofs of the houses, over which a low minaret rose. The other swaths of colour, contained within mud walls, were less brilliant but still a relief for the eye: the blond of wheat, the yellow of mustard and, much larger, an expanse of pale silvery green, which must be the olive grove on this side of the village, the main reason for the company's visit.

As the men approached the grove, teams of skirmishers veered off, clambering over the walls to either side of the track. They spread out into the fields where a few villagers stood gaping, hoes in hand. Elias wanted to follow them into the fields and take an urgent piss, or attempt to, his bladder empty but burning. Then the olive grove was there beside them, across the mud wall, which here was overrun by wild grapes and bougainvillea. Brushing past the purple flowers he noticed for the first time their lack of smell. When your body is rattled do your senses shut down? No, the opposite, your sense of smell, like vision, grows sharper. Fresh goat dung on the path, the vinegary funk of anxious, overheating bodies, and now the fainter smells of the grove instantly returning him to boyhood, first time in Greece, near Pirgos, the rich bitterness of the fruit and also the leaves and resinous bark of the trees, some a thousand years old, as these ones too might be. They have that sinewy look, rheumatic yet thriving, trunks knobby, impacted, as if they've petrified indestructibly. The other groves in Afghanistan are young, planted by the Soviets in the '70s, while this one is said to go back to the time of Alexander the Great, some of whose troops settled in this valley, which must have reminded them of home. They planted grapevines and the olive trees from which these trees were descended, and they remained here when the other Greeks withdrew, so for centuries afterward this would have been a small ethnic outpost of Greece.

Sappers with chainsaws are going over the wall into the grove, shadowed by soldiers lumbering in a crouch, awkward in their kneepads and cyborg body armour. The grove offers the only good cover in the valley. According to Intel, the enemy has been bivouacking here and emerging from the valley at dark to attack convoys on the highway west of the pass. Last week a British contractor was killed and six soldiers wounded by an IED. Intel thinks the enemy has left for now, but the orders are to clear-cut the grove and drag away the remains. The men will pile it up for the villagers to use as firewood or building materials, or to sell. Whatever they choose. Winning hearts and minds. A simple operation—but even a rootless, suburban Greek knows that olives are not like other trees. It's not just their age, it's how families tend them for generations and count on them for their staples: the fruit, for pickling and salting, but above all the oil: their cooking fat, their lamp fuel, their medicine, their butter, their lard, their soap, their lotion, their lubricant. People in dry, poor countries never doubt that fat is life.

"Trif, go in with Barrett and Lozac. Guard those sappers."

"Yes, sir."

"Interpreter's with the group ahead. We're sealing things off, but keep him close in case of locals." Forewarning the village has not been an option, because if any bad guys—some of whom might even *be* villagers—are still in the grove and get wind of the plans, they could ambush the men.

The sound of the first chainsaw grinding its teeth is sickening, a second wave of sickness superimposed on the first, the first being simple fear, what everyone feels, along with excitement and, for a few of the men, visible elation. You too, just a little, admit it. You're following Barrett and Lozac into the freckling light and shadow of the grove. As each saw starts biting into wood, its howling soars several tones higher, as if euphoric. There's shouting ahead. Sergeant Singh is yelling at somebody, out of sight, who's yelling back. You can barely hear them over the saws now whining in chorus, some sappers moving outward, some cutting their way toward you. "Where the fuck's the interpreter?" Lozac cries. Singh is beside himself: "Lie down! Lie down! Lie down!" He's aiming his carbine at the sandalled feet of a villager in drawstring trousers and undershirt, who stands under a tree, bunching the end of a bough in his fist and shaking it—twigs, black olives, long thin leaves—as if trying to press out the oil with his hand. "He's unarmed!" you yell. Everyone can see he's unarmed, but Singh's widened eyes are flitting, the villager could be a decoy, there's shouting from all directions, what the fuck, the grove is filling up with villagers, though it should be sealed off by now. Maybe they were in here already, eating a meal before starting the day's work. Maybe some are the Bad Guys, the worst of them, the cruel lunatic purists. A mist of exhaust fumes and sawdust floats through the grove. The seared flesh of the trees smells like incense. Singh fires a shot into the air. Barrett seizes the villager by the scruff and topples him to the earth, face down.

From somewhere nearby, toward the village, more shots. Singh's head turns sharply, the hairnet black under his helmet. Down on one knee, you're scanning the well-spaced grid of trees in that direction: all intact, though other trees are falling around you, not toppling and crashing like big pines but just sagging over until the pruned canopies meet the ground, or mesh with the boughs of neighbouring trees not yet culled.

A scrawny, white-bearded man gimps toward you, his palms upturned, eyes beseeching, the whites intensely clear in his brown face. *In the name of God what are you people doing?* he must be asking. You're wondering the same thing. You holler at him to stop. He keeps coming. Your C7 snugged against your shoulder, bolt cocked, safety off, you aim at his bare feet. "Now! Please!" "Stand down!" Lozac screams at the man. "Trif, where's the fucking interpreter?" Another spasm of shots. Most of the men look tense but unpanicked, down on one knee, carbines ready, holding back, then peripherally you see one, maybe two, firing shots, not knowing who is shooting or if they should reply. "Hold fire!" A civilian coming at you is the worst possible thing because what on earth do you do? "What's *no* in Pashto?" "What?" A jolt to your shoulder, as if you've been hit. The old man has stopped and knelt and crouched forward, brow to the ground, as if facing Mecca. "Trif!—don't fire again—some of ours are over there!"—it's Lozac, out of sight, the gas fumes and floating sawdust thickening. "I didn't!" you shout, you insist, to him, to yourself—"Loze?—Jesus, did I?" "Open fire," a voice shouts, "they're armed!" "What?" "They're not armed—don't fucking fire!" (Is that Singh?)

On the ground by your boot, a spent shell. It can only be from your C7. The praying man isn't moving. Bullets zip overhead with a sound like shredding paper. You aim at the man with ferocious concentration as if he is playing dead and means to whip out a shank or pistol and rush you, this little olive farmer. *Get the fuck up! I missed you!* Your open mouth, dry tongue, coated with the bitter dust. To your left, more firing, more shouts of "Hold your fire!" The squibbing of shots has replaced the snarl of saws—the sappers all belly-flat on the straw-covered earth waiting out the firefight, if that's what this is. "Man down," you yell, "get medics!" "What?" "Call that in now!" "Roger!" And Singh, to somebody: "Hold your fucking fire!"

Somehow you're there beside the man, rolling him over, straddling the shrunken body, no pulse, pumping the chest just inches from the wound so that it spurts, spattering your throat and face, and you taste blood. Blood on the man's white beard as well. The force of the compressions half-opens his mouth, his eyes. The whites appear, just the whites, like the vacant stare of a Greek statue. You keep pumping, praying, as if you know anything about praying, while the voices of strangers jabber around you, *Trif, Trif, stop it, man, it's too late.*

Sometime later he and Zeke Barrett, that troubled kid, maybe nineteen, who had fired off a full clip, made their way through the ruins of the grove, not sure where they were going or why. Like bushwhacking in dense forest, pushing through the spiny thickets of intermeshed boughs. The sappers were elsewhere, dealing with the last trees. From here the noise was like a swarm of cicadas. They'd been cutting at waist height, probably for ease and speed—there were maybe four hundred trees to cut down. A gore of resin encircled the edge of each stump. The wood tawny yellow, the growth rings uncountable. Stumps the circumference of a big man's torso.

He drifted on—somehow he had lost little Barrett—and passed medics treating a panting sapper, deep gash in the knee, the patella and cartilage glaring white. He must have hit a burl, the saw bucking back. Farther on, a medic with colourless eyes and ginger moustache pumped the chest of a boy, maybe twelve, shot through the forehead, the perforation perfectly clean. His father was kneeling beside him, rocking side to side and wailing. Somewhere a stoned-sounding voice was saying, "They think when they die, they go to Mecca."

Trif couldn't feel the weight of his carbine or armour. Sounds of group lamentation nearby—a different pitch from the chainsaws, though almost in harmony—as if funerals were already in session. Maybe family had gathered around the praying man, back there in the debris. A white goat on its hind legs stood nibbling a fallen bough. As if in imitation, Lozac, his close comrade, now a stranger to him, grey as a corpse, stood holding a twig to his nose. He plucked and bit an olive and spat. "No fucking loss, man." His C7 was propped against a stump. "Hey, Trif, seriously, your dick get hard in the firing line? Am I fucked up or something?"

Twenty or thirty steps beyond, medics were clumped around the female second lieutenant, Moore. One medic held up a drip bag of blood, another a bag of saline. There was a sewery smell. The head medic hunched over the lieutenant's abdomen, blocking Elias's view. A few steps away a villager lay face down in a slurry of dirt and gore, clutching a machete-like tool. Exit wounds shredded his back. The wounds, the body looked less real than in the movies.

A machete. We'll be able to say they were armed after all.

A medic looked up at Elias. The man's eyes rounded. "Soldier? You hurt? Over here!" Elias walked on, olives strewn underfoot like casings. With the shade of the grove wiped out, for a generation at least, the sun, climbing swiftly, was oppressive. Heat bludgeoned down. The immense sky was a desert in its own right, equally arid, equally empty but for a shrapnel sliver of moon hovering over the mountains to the east. Soon the choppers would be flying in. He hoped they would evacuate the lieutenant, an officer he'd actually liked, in time.

The mud wall of the village. A tree that had grown beside the wall had collapsed onto it when cut. On the other side, something moved among the boughs. He didn't raise his carbine, which drooped from its strap, useless as an arm in a sling. He stepped behind the boughs of another amputated tree. An old woman in dark layers—beaked nose, sunken mouth, like a tiny Cretan *yiayia*—was shaking olives off a branch into her apron, muttering and spitting as she worked.

FLIGHT

With a jolt and a stifled cry he wakes from a hard, drugged sleep. Deep in his gut a clot of dread and grief, or something bitter like grief. He passed out around dusk—in spite of several more Greek coffees—and so missed the dinner where he was supposed to meet the villagers. He still can't quite believe in them, or it. Yet here he is. It might be anywhere from midnight to an hour before dawn. The grille-covered window above his face frames a panel of sky so misty with stars it might be a photo taken by telescope. Silence but for the alien song of that bird in the courtyard.

For two weeks now, every time he has failed to stay awake, the dream: he or his eidolon plodding through a labyrinth of high mud walls, sure that there must be a route branching through the darkness to safety. Yet any route he chooses soon defaults into corridors all descending into a kind of arena, or vast atrium, lit up as if with stadium floods: the olive grove, the same bloody scene replaying. How conscientiously his brain works at getting it exactly right, over and over! (But why not work to change it, delete it?) He senses the playback might go on every night for years—an unfaceable future. Maybe it's looping in the back of his mind twenty-four hours a day, waiting for him to re-enter the cinema of sleep.

He sits up, gropes for the jug of water on the floor by the bed, brings it to his lips. He opens his throat and chugs every drop. For a moment he entertains a fantasy of trying to find and rescue the hospitalized Eylül; he would be arrested, maybe shot, long before he reached her. But to let himself be held in these ruins, incommunicado . . . That man, Roland, with his argument about protecting Eylül, it all seems sophistry now in this darkness. Rationalizations are daytime creatures, less plausible by night. He can't just sit here while liars accuse him in absentia. If he means to fight off sleep for the rest of the night, what better way than by getting up and walking? He recalls seeing on a map that Varosha's southern edge adjoins the Green Line, the Republic of Cyprus just across it.

He rushes the jug back to his mouth as he retches, losing most of the water he just downed. On the floor by the bed he finds the candle and matches that the woman delivered after his interrogation, along with a bowl of stewed lentils, a white undershirt, flip-flops so old that the rubber is brittle and light as sponge toffee, a second blanket, folded sheets stamped POSEIDONS INN, a bar of cracked soap and a roll of newsprint toilet paper of the same vintage. Still wearing sunglasses she said curtly, "*Ta podhia sou*," and when he lifted one foot to show her the sole, she looked away and then handed him a phial of brown liquid and some gauze and tape. In a softer voice she told him to put on the flip-flops and led him slowly out into the courtyard, a garden of aromatic herbs, fruit trees and trellised grapevines, enclosed on three sides by numbered rooms and on the fourth side an exposed stone wall framing a wide wooden gate. Pointing toward room number four she said, in English, "The privy." (In his room there's a sealed door that must once have opened on a bathroom, back when this place, obviously an inn, had plumbing.)

He lights the candle and looks around his near-empty room.

Still no sign of his shirt, jeans, or wallet. They don't yet trust him not to flee. In boxer shorts, undershirt and the brittle flip-flops, his feet socked in gauze, he holds up the candle and tests the room's doorknob. It turns easily, as if oiled, though the door itself, when he edges it open, screams on its hinges. The strange bird falls silent. He holds his breath. From the moon-shadows under a lemon tree across the courtyard, a pale shape stirs. There's a rumbling growl. "*Endaksi*," Elias whispers. The growling stops and something begins thumping the ground, a tail.

Several small tables have been aligned to form a long table in the flagstoned centre of the courtyard. On the tables, a few candle ends and empty bottles. In his drugged slumber he heard nothing of the phantom villagers' dinner. Beside his doorway—at his feet—they've left something under an old ceramic room-service cover. He crouches painfully. From the top of the cover he removes a spoon and threadbare napkin and uncovers the food, a dish made with some kind of meat, root vegetables, and greens. Though he feels queasy, he makes himself take a few mouthfuls with the spoon. The food is delicious, velvety with oil and fat. The dog rises and slinks over, not menacing in manner but self-effacing, its ears flattened, tail down. It's not nearly as big or wolflike as it seemed last night. A few steps away it pauses, black eyes alert and shining in the light of the candle he holds. The sweet, eager face of a fruit bat. "*Ela na fas!*" he whispers and the dog surges in and starts bolting the food. He scratches the matted fur of its ruff. The dog makes muffled, ecstatic snorts as it eats.

Elias stands and crosses the courtyard to the gate. The night isn't warm enough for just boxers and an undershirt, but he will be moving fast, he thinks, despite his soreness and sickness. On the face of the gate, a dark iron latch. He tries easing it upward. No good. He tries downward, gingerly, expecting it to grate loudly when it moves. It won't move. He looks over his shoulder: the dog exuberantly licking the plate, which rattles over the flagstones. He turns back to the latch, leans down, holds the candle to a large, medieval-looking keyhole. He tries the latch one more time, up, down. From behind him a light clicking—claws on the flagstones as the dog trots over. Now the door of one of the rooms scrapes open. He tosses down the candle and it goes out and he leaps and grips the top of the gate with both hands, something sharp there cutting his fingers. One scrabbling foot finds a toehold on the latch and for a moment his full weight is on it. It gives with a shocking clank, like an anchor chain snapping. The gate swings outward with him clinging to it. He lets go and drops awkwardly into the street, twisting an ankle. He swings the gate closed before the dog can escape. A hoarse voice cries, "*Stamata!*" He has lost a flip-flop and shakes the other off and runs limpingly up the street to his right, whatever direction that is.

The dog catches him within a block. He hears it gaining—galloping, panting—and feels the leaden panic of a child pursued in a dream. He stops, turns around and braces. The dog bounds past him in the moonlight, then slows and peers back at him, mouth agape and tongue lolling, as if urging him to catch up. It seems to be simply a dog happy for its freedom out here under the moon. The street looks orderly, clear of detritus, the walls whitewashed and free of growth. Now a sound of slapping boot soles and that pea-gravel voice calling, "*Stamata, allios tha rikso!*" *Stop or I'll shoot*. Roland's warning about the dog has turned out to be hollow, but the old soldier seems another matter. Elias turns down an alley, the dog trotting alongside, and by the time they emerge onto another street they're among ruins, the pavement weed-cracked and stony, the gauze on his feet tearing loose, his cuts reopening. His ankle feels more sprained with every step. He pauses, looks up at the teeming stars to get his breath and his bearings, finds Polaris, the moon to the west, sky lightening to the east. He and the dog turn right down a side street, southward. "Argos, *pou eise?*" the pursuing man is shouting from a long way back, and whistling too. "Argos, *ela!*"

They emerge into the overgrown plaza, like the hub of a topiary city made of vines, wild grape and bougainvillea. There are even topiary cars, a few bicycles, a bus. Only the doors and upper parts of the church are free of growth. As they run across the plaza, footfalls, he hopes his own, echo behind them. On the other side he stops and looks back. Nothing. The dog, who must be Argos, is looking back as well, with an air of perplexed concern. "All right, boy," he tells him, "go! *Na fyge!*" Elias turns and continues south along a disintegrated avenue but the dog stays with him, a bit behind now, Elias trying in the moonlight to pick his way through shrubs, weeds, jagged debris, stepping as if on live coals. The tires of abandoned cars appear liquefied, their chassis submerging into the ruins. An owl shrieks close by. When he looks back for Argos (the dog lagging, head down, planting his paws fastidiously) he can see his own feet are leaving a faint, sporadic blood trail.

The overgrown shops and houses thin away. He and Argos pass the cubic hulk of a large brick building, gaping holes for windows. It might once have been a school on the edge of town. Suddenly they're in open country and soon the road is indistinguishable from the parched, stony earth to either side. The light of the moon, which casts long shadows, shows a Nazarene nightscape as if in a Christmas card: a few olive trees, scrubby tamarisks, low treeless hills covered with herbs that he doesn't see but can smell in the cool air, oregano, thyme, sage, Greek mountain tea. There's a hoofbeat clatter and a flash of motion from the top of a knoll. A troop of small goats without bells scrambles away. The dog looks over but makes no move to give chase. Is he trained not to?

The hermit Paris must dwell around here. Could he be tracking Elias and the dog? Elias keeps looking back. The Green Line can't be far. To the southwest a larger hill looms up and he makes for it, on the balls of his feet now, at times crying out involuntarily. His sweat is cold, his jaw trembles. They approach a black and cylindrical mass that seems to swallow the moonlight and reflect nothing back—the crumpled, creosote ruin of a jet fighter. Impossible to read the insignia. Someone has planted a cross beside the remains of the cockpit, and though the wreckage must be from 1974, the cross is white as if freshly painted.

There's a faint yet piercing whistle from behind him. Argos stops and cocks his ears, looks back, glances up at Elias, then turns and bounds away to the north. Now Elias can just make out a figure who seems to be loping southward in his direction. Old or not, the soldier is overtaking him. He can think of no option but to climb this larger hill and hope that from the top he can see the Green Line, and that it's just on the other side. He tries to run. Searing pains in his feet and ankle wring grunts and obscenities out of him. He starts up the slope, rocky and tussocked with gorse and thistle, limps through a tiny stand of olive trees and hopes it might hide his route from the man below. After winding around a few boulders, he has to scramble upward on all fours. Another minute and the slope levels out—he's already at the top. The hill can't be more than fifty metres high. Yet the view from up here is extensive—to the east the sky is brightening over the sea, the southern end of the beach strip, silhouettes of a few last hotel hulks, an abandoned crane. The border that he'd hoped might run just behind the hill seems to lie a good kilometre to the south. It might as well be a hundred. His soles are cut up, his lungs labouring as if he just summited a Himalayan peak. He can just make out the dead zone's fence and beyond it two more fencelines running west to east, framing a road of gravel or sand, pale in the twilight, ending at the shore: the U.N.'s Green Line. On a hillside behind it, a cluster of white houses with a few lights shining, a town in the Republic of Cyprus. He sags onto one knee, then sprawls sideways and lies groaning, looking up at the last stars. There's a panting sound. The dog looms above him, blocking out the sky, regarding him with a quizzically cocked head, then licks his face. Elias hears boot soles crunching over stones. He shuts his eyes and says, "*Kalimera.*" *Good morning.* A harsh, cracked voice replies slowly in Greek, "I was hoping you would run on, so I would have no choice. Instead you lie down and wait for me like a woman."

Elias sits up, pushing the dog back. The man wears a beret over crewcut grey stubble and aims a polished, cocked revolver at Elias's bloody feet. "*Yiati dhen to grafeis st'archidhia mou?*" Elias says. *Why don't you write it on my balls?* The man's heavy moustache hides the expression of his mouth, but his squint tightens and he aims a sharp kick at Elias's swollen ankle. The pain explodes as red-hot light before his eyes.

The sun is high by the time he hobbles back into the wide plaza near the village with Argos, the dog, at his side and his captor behind them, smoking and gruffly singing songs in Cretan dialect, verse after verse, as if to celebrate the capture. Yet the tunes are mournful. So are the words, at least the ones Elias can pick out. Old battle hymns, tragic love songs. Fuck the man for singing them. Fuck the man for singing so well.

Roland and the young woman, Kaiti, appear ahead, approaching them past the front of the church with its bullet-pocked dome. "Ah, Elias," Roland calls out in a thin, winded voice. "I am relieved to see you in a single piece!" He shakes out a thin woollen blanket and wraps it around Elias's bare shoulders.

"*Oriste,*" the young woman tells him, *here,* and tries to hand him his flip-flops. She won't meet his eyes. He doesn't want her to. Now she seems to realize that he can't put the flip-flops on himself and she crouches, muttering "*Panayia mou!*" as she sees his feet at close range. She sets the flip-flops on the paving stones and very gently slips each foot into place. He flinches but won't let himself cry out. She says in Greek, in an impatient tone, "One of you on either side of him—take his arms. Stratis—did you not think to help him?"

The man shuts his eyes and lifts his chin. "He is an escaped prisoner."

"He's not a prisoner. Not exactly."

"I'm afraid he is, now," says Roland, still out of breath. "He won't be able to walk anywhere for some time."

ACCIDENT

She breaks surface but sees nothing. A woman's voice is saying, *Her father had to fly back to Istanbul, Colonel Kaya*, and a man's voice, accompanied by a waft of fine cologne that seems the very scent of that voice: *Are you going to fly her there as well?*

If her condition permits, Colonel.

Eylül wonders if this is a military hospital, unlikely, and she resolves to stay awake and speak to these people, or signal them somehow, but when she tries to speak she can't form a word, her lips won't move. She knows she is in a hospital bed and gravely hurt, perhaps dying. Her mind grasps these facts with the same calm neutrality she recalls from a traffic accident several years ago, on the highway north of Izmir, when the rear of a truck she was trailing too closely (late as always, speeding as always) appeared to rocket back toward her. Remarkable how the mind found time to summon up so many thoughts, regrets, caveats, objections, excuses, in what could not have been more than a second. The passenger beside her, her younger sister, Meltem, screamed, but not even her scream could disrupt the orderly succession of Eylül's thoughts. She didn't normally bother with seat belts, but in Izmir's catastrophic traffic she had ordered Meltem to wear hers, and, after a moment, to pre-empt the sulky charge of hypocrisy she knew to be inevitable, Eylül had yanked her own on as well.

In the moment before her death—what she'd assumed would be her death—remorse had swept through her, as if the accident were a punishment for some unconscionable act she had once committed but could not remember, though in the wake of the accident it would certainly be revealed.

Of the collision itself she has no memory. When she regained consciousness (the car was wrecked but neither sister critically injured), it was with the relief of a dreamer escaping a nightmare. The remorse had really been regret—not for some terrible thing she had done but for the many things she hadn't.

As for how she ended up here, she remembers being at the bar and then outside with the big Canadian, whose troubled eyes made him look older than his years, and whose rare, encompassing grins made him look younger. The sea turtles swarming around them. Then her climax, which took a long time to reach, plateau by plateau, and which—she guesses with a disembodied detachment—might be her last. Then flashlights approaching, the soldiers yelling. Nothing more.

I'll return and check on her in a few days, the velvety voice says now. *If she's still here. I mean—if you haven't transferred her.*

Of course, Colonel, any time! says the female doctor or head nurse, clearly smitten.

DATA SHADOW

He too is a patient in his chilly, twilit cell. Now and then Roland comes in to sweep away cobwebs, check on his ankle or dress his mutilated feet, and Roland, or sometimes Kaiti, brings him food, simple but ample—lentils, small fish, potatoes, mysterious greens cooked in olive oil and lemon—not prison fare at all, unless each meal might actually be his last before execution. (Roland seems bewildered by this joke.)

Elias doesn't bother joking about the pomegranates they keep bringing into his underworld, and which he finds too much trouble to eat.

He leaves all of the meals unfinished.

The reverse of life isn't death but indifference—this coma of the will and heart.

Lying down all the time makes it difficult to hold off sleep. These crumbling old Aspirin, washed down with wine, make it harder still.

Once he's asleep, the dream and its finale: kneeling beside the old man, turning him over, no pulse, straddling the frail body, pumping the chest a few inches from the pulpy cavity of the wound, blood spraying Elias's eyes and lips and the man's sightless face and white beard, *please, please, come back*, men lifting him off, a medic yelling, "Let me do it, move it!" and one soldier, misunderstanding, "Okay, Trif, you got him, he's done!"

Over and over as he flails awake with an animal yelp, pulse thundering and the bedsheets soaked and cold, it's to thoughts of a different kind of escape—a self-escape. Twice after one of these wakings the door screaked open and a man's shape appeared, the courtyard behind him limpid with moonlight. Roland. His room is next door. In silhouette Roland's bedhead of wiry hair stuck up, exclamatory. His speech was thick and awkward: "Elias—Trif? Again the bad dreams?"

Self-exit. Self-departure. Self-deletion. Self-desertion.

His splintered sleeps leave him too exhausted even to look at any of the books Roland has brought him, an odd mix of decomposing paperbacks (Penguin classics, Zane Grey westerns) and a volume of history on Cyprus and the Middle East that weighs as much as a kettle bell. "To fill in the gaps of an American education," the man said. Elias felt too weary to correct him or argue. And why should he argue? In a way, he guesses, it was his ignorance, his innocence, that put him here.

The afternoon heat is a potent hypnotic. Even the small lizards that sometimes skitter across the walls now rest in the corners, throats barely pulsing. Trying to keep his eyes from closing, he leaves his door open for a breeze and does feeble sets of push-ups and crunches on the cool floor of his cell, his hurt ankle propped on his pillow. He's sprawled on the floor panting when Stratis, silent as always, glides past, glances in, no reaction. During the next set of push-ups something jabs Elias's shoulder. With a cry he rolls clear and ends up lying against the wall looking back toward the doorway, breath held.

The children, poised to flee, stand staring in at him. They wear matching blue cotton pyjamas, probably for the siesta. The boy grips a long stick that he now ineptly tries to hide behind his back. Elias sits up. "You must be Aslan," he says in Greek to the boy, and to the girl: "And you're Lale?" They nod gravely, warily. "*To onoma mou einai Trif,*" he says. They look at each other and back at him. The girl says in a brave, croaky little voice, "We know . . . but where do you *come* from?" As he tries to stand, he tries to smile. Instead he grunts in pain. Their eyes widen. They must see a grimacing, dirty, hairy-faced ogre rearing above them. They turn and run. At the same moment a woman's voice calls to them from somewhere a few walls or streets away. He walks to the door—all of four strides—and watches them slip out through the gate.

You've become the sort of man your own mother warned you to flee.

He eases the door shut, lets his forehead rest against the wood. Something in him heaves and shatters, a sinkhole gapes in the ground of his being, he collapses to the floor, hands, knees, and brow against the cold chalky tiles. He sobs, shakes and chokes, he hears himself making unearthly sounds, dying animal sounds, and his attempts to control and muffle them only intensify the attack. He has to give in. As if a lifetime's quota of grief, loneliness, and regret have been concentrated into one cataclysm, he weeps until his eyes swell shut and he lies still and emptied on the floor.

Awake at dawn, trying not to blink back into sleep, he hears very faintly the sonic arabesques of a cantor in a minaret. No, *muezzin*, that's the word. He has almost forgotten about the living city of Famagusta, just a few kilometres to the north. Houses, shops, schools, mosques, and hospitals. One hospital, anyway.

The sound fades and doesn't come back. Hard to believe in an outside world—or to believe in the beliefs of others, their faith, their sense of membership in a flock, a family, a platoon, a village, a movement, a people. A flag. A corporate brand.

Bullshit, all of it. *You belong only to yourself.*

Self-delivery. Self-erasure. Self-extinction.

On the fifth or sixth morning Roland brings news with breakfast. North Cypriot radio has upgraded Eylül Şahin's condition to "serious but stable," a contradiction in terms Elias has never fully understood but is slightly encouraged to hear. Roland examines his ankle and feet, then adds, "She remains comatose, but Elias Trifannis will be back among the living in no time. When you're ready, I will ask the villagers to come in from their houses for a special feast of welcome."

"They must wonder if I'm real. I've been wondering myself."

"Oh, no, they have all seen you! I brought them in the first evening, when you were unconscious."

"All of them, in here?"

"The village is not so big as you might think."

After the man leaves—he walks with his feet turned out, hands linked behind his back—Elias sits up and eats with stirrings of actual hunger: thick, goaty yogurt with walnuts, pistachios and dark honey, a small tart orange, two soft figs, black grapes, a sliced, beet-red prickly pear, a thimble cup of sweet Greek coffee and a glass of water.

Serious but stable.

Are comas perfectly dreamless?

That afternoon he hobbles, wincing with each step, to the "privy" and back without Roland's help, to sponge-bathe with a bucket and an old monogrammed washcloth. At the first splash of icy water over his face, neck, and shoulders, his body surprises him with a deep-drawn groan—a sound of momentary, tentative pleasure. Or is it just relief?

Back in his cell he finds, between the piss-pail and the bed, a bunch of wild lavender and torn bougainvillea stuffed into a joint of bamboo, no water. Apparently the twins have once again braved his cavern. He sets the innocent bouquet up on the window ledge, the better to see it from where he lies.

That night, after losing his battle and crashing into sleep, he remains utterly unconscious until morning. Some hours later he is able to limp out through the repaired gate, to look around. Siesta hour, the village silent. The dog stirs from a doze in the shade of the courtyard lemon tree and follows him. Elias is using a knob-headed black briar cane that Roland found somewhere and which must have seemed quaint even back in the 1970s, or so he guesses (what does he really know of that time, of any time before his own childhood?).

As he inches along in the sunshine, between whitewashed walls that flood his eyes and brain with light, his panic seems to be suspended, curiosity reviving. Maybe it's just that he can move again. For him bodily effort, whether pleasurable or painful, is life.

The village—this one narrow street—is a small oasis of order in a disaster zone. It's remarkable, like a place in a lucid dream: both solid and spectral. Between the courtyard inn and the neighbouring house lies a geometrically neat vegetable patch, while the courtyard of another house has been turned into a tiny orchard: a fig and plum tree, and a few olive trees burled and gnarled as ginger root. A window box of magenta geraniums under closed black shutters. On a flat roof, under a grape trellis, a chicken coop and dovecote. The cool, soft chortling of invisible birds.

The old soldier in his beret seems to be everywhere at all times. Now he sweeps past, swinging his thin but sinewy arms.

Dark moustache, hair like steel filings. An undershirt over a pelt of greying chest hair, patched camouflage trousers tucked into boots, a machete in his belt beside a snared rabbit. He nods and growls—half acknowledgement, half warning. In Elias's belly a sort of power surge. He glares back at the man and spits in the street. Traditional Greeks—the sort his father was—respect frank pugnacity before a polite smile, but Elias's gesture of contempt is not strategic. Rather it seems that in a moment, with a spike of adrenalin, his attacker, this Stratis, has reset Elias's will.

Ten klicks or so south to the border. He will bide his time until he can move properly again. At present his status out in the world might be that of a deserter—no, more likely a suicide, maybe a rapist as well—though all of that must be fading now. A few days of prying interest, a few hundred shares and online comments, then a story dies and what's left of you is a digital shadow. Still, for now, his relatives in Larnaca and Canada must be talking about his death—*grieving* is surely too strong a word, given their slim acquaintance. He and the woman he'd lived with briefly had split up when he enlisted. Of his immediate family, only his sister, an ESL teacher in Korea, remains. Estranged from their father, she did not come back for the funeral, and her last contact with Elias was some months before that. So much for the myth of the close Greek family. Still, if their father were alive, he would be leaving no bush unbeaten to discover his son's exact fate. But he'd died in a hospital bed, Elias beside him, just before Elias's second tour began.

Bored with this invalid pace, Argos cocks his head sideways, chomps the cane and twists it from the hand of the tottering Elias, then bolts away with it in his mouth. Elias finds he can walk back all right without it.

Under the fruit and nut trees and trellised vines of the courtyard, they are preparing for a village dinner, which usually happens only on Sundays and holidays, Roland says. Elias has double-wrapped his ankle and is helping Kaiti Matsakis and Roland pull five small, square tables into line and cover them with a red banquet cloth, then set the table with olive-oil lamps and candles, plates, cutlery, glasses, and pitchers of raw young wine the colour of dark rosé. They haven't asked, much less ordered, him to help—he has offered because he can now, and he can't bear the thought of withdrawing to his twilit room, where he'll just lie on the bed trying not to sleep. Awake and moving, he feels all right.

His returning strength proves useful. The old hardwood tables are heavy, and Kaiti, though she seems fit enough, is petite. As for Roland, he works with the slow, determined diligence and bravely sustained smile of a stoic trying to hide his struggles. Elias overhears Kaiti urge him to go and rest in his room until dinner. "Nonsense, my dear," he replies in Greek, short of breath.

Elias helps them to ready the grill pit. Though the tamarisk wood the villagers burn is nearly smokeless, Roland explains, they never light fires until after dark and then only in the courtyards. The matches, like other supplies with a long shelf life—tinned lentils and fish, tea, sugar, salt and pepper, powdered milk, soap, toilet paper—come from Varosha's abandoned hotel stockrooms and, for a population this size, could last a century.

Kaiti keeps telling them what needs doing next. Is she some kind of young matriarch, or is Roland simply absent-minded and in need of instruction? When she asks Elias to do things, she uses the polite second person and "*parakalo*," *if you please*, keeping a formal distance between them while maintaining the pretext that he's not actually confined here.

Aslan and Lale enter the courtyard and begin setting the table with a quietly dignified air, plainly proud of their duties. The results, though irregular, are impressive for a couple of four-year-olds. (When Kaiti first told him their age and repeated the names he'd already heard once from Roland, he made the mistake of asking if the names weren't Turkish. She was in his room—having left the door open—to rewrap his feet and rub his ankle with a burning liniment. Absorbing his question, she studied him with half-lidded eyes, pale green in a brown face, the skin of her eyelids and under her eyes especially dark. Sharp cheekbones, black hair tied back. She could pass for Kashmiri. She said simply, "*Vevea.*" *Of course.* When he tried asking Roland about the twins the man answered, "Our way here is that villagers tell their own story, yet only if they so choose." Elias assumes the father must be Turkish Cypriot and absent. Or maybe dead? Twice now he has seen her in a black summer dress, like a compromise between mourning and comfort—not quite style. Everything that she, Roland, and the children wear seems dated or second-hand, as if picked up in vintage shops.)

About Roland he has learned only that he was stationed as a U.N. peacekeeper not far from here, in a town above the sea—one of those few towns that survive inside the buffer zone, along the Green Line, and where Greek and Turkish Cypriots continue to coexist. But something went wrong. Roland, who politely demurred when Elias asked today about his last name and which army he'd served in, arrived in the village some years ago and has remained. How many years? The man shrugs, with a weary smile, as if he wishes he could remember.

A feast under the stars at a table laden with good things can numb any trauma for a few hours. The flickering oil light, seen through tumblers and pitchers of homemade wine, makes the liquid pulsate as if alive. There's a platter heaped with wedges of grilled halloumi cheese and a small grilled seabass; there's a large bowl of a stewed meat that turns out to be hare and other bowls full of *fakhes* (lentils sautéed with olive oil, onions, peppers), spinach and eggplant cooked with lemon, fried potatoes, tomato and cucumber salad; there is green, astringent olive oil and a single basket of white bread, about a slice per diner, each of whom ekes out the ration in pained, careful little bites.

The villagers seem oddly small, or maybe it's that most are so thin, streamlined to the specs of another era. If everyone were standing, Elias would loom and lumber among them. He sits between Roland and the little girl, Lale, and across from Neoklis, a tiny middle-aged man who has a bucktooth yellow smile, jutting ears, and bowl-cut hair with a tonsure-like bald spot. Neoklis's short-sleeved shirt is tucked into pants pulled high up his torso and held there with a skinny black belt. His shirt pockets bulge with chess pieces. Because Greek Cypriots use a dialect, it takes Elias a while to realize the man does not just speak Greek regionally but also strangely, at times incomprehensibly.

His parents are the village elders, Takkos and Stavroula Tombazo. They built their house themselves and have lived in it since a decade before the invasion. They refused to leave in '74 when the other twenty thousand Varoshiotes fled. (As the wine flows, the village's history starts to emerge.) Naturally they considered sending Neokli away with the neighbours, but they were afraid of what might become of him, given his condition—he was just six years old and already much afflicted. Then, in hiding, they became still more afraid: "We thought that perhaps the Turks would come and kill us, or take us away to a prison forever," the old man says in Greek, leaning over the head of the table on his elbows. A barrel-chested little man, half the size of his wife, he has a trimmed beard, a drinker's purple nose, and—unlike his son—a full head of hair, white against his spotted brown skin. "At times, the Turks would pass in the street and try the door, but we had barred it, and they made no effort to get in. Here and there they looted, but carelessly, with no clear plan."

"They looted our shop, for the crystal vases," his wife says from the table's other end. Her drawn-on eyebrows and paisley headscarf give her the look of a cancer patient, though one whose body remains stout and solid.

"We sold flowers," the old man calls.

"Far more than flowers!" she corrects him.

"The actor Mastroianni bought our roses."

"In fact, they were irises. The shop was a few blocks over, toward the church."

"Neokli was better off here," Takkos says in a stage whisper.

"No other children around," she adds. "We decided we would not be forced out."

"We thought the U.N. would make the Turks leave Varosha," he says. "So all of our neighbours could return to us. We were wrong. Still . . ."

"Those who fled lost their homes forever."

"Still, not many Turks came in this far, to loot. And then Sergeant Stratis—"

"Taki, enough, we mustn't tell too much yet!"

Staring down the table at his wife he says, "*Then* the sergeant joined us, and *then* they stopped entirely! Elias is Greek, we should trust him!"

"Some Greek," Stratis says, scowling under his brows, wall-eyed with wine. He keeps filling his glass and draining it with choppy, angry movements, squinting out through the fumes of cigarettes that look desiccated with age. Elias tries to ignore his stares. They remind him of something, and then he gets it: the Turks and Turkish Cypriots eyeing him and Eylül in the bar of the Palm Beach Hotel. Yet apart from Stratis Kourakis, the mood seems festive. Are village dinners all like this or is the novelty of hosting a stranger a sort of tonic? They keep referring to him as *ksenos*—stranger, or guest, or both. His Greek now returning to something like fluency, he's answering their questions about the outside world. With the conspicuous exception of Kaiti, they seem especially gratified by answers that depict it as treacherous, hypocritical, overwhelming, violent. Most of his answers do. As the night progresses, everyone wants to refill his glass and address him, even Myrto—a nervous, bony, brittle-looking woman who talks sparingly and formally—and Kaiti Matsakis. Tonight, just once, she calls him Trif. In huskily accented English she adds, "I wish you to speak to Aslan and Lale, to learn a little English. For their futures, maybe."

"Is that an order?"

She looks mystified. "Pardon?"

"Sure," he says, "no problem. They don't seem to understand my Greek."

"I think only Neokli understands," she says—no smile, though she does unknot her brow in response to his grin, which he feels in his cheeks as if he's working a muscle group long out of use.

Now Kaiti and Stavroula are setting out dessert: pistachios and almonds in their shells, a gleaming wedge of honeycomb from the village hives, apricots, cherries, quartered cantaloupes, grapes, and mespila—golden, large-stoned fruits that apparently grow wild everywhere in the ruins. Takkos Tombazo raps a spoon on his plate and proposes a toast: "Now that we know Elias Trifannis will be staying with us for a while, perhaps a long while, let us welcome him properly." He raises his shot glass of raki. *"Stin iyeia sou—ke banda na 'se gala!"* The second half is in Cypriot dialect, but Elias gets the idea. *Your health and may you have it always.* The old man flings back his shot. The others, except for the glaring Stratis, also cry "*Iyeia sou!*" and drink, even the twins—one on each of Stavroula's knees like grandchildren—who hold thimble glasses of wine. Myrto calls out that if Elias needs books, English, Greek, she has many to borrow. Neoklis stares at him with a frank and famished absorption, now and then seeming to grope at his own lap. He smells distinctly goaty.

Stratis butts out in his dinner plate and leans across the table toward Elias. "You were with a Turk on the beach!" he cries in Greek, as if he has only just now learned of this outrage. Silence breaks out. All the villagers—even those who wear pained looks, Roland, Stavroula, Kaiti—hungrily watch the two men. "There in America," he says and jabs a long finger westward, "your blood has so thinned, you don't even know how to hate anymore!"

"Maybe you should try listening to the news on Roland's radio," Elias says.

"This he will not do," says Roland, in English. "Though he does keep many journals in his room, from 1974. Strati, *parakalo*—"

"To hate one's true enemies, I mean—to hate purely the enemies of your blood!"

"I'm finding enough to hate," Elias says, "without inheriting it from my—"

"He who cannot hate purely, how can he love?"

"*Kai vevea!*" Takkos exclaims, helping himself to more raki. "Stratis speaks well here. It's as if life could exist without death . . . truth without lies . . ." But receiving some signal from his wife he adds, "Then again, our guest is only young, and a soldier on leave."

"Anyone paid to kill the enemies of rich men and presidents, not the enemies of his own blood, is no soldier but a mercenary!" Stratis thumps the table on his last word.

A few seconds of pregnant silence, then Elias says, "You're right."

"What?" Stratis turns his head, cups an ear with his hand. "Your Greek . . ."

"I said you're right."

As if vanquished, not vindicated, Stratis deflates back into his chair. Stavroula Tombazo calls out something in dialect and within seconds, in the Greek way, the mood has swung full compass again, although Elias's nerves stay on alert, and Stratis, low in his chair, keeps brooding and muttering. Kaiti brings out another pitcher of wine. Roland appears at Elias's side with a battered little guitar and says, in English, "I believe you mentioned that you can play?"

"I did?"

"You were half asleep."

Just weeks ago he was singing for his platoon, yet that now seems like another man's memory. Roland says: "I can only strum quite roughly, Trif. I am not musical. Play for us."

"An order from my captors?"

"You know it's more complicated than that. And this is hardly Babylon."

Elias takes the small guitar and turns it in his hands. "Quietly, right?"

"We are in a courtyard and a thousand walls are between us and the outer fence. Sing as you like!"

"So we're really in no danger?"

"Ah, very good, you said 'we'!"

"If the soldiers come, I'll be in trouble too. Maybe worse than the rest of you."

"Please," Roland says. "The colonel looks out for us. Rarely, a military airplane flies over, far above, and we have to stay indoors. But foot patrols are few and quite peripheral. Stratis would disagree—he has always believed our risk more urgent, and perhaps he likes to think so—but I believe the only real danger now is *you*, were you to emerge and reveal our existence."

"If I talk when I leave here, it won't be about this village. Who'd believe me?"

The bass E is missing, the other strings rusted and a tuning peg chipped off, yet the old guitar's sound is not bad. The courtyard acoustics help. Before long his heavy sleep debt, along with the wine and the deep strangeness of the situation, make him feel like he's playing songs in a dream, as he often used to back when his dreams were like other people's. He keeps blanking out on lyrics and chord changes he has known for years, but his audience, these genial jailers, don't seem to notice. They drum the table, applaud and cry "Bravo!" Even Stratis looks a little appeased, though when he asks Elias to play certain traditional Greek songs and Elias admits he doesn't know them, the man locks his ropy arms across his chest and sags deeper into his chair.

Another round of toasts. Elias's tenor, a high voice for a large man, grows bolder and his playing more instinctive. For the first time in a while he feels almost part of something. To his medley of blues, including "St James Infirmary" and "Ain't No Sunshine," Roland tries to sing along. Every song picks its sequel. Now he is being urged, of course, to play Leonard Cohen. "It looks so small in your large arms," Myrto says and he wonders if he has misheard her Greek. The self-enclosed Kaiti permits herself a wry smile and claps in time, the girl Lale off-time. Aslan clings like a jockey to the back of the dog. They lap the table and Argos peers up with a strained but tolerant expression as Elias sings about The Partisan—that soldier who has often changed his name, lost wife and family, is a prisoner of the borders . . . All the faces seem lamped from the inside too, even that of Stratis nodding in his chair, a dozing sentry, and this could be decades ago, everyone dressed in period clothing, or it's another age entirely, the folk of a remote village crowded around the outsider who brings gossip, music, and fresh blood.

At the end of the night as he gets up, the wine-dulled pain in his feet and ankle rebounds and he can barely stump back to his cell, or room.

He wakes to the manic, whistling chitter of that strange bird—a nightingale, Roland has told him—coming from the courtyard, but louder and clearer. The door is open, a golden runner of moonlight laid over the tiles. The bed trembles. Someone is kneeling against it: little Neoklis, that unmistakable centaur smell. Did he climb the courtyard gate to get in? *Where is my guard when I need him?* Still drunk, he feels paralyzed. Neoklis drapes an arm over Elias's bare chest, then rests his ear and cheek on the arm. His left hand moves in his own lap, in the dimness beside the bed.

"*Parakalo,*" he is panting, *Please, please.* His breath smells of sour wine and cloves. "Neokli," Elias whispers, afraid of what will happen if he pushes him away—will there be screams, cries for help? "Neokli, *stamata tora, parakalo!*" *Stop now, please!* But hearing his own *parakalo* echoed back to him seems to excite Neoklis further and now he repeats ardently, "*Parakalo!*" The mattress vibrates faster. "*Parakalo!*"

Elias exhales, resigned, and gently rests a hand on the burning, upturned side of the little man's face. In next to no time, Neoklis is standing in the doorway, nodding, his face blacked out by the moonlight behind him. "You play Leonard Cohen for us again tomorrow?"

NOVEMBER: THE TENNIS SET

As Kaya walks toward the red clay court behind the club, lazily smoking, he sees something remarkable: no sign of Captain Polat. He checks his watch: 12:11. Timur Ali has told Kaya that the earnest young captain usually arrives at the court a good twenty minutes early. Kaya himself tends to arrive five or ten minutes late, not so much as a gesture of authority or because he dislikes Polat—though in fact he dislikes the captain more all the time—but because he is metabolically incapable of hurry.

He sits down on the bench between the net post and the court's high chain-link fence, unzips his racquet cover and notes a second surprising thing: he's feeling edgy, impatient, as if he has smoked a full pack of cigarettes in the last hour, instead of just this one. After a final deep drag he flicks the butt through the fence and glances at his wrist: 12:15. The huge shadow of the Odyssey Hotel that looms behind the court's west baseline is already advancing toward the net. He has made Polat play on the west side for game after game, partly out of fairness (the sun is a real handicap, especially when you serve), but also because he, Kaya, so loves to feel the sun on his bare torso and face, especially at this time of year, when the hours of light are shorter.

It strikes him that he can't remember the last time anyone kept him waiting, whether on-duty, off-duty, or in his pre-army days. It seems everyone hankers to please him. Even his superiors. For years he has felt it. But this captain, Aydin Polat . . . there's something different about him and it's worrying the colonel more and more. Among other things, he keeps asking awkward questions about the restricted zone and the (officially dead) foreigner.

Kaya pulls on his headband too forcefully and it slips over his eyes like a blindfold. For a moment he sits there, slumped. *Why did they have to send me this man?* He hears footsteps now, amplified by the ruins—the loose clapping of Polat's feet in the over-large tennis shoes Kaya has lent him.

Kaya thumbs the headband up off his eyes. Captain Polat halts in front of him, salutes stiffly. He's gasping, his plump, pitted cheeks red. The loaned racquet and white shoes—their uppers oddly breaded with sand—go comically with his uniform, pistol belt, and that big peaked cap on his massive head. As always, he looks like a child kitted up as a soldier.

"My apologies, sir! We were to start at 1200 hours."

"Don't mention it, Captain." Then, to his own surprise, Kaya adds, "Why the delay—was there a problem?"

"No, sir." Pause. "Yes, sir—there was—that is, there might well be." With owlish insistence he stares down through his little glasses, as if Kaya ought to know.

"Well, what is it, Captain?"

"I took the liberty of re-inspecting the perimeter to the north, sir, metre by metre. I found something unusual, at one of several places where the fence is . . . the fence is in urgent need of repair, sir!" Polat's voice gets louder as he goes, as if righteous disapproval is overcoming him. "There are signs—faint footprints, also larger impressions—that a person has slipped back and forth under the fence. Possibly several persons. The bottom of the fence can be lifted right out of the sand!"

"I see." Kaya assumes he means the place where the villagers slip through and down to the water on certain nights, to bathe and fish. "Probably it was just a couple of the guards going in to have a look around," he says. "I'll have Ali speak to the sergeant about it. Shall we play now?"

"You mean, guards have been *looting*, sir?"

Kaya sighs under his breath and looks beyond Polat, as if an ally might materialize out of the heat waves rising off the clay.

"Sir, if they are looting—looting is a crime!—they ought to be—"

"I know, Captain—looting is a crime. As I said, I'll have Ali—"

"Possibly it's the foreigner, sir."

"What, the Canadian?"

"He could still be at large in there!"

"But Captain, I told you, I sent men in to search." As he lies again about a search, Kaya stands up and looks down at his adjutant. "As I told you, they found blood but no body. We can only assume he's long dead—he was wounded, there's no water in there, no food, nothing. Just think for a moment. If he'd lived and escaped, he'd be all over the news by now—in newspapers, TV interviews, especially once they got him home. But even in Canada they're saying he drowned, likely a suicide."

Kaya is a touch surprised at how readily the young man's government has accepted the official Turkish line and given up on him; it seems they're eager to avoid offending a rising economic power by pursuing the matter.

"Right, then," says Kaya. "I'll take the sunny side."

Polat, still wearing all his gear, meets Kaya's eyes with something close to insolence. His patchy moustache is dewed with sweat.

"May I ask, sir, how the radical journalist seemed this morning?"

"How did you know I went to the hospital?"

"I questioned the chef, sir."

"Frankly, Captain, it's none of your business!" As usual, Kaya finds it impossible to speak curtly for more than a phrase at a time: "Since you ask, though—her vital signs are stronger and the doctors are reducing the barbiturates. She should be conscious within a few days. But I'd rather—"

"Then you'll interrogate her?"

"Interrogate her? I'll inform her about her lover's drowning and confirm that she doesn't mean to talk about the incident back in Turkey. Which she won't, I'm sure."

"But she has a *history*," Polat says excitedly, "as a troublemaker! About Cyprus, of course, but—but also about the, the—as she calls it—Armenian genocide. And our troops defending themselves in that Kurdish village, last winter."

So Polat has been digging online when not re-inspecting the perimeter.

"This is different, Captain—it's an intimate matter. The woman's personal reputation is at stake."

"Nevertheless, sir, I want . . . I would like to accompany you."

Kaya tries switching tactics. Improvising an easy grin he says, "Captain, I *order* you to strip, put down your weapon, and pick up your racquet."

Polat's baffled eyes blink behind the spectacles, but after a moment he salutes and obeys.

On the court he is inept. Until now he has seemed deaf to any advice and exempt from all improvement. He's all head, his small body a mere extension or prosthesis; he's visibly thinking and rethinking every shot and then, too late, trying to get his limbs to obey. Usually Kaya deliberately blasts some of his own forehands long, lets Polat's better shots get past him, and even double-faults on purpose, all to make sure the little captain wins a couple of games per set. Despite his feelings about Polat, he can't help encouraging him, calling out sincere praise at his infrequent good shots.

But today the captain is playing much better, with a kind of possessed intensity. Though he runs as awkwardly as ever—his loaned shoes clownishly flopping, his glasses held on with a strap—he's getting to the ball faster. He grits his teeth as he lunges for shots. Each flailing serve, forehand smash or two-handed backhand is punctuated by a grunt that echoes off the ruins. There's even topspin on his forehand. Kaya was intending to spot him the first couple of games, a gesture of conciliation, but Polat is playing so far above his level that he actually earns the wins. True, Kaya is not himself. By game two his double faults are unintentional, partly because he refuses to go lighter on the second serves. His forehands are harder than usual, and less accurate. The conversation before the set has left him shaken. It seems Polat will not relent or be finessed in the required direction.

Kaya wins the third game easily and decides he'll spot Polat a lead in the next one before getting serious and sweeping the game and the set. But a few more flubs on his part, and a sharp, sideline-kissing return on Polat's, and Kaya is down 3–1.

Polat is showing clear signs of growing confidence. Awaiting Kaya's serve, he crouches low at the baseline, grimacing with concentration, racquet poised (it's Kaya's racquet, actually—his best one). As for Kaya, he's watching himself grip the ball and toss it up and pull back his racquet, all with debilitating self-awareness. Although he's no veteran player, during officer training he mastered the game's basics with his usual ease. His ability to relax, even when learning new things, has made him a quick study all his life. Now something is wrong.

He smashes the serve long, sends the second one straight into the net, and for the first time in his life while playing a game he utters an obscenity. Then he double-faults *again*. Trudging numbly along the baseline, pulling a ball from the pocket of his shorts, he hears Polat call, "Should we switch sides after this game, sir? It's unfair for you to have the sun in your eyes every game."

"I'm fine, Captain. But thank you. Are you ready?"

"Yes, sir."

He drills in an ace, one of his best serves ever, a beautiful point. But on his following serve, trying for a repeat, he fires wide, and then, still refusing to lighten up on his second try, he double-faults again. Fifteen–forty. He scores another point—rushing the net for a smash when Polat returns a serve too softly—but then loses the game when he tries to repeat that nice play and sends the ball just long.

"Was that in?" he calls, though he's almost certain it was not.

"Ah, no, sir. Just out."

He can't imagine the high-minded captain fibbing about such a thing.

"Good game, Captain."

"Are you sure we shouldn't switch sides, sir?"

In the deferent tilt of the man's head is there something taunting? His features are unreadable because of the sun in Kaya's eyes. At any minute, though, the sun will be dipping behind the ruined penthouse of the Odyssey Hotel and today Kaya, losing 4–1, is happy about it.

In the next game he breaks Polat's serve, and in the game after that, serving without the handicap of the sun, he plays better, calmer, and wins again, after several decent rallies. Polat still leads, 4–3, though the momentum is Kaya's.

In the eighth game Polat plays with frenzied determination, grunting like a wounded man on every serve and shot, his face ominously reddening. He gains a point with an ace, his first ever, then earns another with a weirdly backspinning return that fools

Kaya. But then Kaya comes back with two quick points. The sound of Polat's breathing resounds off the ruins, so the court feels ever smaller, a squash court. An exchange of points and they're at deuce. A long rally ensues, the best ever, ten, fifteen, twenty shots, and Kaya begins to feel exhilarated, as if by the growing skills of a protégé. Finally he sweeps a gorgeous forehand into the back corner and Polat dives, misses, and lies sprawled near the baseline, his glasses knocked askew. Kaya feels a twinge of regret that the rally is over and Polat, it seems, utterly beaten.

"Are you all right, Captain?"

Polat says nothing. He adjusts his glasses, retrieves his racquet and pushes slowly upright, his hands on the clay.

"Good rally, Captain."

"Thank you, sir," says Polat thickly. "Your advantage, sir." Polat limps back to the fence to collect the balls. He frowns down at his watch before positioning himself to serve. One knee of his fatigues is torn. As always, his windup is tight and ungainly, but the serve is respectable. Kaya returns it smoothly and not too hard to Polat's forehand—it seems deep down Kaya would like to share another good long rally before finishing the man off, though at this point in the set he really shouldn't risk it. Naturally he risks it. Polat hacks furiously at the ball and it sizzles back over. Kaya is too far up. For a moment he thinks, *Volley it*, then decides to back up instead, then realizes the ball will probably go long. He lets it whistle past. He watches it meet the clay at the very back of the baseline, a fraction out of bounds, he hopes, he thinks, although it's a close call—a linesman's call.

"Sir? Was it in?"

It was out, just barely, almost certainly, he thinks, and he need only say so and the game will be won, the set tied. Against his own contorted will he calls back, "I really can't be sure, Captain. It was a very nice shot. A centimetre long, I think, but I can't be positive."

"It did look in from here, sir."

He watches Polat carefully. Both men stand motionless, like duellists awaiting a signal. "In that case, Captain, we'll replay the point." Kaya lobs a ball across the net so Polat can repeat his serve. Without moving, Polat catches the ball off the bounce, then looks down and inspects it, as if hoping to find evidence of some kind—a speck of baseline paint?—and suddenly this angers the colonel very much.

"Captain, I believe your shot was long, but I'm giving you the benefit of the doubt. You may repeat your serve now." *And good luck to you*, thinks Kaya, who means to show no mercy the rest of the way. But Polat is still studying the ball in his hand. No. It's his watch he's looking at, again.

"Sir, it's already 1300 hours."

"That's fine, Captain—Ali will tell Ömer to hold lunch for us."

"If it's all right with you, sir, I think I will miss lunch today."

"Miss *lunch*?" Kaya can't imagine why anyone would consider doing such a thing. For a moment he forgets about the past forty minutes: "It's cannelloni today, Captain! And pastries and grappa for dessert. Are you unwell?" In fact, Polat appears to be on the verge of heatstroke. Maybe he really should stop playing. It's unusually hot for mid-November and Polat stubbornly declines to drink water between games.

"I've just realized there's some—there's a task, sir, I've left undone."

"That doesn't sound like you!" *Ha ha*.

"Request permission to be dismissed, sir."

"From a tennis game?"

"It's 1300 hours, sir."

"Captain Polat . . ."

"Perhaps we could finish the match tomorrow, sir."

"Set, not match. We can finish it now. It won't take long."

Silence. Polat still hasn't moved. He seems to be staring hard into the net.

At last Kaya exhales, lets the racquet droop in his hand. "All right, Captain, go ahead."

Kaya has a swim and a shower and by 1340 is dressed and at the table on the club's shaded veranda. The smells of garlic and basil from the kitchen are marvellous, but when the cook, Ömer, brings out the cannelloni, Kaya can't savour it in his usual way. Timur Ali is dining with him. This used to be an occasional arrangement—one with which Ali has never seemed fully at ease—but since Polat's arrival, Kaya has had Ali dine with them daily. After a week or so, Kaya realized he was insisting on this routine mainly to tweak Polat, who thought it irregular and improper. Better yet, Polat is intimidated by the old orderly, who glares at him with bloodshot eyes, mouth hidden by his moustache, whenever the captain asks Kaya too many questions. (Ali himself probably finds Kaya too lax but is of a generation where obedience to a superior is unquestioned.)

Without Polat here to badger Kaya, the meal passes in silence, and slowly. The non-drinking Ali is no talker and today Kaya is preoccupied. A few steps off across the chrome-bright sand, the sea appears stuporous, unmoving in the heat, not a wisp of wind. At least when Polat is here, Kaya can enjoy the sport of trying to make him laugh, to win him over. As Kaya glances at Polat's empty chair and unused place setting it hits him: he has finally encountered someone who is immune to his charm.

"*Efendi?*" Ali clears his throat. "Another glass of retsina?"

Kaya is gazing into space and seeing again the net stretched between Polat and him, at the end of their unfinished set—Polat staring into the mesh. And it hits him. The fence. The fucking *fence*. His intuition seems both unlikely and overwhelming. He whips his mobile phone from the front pocket of his beach shirt and tries Polat's number. No answer. It's 1430. He pockets the phone and stands up. Ali is already on his feet.

"*Efendi?*"

"Ask Ömer not to serve the pastries and grappa yet. I'm afraid the captain may have gone into Varosha."

INVASION

Sleeping for longer stretches now, able to pass a wild olive tree without flashing back to the exterminated grove, he has been exploring farther out in the dead zone. He's chaperoned by Stratis and Roland or Kaiti, along with the dog, who on these outings drops his goofy village demeanour and assumes a kind of heraldic dignity, trotting tall, head erect, eyes hooded and hunterly. Elias still uses the cane, though he could probably gimp around without it. He has come to like it, though. Above all, in preparation for his next attempt, he must maintain an impression of near-helplessness.

A few blocks north of the village a small orchard grows: not of olive trees but almond, cherry, and pistachio. At the time of the invasion this was a traffic island in the middle of a large roundabout, with a small fountain built over what had once been a well, and is now again a well, sheltered among the trees. Beyond it stands a grand-columned neoclassical structure, like an enormous crypt. In the stone of the pediment over the tall wooden doors, an inscription in Greek: LIBRARY OF THE PEOPLE. No other village in the world can boast of such a facility, Roland jokes, and he promises to take Elias in soon. When Elias asks how they keep out the rats, he says, "The place is marble and well-made. In the first weeks after the invasion, some Turkish troops stole old volumes and manuscripts, and rats afterward found their way in and ruined some books. But the looters stopped coming in this far after one of them . . . well, he perished."

"You mean with Stratis's help?" Elias asks.

Silence, then Roland says, "At any rate, all damage from vermin ceased when Myrto became 'librarian,' so to speak, on her arrival."

One day, after assessing his feet and ankle, Kaiti declares deadpan that it's time to go shopping. She sets out briskly and pulls ahead—like most small women, she's a fast walker—while the twins trot on either side of him, peering up at him gravely like munchkin jailers. Both take after Kaiti except for their eyes, which are almost black and set close together. Both have hair to their shoulders. Sergeant Stratis and the dog shadow them for a few blocks, then vanish. The man might be hovering nearby or he might have gone foraging, snare-lining, water-hauling. He knows, of course, that Elias still can't get far. Maybe he thinks he no longer means to.

Between the plaza and the village is a warren of narrow streets lined with the remains of shops—a dystopian bazaar, oddly beautiful, the storefronts overgrown with creepers, bougainvillea, jasmine, wild grapes. There are shoe stores, souvenir shops, cafés, clothing boutiques, a hand laundry, and two used bookstores from which all stock has long since been moved to the library. In the ruin of a menswear store Elias chooses a few shirts from the rack, their shoulders dandered with dust, then a few pairs of Bermuda shorts and cigarette-leg khakis, like things he dimly remembers his father wearing. Also an extra-large sports jacket with padded shoulders (they all have them). The twins are trying on fedoras and straw hats far too big for them and standing in front of the warped, blotchy mirror making faces and giggling. Kaiti watches with maternally amused eyes, then some worry eclipses her face, cleaving a line between her brows.

"They do seem to like it here," he says in Greek, meaning both Varosha and the store. "How does this look on me?"

"You must ask a wife if you want flattery."

"Marriage must work differently over here."

The left corner of her mouth lifts, just. He gets a glimpse of white teeth. Does it count as a smile? He has not yet been able to make her laugh.

They pass through another gaping entrance into a men's footwear store. It smells like a crawlspace. A rat scutters out of sight. The uppers of leather and canvas shoes have all been eaten away, but the rats have left some vinyl tennis shoes and deck shoes undamaged. Time has discoloured them from white to dirty cream. Kaiti unlids a plastic bin of socks, also underwear, saying, "*Oriste*—take what you need." He picks out a few pairs of dark dress socks, then stands holding a pair of white, bikini-style briefs in front of his face. They look like a joke gift. He hears Kaiti chuckle and he looks over: actually she's watching the twins, who are playing in the dust, making a trail of hoofprints with the cloven forms of shoetrees.

"All right, that's enough," she tells them in Greek. "This mummy dust might make you sick."

"Do they ever get bored?" Elias asks quietly, so they won't hear.

"Now and then, of course. But the village is all they know. As for myself . . ." She trails off.

"What?"

"At first I thought only of the things and people that we . . . that I was protecting them from. Now, I think more often of what they're missing. Even the less healthy things, the TV, the junk food. I miss those things too."

"Why did you come here? I mean, how did you even . . ."

She regards him as if he has forgotten his place—or has the question simply startled her?

"Ah, right," he says. "I'm not allowed to ask."

"I might choose to tell you sometime." Silence, then she blurts out, "What happened to you in the war?"

"Am I being interrogated?"

"Hardly—I have no way to force you to answer."

"You could tell me your story first."

"If I wished to." She looks back at the twins, now watching her and Elias and trying to hear. "Go ahead," she tells them, "make more of your beast tracks."

"Devil tracks!" they cry back at her.

"Why not just *let* me leave," he says softly, "instead of forcing my hand? I promise I'll do nothing to hurt you out there—you and the villagers."

"If you went back now, people would know you'd survived in here and they could find out about us."

"Hurting you—you all—or anyone—it's the last thing that—"

"And Kaya would be compromised too. No—neither he nor we could allow it. I'm sorry, Trif."

"I'm not asking if it's allowed."

"Your Greek gets clearer by the day." Ghost-green eyes still locked onto his face, holding him there, she calls out, "*Endaksi*, enough games for now! Time to go home."

Returning with their loot they pass through concentric zones of lessening chaos, as if walking back in time to the prewar Varosha. She sees him to the gate and bids him good afternoon—"*Kala apoyevma*"—with a stiff, dated sort of formality, though her gaze is less reserved now, perhaps even sympathetic. The twins take her hands and the three walk back up the street toward their house.

In the courtyard Roland and Neoklis sit under the pistachio tree playing chess. As Elias comes in, Roland lifts a hand with the index finger raised: *One moment, I've something to tell you*. Neoklis is squirming in his seat, puffing and grunting, his hairless face, just above the wooden board, shining with sweat, his shirt pockets stuffed with the pieces he has seized. In fact, he's a prodigy. Roland sighs, sits back and grins broadly in his beard. He picks up his king and hands it over.

"*Na paiksoume pali?*" Neoklis asks. *We play again?*

"Certainly!" Roland says, then turns toward Elias. "Trif, I've some news."

"Eylül?" he asks. Roland's reports on her condition have grown infrequent as Turkish Cypriot radio has moved on to other stories. But now, he tells Elias, there's an update: "Although unconscious still, she is showing more hopeful improvements."

As Elias takes in the news, Roland studies his face. "Why, Trif, you look as relieved as if she . . . Or is it simply that you yourself are improving? As you came in and I saw you from the corner of my eye"—he says it like *coroner*—"little sign of any limp! Perhaps now we must watch you more closely?"

"Or have Stratis break my other ankle."

Roland cocks his head pensively, as if considering the proposition, but then says, "To be honest I would be quite sad now if you also were to leave us."

"Trif is back!" Neoklis announces in Greek, as if only now realizing.

"Who else is leaving?" Elias asks.

Roland smiles unhappily. "*Pios kserei?*" he says—*Who knows?*—as always switching to Greek when he wants to equivocate.

The feeling is strange, almost painful, like a collapsed lung reinflating: a gutted heart starting to refill.

In some ways he will be almost sorry to leave. This pocket in the ruins of a dead city seems more and more like a singularity outside time, so that past events out there beyond the mouth of the wormhole are coming to feel, by light of day, like hallucinations. Another few months and they might seem to belong in the bio or obituary of a stranger—though by then he will be back out there and dealing with the fallout of the real events. For one thing, now that the past month has fully estranged him from his comrades, he feels ready to testify at the inquiry.

Afternoons he passes out in the narcotic heat, to the alpha-wave hum of the crickets, and these sleeps are unshattered. Then last night again he slept through until dawn. He woke to the throttled squawk of the rooster from the Tombazos' roof. Something has been done to the bird to keep it from crowing. Smells of coffee and blooming cyclamen wafted in over the transom with a pleasantly cool breeze. Mid-November. He pulled on Bermuda shorts and flip-flops and unblocked the door—a ladder-back chair tilted against it to hold off Neoklis—then limped out into the courtyard and picked an orange. Through the open door of room seven, the "kitchen," he got a glimpse of Stratis boiling Greek coffee over the two-burner camp stove.

In room four the smell of the long drop is strong but today for the first time it reminds him more of summer-camp canoe trips than army pit latrines. On a wide shelf under a spotty mirror, small wrapped bars of hotel soap are stacked beside a jug of water, a wash basin, and a bowl of the tooth powder the villagers make out of baking soda and cloves. Two pairs of his preposterous briefs are drying on a line by the window, where he hung them last night. He shaves with a straight razor that looks like a stage prop.

After helping Roland hand-squish potato bugs and pick tomatoes in the garden, he stumps slowly north to the library, knowing it's open for only an hour or two around midday, when enough light enters through the skylight's cracked, dirty panes. He hopes to find compilations of songs in English. If the library has any, they will be pre-1974, but he likes plenty of that older material. Nightly now he plays for at least a few of the villagers. He means to expand his playlist, add some Greek songs, and Roland would like him to learn a few traditional western numbers like "Red River Valley," to which Roland knows German words. "Ah, then you're German—or Austrian?" Elias asked. "Or possibly Swiss," the man replied, in Greek.

The library's grand front doors are sealed along the bottom to keep out rats. He enters through the side door and negotiates a gloomy maze of meandering shelves. More than once he has to backtrack. He emerges and crosses the atrium to the desk under the skylight, where Dr. Myrto Nicolaides is leaning over a chaos of layered papers, gnawing a pencil (the library is the one place where she will not smoke).

"Sorry to bother you," he says. She peers up: startled eyes with dark pouches beneath. She looks more like a sleepless scientist than a librarian. For years she was a junior professor in classical philosophy at the university in Nicosia—this much he has learned. Also that she spends her daily two hours here (four or five in summer, when the light is better and this is the coolest spot in Varosha) planning and executing an Augean labour of reorganization. During his first visit, with Roland, Myrto explained in stiffly accurate English that in her view, books ought not to be shelved in exclusive sections, by genre, each genre internally alphabetized, but instead in a sort of rolling continuum, according to *essence*. Thus Ovid's *Metamorphoses* belongs not in Poetry or Classics but between books concerning dreams and books concerning psychology, especially those by C.G. Jung and Hermann Hesse. Those books then shift by degrees into neurology, then physiology, anatomy, evolution, geology, teleology, philosophy. Marcus Aurelius and other laconics, as she calls them, shade into the authors of haiku, then the Buddhists, the Hindus, the Sufis, the Christian mystics, who are many aisles removed from St Paul, who resides with Descartes and other dualists . . .

Now in a crisply satisfied tone she corrects him when he asks about the music section. The shelving, she repeats, is fluid, a moving river of associations! Alas, this has led to certain problems. Knowledge does not form a single, linear spectrum—it branches, it forks. Evolution not only leads into geology but also diverges into neurology, not to mention chemistry, or genetics! For several years, she says, Roland has been helping her move the wheeled but heavy shelves into looping, labyrinthine configurations, trying to shape an essential continuum that is unbroken except for those places where a "synapse" must be left between shelves to permit visitors to pass—yet still in several places the project has stalled, the shelves like dead branches, and each "solution" leads to other problems, other dead ends. "I misjudged the difficulty," she tells him now, the overhead light showing the grey in her tied-back hair. Her mouth moves little when she speaks, her teeth never showing.

"Come." She guides him back into the stacks. "I can lead a borrower directly to any book in particular, by memory." And she adds that she is compiling a vast alphabetical catalogue, lest she be the only one to know where each title can be found.

The shelves close around them. Dust motes drift in eddies of air, the detritus of countless volumes slowly atomizing. They pass a lone shelf that juts from a line of shelves. On the dead end of it, a brass plaque reads POLEMOS PATER PANTON—*war, father of everything.* Unlike the others, this shelf is bare.

"This used to be Military History?" he asks.

"The books have been redistributed. For now, I leave this shelf labelled but empty, a symbolic gesture, war as a dead branch. Consider what it did to my city!"

"So you don't agree with the line."

"*Agree?*" she says, as if she rarely agrees with anything. "You've been sweating," she says, now in Greek, and her small, comma-shaped nostrils flare. Once he's sure that he hasn't misunderstood, he says, "I was helping Roland in the garden."

"Yes, in the sunshine. I smell that too. It seems so far away when I'm in here."

"Sorry, I didn't have time to wash."

"Not at all," she goes on in Greek. "Please, say no more."

He doesn't know where to look. He crosses his arms over his chest, as if to seal shut his armpits, which are abruptly damper and chilled in this twilit space. He shivers. Like any large man, he finds frail people more disconcerting than the strong. They're trickier to read. He says, "Didn't Charles Manson say his father was the war?"

"Who?" she asks. She's edging closer with no visible motion and he can see the lines like fine print in her olive skin, how her eyebrows are faint, pencilled arcs. In this moment she seems inseparably part of the library, a creature of its gloom and of the past, all language and knowledge. He himself was a bit of a bookworm before learning to hide it as a boy, so as to *pass* as a boy, a jock, and to gratify his father, which of course is what eventually brought him here.

"I'm not sure I want to go back," he hears himself say.

She steps forward, kisses him on the lips. He loosens his tight arms, opens them and wraps them around her thin shoulders, less like a lover than like a boxer clinching to avoid further blows. She feels cold under her flimsy blouse. She kisses him harder. Briefly, reflexively, he kisses her back, this woman—maybe close to the age his mother was when she died—then turns his face away, cups the back of her head in his large hand and brings her cheek to his chest.

"*Lipameh*," he says. *I'm sorry.*

"For what? Such a kiss? That was nothing."

"Then for nothing."

Their speech and the sound of her breaths are amplified high above in the coffers of the ceiling, from which dead electric lamps hang down. They stand together amid piles of unsorted books, the shelves towering around them. She smells of graphite and cigarette smoke.

"It's not war," she says, speaking Greek now, "but simply hate."

"What is?"

"The father of all things. Hate is. Also anger, envy, failed love. War . . . it's just a symptom." In Greek the phrases sound not rhetorical but natural, as if the language has evolved solely for the use of orators, lovers, eulogists, singers and poets. "When I came here, I told myself I was at the end of love, thus at the end of life. I would disappear into the aftermath, alone here, and not return—die, I must have thought. I was mad with grief and shame. I never knew there were people in here, nobody knew. But I remembered the city—I grew up here, a very happy time, I was twelve years old when we had to flee. I never forgot this library. I decided—no—I decided nothing—I simply acted—I fled *back* here when my life collapsed. The man was married, a senior colleague, four children, married and with other lovers, or so I learned at the end—he lied to me for nine years, six months and two days. My God, the promises! A life with him, children of my own, children of our own—common promises, I know, a trite little tale, but to me at that time, somehow it seemed unique, our own epic! I was little older than you when it started. It was after my marriage died. I see now that he never took me seriously, not because I was a woman but because I grew up poor, by his standards—my father worked with his hands. You wouldn't understand, you have no class system in America, not like here."

"Well," Elias starts, but he stops himself so as not to stop her.

"In the end—I never believed it possible and yet I could see how easy it was for him to give me up, a mildly disagreeable bit of business, like sacking a difficult, minor employee. I did things to injure him then, things one should never do, not even to men like Manoli. I was out of my mind with the loss. I did terrible things! No one died, but I lost everything, family, friends, my position, the children he never gave me, also the two he made me cut short, 'too soon,' he told me, 'not yet.' He meant, 'not ever.'"

She brings amber fingertips to her mouth, the nails closely bitten. The lines arcing from her nostrils to the corners of her lips channel tears.

"But, look, I said I was finished with love, this kind especially, and here I make myself a liar, throwing myself at you."

"It's all right," he murmurs.

"I've begun to dream again lately," she says. "I mean, dreams of love."

It hits him that he too had an erotic dream last night—no war dream. But who was the woman? The face was blacked out like a redacted word in a vital document.

"In the dreams, however, I'm not too old for one of your age."

"You're not old," he says, although he can't help thinking, *Yes, she is old*. "It's just that . . ."

"Or you think I'm half mad. All the others do."

"I *like* your library," he says.

"The twins even fear me. They believe I'm a *magissa*—I will catch them among the shelves and turn them into moon moths and press them into books. If only I had such powers! What would I have done to Manoli, I wonder?"

She kisses his cheek and he feels the hot tears. He hugs her—keeping a slight distance at the waist—and the buckling of her delicate skeleton startles him, as if a little more force might have snapped her spine.

He returns to the courtyard as the afternoon heat builds and siesta settles over the village. His words to Myrto—"I'm not sure I want to go back"—surprised him at the time and surprise him now. He will have to flee before his resolve weakens further. His ankle hurts too much to run, but he can manage a walk. It will have to be enough. As he opens the gate and enters, Argos, on his side under the lemon tree, lifts his head slightly, looks over, lets his head flop back into the dirt. Elias leaves the gate slightly ajar. Roland can be heard snoring in his room. He has said this is the hottest autumn he has ever known in Cyprus. As Elias enters his own room, he glances across the courtyard at Stratis's half-open door, then lies down to wait until the siesta deepens and even Stratis must be asleep. Instead, after a few minutes he hears the man emerge, cross the courtyard to the gate to shut and lock it, then go back into his room.

Elias lets his body loosen, his heavy eyelids droop. It's as if he has eaten *lotos*. He decides, if *decide* is the word, to leave things to fate for now. Wait and see if Stratis begins to snore. Jumping the fence with this ankle will be tricky. Maybe try tonight instead? Or after the Sunday dinner, so as to see Kaiti one more time.

A rapping like a burst of semi-automatic fire wrenches him awake. The door swings open. He has been sleeping hard for maybe an hour; the shadow of the window grille has crossed several tiles. He expects to see Neoklis, maybe Myrto. Stavroula Tombazo barges in, flower-print housedress, meaty arms and monolithic bosom, and Elias thinks, *My God, you too?* Woozy with sleep he addresses her in English, which she doesn't speak: "What is it—everything okay?"

"Get up and dress. Roland and Sergeant Kourakis need your help. Are you not a soldier? The hermit warns that an armed Turkish officer is approaching the village."

Roland and Elias pass through the derelict bazaar to the plaza and then across the open square under a withering sun. No one should be awake and moving out here. Roland walks as always with his head stooped, hands linked behind his back, feet turned out. His straw sun-hat goes oddly with the remnants of his peacekeeper's outfit: that faded blue shirt with the cloth epaulettes. On his belt a primitive-looking walkie-talkie. His eyelids are puffy and he's already red and winded, lucky for Elias, who's struggling to keep up on his ankle and tender feet. But Elias is not unwilling to be out here, aiding his captors; he'll be in far more trouble if captured by the Turks.

Roland explains that Stratis and the dog are up ahead, not far from the Jaguar gate, watching the intruder.

"I thought you said the village was safe?"

"This is a mysterious aberration."

"You're sure it's not this colonel, Kaya?"

"Of course not!" Roland sounds untypically irritable. Or is he simply alarmed? "Come, hurry, Stratis cannot be predicted."

They enter a side street that soon curves away from the plaza, then straightens and runs east—more or less the route Elias followed on the night he entered Varosha. Another block and the Jaguar gate comes into sight. Roland is several steps ahead. Elias repeatedly turns his ankle in the cracks between paving stones. Shocks of familiar agony. He could never have reached the Green Line. An eruption of static and Roland brings the handset to his ear. Elias can't make out a word through the crackling, but Roland replies in Greek, "We're at the gate—not far now. Five minutes." Because of the connection or Stratis's hearing, Roland has to repeat himself: "*Pende lepta! Endaksi?*"

First Roland and then Elias squeeze through the rift between the sedans. Thanks to the village diet, Elias fits through more easily than on his first night in Varosha. Another block and they veer left onto a wider residential street, its asphalt buckled by man-high weeds like giant Queen Anne's lace, some of it freshly macheted. They pass an auto showroom, the glass facade collapsed and replaced by a screen of palm scrub behind which a few homely European compacts, grey with dust, remain on display.

The cratered street opens into a sun-white expanse: a tiny plaza with an old stone church to one side. Roland stops, swabs his face with a handkerchief. In the shadow of the hat brim his eyes, very blue in his boiled-looking face, swivel and search. A voice calls softly, "*Ela edho, vlakes!*" They make for the remains of a building on the corner, its roof caved and a mespila tree growing out of the rubble.

Stratis and Argos are tucked behind what's left of the east wall, Stratis's dark beret tipped low over one brow. He's restraining the dog by the ruff. His free hand holds a mespila bitten to the stone. Behind his moustache he's calmly chewing. Roland and Elias hunker beside him and squint across the blazing square. Elias feels the heat everywhere except in his guts, which are ice cold. At first he sees nothing. Then something moves in the shade on the ledge of the fountain at the centre of the square. A squat palm, like a huge pineapple with ratty fronds, grows out of the dead fountain. His eyes adjust. A man in uniform sits on the ledge, his head and torso slumped forward. His peaked cap has fallen by his boots. His head lolls lower, snaps up. Elbows splayed, he's pressing his hands down onto his thighs, as if trying to push himself to his feet. Again his head droops and this time his body follows, first in slow motion but speeding up, toppling forward off the ledge and crashing into the square.

Stratis stands and releases Argos, who pounces over the rubble and slinks low and fast toward the body. Stratis flings away the stone of the fruit, unpockets his lovingly oiled and polished revolver, and follows. Roland and Elias come next, Roland jogging a few steps to catch Stratis, putting a hand on his shoulder, saying in Greek, "Do nothing that can't be undone!" Stratis jerks free and calls back, "Now do you see this will always be a war zone?"

Argos sniffs at the body and now looks up at the approaching men. Stratis clucks his tongue. The dog backs off. Roland kneels and checks the man's throat for a pulse.

"Dead?" Stratis asks hopefully.

"No—he's hot, and his heart is racing. Put away your gun and help me turn him."

Stratis makes no move to touch the man. Elias squats and helps Roland turn him onto his back. The large head has an inflated look, the plump face so livid you can barely see the oozing welt where his brow just smacked the stones. One lens of his wire-framed spectacles is cracked. There's a tear in his trousers leg, though the scrape there on his knee looks hours old. His holster is empty. He looks to be around Elias's age.

Roland cups a palm over the man's forehead.

"He's bone dry. Heatstroke. He must have been in here for hours. The streets around here are a labyrinth. He'll be dead very soon if we don't help."

"Then we don't help," Stratis says from deep in his chest.

"Don't be a fool! They'll come in here looking for him."

"But Kaya can fix things, no? Isn't that what he does, according to you?"

"This man is a captain in the Turkish army!" says Roland, indicating the shoulder patch plastered with dust and dirt. "Kaya did mention he has a new man—God alone knows what he was doing in here. But if he goes missing, there will be a full search of Varosha and not even Kaya could prevent it."

Behind the damaged spectacles the man's eyes are open a crack. He's exhaling in quick little puffs that keep forcing a small gap between his lips. A thin, almost juvenile moustache. Roland is undoing the buttons of his khaki tunic, the T-shirt beneath it soaked and sour-smelling.

"If we help him and he sees us . . ." Stratis begins.

"That is a problem, it's true, but—"

"It's more than a problem!"

"—but we've no other choice! We'll have to blindfold him, then carry him out. At the fence, you and Trif will stay by him, try to keep him cool. Get some of your water into him. I'll run down John F. Kennedy, then go out to the officers' club and find Kaya."

"But how can we know who else is there?"

"Where, at the club?"

"If anyone but Kaya and his man should see . . ."

"We've no other choice, unless we mean to let this man die. Let's move him into the shadow. Give me your wineskin and the blindfold."

Shielding the wineskin with his left hand, Stratis lifts his chin while closing his eyes and clicking his tongue—the Greek "no" in all its jarring bluntness.

"For the love of God, Strati, don't be a fool!"

"You were an officer, perhaps, but not mine."

"I'm not giving you an order, I'm begging you to *think*!" And Roland mutters in English, "All of them anarchists, and I love this, until moments like now."

"Your hat," Elias tells Roland, and Roland, understanding, whips it off and gives it to Elias, who starts fanning the Turk. Stratis finally pockets his pistol, grips the man's boot heels and drags him into the shade under the fountain ledge. Elias and Roland have to scramble along in a frog-squat, Elias still fanning, Roland supporting the back of the man's head over the pavestones.

"Ah, his weapon!" Stratis says, fishing a black Beretta-style pistol out of the dry fountain. He brings it close to his eyes, like Gollum with his precious ring. "You may order me to replace it in his holster—go ahead!—but this time I will not be so—"

"Just give us the water!" Roland cries, adding some gruff German aside.

Stratis lifts the wineskin high in his hands and squeezes a long stream into his own mouth, then ostentatiously works the stopper back in. "There. There's little enough. May it turn to venom on his tongue, the *malaka*."

With a splash of water Elias dampens the blindfold that Stratis hands down to them. Roland removes the cracked glasses and folds them into a pocket of the man's tunic, then secures the blindfold over his eyes. They remove his boots and wet socks to cool him further, then lug him across the square into a perplex of narrow, swerving lanes and alleys. Stratis and Roland lead, each bearing one of the man's thighs, continuing to argue in Greek as they stumble along. Behind them Elias takes the bulk of the weight, his hands and forearms hammer-gripped up through the man's burning armpits, the back of the man's head lolling against Elias's chest. With every step, pain crashes through his ankle. He has the man's boots slung around his neck by their tied laces and he wears the man's solid officer's cap. Argos trots beside this many-legged formation, glancing up with a look of excited concern and that panting, apologetic grin. *Forgive me, men, I would help you if I could!*

The little captain seems light at first but soon grows heavy. Elias turns his ankle again and groans, "Jesus, fuck!" *It's over*, he thinks. *I won't walk again for weeks*. "Is it your foot?" Stratis snarls over his shoulder. "Does it hurt?" "Just when I laugh, motherfucker," he says in English, and Roland calls, "Enough, both of you!" Small flies appear and swarm in the men's faces, as if knowing their hands are tied up. "This incident," Stratis says in what he must think is a whisper—or maybe not, maybe he doesn't care—"must have to do with Trifannis!" "If so, it's now irrelevant," Roland gets out. The Turkish captain squeaks and moans like a child sleeping out a fever. They set him down on a cracked stone bench covered with dirt and guano. They squirt another precious dram down his throat and then, after a swallow each, heft him and struggle on.

"How far now?" Elias asks. No answer. They turn into the breezy gloom of an alley littered with rubble and rebar and emerge onto a wide, blinding boulevard—gutted cars, buses, the facade of decrepit hotels looming—John F. Kennedy Avenue. In a narrow defile between two towers, a glimpse of the sea. "I've got to put him down."

"It's Kaya," Roland whispers.

Out of a thicket of scrappy palm trees sprouting from a traffic island two figures emerge—one in khaki fatigues, very tall and thin and with a drooping grey moustache, the other slim, fit and graceful, dark hair swept back, aviator sunglasses, zany beach shirt, white slacks and deck shoes. He could be a French playboy off a Côte d'Azur yacht. Neither man looks to be armed. Neither looks at all like a colonel, but Elias assumes Kaya must be the one in civvies.

"Friends," this man hails them, "my friends!—Roland!—what is happened?"

As the groups converge, Argos, his ears laid back, happily waddles up to greet the man who must be Kaya, but the man is pulling off his sunglasses to gape at the barefoot, blindfolded captain, who looks as dead as can be. "But what have you *done*?" Kaya says in densely accented English, and at first it seems he might be addressing the unconscious captain instead of the men who hold him. Now Kaya notices Elias. The brown eyes in Kaya's tanned face widen; speechlessly he points at the captain's hat still perched on Elias's head like a trophy.

"It's all right," Roland says. "Let's get him into the shade."

"He is not dead?"

"It's the heat. He must go to hospital, now." Roland adds something in what must be Turkish.

"Come," Kaya says, then he too switches to Turkish, addressing either Roland or the old moustachioed orderly. Now this orderly and Colonel Kaya—who smells fragrant, almost floral—push in on either side of the captain, and the five men together bear him into the deep canyon between hotels. It's only now, with some of the weight shared out, that Elias's arms begin trembling. Another whiff of cologne. Next to the dashing Kaya, Roland with his straw hat and beard might be a weathered Amish farmer. They emerge into the sun. A roofless olive Jeep has been driven right up onto the loose, twisted fence and parked on top of it, flattening it into the sand.

"He came in this way, then?" Roland asks.

"Here or by Hotel Varosha," Kaya says.

"But *why*, Erkan? Why the devil would one of your men—"

"Because of me," Elias says. "Stratis is right."

"You are Trifannis, most obviously. I am Kaya." Somehow the man's glowing suavity is untarnished by his broken English and the crude, clumsy fact of their lugging a body together. "I hope that my officer either saw or heard you not?"

"I think not," Roland says. "He was like this when we found him. Hurry."

"*Ellinika, poustes!*" says Stratis: *Use Greek, you faggots!*

They deposit the captain, again moaning, onto the rear bench of the Jeep. The tall old orderly digs out a plastic bottle and drips water between the man's lips and splashes it over his face and chest. Then he climbs into the driver's seat and starts the engine. His yellow eyes are impassive, his mouth, like Stratis's, hidden. Stratis spits and walks back over the flattened fence into the dead zone, where he stands waiting, turned away. He lights a cigarette and snaps a command over his shoulder at Argos, who has been striving to get Kaya's attention but now trots over to Stratis, though with reluctance; the whites of the dog's eyes show as he casts yearning glances back at Kaya. Elias returns the captain's peaked cap and Kaya says, over the engine's throbbing, "*Teşekkür ederim*—I thank you so much. And have you his pistol?"

Elias looks at Roland; Roland's beard bunches around his mouth. Turning up his hands he says, "I am afraid it was inadvertently lost, Erkan."

Kaya glances at Stratis's back with a philosophical half-smile.

"But there *is* a mobile telephone," Roland adds, enunciating carefully. "In your man's chest pocket. You must check for photographs. It's possible that he got as far as the Jaguar gate. In fact, you might want to throw a second mobile into the sea—tell him it was lost, like his pistol."

The fallen man squeaks, then puffs a large breath between his lips as if blowing out a candle.

"Go now, Erkan."

"Of course." Kaya hesitates—he seems loath to end the conversation—then vaults lightly into the Jeep. He dons his sunglasses and shows Elias his white incisors. "Oh, and the woman, Miss Şahin! She is more well. Please do not worry. I am sorry for these events. Please stay in the village forever."

Elias assumes he means "for now."

"You are comfortable? You appear to seem hurt."

Elias shrugs. "Listen, I'm not asking this out of vanity, but . . ." When he sees that Kaya can't understand, he turns to Roland: "Ask him if there's any news about me—I mean from back home."

Roland speaks briefly in Turkish. As Kaya answers Roland in Turkish, he looks directly at Elias, punctuating his words with courtly smiles and nods. Roland translates: "You do remain drowned. But—and the colonel is pleased for you—some of the media in your part of America doubt that you really harmed Ms. Şahin. They suspect a Turkish cover-up. However, your government seems eager to let the matter drop, and so they have. And the media have moved on. In this way, things have worked out for everyone."

"Better get him to hospital," Elias says, trying to sort out his feelings.

"Ah, and please not to bathe!" Kaya adds. "I mean . . . not to go through the fence there, either here, for bathe or fish, until I notify."

"*Ja*, of course," says Roland.

The Jeep reverses off the fence, spattering sand, some of which strikes the back of the rigid Stratis. The fence remains flattened. The vehicle judders away up the beach toward Famagusta, its gears grinding up and down the scale. Before long it blends into the thermals pulsing up off the sand. Roland and Elias turn and for some moments stare at the sea; then they exchange a look and, despite Kaya's request, tramp down and wade into the shallows without undressing.

This small triumph over a Turkish invader renders Stratis even more spry and vigorous than usual. He applies his machete to a hooked acacia branch to make a rough crutch for Elias before loping ahead to the village to bring the news. Argos runs after him.

Elias and Roland straggle homeward, stopping to rest wherever they find shaded places to sit. Elias is in too much pain to say much, though if he did, he might admit it's some consolation to hear that people back home don't buy the rape story. The real world seems spectral now, almost fictional, but there are still a few souls out there whose opinions matter to him: relatives, a few ex–mess mates, the woman he'd lived with, some clients at the gym where he worked as a trainer. And that troubled military shrink. As for his ex-commanders, he doesn't give a shit. Speaking of whom: this leaves just one piece of unfinished business out there in the world of the living.

Near the village he stumbles, the crutch snaps, and he yells something that shocks even him; working as a trainer he learned enough about injuries to guess that what he has here is a stress fracture at the very least.

"Trif? I am sorry for your pain, but if it might give you solace . . . you may have helped to save the village just now."

"Like a POW who helps fight a fire in a prison camp?"

"But look, you smile as you say it."

"I believe that was a grimace."

"We are close now."

"Anyhow—happier ending than with the last village we tried to save."

"We?"

"Over there. In the war."

"Ah," Roland says. "I did wonder if what occurred . . . might be of that nature. Involving civilians." He pauses to catch his breath. "In Vietnam, I think, an American officer said, 'We had to destroy the village in order to save it.'" When Elias doesn't respond, Roland adds, "In a quieter way, it might be too late for this one also."

"What do you mean?"

"Ah, there, she is waiting for us!"

Kaiti comes up the street toward them. For just a moment he wonders if the unguarded gladness on her face and in her gait might be on his account, but then he realizes, no, of course not, it's for Roland, she and he are like daughter and father. "*Ela, pedhi mou!*" Roland cries, opening his arms. As she and Roland embrace beside him, Elias can smell her, a faint melon-like sweetness, and even the rich oils of her scalp. Now, to his surprise, she turns to him, Elias, and rises onto her toes, puts her fingers lightly on his shoulders, touches her cool lips to both sides of his jaw. In Greek she says, "Trif, I hear you have re-injured your foot."

"Has the sergeant been expressing his concern?"

Her cheeks dimple slightly, an interrupted smile; she says, "Do be careful, Trif. Stratis can't live without quarrels the way some men can't do without love." (Does she mean sex?) "He seemed upset just now, when the women agreed that you deserved gratitude for lending us your strength."

Dusk finds him and Roland drinking under the pistachio tree, alone but for the dog, who lies snoring on the cool flagstones among fallen lemons not yet gathered by the twins. Takkos has taken the twins and Neoklis back to the Tombazo house. Stavroula and Kaiti are finishing a rabbit stew for tonight's impromptu celebration and Myrto has forced her assistance on them, though usually they chase her out of the kitchen, insisting they need no help and then, in her absence, cheerfully concurring that she is perfectly ignorant when it comes to food. As for Stratis, he drank with them for an hour, but as Roland and Elias began to grow animated, he fell silent, finally leaping up and stalking away to his room.

"The wine is very good, the wine is *wonderful*," says Roland, drinking steadily and leaving the appetizers untouched, his accent thickening in a way Elias hasn't heard before now. "But happily I would walk the fifty kilometres to Nicosia tonight, to the U.N. bar in the Ledra Palace, for one certain drink."

"Beer?"

"*Ja*, exactly—cold beer in a cold glass!"

"If we could get some we could keep it cool," Elias says, indicating the bucket of cold well water in which his foot is soaking. He asks, "What would happen if you actually went back to that bar?"

"Oh, they would arrest me immediately." Roland stops himself, looks cannily at Elias, one side of his grey-streaked beard curling upward. "Ah, I see, you intended to trick me! A good try. But I tell you nothing more now."

"Were there women in that bar, or mainly men?"

"No, always we have women." *Always vee haf vimmin.*

"You must miss that sometimes."

Roland tilts his straw hat back off his brow. "In the night, sometimes, *ja*, of course. But I was married very young, I was married a second time, and I had also a woman on Cyprus, in the Greek–Turkish town, before I come here. So . . . maybe I have had enough. I have the strong memories still."

"And that's enough? I mean—"

"Why ever not?"

"Memory, I don't know . . . it's like a gallery of ghosts."

"But such ghosts! The women were real to me, always, and so they remain now. The problem is, if one pays too little attention at the time. Then one has just a shadow of a shadow."

"I doubt I've paid enough attention."

"*Ja*, probably you thought each could be replaced."

"Or I was too lazy—half asleep."

"No! You thought each could be *replaced*, just as you thought time replaceable, from endless supplies!" He seems deeply drunk now, his voice all but booming, his usually calm, recumbent hands moving in the air. "For centuries we Westerners are all people of the clock, and I also, naturally, before Cyprus. Consult a clock and you think you control time—you measure it, you make it, you take it, you give it, you save or waste it, you pass it, you hurry or slow it—you even think you 'kill' it! Here in Varosha my watch failed some years ago, but I had ceased to wear it anyhow . . ."

"What makes you think you know how I felt about women?"

"All young men are likewise! They think they have endless time! They can't see that each woman is the last."

Elias tries to think about these important-sounding words, but his mind won't focus. Something else occurs to him. "Wait—was it Paris that warned us about the Turk?"

"Paris?" Roland's high forehead creases. "Ah, Paris! *Ja*, I believe it was he. Forgive me, the wine. Will you take another glass?"

Somewhere in the boughs of the lemon tree the nightingale starts performing on his pan pipes. Elias gulps another draft of the delicious rhubarb-pink wine. Despite his pain and fatigue a strange feeling is brimming in his body: well-being, serenity, almost a sense of belonging. Is it just the drink?

The gods being ironists with impeccable timing, Roland chooses this moment to break some news.

"Ekaterini, in her four years with us, I believe she missed—*has* missed, I should say—many things. Her life in Nicosia, a few friends, her work before they had to come here. Now she is considering to leave us in the new year, or sooner, with the twins. And if her mind is made, she will do as she will. Her *will* . . . that's what brought her here in the first place! This thought is a stone on my heart. It might even finish Varosha—this second Varosha. The rest of us are old, or unwell—I'm unwell, I know you see this—and what young people, even if they must flee here, will ever stay without the *technologia* they all live with now?"

Elias realizes he has missed those things far less than he'd have expected. But Kaiti and the twins he might miss, if he stayed here. He says only, "You could always seize more young people at gunpoint, like me."

Roland seems not to hear. He wobbles upright, doffs his hat, sets it on the seat of his chair. "Now, if I may, I really must excuse myself." He makes for the privy with effortful dignity, arms out to the sides as if feeling his way up a dark tunnel.

Stratis's door opens as if on cue. He comes striding out, straight toward Elias, his head down like a bull.

"*Allo krasi?*" Elias says, lifting the wine jug as the man halts in front of him.

"So—now the wine is yours to offer?"

Never engage with an angry drunk.

"Remember your place," Stratis says harshly but quietly, apparently not wanting the women in the kitchen to hear. "You're not one of us, whatever they say, however drunk and full of yourself you become. I am the soldier here, the guardian."

"And I'd salute you if I wasn't a civilian."

"You're a deserter, as I hear it."

"More like a hostage."

"And like Kaiti, you're of a generation that lacks a sense of duty. She too assumes herself the equal of her elders. And you—treated by doctors for the distress of service! We fought a battle in the bowels of hell and without the luxury of doctors and beach holidays afterward. Most of us were in our graves!"

"I was in a battle too," Elias murmurs. "But there was no enemy."

"What?"

"It doesn't matter."

"In any case, battles today are not what they were."

"How the fuck would you know?"

As if waiting for this insult, he steps forward and slaps Elias across the face. Elias tips backward in the chair—mostly because he has recoiled, trying to slip the blow. As he falls back onto the flagstones his foot twists in the pail, the pain flaring. The pail topples back toward him, icy water drenching his legs and crotch.

Elias looks up, his chest heaving. "Planning to shoot the lame civilian now?"

"That was a warning."

"All right, and here's mine. You've hit me twice now. There can't be a third time."

Stratis's eyes blaze down from under his unkempt brows, but before he can reply, Kaiti, in the kitchen, can be heard telling Stavroula she will return in a moment. Stratis turns and walks straight back to his room. Elias scrambles to get himself, the chair and the pail upright. He sits on the chair, sticks his burning foot back in the pail, grabs Roland's hat and sets it over his soaked crotch as if hiding an erection. Kaiti comes out holding a lantern, her black curls tied back under a kerchief. She sets the lantern on the table and sits on Roland's chair. "Do the weary warriors require more wine?"

"You're sure there's enough, even for prisoners?" His words sound more sarcastic than he meant, but then he's still furious, his face hot, chest constricted.

"More than enough," she says. "You chose the right month to arrive."

"I've hardly chosen a thing in my life."

"But you chose . . ." She stops herself.

"What?"

"Nothing. I'll refill the jug. Are you all right? You look—"

"I chose what?"

She tilts her head above the lantern and gauges him. Its light gives the effect of an ultrasound scan: dark hollows under the pale eyes. Yet it clarifies nothing. "You chose to cross a line. On the beach. The woman, she was a Turk."

"What, you think that's bad—you as well?"

"I never said that!"

"For me, it's not crossing a line. For you, maybe."

She stiffens, juts her chin at this gaucherie. *If only we could speak English*, he thinks, adding, "I just meant, you know—I'm not Greek in the way you are."

She stands and picks up the lantern. "I am *Cypriot*," she says.

"Wait, Kaiti . . ."

"I'll return to the food. It's almost ready. You look famished, as always."

And she's gone. Then Roland can be heard opening the door of the privy, singing softly and off-key, "*Oh, Shenandoah, I love your daughter . . . Avay, you rolling river . . .*"

As he returns he looks in puzzlement at his hat in Elias's stained lap.

THE ICE BATH

Kaya looks down into the deep stainless steel tub where Polat lies immersed up to his hairless chin in water clacking and popping with ice cubes. An intravenous tube rises from Polat's pale arm, which is belly up on the surface, to a clear bladder of fluid slung from a wheeled armature. The room is aggressively air-conditioned. Kaya shivers, longing for the last of the day's sun. The ice crackling around the patient puts Kaya in mind of his late-afternoon cocktail: Scotch on the rocks, or a raki and lime juice over shaved ice.

The doctor has stepped out for a smoke. Kaya longs to join him but dutifully remains with Polat and a gigantic male nurse, who holds a thermometer and simply cannot stop talking to Kaya. "The patient's core temperature is down, close to forty degrees Celsius now, due to the ice bath. *Inshallah*, he will be conscious very soon!" This man has a fleece of black curls on the backs of his hands and bristling up over the neckline of his scrubs. He goes on chattering—the unseasonal heat is his next topic—and Kaya politely nods and smiles at the appropriate cues, all the while pursuing his own thoughts. Polat must have been active under the sun from 10 A.M. onward: inspecting the perimeter fence for several hours, running back, late, to the club, suicidally hurling himself around the tennis court, then returning to his explorations and entering the maze of the dead zone in the worst of the day's heat. No break, no lunch, no water after their set. Small wonder he almost died.

Reluctantly, Kaya has to accord some respect to this determined little man, this comic Napoleon. Whatever his physique, there can be no question that his will is strong, much stronger than Kaya's, and this fact is unsettling, as if Kaya wasn't unsettled enough already. So far he has been too lazy to do the paperwork and lobby Ankara to try to have Polat sent elsewhere, and now, if he does, the man might make trouble. For one thing, he has probably deduced that most of the funds earmarked for maintenance of the decaying perimeter fence are being siphoned quietly into the tennis court, the putting green, the beach bar, the rooftop garden . . .

Worse, Polat seems obsessed with searching the dead zone.

Kaya does not want to leave before Polat revives (he needs to debrief the man), which means dinner will probably be delayed—one of Ömer's specialties, a fresh dorado in vindaloo curry, followed by the pastries postponed at lunch. The shaggy giant blabbers on and Kaya continues to camouflage his inattention with gracious smiles. Finally he tells the man, "I'd like to check on another patient, if I might. Please let Dr. Günsel know that I'll return shortly."

"Of course, *efendi*."

He walks to *Bayan* Şahin's ward. Having rushed away from lunch to rescue the captain, Kaya is not in uniform, but some members of the hospital staff recognize and hail him warmly. One doctor, presumably a former army medic, even salutes.

The door of her room is open. An olive curtain separates her space from the part occupied by another comatose patient he has never yet seen. The room is warm. A small fan mounted on the wall swivels from side to side like a security camera. A sheet and a cotton blanket shroud her up to the V-shaped concavity at the base of her throat. That vulnerable hollow seems deeper than it was last week. Is she melting away, despite these drips and tubes? They were unable to revive her from the induced coma, but for two weeks now they've been predicting that she will surface on her own—all the omens suggest it. Nevertheless, this sleep. The singularity of her condition has made them reluctant to fly her up to Istanbul. Last week, instead, two specialists flew down here to see her.

Kaya stands over her. A face crowded with beautiful bones, the lips somehow sensual despite their thinness and present condition: pale and flaking. Everything about her is too thin for his tastes, yet he can't help but envy Elias Trifannis a little, yes, in spite of the outcome of that tryst on the beach and the young man's current detention, if that's the word for it. And now (Kaya's mind helplessly clicks on the next link) Trifannis might fall for that plump young Cypriot Greek, she with the soft shadows under pale green eyes, unforgettable eyes! Kaya had admired her four and a half years ago when her lover and Roland had brought her, in labour, to the officers' club, at Kaya's invitation. He had given the maid and the groundskeeper two days off and sent Ali to Famagusta to fetch his own personal doctor, somebody Kaya knew he could trust deeply (and bribe slightly). No doubt the doctor had assumed Kaya was the actual father.

Kaya had been surprised and a little ashamed by his bodily response to the sounds of the labour, which were loud enough to reach him from the guest room at the far end of the hall. He was lying in bed at 2 A.M. He had turned forty a few days before. The young Cypriote's groans and cries sounded at first like cries of intense pleasure, slowly mounting to a crescendo both horrific and arousing. It also induced in him a feeling of loneliness so intense it was almost sickening, which seemed odd, because Kaya was, and is now, so seldom lonely. Mostly he prefers the company of his own happy senses to that of people with their many grievances, obsessions, expectations, and demands.

When he heard, more faintly, infant mewls, just after 4 A.M., he dressed and walked down the hall and knocked quietly and, when the doctor opened the door a crack, asked if everything was all right. "Twins," the doctor said in his usual manner: unsmilingly facetious. "Fat and loud and liable to thrive for a century." Kaya nodded to acknowledge the remark, thanked the doctor, and turned away, inexplicably overcome.

Now, hardly knowing what he's doing, he leans down and tenderly kisses the patient's cracked, white-crusted lips.

"*Albay* Kaya, is that you?"

Kaya recoils from the face as if bitten and turns around. The head nurse of the ward stands in the doorway, her chins reddening along with the earlobes poking out from under her headscarf. "I was just passing the room," she says. "I saw—someone. I mean to say—I didn't realize it was you, *Albay*, without your uniform. You look like you're on holiday!"

Kaya feels compromised by the blood surge in his own cheeks and ears. "I didn't expect to be coming in," he says. "I mean, to the hospital. I was just trying to be sure she was still breathing. She seems so *still*." With an inadvertent note of accusation he adds, "Weren't the doctors saying she should be conscious by now?"

The nurse puts a finger to her lips, beckoning with the other hand. He walks toward her, leans in to listen.

"She may well be conscious, sir, but not able to show it!"

"Excuse me?"

"Her vital signs are normal, sir, more or less. Her brain scan too. The doctors think she may be conscious at times but 'locked in.' Still, because of her physical improvement, they remain optimistic that she will waken fully."

"Ah, well . . . in that case, so do I." He thinks of something and adds, "Do we have to whisper, though? Might she not be asleep right now? Wouldn't she have sleeping and waking times within that state?"

"Yes, sir, but we can't be sure without a scan, and even then . . ."

"May I ask one favour?"

"Anything, *Albay*."

"If she does waken fully, please allow no one else to speak to her—especially any other patient—until I speak to her first."

Hurrying back from the west wing to Polat's room he passes a high window. A lava-red sun is merging into the plains of the Mesaoria, which fade away into the island's interior. Desolate borderlands. He longs for his beach club. The dinner hour is fast approaching. He breathes, summoning his credo back to mind: Things right themselves—they always do.

The giant nurse is wheeling the ice bath out of the room as Kaya approaches. The man grins broadly in his beard, which starts just below his eyes. No sign of Polat.

"Is the captain all right?" Kaya asks.

"Yes, sir—and conscious! I'll be back in just a moment."

Polat lies under a white sheet on an adjustable bed, the upper part slightly raised. Beside him Dr. Günsel stands scribbling on a clipboard. Hypodermic drips still feed into Polat's arm. His soft face has cooled to a blotchy pink-grey, the old acne scars visible. As Kaya stops in the doorway, Polat's eyes—drained of their blue now, almost translucent—meet Kaya's, then flick away toward the ceiling.

The doctor intercepts Kaya and ushers him back outside.

"May I not speak to him, Doctor?"

"Of course, Colonel." The man hesitates, as if obliged to deliver bad news to a relative. His lab coat is spotless except for a sinister rusty stain at mid-thigh level. "Just one thing first. The captain just now informed me that he means to leave the hospital tonight or tomorrow and go back into Varosha. He seems clear in his mind now—no longer delirious—and he insists that there's some urgent task he needs to complete in there."

The doctor pauses nosily.

"Please go on," Kaya says.

"Colonel, a heatstroke victim is sensitized to high temperatures for as long as two weeks after recovery, and as you know, we're having a hot autumn. I'm afraid the captain is going to require some time off, in a cooler place. I realize you might not be able to spare him for long, but—respectfully—I would suggest that he be sent for a one- to two-week convalescent leave, perhaps at a mountain resort near Agri, or on the Black Sea."

Nodding sympathetically, Kaya says, "I hear Trabzon is cool at this time of year."

"Yes, it is—Trabzon! You don't object, then, to sending him there once we discharge him?"

"I'll defer to your advice, Doctor. If you could just put it in writing? And let's make it two weeks, shall we?"

"Good, yes, of course. Oh, and Colonel? On the captain's return in December, even if it is cooler—and I'm sure it will be—please try not to work him so hard on the tennis court? He's not a natural athlete like you!"

Kaya bows slightly, then asks the doctor to give him and Polat a few minutes alone. He re-enters the room, eases the door almost shut, drags a folding stool over to the bedside. Polat stares fixedly at the ugly sacs of fluid dangling above him. Kaya wonders how much he can see without his spectacles, which lie on the bedside table, the broken lens removed.

"I'm happy to see you recovering, Captain. How do you feel? Are you chilled in here? I find it chilly."

Polat's face and body are still, but his irises flit over to meet Kaya's gaze. "I think the foreigner is in there, sir."

Kaya is not to be spared, it seems. Wearily, stalling, he says, "What . . . you mean in the dead zone?"

"There might be others in there too!"

"Surely you don't mean you saw people in there, people living in there?"

"Signs of them—before I fainted."

"Fainted? You almost died before Ali and I found you!"

"I'll take water next time. In a few days, maybe. Near where the fence is unsecured I saw signs—signs of a trail. My phone—where is it? I took pictures."

"You had no phone when we found you. No pistol either."

"Maybe they took both!"

"But who would take them, Captain? They must be lost—you must have been staggering around for some time before you collapsed."

"We can find the phone."

"But Captain," Kaya lowers his voice, "it could be anywhere in there."

"Or will you order me not to go in again?" The weak voice is thinning as Polat tries to inject volume into it, like a querulous old man on his deathbed.

Kaya, almost whispering, replies, "The doctors want you to go away, Captain. On leave. For at least two weeks, maybe three. Somewhere cool. They're quite insistent."

"But, sir . . ."

"They feel the Black Sea would be ideal."

"Sir, I heard voices!"

"What, before you fainted?"

"Sometime after, I think."

"But you were unconscious! Ali and I carried you out on a stretcher! And we said nothing—the work was too hard, frankly—and, frankly, Ali was too angry."

"Greek words. English too, I think. They were carrying me in their arms, a number of men. Five, maybe six."

"I told you," Kaya leans closer, "we used a stretcher."

"I even heard his name—Trifannis!"

"Captain, please, calm down, you're confused. You were delirious. You were in a sort of coma—your temperature was over forty-one when we brought you in here!"

"It felt real."

"Hallucinations do," says Kaya, as if he knows.

"I was sure they were real, those men."

"No. Just Ali and myself."

"And a dog!" Polat cries, re-excited, flushing now as he tries to sit right up. "I saw a grey dog just before I fell!"

"Colonel?" the doctor calls from the doorway.

"I know," Kaya says, "I'm sorry. The captain must rest."

"If you don't mind, yes." Dr. Günsel walks over and stands beside Kaya, who is still sitting. Kaya says to Polat, gently, "There could be a few wild dogs in there, Captain—that's quite possible. The rest was a dream."

Polat doesn't reply.

"I have to get back to Varosha." Kaya stands, slipping his aviator shades out of the pocket of his beach shirt. "Please try to sleep. You're to follow all of Dr. Günsel's instructions. I want you fit and healthy on your return."

IN CYPRUS THE NIGHTINGALE WON'T LET YOU SLEEP

In due course he will remember the portent: three vultures tracing leisurely spirals in the sky above Varosha's northern quadrant.

With the help of two wooden crutches—real ones that Kaiti found for him in the storeroom of an old pharmacy—he's labouring toward the library after a morning of work: kneeling in the vegetable rows on potato-bug detail, then sitting on a chair to help sort olives and squeeze out pailfuls of the sublimely bitter, chartreuse oil. The villagers use an old hand press that Takkos Tombazo recovered years ago from a goatherd shed. It requires a lot of strength and stamina, and Elias is happy for the work, physically hard, shared, and steeped in that heady smell—work with a palpable, precious outcome. If only there were a dozen loaves of fresh bread to tear up and soak, hank by hank, in that throat-burningly potent, spicy oil!

First a cane, then a crutch, now crutches. What next, a walker? Maybe the vultures have their eye on him. Yet he feels almost cheerful. The drugs may be helping a little (in lieu of any painkiller besides Aspirin, Roland has traded frogs' legs for sedatives, stale-dated and labelled in Turkish, left by some visitor at the officers' club). Or is it the dead zone's pacifying silence, in fact a manifestation of constant sound, non-human, unthreatening: the bees and field insects humming, steady breezes, the overlapping calls of the birds.

In a cloth bag over his shoulder he carries books to return to the library: Kazantzakis's modern sequel to the *Odyssey* and an anthology of twentieth-century Greek poets. Both books are a couple of days overdue. He has been putting off returning them and thus being alone again with Myrto. He goes first to the well on the large traffic island among the nut and fruit trees. On a line between two trees plucked clean of their cherries, the villagers' washcloths hang in a row like prayer flags, each a distinct colour. A wide bolt of blue cotton has been wrapped most of the way around a circle of trunks to make a semi-private bathing area. In the narrow gap beneath the ground and the bottom of the fabric a lone wet foot stands next to a basin and a pair of flip-flops—one of Kaiti's feet, brown and longer, slimmer than you would expect, given her size and shape. At last her other foot, wet and clean, steps down into sight beside the first. She's humming softly. It hits him that the tune is a fair facsimile of one he played last night, "Ain't No Sunshine." When she emerges in a loose dolphin-pattern sundress he nods to her, lowering his eyes—her own seem offended, or just startled—and she says, "You should not be so quiet, you might surprise someone!"

After she leaves he draws up a bucket of water, sits on a wooden stool, strips off his shirt, and swabs his torso clean of the sweat that Myrto said she liked. Then he limps over to the small mirror secured to a branch and ducks down to inspect his face. With his brush cut growing out, the premature retreat of his hair at the temples shows. Has this difficult year made a difference? He can feel a thinning at the crown as well. And yet somehow he looks younger and healthier than before, his face deeply tanned, the whites of his brown eyes uncannily clear.

Crossing to the library he scans the sky. The birds are gone. Above the desert in Kandahar the empty skies were never quite empty: there were always a few carrion birds, sometimes dozens, orbiting above roadside wreckage or the fuming remains of mud-brick structures. An embedded journalist there mentioned a detail too curious to be untrue: unlike other creatures, which eat good-smelling food and produce stinking excrement, vultures devour rotting flesh and then leave droppings that are odourless.

Elias nods warily to Myrto and sets the books down on a front desk cluttered with papers on which handwritten lists, mystifying diagrams, and long columns of addition and multiplication appear. The high, pencilled arches of her eyebrows make her look preternaturally wakeful, expectant.

"Sorry," he says. "They're a bit late."

"But it was *Roland* who borrowed them," she corrects him with obvious pleasure, "on 11 November."

"But he borrowed them for me, and I'm late, so I guess you'll have to fine me. I hear there are fines?"

"Certainly, of a sort. But it's only two days, and we realize you are having trouble getting around. Did you read the famous poem by Seferis, the one he composed in Cyprus about the nightingale and the Trojan War?"

"That's why I wanted the anthology," he says. "To read that one. I'm not much for poetry, to be honest, but in Paphos a doctor told me I should read it. Prescribed it, really." Dr. Boudreau had broken down during that session and Elias had tried to comfort him, which seemed to help the patient slightly, if not the doctor. *For a shade, an empty tunic, we slew and died.*

"Did you find the Greek at all difficult?"

"The Kazantzakis was harder. You're sure about the fine?"

She lifts her chin, shuts her eyes. "*Ochi!* You owe me nothing."

"How's the project going?"

"Very well, thank you! Would you come and help me reposition a few of the shelves now? This will be your penance." When he hesitates she adds, "I told you, Elia—I'm no *magissa,* I will not try to make you do things against your will!"

"No, no, it's just that I'm on crutches, and—"

"When you gave yourself to me among the shelves," she declares in Greek, as if reciting from a poem, "it helped to shake me from a slumber—that's all. But of course I knew even then that you were not the man for me. Forgive me, I'm always perfectly frank." As she goes on, he nods slowly, as bewildered as he is relieved. Does she believe that something happened in the shelves other than a kiss, more or less delivered by surprise?

"It's not so much your youth, however, it's your *era*. I mean that you are a man of the present day, soft, a little shallow, as was Manolis, in his own fashion. I am finally happy, here in the past, and the men who've lived in this place for some time—now that I recognize them again as men—well, they too inhabit that other time, each in his own way. So now I can have a man again."

"You mean Roland?"

"Roland I care for, naturally I do, yet something in him has moved beyond eros. No, but when Stratis Kourakis returned ahead of you two, after confronting that Turk, and I saw the gleam in his eyes, the unsmiling pride in his bearing . . . You seem astonished, as if you've never looked at someone you've known for years and then, suddenly, it's as if your eyes rightly focus! Stratis is a man of the old ways, he grew up in a mountain village in Crete, he has that unwavering stare, he smells of earth and woodsmoke. He can hardly write his name—I doubt he has written his name, or anything else, in years!—but he knows some thousand verses of the *Erotokritos* and he can recite all the great poets. Stratis is simply *steeped* in time . . . But come now, help me with the shelves," she instructs, as if she has forgotten about his injury. "I've been reconsidering the place in my schema for the dictionaries, grammar texts, and language primers."

As he limps back from the library, it hits him that his "I'm not much for poetry" was nothing but a reflexive disclaimer, typical macho bullshit. He had liked the books and as he struggled through them he felt something in him thawing, softening.

After the siesta he emerges and sheepishly scans the courtyard for Kaiti, half-hoping not to meet those jarring, jade-pale eyes; he has just had another dream of slow, tender fucking and this time the woman's face was not disguised. No sign of her now. Under the pistachio tree a chess game is about to start. Neoklis hunches a few inches above the board as he stations each piece in the exact centre of its square. Elias crutches himself over to the kitchen to brew coffee over the propane stove, then sits watching the game as he peels a mess of potatoes for the Feast of St Ekaterina—Kaiti's name day. He works slowly while high in the lemon tree a final cicada laments her vanished kin.

Stratis requires little sleep and like all such men he will mention the fact on the slightest pretext, but today he seems to have skipped the siesta entirely. He wanders in through the gate, lax-limbed, glassy-eyed, a flush on his leathery cheeks and throat. Usually on seeing Elias he will grunt a greeting, ask coldly how his ankle feels, then try to pick a fight. Today he sits down beside the younger man and says nothing. He seems lost in a kind of happy shock.

Evening is falling, limpid, cool and perfumed. Stavroula admits a rosy surge of sunset into the courtyard as she enters through the gate with the long-haired twins, who are scrubbed and got up, Lale in a frilly cream dress like a wraparound doily, Aslan in a pale blue dress shirt, grey flannel shorts and black knee socks. Stavroula collects the pail of potatoes and summons them to Kaiti's name-day service in the cathedral, as Stavroula calls it—*kathedrikos*—where Takkos sometimes officiates as lay priest.

Robed in ceremonial vestments that the real priests must have abandoned in their flight, Takkos, clearing his throat and sneezing in the dust, is trying to recall the liturgy. He seems oddly nervous and at least a little drunk. The dusk-dim church is lit by a half-dozen tapers, their glimmer trembling over the solemn faces on the *ikonostasis*: Christ the Pantokrator, Agia Maria, Agia Eleni and other Byzantine saints painted in sumptuous if faded golds, greens, indigos, scarlets . . . Kaiti Matsakis wears a high-necked, sleeveless lavender dress, which in its dated modesty is movingly attractive. Eyeliner and lipstick. Her curly hair is braided and coiled up onto the top of her head, an ebony tiara.

Kaiti kneels at the communion rail with the twins on either side. Then Stratis and Myrto kneel pressed together, her wavy, greying hair fanned across her bony shoulders. Unlike him, she doesn't take the bread and wine. Neoklis, with his poignant bald patch, looks especially small up there next to his mother. He seems not to notice how she struggles to regain her feet, her calves so swollen. Takkos notices but does nothing, as if fearing that his helping her might compromise his temporary status and relegate him to husband. Elias—in khakis and a wide-lapelled white shirt manufactured years before his birth—gimps up to the communion rail. As usual, he's uncertain of what he's doing, why, and what it means. First communion in twenty years. Memories throng back. Sitting in the pews pressed into his mother's soft side, her smell of menthol cigarettes and rosewater, she separating him from his father, who has a flat-top haircut like a Green Beret, while on Papa's other side sits Trif's big sister, Sonya . . . Elias tips his head far forward as he kneels, deeply pious, it must seem, although actually he's trying to hide his own thinning crown from the congregation (in other words, from Kaiti).

Roland stays seated, his expression gently ironic, maybe a bit rueful. Is he too finding the service valedictory, as if it's really a kind of blessing before a journey?

***

On the pavestones of the plaza, in the falling dark among the topiary ghosts of buildings, vehicles, and the great tree, a soccer game erupts. The twins start out in their Sunday best, but Kaiti and Stavroula chastise them and soon they're barefoot, Aslan in his shorts, Lale in underpants and camisole. Stratis Kourakis now reveals another hidden capacity, dribbling the ball with a lanky and looping grace. Roland instantly joins the game, despite his health troubles, whatever they are. At the chessboard he's a calm player, but not out here. Shoes smacking the pavestones he charges around with a fierce, fixed grin as he tries to strip the ball off Stratis. (After a few minutes, he stops and withdraws, his eyes glazed, mouth open as he pants.) Takkos, back in layman's gear, tends goal and is hard to beat, partly because he keeps nudging the goalposts, Elias's shoes, closer together. When Elias catches him at it, the man grins ear to ear. Now Kaiti peels off her flats and joins in, running high on her toes with the flying lightness of a figure on an urn. As for Myrto, with an Old World scholar's scornful gravitas she declines to run, but when the ball comes to her she giggles in startled delight and blindly kicks it.

On his crutches Elias plants himself so that on the rare occasions he gets the ball, he can cross it to Lale or Aslan in the goalmouth and they can score, which is easy, as Neoklis just stands there frozen, only lunging to stop shots a second after they've gone past, then tragically exclaiming, as if he barely missed. Now Stratis lopes around everyone, the chafed leather ball seemingly glued to his boot, until Elias, suddenly determined to challenge, hobbles into his path and manages to kick the ball with his good foot. It skitters off across the plaza, Argos in pursuit. The dog pins and savagely bites it, as if it wasn't deflated enough already.

The two men sit sprawled after their collision, Elias wincing and grinning and holding his ankle, and for a moment Stratis reverts to his old self, knotting his brow, muttering behind his moustache. The twins—who always steer shy of Stratis—each grab one of Elias's hands, trying to pull him up. When Aslan bumps his ankle, Elias yowls and the twins burst out laughing, as if he must be fooling around.

Lale asks in Greek, "Can we play more?"

"Sure," he says. "Just a second."

But Kaiti looms over them. "Better to stop now, before someone gets hurt."

"I guess you're not counting me?" he says, trying to make her smile, but her face hardens. Switching into effortful English, she says, "I wish you not to try so much to make them love you!"

"What are you talking about?" He can feel Roland watching them, everyone watching them, though only Roland and Myrto can understand.

"I must return them into the world," she says. "Can you understand this?"

"I didn't realize the decision was made and final."

"What, pardon?"

"I'm not trying to stop you, Kaiti."

"Of course you will not stop me!"

"I'm not even a citizen here, I'm a . . . I don't know what I am."

"Pardon?"

He repeats himself in Greek. In English she replies, "And yet I think *you* wish to live here now more than I!"

"What makes you think that has anything to do with you?"

Her eyes widen. "I never say this!" Then, in Greek, in an undertone: "Simply respect my wishes and don't make them so attached to you that it will be even harder for us to leave. *Ela, pedhia,*" she summons the twins, putting out her hands, keeping her eyes on Elias. Then, in English: "Try to understand this, Trif."

***

By lamplight in the courtyard the villagers feast on a great mullet stuffed with unpeeled lemons, Neoklis's cherry tomatoes, olives, shallots, peppers, garlic cloves as fat as Concord grapes. There's *kohli*—snails with garlic and anise—and grilled halloumi that squeaks like curds on the teeth. And bread—two warm crusty loaves baked from the villagers' little trove of Turkish army flour. Quickly the company exhausts the wine chilled in well water and starts drinking it warm, chased by tiny glasses of raki. And so the toasts begin. Elias feels his heart lightening again, like a man at a funeral that's turning into a wake. What's done is done, what's dead is dead, and the night is still to come. He brings out the guitar and takes some requests—"Hallelujah," of course—then backs up Stratis and Myrto as they sing the male–female duet of the *Erotokritos*, or at least the half-dozen verses Myrto knows. Tone-deaf, she shrilly chants the words more than sings them. Stratis's vocals have their usual power—the raw-souled voice of a peasant recorded in wax by an ethnologist a century back—but tonight there's an extra layer of trembling resonance. His cracked rasp seems a signature of passion, not age. A younger part of him is harmonizing with the old. All his traits are open to reassessment. The wine-vinegar pong of his sweat always was a virile musk; his glowing aura makes his hair and luxuriant eyebrows sterling, not grey.

Elias must be the last one here to know about the lovers.

The night contracts and clarifies into a series of panels: Kaiti kneading Stavroula's bloated bare feet, which rest in her lap on a towel: Roland appearing behind Kaiti's chair, kissing her braided crown as she peers upward and to the side, a small girl trying to guess who is there. Her eyes encounter Trif's and for a few seconds don't look away. *Try to understand this,* they seem to repeat. Neoklis refuses to look at Elias at all, but he drums his fingers on the table to his playing. The new lovers, chairs together, lean back and smoke their atrocious cigarettes with voluptuous languor, Myrto exhaling through her nose and giving Elias a warm smile, permitting a glimpse of the small, stained teeth that he now senses she hates. Takkos and Roland dance with their jackets off, sleeves rolled, raised hands linked by a scarf, Takkos's eyes sealed in the ardour of his trance, Roland watching the man's quick little feet and trying to keep step while beaming as if this is a wedding banquet and he's the father of the bride.

"*Na pethanei o Charos!*" Stratis calls, swaying in his chair, glass raised. *Death to the Ferryman!* Then Takkos, breathlessly: "To Ekaterini—in thanks and with love. How terribly we will miss you—you and the twins!"

When it ends and the lamps are snuffed and everyone has turned in, Elias, drunk, sprawls on his back on the flagstones beside the still-littered tables, under one of which Argos lies twitching in sleep, the dead soccer ball beside him. No moon. The stars are impossibly dense. It's almost December. A new coolness is settling over Varosha, the Milky Way like a winter cloud and every star a falling flake. More sounds of lovemaking from Stratis's room drive Elias into his own cell, where the bed opens and swallows him.

OUR QUIET EXILE

As the serene, sunny days and cooler nights of Polat's absence slip away, it becomes clear to Kaya: he will have to take whatever steps are necessary to have the man transferred elsewhere as soon as possible after his return, or before. It won't be easy. The army's sprawling, inscrutable bureaucracy poses a challenge even for the well-liked and well-connected, and Kaya has let most of his connections idle and rust, having been too content, here in Varosha, simply to live from year to year without carefully banking favours. What's more, Polat is sure to see any transfer that Kaya might arrange as exactly what it would be, and in reprisal he would likely pass his suspicions and grievances on to higher powers, if he hasn't done so already. This likelihood in mind, Kaya has been having the perimeter fence mended, under Timur Ali's supervision. And if Polat should claim he has seen things and heard voices inside the dead zone, well, that can be explained away. As for Elias Trifannis, the authorities are content with how efficiently Kaya dealt with the problem, though of course they don't know—and don't want to know—the details.

The real danger is that the returning Polat will insist on going back into the dead zone and there discover the villagers. Conditions now favour such a mission; the heat wave has broken and the first autumn rains have fallen, bringing into flower the late yellow narcissi and Cyprus cyclamen that Kaya so loves and looks forward to every year. In the morning they scent the sunny but cool veranda of the officers' club, where he sits sipping his Turkish coffee, smoking a cheroot and reading the *Hürriyet*, which Ali brings him from Famagusta at eight every morning, about four hours later than it would be delivered in Istanbul. Turkey's major centre-left daily. Kaya always reads the sports section first, especially articles about Fenerbahce, his favourite team in the Super League, and about tennis (he adores the Williams sisters). He keeps his laptop computer open and ready beside his glass, a clear jug of ice water, and a plate of miniature croissants, so he can follow up on the stories and watch video replays. For this reason it always takes him until after 9 A.M. and his fourth sweet coffee to get to the news in the front section.

This morning he delights in the sea-wind's freshness on his clean-shaven face after a night of rain, and he's basking in the odour of fall blossoms, the syrupy scent of overripe muscat grapes above him in the trellised vines. He's happily languid after last night's hours with a chubby and jovial, blonde-dyed Romanian dancer from the hotel, who seemed pleasantly surprised by his manners, hospitality, and intimate stamina. He feels like himself again—that deep, almost subatomic sense of well-being—so the fact of Polat's return can be brushed away, at least temporarily, like these drunken wasps that keep alighting on the sweet rim of his cup. For a moment he considers replaying highlights of Serena Williams's recent matches in Istanbul, but then, with a vague sense of adult obligation, he picks up the front section of the *Hürriyet*.

Within seconds he's sitting straight up in his chair. Tearing off his aviator shades he gropes for the reading glasses he uses only when he's not skimming.

Things right themselves—they always do.

Kurdish partisans in Assad's roiling Syria are now pretty much in control of the northern region along the Turkish border. A number of them recently slipped across the border and joined up with Kurdish guerrillas concealed there. Yesterday morning a group of sixty or more Kurds ambushed and routed a Turkish patrol—three killed, six wounded, the rest apparently taken hostage—before withdrawing south across the frontier. So, as of now, Turkey's latest truce with the PKK is in tatters. The *Hürriyet* quotes the regional Turkish commander as saying he intends to pursue the enemy across the border with a large body of commandos and regular troops, even some armour, to rescue the hostages and to destroy the enemy. He expects the operation and its aftermath to take some time, given that there are several thousand armed partisans waiting just inside Syria and they will not shy from a fight.

Within minutes Kaya, having called to Ömer in the kitchen for another coffee and a shot of raki, lights a fresh cheroot and starts an email to one of his few remaining contacts in Ankara, General Dogan Yilmaz. Kaya and Yilmaz were drinking companions some years ago when they were both stationed in Edirne as first lieutenants. Yilmaz was married here at the club seven years ago and since then has twice returned on holiday, most recently three years ago.

After prefatory salutations, remarks on the belated change of weather in Cyprus, and good wishes to the general's wife and three sons, Kaya gets to business: *At any rate, I've been sensing in my adjutant, this Captain Polat, an increasing restlessness and dissatisfaction. As you know, I've managed to adapt myself to the quiet administrative, custodial nature of this posting, but the captain is utterly bored. He finds it hard to accept that some duties, such as those of our quiet exile here, are of an undramatic nature. Put plainly, he's a young idealist (he's 29), and the kind of soldier who is impatient to test his mettle. Here, of course, he gets no chance. His qualities are squandered. His passion lies fallow. It's a shame. Not only does he crave larger challenges but also, I feel, truly needs and deserves them. Though physically unimposing, he does not lack for courage. He is dutiful and honest—almost inhumanly so. You wouldn't much like him—few would, I think—but he has the makings of an excellent officer, in the traditional mould.*

Kaya stops and takes a drag on his cheroot, amused in spite of himself. By "traditional" he means, basically, "medieval."

I also believe he is deeply ambitious and craves opportunities for promotion . . . Seeing how this phrase could be misconstrued and make Yilmaz uneasy, but loath to backspace, rethink, and rewrite, Kaya simply expands: *Ambitious and yet unselfish—the army is everything to him. To speak plainly, old friend, Captain Aydin Polat, both for his own good and, frankly, for mine, needs to be dispatched to some place where he can truly apply his training, and also cultivate his qualities as a leader, for which he has considerable (and, here in Varosha, utterly untapped) potential.*

I understand that within weeks, or days, a punitive operation is likely to be launched against the PKK and PYD along the Syrian border. If you could somehow arrange to have the captain transferred to one of the units that General Özel means to deploy in the mission, I would be greatly in your debt. More importantly, I think the captain himself would be so gratified by the transfer, and the possibilities it might afford, that he would not for a minute resent it, or see it as anything less than what it is—(Kaya takes another long, pensive drag)—*a kind of situational promotion. All the same, I think it would be best if he did not know that the idea originated with me. And please forgive me for not going through regular channels, but in such a situation, there is no time to waste. At any rate, if you can arrange for him to join the operation, we can only pity the Kurdish fighters who will be subjected to the ferocity he has stored up while raring for action down here . . .*

Yes, and pity the *Turkish* ones who might have to endure his high-minded little tyrannies. And now it strikes Kaya that if Polat actually *were* to see action as an officer, he might send some recruits to unnecessary deaths, or be shot or blown up himself (the Kurds know to pick off the officers and NCOs first). Troubled by both possibilities, he simply changes the subject on himself, using for distraction the taste of his raki on the rocks, the aromatic tang of fennel in the bouquet. Then back to the email: he writes that Polat is now actually in Trabzon, enjoying a short holiday after injuring himself by training too hard during the recent heat wave. *The PKK will never know what has hit them!* He concludes by urging General Yilmaz to be his guest again before too long and tacks on a lyrical, loving description of the beachside patio in mid-morning, the new narcissi, the smell of Ömer's cooking as he begins preparing lunch: beef shashlik on saffron rice.

Like a stockbroker sealing a briefcase after closing a deal, he snaps shut his laptop with a flourish. He peels off his shirt and walks out from under the trellis into full sunlight. Not a cloud over the sea between this empty beach, his own personal beach, and the mountains of Syria beyond the horizon. He cracks his neck and his knuckles as he strolls down to the water and wades in—the shallows cool but still pleasant—and starts breaststroking along the shore.

On his return he finds a brief but friendly reply waiting. Yilmaz misses Kaya and hopes to visit the club again soon, perhaps with his family. Meanwhile he will try to get Kaya's "seemingly mis-posted" adjutant transferred. He can guarantee nothing—he knows that Kaya understands—but he will do his very best. (Kaya believes it; his old friend is not only discreet but conscientious to the point of obsession.) Kaya has also received a message from his ex-wife, Pinar, with good news: the children can come to stay here for the New Year holiday. Now if only there were a third message from the hospital, to say that Eylül Şahin has surfaced from her coma or "locked-in" state! Since Kaya's last visit it has been the same puzzling story: strong vital signs and sporadic high-level neural activity, but, still, this coma. Of course, he remains a touch concerned that she might have been aware of his kiss, but more and more he thinks it unlikely. After all, he himself was fully conscious and yet the act now seems unreal to him, like the vestige of a reverie or spell of deep inebriation. Anyhow, he can talk his way out of trouble if necessary.

Just five days later—the day before Polat is scheduled to fly back from his leave in Trabzon—Yilmaz emails Kaya to notify him that the transfer has been approved. The captain is to report back to Kaya, collect his belongings, then fly through Ankara to Diyarbakir and report to General Özel. When Kaya receives this email on the patio, his happiness is extensive, even by his standards. He gathers that some people see joy as little more than relief in disguise, a remission from worry and pain—but while joy for Kaya is a true presence, not just the absence of suffering, he finally understands the concept.

At 5 P.M. on the day that Polat is scheduled to report back (Kaya expected him by noon, but there's no sign of him and his mobile is switched off, so maybe he's on the later flight) he receives a call from the hospital. It's the helpful head nurse, delivering good news in a hesitant tone, as if bad news is to follow. *Bayan* Şahin has been conscious since early this morning. The nurse apologizes that she herself was not on duty at the time, or she would have called the colonel at once, as promised. She says, "Praise be to God, the patient is doing very well!" and adds quickly, "She has had visits from several doctors and therapists, as well as someone from the military."

"The military?"

"I'm afraid . . . the new nurse on the ward this morning failed to receive my instructions and call you, as promised, *Albay* Kaya."

The woman is audibly cringing, frightened. It's widely understood that the army here deals with troublesome Turkish Cypriots by arranging traffic "accidents." Last month, the north's only visible gay activist was run down and seriously hurt by a commissary van in north Nicosia, and Kaya fears it must have been deliberate.

"Don't worry," he says. "Please. It's not your fault. Tell me, though, who was it who came in? And what time?"

"I'm not sure, *Albay*, I'm so sorry. The new nurse says it was an officer. I'm afraid she failed to ask his name."

"But no journalists yet? No family? I need to speak to her first."

"Her father is flying down now. The news people . . . they don't know yet that she is conscious, and she asks that we not admit them once they do." (That sounds promising, he thinks.) "Shall I try to find out who the officer was, *Albay*?"

"It's all right—I'll come in right now."

"Now?"

"I know visiting hours are over," he says, "but . . ."

"Of course, *Albay*! I'll be here at the desk myself."

He's about to don his resplendent dress uniform and boots, but then—not wanting to remind a victim so vividly of his connection to her attackers—he demotes himself to beige khakis, a crisp yellow shirt, and laceless polished brown shoes. Ali drives him up the beach to Famagusta. They barrel over amber strips of sunlight lancing from between the corroding towers, beyond which the sun is sinking into the dead zone.

In the hospital the head nurse, in her kerchief, with double chin and earlobes reddening, keeps apologizing as she hurries with Kaya to the patient's room. He tells her again not to worry, everything is fine.

He enters the room alone, eases the door almost shut. Eylül Şahin is sitting up, two pillows behind her, the bed in its raised position. She is sallow, very thin, the bones of her face seemingly trying to break surface, but on the whole she looks well for someone who was in a coma just twelve hours ago. Is that a trace of a smile? He is seeing her eyes for the first time, dark, calm and acute, enormous in her diminished face. Her body and head still bristle with tubes and wires. A monitor displays numbers in flux, which must represent her heart rate and blood pressure, though Kaya knows little about such things. The curtains that divide the room in two are open, the other bed vacant.

He performs a courtly bow. "Forgive me for disturbing you."

"All right," she gets out in a dry, constricted voice. The faint smile is gone.

"I'm Erkan Kaya, superintendent of the Varosha Restricted Zone."

"Hoped you were my father. He should be here in an hour or two."

"I'm sorry, no. But I'm pleased to hear he's on his way. Would it be absurd to ask how you're feeling?"

"Not as rested as you'd think, after a sleep like that." She reaches for the red-framed glasses on the bed table next to her mobile phone and slowly fits them on. "You're the colonel?"

"Call me Erkan, please. May I get you anything? A drink?"

"They're taking care of me." She lifts a white plastic container and fits the straw between her lips. He sees her mouth and long, sinewy throat working. Her shrivelled arm works, too, to hold up the container, which trembles slightly. With her eyes she indicates the chair to the left of the bed, next to the monitor. "Go ahead."

He sits. "*Teşekkür ederim.*"

"I'd prefer to stand," she says, "after all this. But my legs. Still, I got around the room today, with help. Started exercises. Tomorrow I'll walk on my own."

"Is that what they told you?"

"I told them."

"I see."

"They say muscles recover fast, at my age. I mean to leave here and fly home with Baba in a few days." She pauses, sucks up more water. "They say that's impossible, or at least unlikely."

"It does seem soon."

"I can't leave here soon enough. And unlike you, Colonel, I don't have to take orders." He sees now—the eyes are all iris, the pupils tiny with scorn. How rarely has Kaya received such looks in his life! Does she know of his indiscretion? More likely she simply sees him as yet another soldier—and long before that incident on the beach she was critical of the army in her writing, often, in fact, in the *Hürriyet*. If only she understood that Kaya shares many of her views! He too detests the Polats—and Erdogans—of the world. Not that he can say any of that to a journalist. She adds, "And I've work to do in Istanbul, as I told your colleague today. When I explained, he seemed quite upset."

The numbers on the monitor are rising: 84 and 127/76.

"Who was it you saw?"

"A Captain Polat."

I knew it.

"He said he helps you with Varosha but has just been transferred."

"I'm very sorry for this. Captain Polat was meant to report to me today. He has been . . . on leave, unwell. What did he want?"

"To hear what happened. My story."

"And you told him?"

"Yes."

"The truth?"

She looks shocked by the question.

"Forgive me," he says, "but—"

"He told me your version too. I was being raped, violently. Your men saved me. At least until they shot me."

"By accident! And it's not my version, it's—"

"Your captain embraces it despite all its absurdities"—she pauses for breath; he resists speaking—"and my own objections. Honestly, Colonel, why *would* I want to protect a rapist?"

"I never believed that part myself"—he's thinking quickly—"but you can see how the men, in the dark, might have misunderstood whatever was . . . taking place between you and . . . You understand, I hope, that they didn't actually mean to shoot you?"

"He wanted to know what I'll do with this truth."

"What did you say?"

"First tell me. He's alive? Trif? Your man kept saying 'missing, officially dead.' You're holding him?"

"Of course not, no. He's dead. I'm sorry." The lie sickens Kaya—it's harder to tell than expected—but it's necessary, for the best, for everyone. No use making a fetish of truth; lies are often the more human thing. "I'm sorry. We assume he drowned. Fled and then drowned. We found his mobile in the sea and his clothes on the beach, washed up."

"No body, then," she says, just audibly.

"Well, it may surface, in time."

"If he is dead, it was your men." The rates rising: 92 and 134/81. "If he drowned, they forced him in. Or shot him and threw him in."

"We found no sign of that. It could have been suicide, too, I'm afraid. We gather he was on leave, being treated for some kind of, uh . . . shell shock, or depression. Believe me, please, I'm deeply sorry for everything that has happened. The army will certainly compensate you for your—your trouble, your suffering. But I hope you understand . . . how can I put it . . . ?"

"You hope I'll say nothing."

A sudden draft chills his damp brow and he glances toward the door, where that wall-mounted fan swings side to side, as if recording everything they say.

"Your captain hopes the same," she says. "He was less polite about it."

"But surely it would be best, especially for you? You don't mean to reveal that you were . . . that you and this Greek, whom you'd only just met . . . I mean, not that I myself have any . . ."

"You two are very different."

"What—I and the Greek?"

"You and the captain. When I said I'd write an article, or book, he tried—"

"A *book*?"

"—to appeal to my patriotism. He said, did I want to disgrace the army, humiliate Turkey? Though it's the army he cares most about. Its 'prestige.'" She has been talking expressively enough with just her mouth and eyes, but now she manages to involve her long-fingered hands and wasted arms, lifting them off the bed. "He kept using that word! How I hate it! The army's 'prestige'! When people start using 'prestige' . . ." She has to pause for more water. She sucks on the straw as if it were the day's first cigarette.

"I feel the same," Kaya murmurs, "just the same."

"I told him—if embarrassing your army helps get it out of here, so the Cypriots can reunify . . ." Her hands collapse onto the coverlet.

"You're exhausting yourself, Eylül—Ms. Şahin—please."

"You've no idea—just to be talking, even this way, arguing, angry, remembering what happened—just talking!—it's a kind of pleasure. I've been conscious on and off for days, thinking things, but unable . . ."

The soaring rates could now be Kaya's: 95 and 141/82. He glances at the door, leans forward and says, "Our army, rightly or wrongly, will never leave here. That's just a fact. It can't be changed. It's not worth exerting yourself—inviting hatred and scandal on yourself, not to mention on Turkey—for the sake of a truth that, frankly—"

"You admit it's the truth?"

"How can I know for certain, beyond a reasonable doubt? It's their word against yours! And as commander I have to assume that my—"

"But you know it, deep down."

"Truth is not the issue! It's a matter of—what simply *is*. I have no choice but to support my men, and there are a number of them, while you—you're alone. I'm so sorry. And what if I did believe you? It would make no difference—the public would believe them! The public would want to believe them, most of the media would tell them to believe, and so they would believe."

"It doesn't gnaw your conscience . . . he's now officially a rapist?"

Kaya deflates. He never felt right about that part but could see no alternative.

"He was a good man," she says. "I saw it."

He wants to touch her olive-pale forearm, from which the port for the saline drip protrudes, but she wards him off with a look of distaste that pains him very much—a patrician hauteur undiminished by her helplessness, those shaved spots for electrodes among the black roots in her hair, a forlorn blonde dye-job growing out. He says, "Please listen. If you really are willing to face the hostility of, of reactionaries, millions of them, well . . . maybe you could state publicly that the men were mistaken—that it was no rape. But *honestly* mistaken—they must have been! You'd have to state that too. It was very dark on the beach, after all, and the Greek did assault the sergeant—I saw his wounds."

"So he's 'the Greek' now."

"Ethnically Greek."

"They knew it was no rape. They knew I liked him. They followed us out of the bar."

"But—might they not have been concerned, and for good reason? That's what they'll claim, and the nation will accept it. The Greek—the Canadian—he was a big man."

"So you've seen his body?"

"No. The men all said so. And I saw a photo of him in uniform, on the internet. Ms. Şahin, if you do mean to tell your full version—

I have to be completely frank—I fear you'll be putting yourself in danger."

"Are you threatening me . . . you too?"

"Of course not!" Kaya is aghast. "That idiot threatened you?"

"It was nothing specific."

"When was he here?"

"Around noon."

So where has he been since noon? (102 and 142/84.) Kaya leans in closer to her, his hands on his knees. "When the captain reports to me—I expect he must be at the club now—I will speak to him severely, but I'm afraid he might have talked to others by now. Told them what you mean to do." Gone over my head, Kaya means.

"Some people don't have the luxury of not saying what they know to be true," she says.

"You mean *him*, Polat?"

"I mean myself. I couldn't forgive myself."

It's clear Kaya has underestimated her, as he underestimated Polat in a different way. Not everyone is like him, Kaya—happy to let the world just drift along the way it is. For a moment he looks helplessly inward, in a way he is unused to and finds deeply unpleasant, then hears himself say, "I don't suppose there's much I couldn't forgive myself for." Now the feeling that gripped him just before the kiss steals over him again. As if all the world's suffering were concentrated in a single sleeper, whom only he, Erkan Kaya, could save. What nonsense. She's implacably sincere. He can't help or protect her. Still, he tries: in a shaky, almost pleading voice he says, "Would it make any difference if I told you I could likely arrange for . . . considerably greater compensation, if you'd just . . ."

Silence.

"I didn't think so."

"For me," she says, "one good thing's come from this. I went through withdrawal in the coma. I mean cigarettes. I've finally quit."

"Good, good," he says quietly. (88 and 136/79.)

Her eyes drift toward the other, empty bed. Voice now whittled to a whisper she says, "Nurse told me they took away my roommate. Yesterday. She had a crisis. Died in the operating room. Odd to think we slept side by side for weeks . . . such intimacy, in a way . . . yet I'll never know her."

How I wish I could tell her Trifannis is alive.

"You're worried about the kiss, aren't you?"

"What?" Momentarily Kaya means to lie, as he did to Polat in the other ward—*you just imagined it all!*—but she is speaking again:

"Don't worry, I'll say nothing. Not about that."

Two raps on the door. It swings inward. The head nurse's blushing face. "Forgive me, *Albay*, but our patient . . ."

"I know—I'm tiring her. We're almost through."

"Of course, *Albay*." She withdraws and leaves the door ajar.

"You see," Eylül whispers (he's relieved now at the weakness of her voice), "I'm almost grateful." He has to wait as she goes through the laborious mission of getting more water into her. "The loneliness . . . once I was conscious, it was hard. Hard beyond belief! No one I knew was here for the first days of it. You can't imagine. I don't know why you did it . . ."

"Nor do I, I swear. Forgive me, please."

"But I felt that that man . . . he knew I was conscious."

"I didn't, I'm afraid."

"As if he was whispering in my ear, 'You'll live!'"

"I think, maybe, in a way I was."

"And then took no other liberties."

"Of course not!"

After a few seconds Kaya adds, "Please—think carefully about everything I've said."

"I've made my decision, Colonel."

"At least say nothing yet to your father! Not to mention the media—I gather you don't mean to talk to them?"

"I'll break this story in my own way. As for Baba . . . no. He'd try to stop me too. Poor man."

"I will need to take steps to protect you."

A corner of her mouth barely lifts. This atrophied smile—is she simply exhausted (her chapped eyelids have grown heavy, her hands lie flattened) or is she mocking him? "I know you mean to be gallant, Colonel, but I don't want the army's help."

"Mine, not the army's!"

"I have to rest now."

"Of course."

(71 and 118/72.)

"I'll be back."

Leaving, he pulls his sunglasses out of his shirt pocket and slides them on firmly.

When he and Ali arrive back at the club in the deepening dusk, no Polat. Ömer emerges from the kitchen in his apron and a chef's hat that looks like a huge puff pastry. He hands Kaya a Scotch on the rocks and says the captain arrived by Jeep not long after Kaya's departure. "It's odd, sir—you must have barely missed him on the beach."

"Where is he now?"

"His flight to Ankara departs any time. But he left this for you." Ömer draws a small, square envelope from his apron pocket.

Kaya trades his emptied glass for the envelope and walks away, heels clapping on the tiles as he tears the envelope open. He sits at the bar under the large, smirking portrait of Atatürk. On army stationery, a handwritten note, the ink black and heavy, as if Polat has gone over every letter twice:

Dear Sir

If you are reading this note I was unable to report directly to you. Forgive me. I suspect that by the time I arrive you will be at the hospital visiting the journalist and I must leave soon for Ankara. As you know I am being transferred to General Özel's command on the Syrian border. I am very pleased. I am grateful for any role you may have played in this transfer. As you know I was to have reported to you after my flight arrived but I decided to stop at the hospital on my way so as to check on the journalist. To my surprise I found that she had recovered somewhat and was able to talk. I spoke to her briefly. It was distressing for reasons you are probably aware of by now. For reasons I think you will appreciate I then went directly to HQ near the hospital and spoke to Colonel Nurettin and several others before proceeding to my quarters to collect my belongings. I think the officers I consulted will be in touch with you to discuss the matter. Of course this all took quite a bit of time and hence my delay. I did consider calling you but felt it too informal under the circumstances and also wished to better organize my thoughts.

Perhaps after the insurgents are eliminated on the border I could be transferred back to your command as I might be able to assist you further in securing the perimeter of the Restricted Zone and ensuring it is not being violated in any way. Colonel Nurettin may now have some concerns of his own in this regard and may wish to discuss them with you.

I remain your loyal captain and loyal above all to the Army of the Kemalist Republic and to the Republic itself,

(Captain) Aydin Cingiz Polat

First thing the next morning, Kaya reaches the always-nervous, careful Colonel Nurettin, by landline to Famagusta HQ, and suggests that he, Kaya, be allowed to handle the situation with Ms. Şahin. Nurettin says he has already referred the matter to Brigadier General Hüseyin in Nicosia, so it's out of his hands now, but in the meantime Kaya should certainly go on trying to persuade the woman to say nothing, which naturally would be the ideal outcome. General Hüseyin has said that his agents will be visiting her, possibly here, and certainly in Istanbul once she has recovered. Pressure will be brought to bear, albeit with delicacy, since clumsy overtures might simply provide her with more material for her inventions. (*Delicacy,* thinks Kaya; not something the army is known for.) The man adds that Captain Polat seems to be entertaining some rather unlikely notions regarding the Restricted Zone, but Nurettin realizes that he was recently ill. Still, Nurettin adds, Polat may be correct in feeling that the perimeter fence is in need of upgrades, so perhaps it is for the best that Kaya has now undertaken that project. Not that Nurettin means to interfere in any way, shape, or form; Famagusta is his responsibility, Varosha is Kaya's.

Kaya returns to her that afternoon, and again the next day, and is stunned by how quickly she's improving, filling out, her skin regaining a bit of colour. They talk for some time on both days, but he makes no progress, although she does seem to be warming to him a little, starting to enjoy their debate about the nature and value of truth, seeming to relish her own spirited rebuttals as she recovers her strength and wit. Kaya's own interest in politics and ideas is slim, but discussing them with a woman keeps him engaged. Still, he's forced to admit defeat. She is going to publish her version. All he can do is hope that if she is widely believed and the story explodes, goes international, the worst of the scandal will bypass him. (Things right themselves: there's a decent chance that if he has to, he can focus blame on those who really deserve it, her attackers.) "Never mind, Colonel. The officers from north Nicosia who came this morning fared no better than you and amused me far less." The head nurse, she adds, finally asked them to leave. Kaya warns her again that she must be careful and asks if he can accompany her to the airport when she goes. She seems tickled by the offer, as if it's a proposition in disguise, but Kaya is truly worried. "No," she says. "Thank you. Anyway, my father and sister are here now." "Please," Kaya says, "allow me!" But she says she will accept nothing from the army: not threats, not bribes, not protection.

He speaks finally to the head nurse—at least there's someone around here that he can still charm and persuade—and makes her promise to give him a few hours' notice before the patient is discharged.

"As you wish, *Albay*. I will not set foot off the ward."

"Really? But you mustn't put yourself out . . ."

"Not at all, sir! *Bayan* Şahin is very determined. It may be as soon as tomorrow."

ACCIDENT

Her sister, Meltem, has gone ahead to fetch the rented car. Her father accompanies her out the hospital's rear door. For his sake more than hers, she allows him to brace her by her left elbow—his hirsute little hand almost encircles it—while she with her right hand wields a nondescript, lightweight aluminum cane. This geriatric appurtenance ought to embarrass her but instead amuses her: since it's temporary, she chooses to see it as a campily stylish prop and deploy it with a slight flourish. In every other way she feels helplessly unstylish, her skin jaundiced, lips flaking under the lipstick, skirt and blouse still baggy.

Her father suggested rolling her out to the car in a wheelchair, but she told him no, absolutely not—she will not be photographed in a wheelchair, and even slipping out this back way they might get ambushed by a few of the reporters who for three days have been trying to talk to her. If any *are* out here waiting, she will tell them politely, "Wait a bit longer." The story is important ethically, politically, and for her career as well, and she wants to ensure that readers—liberals and reactionaries alike—are waiting for her version, full and unscooped.

As they emerge from under the awning, the late-morning sun greets her with a fanfare of light and she stops and looks upward, sneezes hard and feels it in the healed wound in her lower back, a centimetre right of her spine, the muscles there seizing.

"Eylül?"

"It's all right, Baba."

"Meltem will be here any moment."

"See, nobody's waiting, Baba—we fooled them."

"I would not let them near you!" her father says from deep in his body, as always embroiling himself in a conflict that has not yet flared up and probably won't. He has rammed a cigarette into his mouth and holds a quivering, gold-plated lighter under the tip. The last month has grizzled him further and deepened the cross-hatching of lines in his nicotine-orange cheeks. He is shorter than she is, even now with her listing to the right over her cane.

Since regaining consciousness she weeps too readily and now at the back of her throat again she tastes tears: joy at the daylight on her skin, her father's touch, her baby sister's obvious pride, ten minutes ago, at being asked to go and fetch the car. All of it balled up with regret. Her article or book, for one thing, is going to shame and hurt Baba a great deal. This will not be the first time but it will be the worst. And still he will go on loving her, in his angry, ardent way. "Where *is* that Meltem?" He is forcing his voice up over the noise of the city, the heart-monitor beep-beep of distant worksite vehicles backing up and, to the right, somewhere along this side street of parked cars, the chug of an engine idling. A hundred metres farther up—on the avenue that meets this street at right angles—small cars are pelting along, horns bleating, as a policeman walks his scooter through the empty crosswalk. Probably it's quiet here compared to Istanbul, but to her ears, after the hospital, the din is formidable.

"There, it's all they had," he says disgustedly. "You'll sit in the front."

A diminutive olive-green cube on wheels bucks to a stop along the curb across the street, in front of a shuttered cybercafé. Oddly, all of the storefronts across the street are shuttered, the sidewalks deserted. Meltem checks her hair in the rearview mirror and glances out the driver-side window with a cocky grin. Eylül and her father step off the curb. She plants the rubber stub of her cane on the sun-hot tarmac. It sticks a little as she pulls it up. From down the street comes a soul-shattering roar as a small delivery truck launches out from the curb and bears down on them. She tries to lurch forward, toward Meltem, whose mutely screaming face fills the closed window of the rental car, but her baba is tugging her backward, toward the curb, and they offset each other, stay frozen. Grunting "*Idiot!*", surely at the driver, he swings Eylül in front of him to bring her onto his left side, away from danger. The truck—low sneering grille, high windshield, the fat, bearded driver in sunglasses and a prayer cap—looms huge as a train. The impact feels not like steel and glass but like the shockwave of an explosion. She is weightless for a moment that's crowded with thoughts. The sun arcs overhead, the street rushes up to slam her back, though not her skull—something softer intervenes, some part of her baba. The smell of his cigarette still burning somewhere. A sound of vehicle doors flying open, almost in unison, shoes smacking the tarmac. Then Meltem, close by, sobbing *Baba, Baba, Baba!,* as if Eylül is not lying here too.

At the edge of a shrinking visual field, Kaya's handsome face appears under his colonel's cap. Beside him, a tall man who seems to be a moustachioed relic of Atatürk's time. Kaya kneels closer, his hands open, fingers splayed out near her face, as if he means to finish her off, throttle her right here in broad daylight. "It was you," she whispers. He is shaking his head—*no, no!*—his eyes for the first time completely naked. Those hands . . . maybe he wants to touch her but is afraid?

"They came out of nowhere," a stranger's voice is insisting, nasal, Ankara accent. "I couldn't stop in time!"

Kaya looks back over his shoulder toward the sound, then rises out of sight. The crisp sound of a blow, then Kaya's voice: "Assassin!"

"Baba," she calls as the talking faces of paramedics occur in a shrinking circle of light. Then the faces are blacked out, though she can still hear their prattle. Then the import of the words is harder to make out, then it's lost altogether and even the sounds are gone, along with the knowledge of her name, September—sunny month of black plums—and every part of her seems to vanish.

SEEKING LETHE

Every language has a word that expresses its meaning better, or more beautifully, than the equivalent word in any other tongue. Sometimes the beauty is conceptual, as in the case of the German *Lebenslüge*, or life-lie—the convenient if sometimes fatal fiction around which you build a life, or a nation shapes its identity. Sometimes the beauty is acoustical. Listen to the Greek for winter, *himonas*. What other word so encloses the cold season in its very sounds? That long middle vowel echoes the moaning of north winds and evokes the *O* of Boreas's blue-lipped, puffing mouth in those drawings in the upper corners of classical maps. And the guttural *ch* of the word's opening: a harsh, raw, throat-clearing sound, the rasp of winter illness, colds and coughs. Then the dwindling hiss of the last syllable, snow blowing over a sheet of ice.

Or take the Turkish for friend, *arkadash*. You could say, "A beautiful-sounding word for a beautiful concept" and leave it at that, but there's more. *Friend*, or even *ami* or *philos*, seems too brief, clipped, and uncomplicated to house all the qualities of a true friend. *Arkadash* is a roomier word, an atrium of rich sounds, the last syllable lingering in a *shhhh* that extends the life of the utterance, delaying the silence to follow. A secretive sound, too—hush, say nothing to the world about this friendship, it's ours alone. And in the opening *ark* you might hear *arc*, the span and scope of a lifelong connection. But mainly you hear how the word prolongs itself, in the same way that love, never a great respecter of borders, extends beyond death.

Something hauls Elias out of his siesta. Roland stands in the doorway, his hatless head partly bowed, his features blacked out by the daylight behind him.

"I'm sorry to upset you, Trif," he says in a guarded monotone that Elias instantly recalls from their first interview.

"Sorry to wake me, you mean."

A limp quip, to appease the gods. Roland's pale eyes, resolving out of his dark face, drill into Elias's brain. For a moment he thinks, *Kaiti*—she isn't waiting until the new year after all, she's leaving today, has just left. Then his mind unclouds.

"It's about Eylül, isn't it?"

"When I awoke from my nap, I turned on the radio. Something made me do so. I don't know why. I don't believe in such things. The news is bad."

"But you said she was conscious again—she was improving!"

"*Ja*, and they released her today. She was run down outside the hospital."

"What? Is she . . . ?"

"Killed, I'm afraid."

"She's what?"

"Killed!" *Kilt*, it comes out again, and somehow this enrages Elias.

"You mean *killed*?"

"So they are saying."

"Oh, fuck." Blood roars in Elias's brow. "Fuck!" He pounds his fist into the mattress. "But this can't have been . . ."

"An accident? Hardly. Her father was with her, crossing the street. He, too."

"He too what?"

"Was killed."

Stop saying fucking "kilt," he thinks. "So, this has to mean . . ." He can't sort it into sound, but he knows.

"She meant to speak out," Roland says, "and tell what really happened. Perhaps she already has. If so, we will soon know, unless they intend to silence too anyone whom she told. You see, we were wrong. We didn't think she would be willing to say what really—"

"You were wrong. I said nothing. I'm not surprised. Not by what she did, not by what they did. This is what they *do*. And she . . ."

Roland seems to be waiting for him to continue. When he doesn't, Roland says, "You speak as if you knew her well, but you didn't. None of us could have known."

"I could have helped somehow, maybe."

"No."

"Was this Kaya's work—could he have been involved?"

"I think no, unless I have been very wrong about him. Certainly he loves his position and would do much to preserve it, but I believe he has a good heart—no violence in his soul—I've seen it! But, I have been mistaken in such things before. About myself once, even."

"We should pay him a visit."

"Don't be foolish, Trif! I'm sorry we were wrong—wrong about Eylül—but we did our best."

"That's what they told us, in the desert, after what happened." The comparison is dubious but his memory of the debriefing returns anyway. It was an accident, these things happen, they hadn't meant to kill civilians, only to confront any bad guys and eliminate their hideout—and why were those villagers letting bad guys hide there in the first place? (Maybe because they had no choice, were caught in the middle, between the fanatical and the ignorant, like villagers in any war.)

"Even if Kaya wasn't involved, he'll know what happened, won't he?"

"I expect he will arrange a meeting, before the day ends, to formally break the news." Roland leans forward a little, as if meaning to enter the room, but his feet stay planted on the threshold—bare feet, very white, hairless, splayed. Elias has never seen these feet before. Roland looks down at them now as if astounded to find them bare.

"*Lipameh poli,*" he says, backing away and easing the door shut.

Eventually Elias cracks the shutters. Something has changed—a breeze out of the north. It chills his bare chest and he can't seem to move or think. The wind brings down from Famagusta the faint harmonic trills of a muezzin summoning the faithful to prayer. From the flat roof of the Tombazos' house he has counted seven minarets, their spires just visible in the distance. The prayer call is likely a recording, not a living voice. His own reverent vocals seem bogus in retrospect—never quite looking at Kaiti while in fact singing to her, as if a song might convince her to stay. Lines from that Doors song about stealing another kiss, a kiss before unconsciousness . . . The few objects in here, bed, chair, faded Turkish carpet the size of a prayer rug, water jug and tumbler, piss-pail, candles, a few books, the guitar, all absorb his numb gaze with a terrible stillness and detachment. The prayer call fades. Roland's black-boxed volume of Levantine history—that chronicle of atrocities, which Elias has finally been reading—squats on the sill like an IED. With bitter clarity he seems to see how all the ways that people have tried to organize and justify themselves, to sedate their fears, to make sense of life and death, have failed.

Imagine being able to pray.

The night of his own father's death, Elias in jeans and T-shirt lay down beside him, impossible, two men of their size lying side by side on a hospital bed. Elias's aunt Roula was asleep in a chair, and his stepmother, now separated from Papa, would be coming back later (too late, as it happened) with Elias's half-siblings. He worked his arm gingerly between the pillow and Papa's hog-bristle nape so that the man's head could rest on his shoulder. That ear and his nostrils were filled with whiskers, all the openings between him and the world growing in. He couldn't speak anymore but if you addressed him he seemed to hear—he would close his fist around your fingers. Naturally, a fist, his final gesture. And earlier when Elias, dutifully sticking to the deathbed script, had forced out the half-lie, "I love you," the man had opened one faded eye and whispered, "I know . . . I wish I could say it too."

That evening in the courtyard nobody speaks to him about Eylül, though of course they all know. This silence could be discretion, but to him, now, it feels like indifference. He seems to be a captive again, or at least an outsider. Everything seems altered. Argos keeps jerking around to gnaw a raw patch at the base of his tail. The twins, in puffy wool cardigans, fling marbles in the dirt, their high voices vexed and aggressive. They glance now and then at their mother, who has a heavy cold and keeps blowing her nose into a rag. In profile she's almost plain, her features a stranger's. She and Stavroula are arguing in a whisper, slangy Cypriot Greek. Is the old woman trying to convince her to stay? Elias realizes he has hardly thought of Eylül in days and suffers a pang of guilt, as if his thoughts might have formed a kind of protective field. Now the twins chant, "Stop talking, stop talking, stop talking!" and Kaiti twists in her chair and scolds, "*Kopse to!*" Myrto and Stratis too seem pensive, riled into sidelong glances at the twins, as if tonight there's something uniquely foreign about them, *Turkosporoi*, Turkish seed. Elias—unsure he won't explode at the slightest provocation, real or imagined—is careful not to look at Stratis at all.

After dinner a chilly drizzle starts and disperses them to their separate spaces. By candlelight Elias unwraps and examines his ankle. Still too soon, and yet now, again, it's clear to him: somehow he must flee and whistle-blow, in the way that Eylül herself meant to do. The inquiry might start at any time, and now there's a second army he needs to embarrass. But the rain is thickening on the roof and shutters. Tonight is impossible. Tomorrow somehow. For now, rest. But when he falls asleep—rapidly after the wine and two sedatives—the olive grove is waiting for him, like a reserved room in hell. *Nice to have you back, Master Corporal.* The rerun won't let him slip lower into real sleep, though it does permit him to wake intermittently in a glaze of freezing sweat. Eyes open, eyes closed, it's the same shuttered dark, with the sound of the autumn rain. He stays awake.

When he doesn't emerge by late morning, Roland appears in his doorway and squints into the gloom, as if wondering if he's still here. It seems Kaya has released a statement: the journalist's last words to him, in hospital, were that she was not raped. She insisted the soldiers must have been honestly mistaken in thinking the young Greek was assaulting her. She and he were simply chatting on the beach. However, not wishing to impugn the integrity of four brave, well-meaning men (whom she fully forgave for the accidental shooting), and given that the Greek was unfortunately deceased, *Bayan* Şahin had no intentions of speaking publicly. But Colonel Kaya—according to his statement—felt that now, under the circumstances, her words should be known to all.

"He's quite a dancer, our colonel," Roland says. "He knows people will understand him to mean that she did intend to speak out—why else would she have been run over?—and so he puts it in such a way that she gains credit for her courage and honesty; you, the 'Greek,' will be posthumously excused; and he protects himself by not subjecting the army to . . . any exposures or embarrassment."

"People will know she was killed on purpose?"

"In North Cyprus, certainly. Many in Turkey as well. But I doubt anyone will dare challenge the story. Trif, may I bring you something to eat? Stavroula has picked some soft figs from her tree. May I open your shutters? Why not join Takkos and me in the kitchen for sweet coffee? It's warmer in there."

Elias says he feels ill, might sleep a little more. That's a good one.

He cracks a shutter for light, opens the top of the Aspirin bottle—five left. Then he unscrews the vial of sedatives and tips the remaining pills into a hollow in his pillow. Just four. Five and four may be too few to dull the pain fully, but enough to get him to the beach, a half-hour hobble, unlike the much-longer trek southward through the ruins and the hinterlands to the Green Line. His plan, if you can call it that, is to swim for hours south along the beach and that parade of dark hotels. A long swim, but he's a solid plodder, naturally buoyant, rarely getting cold.

He sits and watches the light slowly wane and sometime after dark, when the north wind brings back the summons of the muezzin for the bedtime prayer, he bolts the pills. Listens to the slowing trudge of the pulse in his skull until he's certain the village is asleep, even Stratis. (Lovers sleep so much better than soldiers.) He leaves a note on the bed: *Roland, thank you for having me. No irony intended. I've come to like my prison colony. Maybe love is the word. I will keep the secret safe. Trif.*

In his flip-flops, shorts and undershirt, and with the cane, he goes out into the sodden courtyard. By the door, as on his first full day here, they've left a meal under the old room-service cover. At the sight of it, his eyes sting and blur. Argos has been nosing at it. Now the dog peers up at him, backs away and then—ignoring Elias's whispered pleas to stay behind—follows him out through the gate. Stratis has been leaving it unlocked so that Myrto can come and go at night. Besides, who would expect Trif, still crippled, and now seemingly contented, to flee again?

A drizzling mist. Famagusta fills the clouds with enough light that he can see his way. He limps through the dead zone's serene desolation, increasingly stoned, the drugs hitting him harder than he'd foreseen, but then he has eaten and slept little in the past twenty-four hours. The plaza under its parasitic green cladding could be a lost Mayan city. Near the spot where he first glimpsed the dog, he stops and begs it to go back, even tossing a few small stones and saying, "Leave me alone!" Argos easily dekes the stones. Elias pushes on, the dulled pain in his ankle like the fading echo of a piercing sound. Argos follows. Elias stops, turns, lifts his fist, attempts to curse the dog—that earnest, fruit-bat face—and finds himself sobbing. Finally he walks onward without looking back.

He crosses John F. Kennedy, enters a chasm between hotels, plods zombie-like over rubble that he should be able to feel through the flip-flops but can't. Perfect. He leans the cane against the repaired fence and climbs it without pausing for a look, slicing his fingers and calves on the barbed wire. Vertigo flings him sideways. His ear and shoulder bury into the sand on the far side—no pain. At least the fence has stopped the dog, who is whining with all his heart a few feet away. Elias gets up, steps out of his flip-flops, slouches toward the sea. Intense feeling of being observed, though not by the dog. The hermit Paris, at last? For the first time he wonders: could Paris have been watching while he and Eylül were having sex on the beach, not far from here? Her body so alive beneath him.

The water burns like jellyfish stings in his cuts but the sea is warm, warmer than the air, and he wades in without stripping, some modesty about his body being found nude if he doesn't make it, though they say if you drown the sea strips you anyway. *You're not going to drown.* He starts swimming south. Soft rain dimples the wavelets and kisses his cheek as he turns his head up to breathe. A dog is barking in a dream and he treads water and looks back. Pale form in the shallows. How did he get past the fence? *Stay there.*

Good boy. Elias sets out again but realizes he's being shadowed along the beach, so he turns eastward and swims straight out to sea. Ahead now, no telling where sky and water meet. To his left the lights of the Palm Beach Hotel, of Famagusta, of a carrier ship outbound from the port and lit up like a casino. He turns south again, navigating by a few lights to the southwest that must be Kaya's beach club. No sign of the dog. He swims steadily but keeps veering east, into open sea, probably because his right arm is stronger, his left ankle useless. Several times he corrects course. Then, for a while, the drugs metastasizing as if he has downed a dozen, not a few, his awareness lags and he crawls on, still warm and growing warmer, limbs pleasantly emptied, his rhythm hypnotic, the soft swell rocking him.

When he looks up for the lights of Kaya's club, expecting to be abreast of them now or beyond, they're still off to the southwest and seemingly *farther* than before. Much farther. He has drifted a long way out, or a current has caught him. No idea how much time has passed. He turns southward again but keeps losing his bearings. He's confused but too drugged for panic, exhausted but too drugged for pain. Trying to rouse himself, he starts working at the water, urging his limbs to wake and fight, and he keeps at it, but over and over the coaching words in his head grow garbled and fade, until, quite suddenly, utterly, his will too seems exhausted. The Green Line is just a figment, a border on a fantasy novel's whimsical map. The shore itself now seems too far to go—another fiction. *Your plan is hopeless, your judgment shit*, his father whispers into his ear. Go ahead, say it. It doesn't matter. He lets himself slip under, opens his eyes: in the blackness his body radiates blue-green light, maybe a pre-death vision, pure psychedelia, then a part of him wakens: it's bioluminescent plankton, tracing the paths of his slow limbs in photons.

Something the size of a large child flashes past. His stinging eyes open wider. White missiles in sheaths of glittering light are bolting around him, their wakes fading behind them like comet tails. Muffled squeaking, a chorus of eerie moans. From his ankle the gauze wrap has unravelled to trail away downward. Beneath it, small fish in a dense school are swooping and banking while the dolphins herd them and pick off outliers. He sinks deeper while he stares. He clambers back to the surface, gasping. Around him the swell churns with bottlenose dolphins, one and now another breaching, snorting jets from their blowholes, a sardine stink in the air. Round eyes and rubbery, clownish grins. Helplessly he grins back. Everyone has heard these stories, how pods of dolphins will gather around drowning men to guide or carry them back to land.

Something slams into his midriff like a tackle on a rugby field. He doubles over in the water, clutching himself. Before he can interpret the pain he's buffeted again, in the ribs under his arm, and this blow revives other pains, his barbed-wire cuts scorching. He gapes for breath. A glancing blow against his right thigh, powerful backwash, a maelstrom of light swirling. A dolphin scuds past his belly and the truth gets through to him. They're attacking, they're trying to drive him off, maybe hurt or even kill him. Dolphins never do that, he thinks, though they do attack sharks this way—so he has heard somewhere—so maybe they do kill people, who can say? Who would ever know? A dolphin torpedoes straight toward his chest, swerves away at the last moment. He's defenceless, can barely shift his limbs, and maybe he shouldn't bother, maybe this is what he deserves. Then suddenly he's just pissed off. *Stop it, bullshit, leave me alone!* He turns back toward the island, who knows how distant, the western horizon black now, darker than the clouds above, a few stars showing in a swath of clear sky mounting over the Cypriot coast.

He breaststrokes, head up and chilled, afraid of being struck again, his belly and crotch cruelly exposed, the dolphins electric around him. A few strokes ahead, one breaches and blows. Its long grin now seems taunting and smug. "Fuck you," he gasps, another personal first, who has ever told a dolphin to fuck off? One soars under his belly in a knifing flash and the tail fluke scrapes him. He feels for his belly as if it might be slit open, spilling entrails into the sea. He puts his face under to check: his glowing hands are a stranger's burning after a phosphorus bombing.

Abruptly the seas are emptied, lifeless. Awake though heavily stoned he flops westward, instructing his arms to move, like limbs gone to sleep, pins and needles. His legs and feet sink over and over until he remembers to instruct them too. Ahead and to his right, the lights of Famagusta and the Palm Beach Hotel don't seem to move; the fainter lights of Kaya's club grow no clearer. Maybe, despite his efforts now, the currents are still tugging him east toward the coasts of Syria and Lebanon. Or he is dreaming it all. Yet some pocket of his consciousness seems aware and focused.

Overhead the cloud wall like a stadium roof is hatching open. The Milky Way appears, a glowing Gulfstream. Time and again he loses track of himself in a twilight torpor through which his body keeps crawling west. [. . . . .] Now the warm lights of Kaya's club do seem nearer. They're straight ahead. The sky less dark. When he tries to look behind, to check if dawn is approaching, a wave slaps him in the face and he sinks and flails back up, coughing brine. He tries to swim but his limbs are too cold, cramping, his torso shivering. A dog yaps out of the gloom. He struggles to see ahead. The salt blinds him. He tries to sidestroke but his dead legs keep dragging him down. He's finished, but he keeps on trying, goes on ordering his limbs to function. As he sinks again, the irony hits him—he's drowning himself in perfect accordance with the official story and will now helpfully wash up on the beach.

But he stops sinking. Though his feet are numb he seems to feel or sense something pushing up at them from below. Sand, pale sand. He's touching bottom. He wobbles upright, arms outstretched like a teetering drunk. His head and the top of his chest are above surface, chilled by a breeze out of the clear west, where Venus is setting. His chest bare. At some point in the night his undershirt has disappeared, his shorts too. He's still a ways out from the beach, Argos barking but invisible. A white building that must be Kaya's club looms in the twilight, two windows aglow.

Something slides out across the water, straight toward him. He peers into the gloom. A silhouette morphs into the splashing head of a monstrous hippopotamus . . . then two figures kneeling, digging at the sea with short-handled shovels. No, paddles.

Two men paddling a Zodiac.

"Trif . . . *Gott sei Dank*, it's you!" a man calls in Roland's voice.

"*Kalimera sas!*" the other calls, heavy Turkish accent, Kaya. "You are alive in the end!"

The Zodiac slows, averts its bow, softly bumps Elias's shoulder. Hot hands are on him, trying to drag him aboard. He can't give them any help.

"He is cold as ice," Roland says.

Thank you, Elias tries to say, but his lips are numb, teeth chattering too badly. And so they fish him out—mute and naked and cold as a corpse—and haul him back to shore.

TWO

The Green Line

He was collaborating with Death. You could have said that Death had a contract with the captain.

—CÉLINE, *VOYAGE AU BOUT DE LA NUIT*

He who digs a grave for another falls into it himself.

—GREEK CYPRIOT PROVERB

Odd to consider that an action—say, the soft, involuntary squeezing of a trigger—is as irreversible a moment after it happens as it is a day later, a year, a century. Hard not to believe that as time passes, completed actions somehow solidify, are embedded ever deeper in history's weave, just as the dead seem ever more dead with passing years. It's an illusion. No momentary molten state separates the event from its registration in permanence. No penumbra, no quantum wobble. A nanosecond after the trigger is squeezed, the accident is a finished fact, and the dead will never be more dead than they are now.

ARKADASH

Kaya's eyes are open under the hot, sodden towel that clings to his face and throat as solidly as wet plaster. The light of the morning sun rainbows the cotton's tight weave, which he sees as through a microscope. He hears Ali stropping the razor. Nine crisp strokes, as always—three superstitious sets of three. Kaya half-dozes under the towel.

At 4:00 this morning the German, accompanied by that filthy, fawning dog, arrived at the club to ask Kaya to help find Elias Trifannis. After fishing him half-dead from the shallows, they helped him into a tubful of water as hot as they could draw it, then put him to bed in one of the guest rooms under every blanket Ali could dig up. The German had asked if, once he'd gone back to the village and reported the news, he might return to the club and stay until Trifannis awoke. Kaya agreed and asked Ali to install Roland in a room on his return, and also to send the maid and groundskeeper home for an early weekend when they arrived at 8:30.

Kaya went back to bed for a few hours and woke refreshed but uneasy in his heart. *Was* the Greek trying to drown himself, or simply to run away? When rescued, Trifannis could hardly speak, but his lipless glaring at Kaya said plenty. It's unsurprising he would suspect Kaya was involved in Eylül Şahin's "accident." While Kaya assumes he will be able to convince the man otherwise, for now the animosity is upsetting. Kaya can't bear to be on bad terms with anyone.

Ali shaves him daily on the club veranda—Kaya lounging in a deck chair while Ali perches on a stool—except for some mornings in January and February when the north winds keep them inside. Ali now unpeels the towel and Kaya sighs with forgetful contentment: the air's bracing coolness on his cheeks, his skin feeling new-formed, flushed and fresh. The inside of his eyelids glow golden red as Ali lathers him with sandalwood soap, then gingerly scratches at the modest growth. He's searching for whiskers as much as shaving them. Kaya has a curiously sparse beard and the daily shave is more a luxurious ritual than a grooming necessity.

Ali pinches and lifts Kaya's nose, sealing the nostrils, while scraping downward over the skin between nose and upper lip—a curiously intimate proceeding. Above all, Kaya loves the icy freshness of the sapphire aftershave Ali pats onto his cheeks and chin and throat, a concoction of alcohol, menthol and Marmara frankincense that Kaya orders into the club from a gentlemen's shop in Izmir.

"*Teşekkürler*," he thanks Ali, who as always says nothing, only salutes. Kaya then declines a tempting offer of the *Hürriyet* and coffee. He really ought to go and see if Roland—who was out wandering the dead zone for half the night—is awake.

He taps on the man's door. After a moment he tries the handle and finds, as expected, that Roland hasn't locked it. He glides the door open. The bed is made, impeccably. The bathroom door is ajar, no sound or light from behind it.

Kaya pads up the hall to the next room, the largest, where four years ago the green-eyed Cypriote delivered her twins. For fear of waking Trifannis, he doesn't knock, just opens the door gently. The room is warm and stuffy. Trifannis—assuming it's not just some pillows arranged anthropomorphically under the blankets—is buried under the layers, no part of him showing. Roland, his back to the bed, sits in an armchair facing the closed window, the drapes parted just enough to give a view over the choppy, sun-bejewelled sea. Roland's booted feet rest flat on the floor, his hands splayed on his knees. After a few seconds, as if wrenched out of a trance, he slowly turns toward Kaya. His beard looks combed but his hair is flared awry. "Good morning, Erkan."

"Good morning! Why not you . . ." Kaya begins awkwardly in English, then switches to Turkish, which the German speaks more than passably: "Why don't you go back to bed for an hour or two? I doubt he'll wake up any time soon. Ali and I can keep an eye on him. Please—you look unwell, pale."

"I thought I should be here when he wakes up. He will be confused, I think. You seem to be bleeding."

Kaya touches his chin and examines his fingers.

"This might be the first time ever that Ali has cut me."

"He must be weary too."

"He'll never say so . . . I considered having him fetch my doctor down from the city—for our patient here, not for this scratch!—but on the whole it seemed too great a risk. So many risks these days!" Kaya shakes his head. "Shall I have Ali bring you coffee and a croissant?"

Roland's heavy brow purses, as if Kaya is posing a deep conundrum; then, almost shyly, he says, "To be honest, what I should really like is a hot shave. I used to go now and then to the Turkish barber in the village . . . the one where I was formerly stationed?"

"Of course!" Kaya says delightedly. "You must have a shave!"

"Mehmut, his name was." Roland sounds a bit wistful. His Turkish is courtly, stiffly correct, his umlaut-sounds excellent.

"Why not go downstairs, so Ali can shave you on the veranda? I can stay here with our swimmer."

"I think I ought to stay as well. Perhaps another time for the shave."

"Nonsense! I'll have Ali come up here now. And he'll bring you a coffee."

"*Teşekkür ederim,*" the German says, a tremor of frailty in his voice as if he, not the Greek, is the survivor.

After lunch, Kaya enjoys a *digestif* of marc and a cigarette while reading the paper up on the roof, which gets direct sunlight for another hour after it recedes from the beach. (He has considered dynamiting the two hotels that loom behind the club and steal its sun, but he fears the tennis court would be damaged, along with the little grove of tangerine trees that his children played in when they were small.) Turkish forces are now mustering along the Syrian frontier. Polat, he guesses, will be joining them at any hour. As for Eylül Şahin's sad story, it's fading already. Today, just a couple of lines. *Yet another journalist's accidental death in the Turkish Republic of North Cyprus* . . . The *Hürriyet* knows, but can do little more than protest in this sardonic code.

Ali appears out of nowhere, as usual. "The Greek is conscious, *efendi.*"

"Is he?" Kaya sits up. "Very good. Please take him some water, coffee, and a croissant. No. Several croissants. And two soft-boiled eggs. Maybe a sliced tomato, a few black olives . . ." Though Kaya finished lunch less than an hour ago—baked ziti, Greek salad, zabaglione—his mouth begins to water again as he improvises a hearty breakfast for the Greek. "And a good-sized wedge of halloumi, and a few fresh figs, and a tangerine. And American toast, with butter and honey. He's a big man."

Kaya hurries downstairs to the Greek's room. The curtains are open. Roland has turned his chair around and is seated next to the bed. His pale beardlessness startles Kaya, even though Kaya personally witnessed the beard's removal just two hours ago—and couldn't help sensing that Ali appreciated having real whiskers to attack. The young Greek is propped up in bed, unshaven, puffy-eyed like a battered fighter. He's examining his own torso and prodding a heart-sized, eggplant-purple bruise over his ribs. When he notices Kaya in the doorway his hand fists, falls onto the blankets. Kaya sighs; another interview with a hostile convalescent. In English he says, "I am pleased to see you so alive today. But what happens"—he points at the bruising—"there on your breast?"

"Were you involved in what happened to Eylül Şahin?"

"I've told him," Roland says wearily in Turkish, "you've sworn you weren't."

"You must have known something!" the Greek says, seeming to slur his words, which makes him no easier to understand.

"I, know Miss Şahin? Never before I know this woman."

Roland explains in Turkish what the young man actually meant.

"Ah, no, no, *arkadash*! Of course I know nothing! This death is sad to me also. I am sad that it must happen."

"But it didn't have to happen!"

Kaya looks to Roland; how small and ineffectual the ex-peacekeeper's mouth appears now in his naked face! Roland says something to the Greek, then tells Kaya in Turkish, "He misunderstood. I've explained that you didn't mean, 'She had to die.'"

"'*Arkadash*,'" the Greek says softly. "I forgot that word till now. What does it mean?"

"It is meaning 'dear friend,'" Kaya says. "You know some Turkish?"

"Just that word."

It hits Kaya who must have said it to him, and when. "Friend, believe me, I am so sorry. Also, I am angry toward . . ." He stops himself from saying *Captain Polat*.

"You're not denying the army was involved?'

Kaya looks at Roland, who translates. With a fleck of impatience Kaya says, "Tell him I am truly sorry, but there's not a thing we can do. Nothing! The truck and its driver were unconnected to the army. I assume they were hired—everyone will think so—but there's no way to prove it. And any attempt to prove it—very dangerous. The police here answer to Ankara. He has to understand. He can't reappear yet and actually voice these suspicions, or he could destroy"—long pause—"your village, for one thing, and make you all refugees again, or worse. As it is, it might be hard for me to protect you all if my adjutant—don't say this part—should return from Syria."

When Roland finishes translating, seeming to use a lot more words than Kaya used, Kaya jumps in before the Greek can respond: "How do you do, my tired friend? I commanded a breakfast for you" (he wonders now if the word should be pronounced *breggfast*, which makes more sense to him), "a very healthful breakfast!"

ROLAND'S TALE

Famished to his marrow Elias scours and sops clean the various plates on the breakfast tray. He's marginally aware of Roland seated by the bed, watching. At no point is he able to look up from the food. The tangerine, which he eats last, helps cut the bitterness of the drug that still coats his tongue and palate, along with aftertastes of sea salt and iodine.

When he finishes, Roland—this stranger with the vulnerably exposed, meek-looking mouth—bursts out, "You must never do that again!"

"I'm sorry you had to come after me—"

"Whatever did you *think* we would do?"

"But I'm not sorry I tried."

"Tried to leave, or tried to end your life?"

"If I wanted to end my life, I'd just provoke Stratis."

"You've done so now—he is livid! You really believed you could swim so far?"

"I wasn't thinking 'could' or 'can't.'" A salvo of sneezes rips through his aching body. He won't mention what he recalls only dimly: that his will, his *thymos*, gave out for a while. He let go. He was ready to die. He died.

Handing him the breakfast napkin Roland says, "Well, all the same—gesundheit. I say nothing more of it now. Forget my angry words. Perhaps I am just talking of myself anyhow, as one does."

"I don't follow."

"To flee one's life or to end it—to face this choice! This I understand." He looks firmly at Elias, as if daring him to doubt the words. Clean-shaven, he appears younger and yet wearier at the same time. "In the village in the hills where I was stationed, one whole night I sat and stared at my pistol. I'd put it on the table while I waited for the military police. All was silent, even the dogs and chickens, as if I had killed every living thing . . ." He seems to be doubting his decision, or ability, to tell the story. Then he goes on. "After some hours, when I realized I could not . . . swallow this last meal of lead, I holstered the gun and left for Varosha, on foot. You see, there were rumours back then among the U.N. folk—you would hear these things, like fairy stories, at the Ledra Palace bar. I did not quite believe, but where else had I to go? Ah, but as I left, I unholstered the gun again and laid it back on the table. Never since have I touched a weapon. When the U.N. police came, they would find their evidence waiting, like an exhibit in a courtroom."

Elias is too tired to speak—whether to ask a question or to nudge Roland on—but senses he has only to wait.

"I mentioned before that in the buffer zone there are several villages where Greek and Turkish Cypriots still live together, supervised by the U.N., and that I was stationed in the smallest of these, up in the hills to the west, close enough to Varosha that the very sea here"—he nods toward the window—"can be viewed on clear winter days. These are charming places, with lanes of stairs that mount between the white houses up to a plaza, where you find the main church, a few cafés, a taverna, and always a giant old shade tree. Nearby too there will be a mosque. Turkish Cypriots are mostly secular, so the prayer call is not always heard, but on Muslim holidays at the Al-Asr, the *adhan* will sound through the lanes, rousing the Greeks from their nap as well as the Turks. When you first hear this *adhan* and the church bells overlapping, as if talking at the same time yet never raising their voices, in fact nearly harmonizing—this novelty was one I cherished.

"Never have I loved a place as I loved that village! Every sunlit or moonlit view, down or up streets, across the plaza, over rooftops to the sea, was exquisite. The people seemed warm, for the most part, and at peace, as if somehow the region's terrible history had bypassed them. The only sign of history, in fact, was my presence, and the tiny 'HQ' on the plaza, with its rusty flagpole and a ragged U.N. flag.

"In other ways too the village seemed untouched. Owing to its status in the buffer zone, builder permits were not easy to possess, so it remained free of villa development for the English and Russians. And since the developers' money couldn't flood in, the . . . the velocity of life had barely changed. In fact, at first it was a little too slow for me, though before long I ceased to notice.

"After my university years I'd lived in West Berlin with my wife, Heidi. After the wall came down, we lived on the cheaper east side. We had been part of the crowds—they called us *Mauerspechte*, 'wall-woodpeckers'—that broke holes in parts of the wall, before the full, official demolition of the next year, 1990. The intense euphoria of those hours and days would be hard to exaggerate. For a while, after the unification, I felt as perfectly home in Berlin as I thought possible.

"As an adult, naturally one knows that euphoria must be followed by a subsiding, even a sort of nausea, but for us and our friends—community organizers who had been trying to form ties with others, on the other side—the feeling that began to set in was worse. We'd expected too much. Formerly divided peoples, with their different habits, ideas, illusions—their shared world could hardly be perfect. One colleague from the East said to me, with envy, a little contempt, and much amazement, 'You who've had the freedom to pursue your dreams have picked such poor ones.' True—I myself had longed for authority, power in my little field, a lust which now seems laughable—yet at the same time, my wife and I had hoped the simple kindness, the village unity and festivity we'd cherished, might linger, even in lesser form. In our busyness it seemed to vanish. It struck me that something deep in the northern soul must fear and hate festivity, could not help but yearn for the return of order—in fact, for more walls of a sort! I'd told myself that every wall longs to be toppled, all hearts long to be open and unguarded, and I still believe I was not wholly wrong, though perhaps no more than half right. There remains always the *Mauer im Kopf*, 'the wall in the head.'"

He pauses for a sip of water, closing his eyes as he swallows. He sits with one leg crossed over the other in the European way, the knees close together, crotch unexposed.

"When a shared dream suffers defeat, or just compromise, often it kills the union of the dreamers. Heidi and I seemed helpless not to blame each other for our dream's defeat, and also, perhaps, for its too-hopeful nature. I decided to go away and—still hopeful, in my fashion—become a peacekeeper. I suppose I thought to dismantle other walls with more perfect results. Naturally I first had to volunteer for the army, thus losing whatever friends in the peace movement I'd not lost when Heidi and I separated.

"Two years later I was posted in Bosnia, at a checkpoint where nothing much ever happened. While there I became haunted by the story of a peacekeeper who, not far away, found a chance to kill a man of the Ratko Mladić sort, but felt he must abide by our principle of neutrality. When this warlord renewed his mission of massacre, the peacekeeper, who witnessed the results, could not forgive himself. Within a year he lost his mind. Before he went silent he said, 'I had not even the courage to shoot *myself*, afterward.' This story I could never forget."

Elias peers into his coffee cup—nothing left but grounds—then drains his water glass.

"In time, after tours in other difficult places, I arrived on Cyprus and was posted to Ephira. I could hardly believe my fortune. I've told you of how I cherished the village's beauty, and of how well the two peoples seemed to mix. Certainly you would not say they loved each other—they were too wary for that, and most were insufficiently fluent in the other's tongue. But, together, they loved Ephira, which made for a true bond. And their *way* of living in that place . . . I can say truly that it taught me to love.

"In Berlin too I had loved, in a way, but always it was love 'on the fly,' in hurried passing, or love in the abstract—love of peace, liberty, humanity—or it was love in the shadow of my ambitions, or love postponing its full expression until a future when, somehow, one would be less busy—less driven! To a driven man, others are not fully human, you see. They are a portal to his goals, or a barrier in the path. In Ephira, I realized that affection does not combine well with the ticking clock.

"Some days, once I'd completed the day's work, I would sit for hours in the plaza beneath the spreading carob tree, playing backgammon and taking coffee or icy beer and conversing with the villagers, Greek, Turkish, and the few tourists who passed through. Folk up north might have seen the pleasant sameness of this life—at least once it passed the length of a sunny holiday—as wasted time. I insist there was a value. In the village, everything became real. I'd liked food and drink well enough before, but now the flavours—the intensity of the flavours was shocking! I looked at the people around me and—so it seemed—I saw them truly, heard them, understood them. I grew so patient, I hardly knew myself. For my neighbours I felt a calm and profound affection, even for those I disliked in certain ways, like the mayor, Adamou, and the rich Turkish Cypriot, Şenoglu.

"I was by now paying visits to a widow who kept hens and grew vegetables just south of the village. I loved this Ariadne very much. As I myself was well liked by the locals (though not quite as well liked as I imagined), no one seemed to object to these visits, not even the priest, even though Ephira—like any village in the hills, from Bavaria to Bolivia—was quite conservative, and in ways I chose not to study too closely. You see, I'd resolved not to return to my unified country but rather to make Cyprus home. You'll note the irony: I'd found happiness in a place that was still very much divided and I myself a kind of guard on the wall! Of course, there was no actual wall in Ephira, and I no longer felt like any guard. Like our lazy colonel here, I would forget my uniform more and more often, and never would I bear my gun. Still, each morning I would drive a route around the area in the white Jeep, though often I would stop to talk to people, or deliver a sack of rice or pitcher of wine from old Spyrou's shop to the houses of elders outside the village. Or to the widow's house.

"Now and then, someone would arrive to replace me for my leaves, and I would go to Nicosia to buy a few needed things, mainly English and German books. As you know, Nicosia is still truly divided, as Berlin used to be, so I was always happy to return to Ephira. In due course, I petitioned the U.N. authorities that I might remain for another tour. Request granted. And so, two more years passed in happiness.

"In most places, I think, most people wish to get along without the strife, but everywhere there are a few deeply driven men who, if the conditions come up, will seize their chance. These men are either idealists or cynics, nothing in between. They intoxicate the crowd and fool them into doing the work that a bloody dream demands. From the beginning, I sensed Yiannis

Adamou might be such a man, but I was unwilling to believe he would cause real trouble.

"Adamou was of average appearance, average build, average mind (though clever enough for his purposes)—not someone you would easily recollect if the police asked you to describe a man involved in a crime. Still, one thing divided him from the villagers: he carried himself not like a Cypriot but a Greek from Greece. Greek Cypriots, as you know, are more quiet and reserved, rarely looking you hard in the eye and standing close to dominate you, like *Greek* men—like our Stratis!—for whom that role is part of life's theatre. Was Adamou simply conceited in his local importance? He'd been the mayor since his mid-twenties. But I suspect he had always been what he was.

"Still, when he came to Mehmut to have his moustache or his hair trimmed—he was balding, with a flaking skull, but the fringe of hair grew thick and black—he was civil enough to the barber, who, by the way, was the saddest, gentlest man I ever knew, with drooping dark eyes, always moist, as though he cried eternally for some private sorrow, or for the world. Yet he would smile at jokes and plenty were told in his shop. That banter was a wonderful training for me, in both tongues. In fact, Mehmut's noisy little shop on the plaza seemed the very heart of the . . . the liaison between Ephira's Greeks and Turks, like the tiny parliament of a two-nation country.

"One morning I lay in Mehmut's chair with the hot towels on my face while three Greek Cypriots, Adamou the loudest, argued in terms which made it obvious: this was no new conversation but part of one ongoing, one of which I should have been aware, given a few things Ariadne had said and which I'd missed, or rather *dis*-missed. But I knew I must listen now.

"Over the past year some younger Greek Cypriots had left Ephira, making advantage of the republic's new membership in the E.U. to take work in Europe. In the same period, by coincidence—though the men in the shop had their doubts on that score—there had been an unusual number of births in the Turkish quarter, and a large family had moved down from Girne, permitted to do so because they had relatives in Ephira. As a result, for the first time the number of Turkish Cypriots in Ephira was approaching the number of Greeks—so Mayor Adamou was now saying. Of course, everyone knew the Turks simply had more children. Now they were importing outsiders under dubious pretext, to 'flood out' the Greeks, just as they had in Ottoman times. And now the village's wealthiest Turk, Derviş Şenoglu—a retired hotelier from Famagusta, who had also moved in and built a house, having relatives here—he had approached Adamou and, citing the demographic change, proposed that he should represent the Turkish Cypriots and meet regularly with Adamou. Adamou felt that Şenoglu was proposing a sort of co-mayoral arrangement and it angered him deeply. Şenoglu had not been elected, after all. Of course, in the next election, he might very well be elected, since by then the Turks of Ephira might be the majority!

"As Mehmut lifted the towel off my face—his fingers seemed to be trembling—the men began to argue about what measures might have to be used if the Turkish population really did overtake the Greek. By now, I knew the other voices—Socratis, the owner of a hardware shop, and Andreas, a younger man who seemed never to do anything and lived with his parents. It was becoming harder to follow their words. I think perhaps they were finally made cautious by my presence, though in general, I think, they'd ceased to regard me as 'U.N.' at all. I was simply a likeable, harmless *ksenos* who had chosen to make his home among them. As for Mehmut—I suspect they were so accustomed to him that he'd become invisible to them, like a servant.

"I heard the slap of dress shoes in the doorway and the men fell silent. I realized what must have happened. Şenoglu had come in. I wanted to sit up and look, but I sensed Mehmut hovering close above me with the razor. Evidently, Şenoglu was shrewd enough to interpret the silence but, like Adamou, too proud to be cautious. In Turkish he made a jocular remark to Mehmut. I think the gist of it was that he thought it courteous of the Greeks not to speak ill of him in his presence. Mehmut made no reply. He seemed to be more aware of the moment's gravity. Adamou and his . . . what is the word . . . sidemen?"

"Sidekicks?"

"*Ja*—they all begin speaking at once, whether to each other or to Şenoglu, I couldn't say. I sensed that all three were on their feet. Adamou said something in broken Turkish and Şenoglu replied in broken Greek, calling the man a *vlakas*. I sat up in the chair and ran into the razor, which nicked me and left a small scar"—he indicates a horizontal welt on a part of his cheek previously covered by his beard—"the only mark that the tragedy has left on my person! With my toe, I spun the chair to face the door. As Şenoglu saw me, he seemed both surprised and amused. Ah, he must have thought, a quarrel finally erupts between the two sides and out of the air the U.N. appears! But to Adamou, the grin must have seemed another display of contempt, and he did something very odd—he pinched Şenoglu's nose and twisted. Şenoglu's eyes opened very wide and his black brows drew together, I think more in amazement than anger. He slapped Adamou across the face, terrifically fast. It *was* a slap, not a punch, but hard enough that Adamou staggered backward. Now Andreas, the biggest one there, who by the way wore a moustache modelled after Adamou's, raised a fist to strike Şenoglu, but I called, 'Stop now!' first in Greek, then in Turkish. The Greek Cypriots glanced toward me, while Şenoglu grinned again, spun on his heel and left the shop.

"The three Greeks—all muttering angrily—started out the door, and for a moment they blocked each other's way, like comedians in a soundless film. Feeling ridiculous myself, I said,

'If you catch and hurt him, I will have to arrest you!' Never had I tried to speak this way, not in Cyprus. I was not even sure how to go about arresting anyone. They turned to me and, despite their anger, they began laughing. How those three men laughed! I realized I was still sitting in the chair, fully lathered, wearing a shaving bib, talking my accented Greek out of a St Nicholas beard of foam that must now be dashed with blood. Adamou said, 'Will you chase us through the streets looking like that, Roland? Then arrest us and throw us in jail? And what jail would that be? Anyway, we can settle our account with Şenoglu at a more convenient time. Let him go. Ephira is small.' 'I *will* arrest you if you hurt him,' I said, and then—trying to be even-handed, always an error with a man like Adamou—I said, 'And I'll be speaking to him as well, about striking you.' The three laughed and Adamou said, 'Don't bother scolding him about that slap. His young wife could hit me harder. At least I think so. Perhaps I will find out.' And they turned and left.

"I lay back down in the chair and let Mehmut stop my cut with his pencil of ice, then finish the shave. His hand was trembling and I could feel the blade at my throat as I tried to think. I managed to convince myself the matter might go no farther—after all, had peace not prevailed in the village for years? Still, I did resolve to speak privately with both Adamou and Şenoglu the next day.

"That evening as usual I visited Ariadne. She filled my glass many times, and after the meal—her stew of rabbit, lentils, and leeks, you know the dish, I prepared it just a few days ago—I told her I should go back into Ephira and spend the night at HQ. Naturally, I'd told her what happened in Mehmut's shop—and, just as naturally, she already knew. Now she urged me to stay with her, at least for a few more hours. I insisted I must go, to insure that all was well, but she—how can I put this—she convinced me to stay a little longer. Afterward, I fell asleep, but at around eleven suddenly I woke. Her arm was firmly around me.

I tried to remove it gently, but she held tighter. I explained again that I should leave, must leave, *prepei na fygo!*, and she grew almost angry, crying and pleading with me. I asked what was happening—did she know of some reason I should not go? No, no such reason, all was well, she said—in fact she now recalled hearing that the mayor and Şenoglu planned to meet the next day, to discuss matters. But she would not look me in the eye—this woman whose black eyes never seemed to weary of meeting mine. Would I not please stay for the night? I pulled away. She began to weep and rage. At the door she stopped me and held on, but I, now fearing the worst, I shoved her away and she fell back into the table that was covered with the remains of our feast. She ended on the floor and looked up at me with fury and fear. 'Don't go,' she said, 'for your sake, if not for mine!' But I went, and one of the saddest things about this parting is that I recall so little of our last time together, I mean as man and woman. I had learned to pay such close attention to each moment, but that night—I was distracted.

"I ran up the dirt road under the stars. It seemed to me that the insects to either side of the road fell silent, field by field, as I climbed toward the houses and the cupola of the church. The plaza was deserted, the cafés were all closed, which seemed odd—usually on summer nights they would be open till midnight. The tattered U.N. flag drooped pitifully above the one-storey HQ. I hurried into the back room and found my sidearm, which I hadn't seen nor touched for who knows how long. My sense of alarm was real, yet I felt ridiculous as I loaded it—like a boy pretending to be sheriff of Dodge City, as I had as a boy. I tore off my shirt and pulled on my U.N. one—the faded blue one, you've seen me wear it—and my beret.

"Downhill I ran from the plaza into the Turkish quarter. The lanes were deserted. The front door of Şenoglu's house was ajar, as I'd feared and even expected—you see, everything was now appearing in a . . . an aura of the *expected*, like in some kind of half-conscious dream . . ."

"Lucid," Elias says softly, "a lucid dream."

"*Ja, ja*. So, I pushed open the door and entered. Şenoglu lay at my feet in a shallow bath of blood. He was in a bathrobe and undershorts, very bloodied. His breath was passing in and out of a wound in his ribcage—bloody froth emerging and being sucked back in. There were other wounds too. I thought, 'I must alert the police,' then recalled that there were no police but me. 'I must fetch Dr. Economou,' I thought, but then I heard sounds from up the hallway. I drew and readied the pistol and followed a deep green carpet, like in a grand hotel, so my steps were silent. A door was open on the right. It was a bedroom with a wide bed, modern furnishings, drapes instead of shutters. Yiannis Adamou—I knew him from behind by his wreath of hair—he was arched over the foot of the bed, the toes of his shoes planted on the floor and his trousers around his knees. His shirt-tail hung down and covered his thrusting backside. His thick thighs were like an ape's. I couldn't see whom he was covering but I knew it must be Şenoglu's young wife, Fatim. A very small woman. She was face down, with her lower half bent over the foot of the bed." Roland breaks off for a few seconds, coughs his throat clear, then resumes: "Her cries were muffled, yet they were loud. Adamou was strangely silent. At the foot of the bed, Socratis Costou was simply standing, as if observing these events with the detachment of a . . . a researcher, though now I conclude that he was really in shock, *ja,* I think maybe that none, not even Adamou, had believed their visit would go this far—maybe they too found themselves taking step by step, in lucid dream. As for Şenoglu, I picture him at his door, taunting them, flippant and haughty to the end, never aware he is dooming himself.

"The third Greek, Andreas, stood over beside the drapes, restraining Şenoglu's young son, who was watching in horror and crying (I mean weeping, not crying out—he was making no noise).

No one seemed aware of me, even after I told them to stop. My voice must have been faint, or not audible over the other sounds. I held the pistol out in front of me and crossed the carpet on feet that I could not feel, then aimed at the mayor's temple. Finally the others—though perhaps not him and Fatim, whose face was pushed into the bed and her eyes shut tight—the others knew of my presence. Socratis regarded me with surprise and yet, still, no visible alarm. Perhaps it *was* shock, or perhaps he had so often seen me at my ease, he didn't believe me capable of action. Neither did I. He called to Adamou, 'Yianni?' My vision was reduced to a circle which contained the mayor's face, still oblivious, and the tangled hair, cheek, and closed eye of Fatim. Then her eye—it opened and found me at the same time that Adamou's turned toward me. Her eye showed no relief, only terror, while the mayor's eye narrowed and his mouth curled at the corner—that conceited contempt again! I was still not real to him! He went on thrusting as if I and the pistol were not there, then he panted out his loathsome words: 'The widow was not enough for you tonight?'

"The bullet entered through his temple and killed him so fast, the insolent expression never left his face, which fell heavily on the back of Fatim's neck. She screamed. For an appalling moment, his body seemed to move on her as before, then stopped. Fatim shut her eye and called, 'Derviş, Derviş!'—which was both her son's and husband's name. With my free hand I gripped Adamou's shoulder and tried to lift him from her, but I could only drag and tumble him off sidewise, so he flopped off the side of the bed and lay facing up. I took a step backward. His leering eyes stared up at me. They appeared even more mocking in death—a permanent mockery! I still see those eyes. His member—I tried not to see this—his member still looked murderously inflamed.

"Fatim, having pulled her bloodied nightgown down over herself, had crawled up the bed to the . . . the headboard, where she turned to face the room. She stretched her arms toward her son. Andreas's own arms had fallen limp at his sides, thus freeing the boy, but he, the boy, seemed not to realize, so the mother and son remained a short way apart. The boy was screeching while Fatim called to him, Come! She seemed afraid to move from her spot. As for Socratis, he seemed to be imploring me—his hands were open, he was trying to tell me something, he was speaking very fast, I couldn't understand his words, couldn't seem even to hear him, and I shot him in the chest. I watched my own hand and the pistol shoot him. He flew backward—the carpet all but silenced his fall. Andreas was making for the door in a panic, stepping over the body of Socratis. Andreas I shot in the side of the chest and he fell and curled into a ball and lay still. Naturally I assumed he too was killed"—*kilt,* Roland pronounces the word—"though some days after, I learned that I had wounded him only, and not too badly.

"The son now rushed to his mother and they embraced in a desperate way. I said, 'Please wait here, Madam,' in Turkish, then I yanked a bloodied sheet off the bed and settled it over Adamou and walked out of the room. My head and body felt anaesthetized, no thoughts, no sensations. I passed Derviş Şenoglu—the slit in his ribcage was barely breathing. Outside the house I paused to bend over and vomit, then I ran back up toward the plaza, where I knocked on the door of Petros Economou, the old doctor who served for all the villagers, Greek and Turk. I knocked louder. I could have put my fist through that door and felt no pain. When the doctor came—he was fully dressed and holding his medical bag—I instructed him to go to Şenoglu's at once. He nodded sadly and said, 'So I feared.'

"I returned to the kitchen of the HQ and set my mobile phone and pistol on the table, and at this pistol I stared, as I said before, trying to decide whether to . . . finish a life now finished in every other way. I thought I'd escaped history. Now I saw I had made a sabbatical, nothing more. My little Eden was a dream. I'd just shot three unarmed men, one of whom perhaps I was correct to kill, but the others—both helpless. I kept expecting the police to arrive, then kept recalling that neither those from the south nor the north could enter the buffer zone. At some point, U.N. personnel would come for me. By 1 A.M. I heard ambulances approaching. Both the HQ telephone and my mobile began to ring, which made it still harder to concentrate on the decision I was trying to take. So both devices I silenced in a permanent way.

"Soon afterward I departed. Ariadne's house I passed on my way out of the village. As a light was glowing in the bedroom—I could see it through the shutters—I thought for a moment of stopping to bid her goodbye, but I was still too angry at her. Since then, I have come to believe that she was not only doing Adamou's bidding but also, truly, trying to protect me from harm. She loved me, after all. And to think, the last touch between us was that violent push . . ."

When Elias realizes Roland doesn't mean to say anything more, he asks quietly, "Do any of the others know this story? Stratis?"

"Kaiti I have told, knowing she would understand. Myrto was in Nicosia when these famous events occurred—imagine, a German peacekeeper embarks on a 'killing spree' in a Cypriot town!—but if she has tied the connection between that news and me, she says nothing. The others, no, especially not Stratis. To them, I'm a U.N. corps deserter, that's all." His hand moves suddenly—it seems he might slap Elias. Instead the hand fastens over Elias's brow. "No fever, but you look weary. Far from recovered, I think. I'll go back to the village, Trif, and let you sleep."

Elias doesn't tell him that he looks weary too—utterly emptied.

"The colonel will keep you for a few days—let you stay, I mean, feed you well—until you feel strong. Then Ali will accompany you back." He pushes his palms down onto his thighs to help get himself upright, then walks to the door.

"Roland?"

The man halts in the doorway, like an actor in a drama, though he doesn't turn back around on cue. He waits, as if resigned to what's coming.

"I can't promise you I won't try to leave again."

"Three times is not enough?"

"I have a story, too. People need to hear it."

"Then why not tell us?"

"Because of your own crazy secrecy! At least until now."

As Roland turns to face him, Elias finds himself spilling out a condensed, edited version of what happened in the olive grove. He admits the possibility that he shot a village elder dead; he doesn't admit that he's more or less certain, and he omits the last part, which Roland's own story has brought back so graphically—how he gave up trying to revive the man and let himself be pulled away, shocked by how his efforts had desecrated the body, caving the chest, widening the wound, staining the white beard and yellow teeth. The man's family would think that he'd been beaten as well as shot.

In the doorway Roland says, "I feared it must be something of the kind."

"It's not like I want to bring ruin on your last refuge, but . . ."

"When I was a boy," Roland says, "the frontier scout Kit Carson, he was a hero to me. Years later I learned that when he led soldiers against the Navajo, he obeyed orders he did not love and cut down all of their old peach trees, thousands of them. The fruits, fresh or dried, they were the Navajo's staple! My hero broke their hearts and won the war. Forgive me—it's a poor time for this story."

"That's why I don't follow them anymore."

"What, the stories of history?"

"Orders. From anyone."

"I think, like me, you may need to rest silent for a while. *Auf Wiedersehen*, Trif."

***

An obliterating sleep unshattered by dreams. He wakes in the dark. He could be anywhere, or nowhere. Then he spies through a gap between the curtains a row of three clear stars, Orion's belt lifting out of the sea. He lies unmoving for some time, then gets up with a moan, hobbles into the bathroom and stands in the shower, his forehead against the tiled wall, letting hot water flow and flow over his aching muscles, contused ribs, growling belly.

He comes back into the room with a towel wrapped around his hips. The bedside lamp is on. Kaya sits in the armchair by the bed, where Roland sat before. Beside him, a trolley bearing a large tray crammed with good-smelling food.

"Excuse me, but I think you will be *hungry*," Kaya says with a knowing twinkle, as if delivering a reliable old punchline. He wears a mauve shirt and a black blazer, as if he has dressed for a dinner of his own. And so he has. He explains that he would like to eat here with his guest, if that would be fine. And if Trif would care to wear clothing, Ali has purchased some things in Famagusta (with a courtly flourish Kaya indicates a set of maroon pyjamas, apparently silk, laid out at the foot of the bed).

"Timur Ali also brings pants and a shirt and a jumper and the shoes and other things, as need be. These are in the closet. One question more. Will you care to watch important football as we dine?"

"An important game?"

"My favoured team, Fenerbahçe, plays with Galatasaray."

Relief, or something like it, wells in Elias. To sit up in bed in pyjamas, fill his aching stomach and take in a spectacle whose outcome he could not care less about . . . the luxury of mindless oblivion.

"I may ask Ali to bring the TV. Also DVD. I have many movies."

"Okay."

"So you agree?" Kaya adds with feeling, "You believe me, then!"

"You mean about Eylül?"

"Yes. Miss Şahin."

Elias nods slowly and says, "I guess I must."

Helplessly he falls on the food and for some time barely speaks or looks up from the chicken kebabs and the plates of saffron rice and *horiatiki* glistening with good oil and the warm bread and the *kataifi* and the tumblers of retsina. Kaya observes with a pleased and slightly amused air. Unlike Elias, the man dines with courtly manners that he forgets only at climactic points in the match, when the commentators' voices crescendo and he wide-eyes the screen, full mouth agape, fork and knife held aloft in tight fists.

After the meal, a portly cat with a sour face hops onto the bed, cuddles against Elias's packed stomach and goes to sleep, wheezing electrically. It's the cook's pet, Kaya says indifferently, and offers to throw it out the door. "No, it's fine," Elias says.

The men are on their fourth round of Armagnac when the DVD ends around midnight. The original *Planet of the Apes* is one of his favoured films, Kaya says. He has seen it often. His eyes, by the last scene, are bright and wet. When Charlton Heston kneels on a beach of ruins and hammily declaims, *God damn them all!* Elias mutters, "Amen."

"Excuse me?"

"I just meant . . . It doesn't matter."

Gracious in bafflement Kaya says, "Ah—of course."

"You must have told her I was dead, right?"

Kaya asks him to repeat the words slowly and then, contorting his brow and speaking with great concentration: "I had to say this thing. Yes, I am sorry, but I must."

"If I'd known they meant to kill her, I would have tried to do something."

"What?"

"Something. Anything."

"But some problems . . . maybe they have no solving."

Elias finishes his drink. "I think I should sleep now."

"Yes, please, you must!" Kaya pinches loose the knees of his slacks and gets up. "Please sleep all you may. Shall I put a glass of brandy for the night? A fresh cigar?"

He surfaces from another stint of annihilation and the sun is several hours high over the sea. The good brandy has left him with a bad head. Beside his inflamed ankle, the bloated old cat snores. His crutches have been set against the wall. He stumps to the balcony door and outside. The air is cool but heat is welling up off the ash-white sands three storeys down, where Kaya lies asleep on a beach chair, an open newspaper lapsed over his chest.

Elias goes back inside and then down the hallway in his silk pyjamas, using one crutch. He gathers Kaya's room must be at the far end. The door is ajar. The room is uncluttered, the bed made. A lamp-like water pipe and near-empty brandy bottle share the dresser with propped portraits: the children Kaya was mentioning last night, no doubt, along with an elegant, amused-looking older woman who must be his late mother. A laptop computer—slim, silver, state of the art—sits perfectly centred on the desk by the balcony door. The laptop is open, screen dark. Elias leans down, taps the mouse and brings up the home page, then skims the cursor to an icon. His pulse throbs in the finger hovering over the mouse. One click, then a web address and a password, and he could be looking through seven weeks' worth of mail—a posthumous account that must be overflowing with junk, DND messages flagged urgent, maybe a few notes from old contacts and the morose but kindly Dr. Boudreau. He could blurt a few lines in reply, imagine the effect of that, fresh tidings from the tomb. (Or do service providers delete accounts after they learn of a customer's death?)

He clicks. In the search bar, instead of his mail server's address, he sloppily pecks his name. The search engine corrects him, *Did you mean "Elias Trifannis"*, and below it appears a list of headline links along with headshot photos of two men: Boudreau and himself.

"Oh, no," he says and clicks on a Canadian news service link, then devours the story in convulsive chunks. It's from yesterday, updated two hours ago. The doctor is dead in Paphos, an apparent OD . . . his last act, releasing a statement concerning events in Afghanistan in which his patient, Corporal Elias Trifannis . . . drowned October, possible suicide, being treated PTSD . . . altercation on beach in which Turkish journalist (Elias skips a paragraph here). Then the doctor's statement: reckless nature of company's raid, villagers accidentally killed, one perhaps by patient, historical olive grove destroyed, profound regret encouraged patient say nothing pending inquiry, inquiry then cancelled, wrongly, but now, perhaps, the doctor hopes . . . (The statement includes a transcription of Elias's clinical "testimony," which the military is trying to place under publication ban as a violation of doctor–patient confidentiality, though for now readers can click *here* and read it.)

He stares into the screen, the screen stares back. He'd liked Boudreau as much as he could then like any older man associated with the war. At the hospital in Paphos, even through the meds, it was easy to spot perfunctory solace and mere procedural concern; Boudreau was always sincere. Clearly he was suffering from some kind of intelligent anguish and exhaustion. Now he has gone and proved what he unhelpfully told Trif in their last session: official casualties are a mere appetizer, whetting War's hunger. Any war goes on destroying lives for a lifetime.

There's a sound of boots slowly climbing the uncarpeted stairs from two floors below. He exits the site, closes the search-engine window and snaps down the laptop screen. Then he remembers it was open, flips it up again, grabs the crutch and lurches out into the hallway. Sound-muffling carpet. Pulse punching in his skull. He reaches the door of his room just as the old orderly rises into view, bearing a wide breakfast tray that holds enough food for a honeymooning couple.

* * *

A few hours later Kaya himself escorts him to the Jaguar gate. Kaya doesn't seem to mind the slow pace. Elias wears the new, undersized shirt and slacks provided for him at the club and is freshly shaved, his head too, having mimed instructions to Kaya's expressionless orderly to buzz his hair almost to the bone.

After the order and comfort of the officers' club, the dead zone is a fresh shock. They follow a route new to Elias, having set out from the club, and one of the first ruins they pass is a structure of three storeys, intact but for a facade that has partly collapsed, exposing a honeycomb interior of rooms where a snowfall of cement dust covers everything. When Elias, with a pang of precognition, asks if Kaya knows what the place used to be called, he replies, "I believe this was Hotel Aphrodite."

At the gate, Kaya shakes his hand with a surprisingly lax grip that still conveys a real warmth. He calls him *arkadash* and says he is assured they must meet again soon, *inshallah*. Stratis waits on the far side of the gate, smoking grimly. He will not acknowledge Kaya. He will not even acknowledge Elias, who nods to him as he squeezes between the grilles.

"Well, Stratis, how are you?"

"*Mia hara*," the man mutters, *one joy*, shorthand for the full greeting, "One joy and two traumas." Elias must be one of the implied traumas. "I should strike you now, here," Stratis says, but seeming to glimpse something in Elias's eyes, he doesn't. Instead he leads him back toward the village at a painful pace. Now and then, hardly breaking stride, he hacks down scrub with his machete. "*Koune sou, vre!* Are you coming or not?"

"Where else would I go?" Elias calls, telling the truth. Poor Dr. Boudreau has borne witness on his behalf and left him free to accept his sentence, free to remain captive for now in a place that, as he toils toward it, seems a kind of sanctuary.

"Where's the dog?"

"What? Speak clearly!"

"Where's Argos?"

"With Roland!"

"Where's Roland? I was expecting—"

"Sick! The last few days have been hard for him. Several of us left our beds cold to search for you, but for him it was hardest. His health is not good." Stratis says it with the comfortable disdain of a man who never gets ill. Elias is weighing Greek words for a reply—*If you're suggesting that what I did has made him ill*—but Stratis adds, "Above all, he is sad at the thought of Kaiti and the children leaving. We are all sad. Your latest reckless departure, and other recent events relating to you, have made her see the village as less secure. And she is right! Such at least is my thinking."

"You mean the others don't agree?"

"The others are more generous. But I am the guardian here, the one soldier—I can't risk that laziness."

"You don't even like those children."

"And they look at me as a goat looks at a knife! But I dislike them less now—in their father's absence they seem ever more Greek."

"Was it you who scared him off?"

"A coward needs no encouragement."

Elias hears himself say, "Will she go back to him?"

"God forbid! But the question is not mine to answer. Nor would I ever ask it."

Stratis leaves him at the gate of the courtyard inn. As Elias enters, Lale and Aslan cheer and charge toward him. Kaiti stands outside Roland's door, a short, dark cardigan over her black dress. "Trif, Trif!" the twins cry. He lowers himself to one knee, sets down his crutches and throws out his arms. They barrel into his embrace. He holds off the tears that would betray how this welcome affects him. "*Theio* Roland says you got lost, swimming," Lale says, "but *dolphins* saved you!"

Kaiti stands rigid, her arms crossed under her breasts.

"Were you visiting Roland?" he asks her, in Greek. "I hear he's a bit ill."

"Yes!" the twins answer him.

"I think I'll go see him too. We could play football later, *endaksi*?"

"They may be busy later," Kaiti says, "helping Stavroula and me."

He's still down on one knee like a suitor—a man with little hope, by the looks of it. "Busy all day long?"

"This is not like elsewhere, where small children have all the time they want. We have to work harder here."

"I thought it was the other way around. It's been years since I've seen children play as much as these two."

"You romanticize."

"I've lived out there more recently than you."

She switches to English: "I cannot school them alone here. They have no young friends. No future! I will like them to have . . . *bread* every day, like normal ones. Also, here are some dangers and I have to protect."

"You think it's safer out there? Are you joking?"

"Slower!" she says in Greek. "Your English . . ."

"Do they know you're planning to leave?" he asks clearly.

"Not quite," she says in Greek. "There are still matters to work out. But this is not your worry."

The twins' eyes, solemn, enormous, look back and forth. The village will feel far less like a refuge if it loses its youngest citizens, Kaiti and the twins. But what right has he to say "Don't go"? It's easy to see why she might feel she has to take them out into the world, even a world that in a few thousand days could arm and order them off to legally murder other teenagers for pay. But he doesn't want to believe that the reason for her going is his arrival—that he has upset a fragile equilibrium, tipping the village into terminal decline.

"How is Roland?" he asks in English.

"Not as well as you appear to be."

"I get over things fast," he says, and his sudden curtness surprises him. "I hope you weren't out that night too, looking for me?"

"Of course I was! With Strati. Stavroula, she took the children."

He totters to his feet, grimacing. "Okay. I'm sorry. That was the last time." He's about to say, *There's nothing to go back out there for*, then realizes that while it's true, it's beside the point. He says, "I have a reason to stay."

She's visibly struggling to pin down his meaning. She switches to Greek: "You mean Roland?"

"I'm not sure what I mean," he lies.

"*Elate!*" she orders the twins and stalks past him, lashing out with her eyes. His cheeks burn as if slapped. She has a gold Orthodox cross around her neck now, perhaps for Roland's sake. She puts out her hands for the twins. They glance back at Elias as she leads them off. She stops at the gate and looks back herself, then says in English: "I am tired of making stories for the children, when men go away."

"I understand."

"But I am happy you live." Her black brows twitch inward and she looks down into a basil patch, as if wondering whether *happy* might be too strong a word.

Roland's room is dim, the shutters sealed to keep out drafts, an olive-oil lamp and a candle glowing on the old brass tea table beside the bed. A china pot of tea and a cup, an old Aspirin bottle, a saucer full of pills. In an oversized turtleneck fisherman's sweater, his hair sheaved and rumpled, he's sitting up in bed with a mess of papers in his lap, holding what seems to be a quill. Except for the old transistor radio on the window ledge, this could be a nineteenth-century sickroom.

Argos, at the foot of the bed, quits licking his own groin, leaps up and trots over to Elias, tail flapping.

"Are you all right?" Elias asks. "Is that really a quill?"

"Not from one of Stavroula's hens. It's from the calligraphy shop, by the plaza. It works better than the ballpoint pens one finds everywhere. The ink for this needs only a drop of turpentine to be fresh again. If only it were the same with me!"

"Wait—what are you writing?"

"Not my last will, don't worry. This influenza, or what have you, it has made me resume my manuscript. A history of the village. It's fortunate . . ." A sharp, baying cough shakes his body. He draws in a wheezing breath. "Pardon me . . . I'm writing in English, so maybe you could look over the work, in due course? I read so much English, but to *write* . . . And I'm a poor speller in any tongue."

As Elias approaches, he sees that the lamp and candle have been lending a deceptive glow to a face that's morbidly pale. Amid three-day stubble, the creases from Roland's nostrils to his mouth are sharply carved.

"You see that our positions are neatly reversed," Roland says.

"But you seemed fine when you left me!"

"I was starting to feel less so. I may have caught something from Ali when he shaved me—who knows? For years in our isolation we have had little sickness. Perhaps my immunity grows weaker. I am relieved that you caught nothing, in your frail state."

Elias sags onto the chair where Kaiti must have sat just now. "I never do," he says guiltily. "But you, you were up all night searching."

"Forget this. It was nothing. And had our positions been reversed, perhaps you would have searched for me also?"

After a moment Elias nods.

"Except, of course, I have no reason to want to flee," Roland says.

"Neither do I anymore."

Elias quietly describes how and what he learned about Dr. Boudreau. Roland listens with his head down, brow bulging. Then he says, "But—forgive me asking, Trif—has this not even a little to do with Kaiti? I did hear the two of you speaking out there . . ."

"It has nothing to do with her—she's not even staying!" Silence. "Anyway . . . Do you feel up to coming outside into the sun? These days are short."

"*Ja*, winter solstice. Back home it was my favourite time. But maybe I sleep again now."

"You need a doctor, Roland. Kaya will send his own doctor in here, I'm sure he will, he likes you a lot."

"The colonel likes everyone! I fear it may yet prove his undoing. But I am the medicine man here"—he pauses, grins miserably—"the *medical* man, and I say, considering risks of an outsider, no doctor is needed but me."

"Since when are you a doctor?"

"I had to train myself, upon arrival. A Turkish Cypriot who fled here shortly before I . . . he grew ill. A homosexual, from the north, where the punishment is death! He rather resembled Kafka, the great Jewish Czech author of absurdist stories and—"

"I know who Kafka is!"

"*Ja*, well . . . this person had arrived in a battered state, and he grew worse. I studied books from the library and gathered what supplies I found in the dispensaries—even some morphine that looters had missed in '74. I couldn't save him from the pneumonia—I believe that was what took him in the end—but I helped a little."

"Why didn't he go south, across the border?"

"A Turkish Cypriot homosexual dying of the AIDS would not be welcome with open arms, he felt, except perhaps for propaganda reasons. I doubt he was wrong." Roland brings the teacup to his lips for a sharp, indignant sip. "I've not brought myself to tell you of this Davut Osman, but now I'm writing of him. And the grave—when we're both well enough to walk there, I'll show you. The time has come. No more secrets. It's in the part of the old cemetery we use, though away from our other graves, as Stratis insisted. How furious he was when we voted to let Osman stay!" Another sip and then Roland describes these graves—for a stillborn daughter of the Tombazos; for a wounded comrade of Stratis's who died soon after they hid here in '74; for a woman who became Stratis's de facto wife and died many years ago; and for their child, who died with her.

For some seconds Elias is silent, pondering. Then he says forcefully, "Do you have any antibiotics? No—they'd be way out of date. But maybe—"

"They lose less potency than you'd think," Roland says. "After this long, maybe half, so I double the dose. Of course, the condition may be viral. Please ask Kaiti not to bring the twins again, for their sake, and tell her I am still holding my own. I wouldn't want her to delay on my account."

Elias says nothing, just nods.

"We must not be selfish, however our hearts," Roland adds, as if trying to convince himself. "At least I know that *you're* no longer planning to leave us, or—or bury yourself at sea."

"Just make sure Stratis knows that, okay? Even in love he makes me nervous."

Easter, not Christmas, is the main holy day for the Greeks. Elias gathers that this year's Christmas, celebrated in the modern way on December 25, is even quieter than normal because of Roland's worsening illness.

Elias has once more graduated from crutches to cane but is still not mobile enough to haul buckets of water from the well or to join Stratis and Argos out on the snare lines, collecting rabbits. Meanwhile Kaiti and Stavroula are busy with a new planting of tomatoes. So Elias by default has become Roland's caregiver, the sort of beefy male nurse you might find in a palliative care unit or on a psych ward. He sits with Roland during the day—reading to him when he's not asleep—and at night comes in to check on him every few hours. The man tolerates this indulgence but has drawn the line at Elias's attempt, with Kaiti's help, to drag his own mattress in and sleep in the corner. He forbids it with a feeble stridency that Elias senses he must respect or risk depriving the man of all rights and power, weakening him further. He does ask that Elias, each morning, pick him a bowl of the lemony, chewy purslane that grows weedlike between the paving stones just outside the gate: "Very healthful, Trif. Try some. It was Mahatma Gandhi's favourite green."

The book he has asked Elias to borrow and read to him is one that he says he has read often before: a dog-eared, disintegrating paperback of Graham Greene's *The Quiet American*. He laughs to the point of violent coughing at the sardonic bits, of which there are many. Finally Elias says, "I hope you didn't ask me to read this as some kind of personal lesson? Because I am not this Pyle guy—this innocent. Nobody is. He's a cartoon. The other characters are way better."

"Oh, I quite agree with you," Roland says, even more tickled.

Christmas dinner is held at noon, both for the daylight and because Roland is asleep every night by seven and they all worry that evening festivities—as if the villagers feel festive now—might disturb him. Even Argos seems subdued, spending much of his time indoors at Roland's feet, like a marble hound on a Templar's tomb.

In the little kitchen, the drizzling day after Christmas, Elias sits squeezing some two hundred lemons, using a wooden hand-reamer and funnel, slowly filling three jugs with the pulpy juice. Most of it will be bottled, with raki and honey, to make a thick, syrupy liqueur. With the remainder Kaiti and Stavroula are preparing litres of a traditional potion for the ill, simmering the juice on the spirit stove and mixing in wine, honey, cinnamon, crushed garlic, pulverized dried hot pepper, and another herb he doesn't recognize by sight or smell.

While squeezing an extra twenty lemons at Stavroula's command, he asks Kaiti in English, "Was Paris invited to the Christmas meal?"

"Paris?"

"The hermit."

"Here," she replies in Greek, "please—take this to Roland before it cools."

"*Endaksi.*"

"You're walking better today, I see?"

"Not enough to stray far," he says, adding in English (Stavroula is right on top of them, like a bustling, sighing duenna), "Are you still planning to leave on New Year's Day?"

"Here's a cup for you, too," she says in Greek. "You have to stay strong if you're serving him, hand to hand. It tastes better than it smells."

"I love the way it smells."

"*Kane grigora!*" Stavroula urges, *hurry*, stirring the pot with one hand while the other flicks at her perspiring forehead—a wet crimp of grey hair has escaped her headscarf. She could never seem frail, not with her fleshy arms and heavy bosom, but today she looks her age, and weary, and it strikes Elias that the village is dying out before his eyes. Even the new couple, Stratis and Myrto, are too old to make children.

"*Theio* Roland is quite ill," Kaiti says in English. "So, no, we cannot to leave yet." She speaks firmly, yet there's an opening in her tone, it doesn't fend him off like before, maybe because they've been working side by side for hours—days, really—preparing sustenance for somebody they both care for. Her cheeks are flushed from the steamy heat, which has made her black hair even curlier.

He sees that his question has flustered her, the last thing she needs right now, and for that reason he's glad he asked it.

He looks around for a rag to wipe the lemon pulp off his hands before he takes Roland's drink. Kaiti has the rag—she's dabbing a gloss of sweat from her brow and upper lip. "Here," she says, gripping his wrist—her fingers go only halfway around—and she swabs his palm with the damp rag and firmly pulls his fingers clean of pulp. Each pull sends a shock plunging through his belly down to his balls; he recalls the garlic smell from her fingernails that first night when she tied his blindfold.

"There," she says quietly, "now go!"

When he enters the sickroom, Argos's tail starts thumping the floor. The tail looks shrivelled, the hair worried away. A lone olive-oil lamp glows by the bed. Roland sleeps on his back, one eye half open. There's a hitch, almost a hiccup, in his breathing. Elias leaves the drink on the brass tea table and collects the previous cup, which has already filled the room with the smells of lemon, garlic, and pepper.

He walks back to the kitchen in the early dark, the darkness of a courtyard in a village centuries before electric light, darkness undeniable, a power with absolute jurisdiction until dawn. He still isn't used to it. He speeds up, the pain in his foot forgotten, his extremities tingling. When he enters the warm, lamplit kitchen, Kaiti turns to him. Her expression . . . he might be reappearing after a backstage change of mask, costume, character, everything. Above the gold cross her throat is as red as her cheeks. She smiles, fully smiles. It's like a long-sustained minor chord resolving in the last bars of a song. He takes her hand and tugs her outside. Behind her, Stavroula, muttering and stirring the pot, sees nothing. In the dark between the half-open door and shuttered window he backs her into the wall with his kisses, and she lets him, and her strong little hands clamp over his ears to pull his face down harder into hers.

FINDING PARIS

Kaya's children have joined him at the club for the New Year holiday. Since he last saw them three months have passed, a small eternity in their terms, and changes are visible, especially in Yil, who has just turned fifteen. His sister, Hava, a month short of her seventeenth birthday, still adores Kaya, chirpily chatting with him at meals or while drinking an Italian soft drink on the bench after tennis—but then she'll fall silent, as if these exchanges have deeply debilitated her, and she'll seal herself in her room to text friends in Istanbul, or go up onto the roof to sunbathe and read her magazines. As for Yil, the occasional sulky reserve Kaya noted when he flew up to see the children in September has hardened into an impenetrable sullenness. Yil takes after Kaya physically, but now his face is contorted into an impostor's mask of suspicion and sneering contempt, and he slouches so bonelessly it seems he's trying to grow shorter, back into childhood. Kaya can't understand him. The boy doesn't seem aware in the slightest of what he can have out of life. As if life is a suitor he's rejecting out of fear of being jilted. At his age, or at least Hava's, Kaya had girlfriends and played football and went out with his teammates, and they would talk or bribe their way into clubs in Üsküdar to hear Yeni Türkü and dance with the girls and even, sometimes, the women—impossibly exotic women, he thought then, young American, British, and Australian tourists in pairs or trios who humoured them, bought them beer, and at the end of the night doled out chaste, mildly condescending kisses . . . Yil is always up in the guest room, either doing homework (his marks are reprehensibly high) or hunching in darkness, the curtains drawn, playing American video games, all military in nature. Fate, Kaya understands, finds such ironies irresistible. He has to admit he was happier when Trifannis was staying in the room. He keeps going up and inviting the boy to join him for a swim, tennis, even a hand of poker ("Too tired now, Baba"), then nicely asking him to turn down the volume. Without a word Yil complies, yet within minutes the chatter of automatic gunfire, the pounding of artillery, the screams of the dying are again echoing down through the atrium to the club's lobby and dining area.

At least it's a fitting audio for the news Kaya has been reading in the *Hürriyet*: fighting inside the Syrian border intensifying by the day, several battalions now engaged against the Kurds. Maybe Captain Polat has gotten his wish and is in the thick of it.

New Year's dinner includes the traditional pine-nut and currant rice, *iç pilav*, while the sweets course is a mixed platter of those honey-drenched delicacies, like baklava, that the Greeks, the Persians, the Arabs, and the Israelis all amusingly claim as their own. Ömer has outperformed himself again. Yet Yil hardly touches his food. Likewise the glass thimble in which a shot of celebratory raki shines. As if conscious of his father's post-meal contentment, Yil starts baiting him—the boy's next essay for Turkish History will argue that so-called neo-fascists who want to keep all foreigners out of Turkey have a valid point. Just look what happened to the Ottomans! And American and recent Euro experiments in multi-ethnic societies prove that people are better off with their own kind. Yil realizes that Baba's socialist newspaper will disagree . . .

Hava rolls her eyes and flees up to her room, leaving Kaya alone with this glum, slumping travesty of himself. Kaya flexes his mouth into a smile. "Who knows, Yil? Maybe you have a point! We Turks seem to have a hard enough time not murdering each other!"

The boy sags further, for a moment appearing to lack any lungs or ribcage at all. No fight to be had here, he goes back upstairs to his computer.

Next morning a surprising call from Colonel Nurettin. General Hüseyin, in Nicosia, means to clear all of the old year's business off his desk. He has asked Nurettin to send a platoon into Varosha to investigate the no-doubt delusional suggestions of Kaya's adjutant, Captain Polat. (Kaya immediately wonders why Hüseyin asked Nurettin, not him, to do this, but he says nothing.) "I realize this is absurd," Colonel Nurettin says, adding quickly, "well, not *absurd*, but . . . surprising." Nurettin always sounds as if he fears his calls are being monitored. "Anyway, I'll just send in a platoon to explore for a few hours and take some photographs. A kind of formality . . . but of course a thorough formality! Yes, we shall certainly be thorough. I suppose it might take half a day."

For a moment, Kaya is truly at a loss; then a solution presents itself. "Well, if the general insists," he says, "fine. There's just one problem."

"There is?" Nurettin asks fretfully.

"The troops, even if they take a map, will almost certainly get lost—badly lost, as the captain did himself, if you remember."

"Of course—he almost died!"

"Those maps are of a city that no longer exists. And the dead zone covers some two thousand hectares. No water, no food, areas where buildings are collapsing . . . Your men will need a guide—I mean a *leader*"—Kaya pauses dramatically—"and I am willing to serve in that role."

* * *

On a morning of warm sun and cool breezes, Kaya, cunningly disguised as a Turkish colonel in his beret, aviator shades, camouflage gear, and combat boots, meets Nurettin's men at an old checkpoint at the north end of the dead zone. The absent Nurettin has had his men gear up as if for battle: helmets, flak jackets, packs, new assault rifles that look like large toys made of black plastic. Kaya has left his pistol behind at the club. This decision—meant to demonstrate his faith that Varosha is perfectly safe—seems to have disappointed Yil, who is accompanying him, having astonished him by agreeing to do something outdoors, early, and away from his computer. Of course, it involves soldiers, real ones, and he's studying them now with entranced eyes, although he's far too shy to speak. He wears black jeans and a maroon Galatasaray training jacket.

The platoon lieutenant is of average build except for a disproportionately ample rump that gives him a laborious, waddling gait, as though he's humping a large pack far too low on his frame. He seems to find the boy's presence irregular but dares say nothing to Kaya, who cheerfully introduces Yil to him and the men, then hurries the party through a creaky, wheeled gate the U.N. used to use years ago while making cursory patrols.

Through a webwork of disintegrated streets he marches them, constantly turning corners and changing direction, as if trying to shake a pursuer. Whip-snakes and small lizards zip across their path. These are streets of long, once-lavish bungalows where German luxury cars are docked forever in their snug parking ports, behind cast-iron fences, now trellises for creepers. What a waste, Kaya reflects again—to seize all these treasures and then forbid anyone else to enjoy them, like a brat smashing a precious toy he has stolen rather than using or sharing it. Well, at least he and the villagers have made something of these ruins.

Yil catches up to him momentarily and says in an awestruck tone, "This would be a perfect setting for a video game!"

Within half an hour the lieutenant, puffing and perspiring, gives up checking his compass and the old street map on which Kaya has helpfully marked their route in red ink. This mapped route is entirely fanciful, a mere doodle that corresponds in no way whatsoever to the route they're following, though it's just as labyrinthine. Yil and the men are now totally lost, or would be without Kaya. Yesterday Ali took a letter from him to the Jaguar gate, to advise the villagers about the patrol. *Please clear the snare lines, put brush and vines in front of the door of the church, keep yourselves and that dog indoors and the chickens quiet. Nothing to worry about.*

Kaya's heels snap along at a killing pace. He aims to give an impeccably military impression while wearing out the platoon as fast as possible. Yil must sense the showmanship in his father's speed and manner; the boy scowls whenever Kaya glances back to see if they're keeping up. He's leading them just to the west of the village, past a small, crumbled church, then angling south and bringing them out into the wide square the villagers call the *plateia*. To Kaya, it's apparent that the paving stones on the north side are markedly clearer of debris, but the buildings around the square are so utterly overgrown—if beautifully so—that the place could not look any more deserted.

As the lieutenant snaps a panorama of photos, Kaya says, "You see how absurd it is, the notion of outcasts surviving in here?" The lieutenant's trousers, hitched way up, are stretched taut across that freakishly exaggerated bum.

Kaya takes them farther south, skirting the west wall of the cemetery and thereby avoiding the few markers that have appeared in the northeast corner in the years since the invasion. Yil and the platoon are wilting as he leads them on past the old technical school on the outskirts and south into the open country that Varosha would have swallowed up, given time.

They break for a smoke and to drink from their canteens. Passing his binoculars to the winded lieutenant he says, "That hill over there? We could climb it if you like. The going is steep in places, but the crest is high enough to give a view of the entire zone. Who knows? We might spot a thriving community we haven't been able to find on foot."

"If you insist, sir, though I don't think that will be necessary."

"Let's continue up the east side, then. We can stop in at the officers' club on the way back, for lunch and a cold drink."

"Yes, sir. Thank you, sir."

They round a low crag on which a large olive tree stands, then pass through a meadow of high grasses and waving winter flowers, anemones and Cyprus crocuses. Under another crag on the far side is a collapsed structure, an old shed or hut. A young mespila tree grows out of the rubble, its boughs picked clean of fruit (by the bats and the starlings, he will say if they ask). A scent of rosemary and sage, baked by the sun, fills the meadow and puts Kaya in mind of freshly grilled lamb. This beguiling little spot could not be more than a twenty-minute walk from the club, yet he has never passed through it. Odd. He feels uneasy, like an officer who might be leading his men into a trap. "Let's go this way," he says, pointing north around the ruins, but Yil calls, "Baba, what's this?"

He's parting the high grasses that were screening a three-barred cross, five or six steps from the hut's doorway, or what remains of it. Several cats dart out of the swale grass and run between the men's boots into deeper grass. The lieutenant takes more pictures. The men approach. The cross is of pinewood weathered grey. A few scales of white paint cling to the surface. The heads of the nails securing the longer, middle crosspiece are badly rusted. Between the nails, some characters are etched, very small, as if out of modesty.

This is a memorial that barely whispers.

"I can't read Greek letters," Yil says, leaning down. "They're faded, too."

"Not recent, then," Kaya says.

"I see dates."

Kaya pushes in next to his son, this troublesome doppelgänger. Yil says, "1979, with a small cross next to it!"

"Can you read the birth date?"

"Can't you see?" the boy asks, incredulous. "It's just a question mark."

"So someone *was* in here," the lieutenant says.

"But years ago," Kaya says. "Someone must have stayed and hidden here after the, ah"—he almost says *invasion*—"liberation. Which explains some of the rumours we've heard over the years." *Explains and lays to rest, forever.*

"What was his name, Baba?" Yil's voice packs into this rushed phrase all the earnest curiosity he seems to have lost over the past two years. Kaya leans closer (he has needed glasses for some time now but fears they'll make him look his age) and sounds out the Greek letters. He is mystified. Roland has never said a thing about this. Maybe Roland doesn't know.

"The dead man's name was Paris."

RED RIVER VALLEY

"And how are you doing, *Kyrie* Trifanni?"

"*Mia hara,*" he says.

"Two traumas as well?"

"None till the morning."

"You've picked a good time, then—the nights couldn't be longer."

"I'd better go check on him."

"Let me go this time, Trif."

"No, no, he doesn't want you to get sick."

"Wait an hour, then—it must be the coldest night of the winter!"

"You call this winter?"

Lying on her side, facing away, she's jutting her naked backside into his groin, sighing, tugging the layered blankets farther over them. "Your skin," she says in that husky Greek voice, like a permanent sore throat. "You're hot as a bread oven."

"I thought that was you."

"Shhh—too loud."

"I forget they're there," he says, meaning the twins.

"A man can forget."

A few minutes later she asks, "Do you miss the winter, Trif?"

"I'd take you way out onto Lake Nominingue, skating." *You and the twins,* he almost says, but senses before him another border he shouldn't cross.

"You'll be able to go back by the end of the year," she says. "This new year. I'm sure. Roland thinks that will be enough time. For Kaya and for us."

"You say 'us,' but you won't be part of the village then."

No reply. Too dark in her little house to see. If the twins come up the hallway to the door, they'll have no idea that he is here, third night in a row.

"Anyway," he says, "I don't have to leave anymore."

"Because someone 'broke' your story for you? Yet you won't tell me!"

"If you knew the truth, you'd understand me better but like me less."

"Who in the world doesn't feel that way?"

"Maybe hate me. Once you're out there, you can find out the story if you want."

"Stubborn as a ram," she says. "I'll go check on Roland now."

"If you do, he might figure out we're together here. You don't mind?"

"It might please him." She reaches back to stroke his cheek and stubbled scalp. "Might help him feel better."

He grapples her tighter with his left arm and docks his face in the armpit she has just exposed, whispering, "No, *I'll* go. Right now. But you—stop pretending you don't understand my Greek—what I said about the village."

"They all mean to die here, Trif. I don't. Since Tansu left us, it hasn't felt the same."

"Of course," he says reasonably, while his heart roars objections. He breathes her in. Sweat like cracked peppercorns and fennel. Her hair, washed just twice a week or so, smells only of her. Her skin sweet and hot. To think he was alone and freezing in the open sea not so many nights back.

"I need to shave them again," she says. "These useless razors . . ."

"Shhh. I'd better go."

She pushes harder into his lap, reaching between her legs for him. "A few more minutes."

"Kaiti, you're making me miserable."

"Am I?" she asks in a gratified tone.

Leaving the house later he instinctively feels the walls for a light switch and finds one, which of course hasn't worked in decades. Outside, no moon. The stars in swarms cast down their icy lustre, dimly frosting the roofline of the city. Limping slightly in the cold he approaches the inn. The nightingale, even in January, makes a beacon of birdsong.

He may not have told her his story, but she has now told him hers. When border regulations were first relaxed, she became a guide in Nicosia, meeting Turkish Cypriots at the Green Line crossing to lead them on a walking tour through the Greek half of the city she loved. Hardliners on both sides hated this initiative, but it proved popular. Tansu was part of a group of engineering students whom she guided one day and who—except for Tansu—all flirted with her in a clumsy, endearingly formal manner. A week later he reappeared and joined one of the tours on his own. During the rest break at a café in Laiki Geitonia, he asked her, in rigid, rehearsed Greek, if she might wish to meet for coffee.

Border controls were being further eased, and soon it was possible for them to cross to each other's side and meet often, and then daily. Predictably, both families disapproved. Still, the slight thaw in relations between the north and the south gave the new lovers some hope. Surely they would not be forced to play Romeo and Juliet to the last scene? What followed was a terrible surprise. Kaiti had believed her friends to be as progressive as the ideals they championed, yet only one of them accepted Tansu. And when Kaiti, now pregnant, confided her plans to marry Tansu, this friend too urged her to terminate both the pregnancy and the engagement. Then her parents warned her that if she went ahead, they would have nothing more to do with her.

But if it was bad for her, for Tansu things were even worse. His uncle, having close connections in the government and the police force, was hostile to any form of détente with the Greeks, whether political or personal. One night after crossing back into north Nicosia, Tansu was attacked and beaten up by plainclothes cops. He realized that he would have to give up either Kaiti or his community. But to live together in the south seemed no better a choice, and besides, Kaiti, proud and impetuous (not her words: Elias's insertion), now wished to have nothing more to do with her family. The couple thought of retreating to Ephira or one of the other mixed towns in the buffer zone, but having no relations there they would not be allowed. They were out of money and pondering the risk, for Tansu, of going somewhere else in the E.U. when she recalled hearing a rumour from a guide who had led tours along the Varosha fenceline (the tours had ceased for lack of business: tourists found the spectacle too gloomy). By now desperate, receiving daily threats, the couple fled to Varosha and reached the village, where they were welcomed unconditionally—or so it seemed to Kaiti, who after their ordeal found the enclave's peace, order, and seclusion paradisal. The twins were born secretly in the officers' club five months later.

Less than two years after that, Tansu departed, claiming he had never felt fully welcome or at home in what was really a traditional Greek Cypriot village. He missed speaking Turkish—Kaiti's tour-guide Turkish didn't count, it seemed. He struggled mightily with Greek. Stratis Kourakis terrified him. He missed his hateful family. ("His family," Kaiti says unforgivingly, "was us.") Tansu, she'd come to realize, was still a boy in all the important ways. She had no idea what lies he must have told after his return. She had no idea what her own community thought of her disappearance. "They're not the reason I'll be taking the twins back into the world. We may not even see them, or Tansu either. They've all surrendered that right." She says these things with a confident severity, as if her heart is not bruised.

Elias unlatches the creaky gate and swings it inward carefully, inch by inch. Stratis's door opens a crack and he looks out, face deformed by the underglow of a flashlight. He grunts a phrase in Cretan dialect—if Elias is not mistaken it's something like "May you vomit crabs"—and withdraws.

Argos is snoring and twitching on Roland's floor, while Roland—sitting up in bed, surprisingly—squints at a manuscript page by lamplight. His beard is growing in greyer. The room has a clean, antiseptic smell, though not from medicine: on Christmas Eve along the snare line, Stratis, instructed by Myrto, cut down a pine sapling as a Tannenbaum for Roland, then nailed together a cruciform base and stood it in the corner.

"You're feeling a bit better?"

"Odd to be awake in the night, but then I've been sleeping so much . . . You were outside the courtyard to observe the winter stars? I heard the gate."

No secrets in a village.

"You're really thin, Roland."

"So will you be, if you will not permit yourself to sleep through a night!" Illness is making him ever more prone to philosophical amusement at human folly and foolery, so at first his remark sounds like a reference to Elias and Kaiti. Has Stratis already figured things out and told him? Or is Roland simply referring to Elias's constant checking on him? With a wry smile the man nods at the silent radio. "Interesting news today. Due to the latest conflict with the Kurds, the Turkish government is determined to maintain its ban on the letters *w*, *q*, and *x*."

"They've outlawed *letters*?"

"Used only in Kurdish." Roland's chuckling hoarsens into coughs that riffle the page he holds close to cover his mouth.

"We need to bring in a doctor now," Elias says.

"Don't trouble yourself, Trif—it's of no consequence."

"I hate it when people say shit like that!"

"But, you know we can trust no stranger to keep the village a secret—Kaya's doctor, he's part of the army."

"Secret? This place is almost finished. You're ill, Kaiti's planning to leave with the twins, the Tombazos are old, and Paris—he might as well not exist. I can't see another village destroyed. We have to risk it."

"I refuse to see Kaya's doctor, Trif."

"Please."

"Let's just consider how I am after a few days, *ja*?"

Elias cups a hand over the high bluff of Roland's forehead.

"Really, Trif, you shouldn't touch me, even if you're strong. You might take it back to somebody else." His altered face is a disguise with eyeholes through which his own ironic eyes peer out, now seeming to scan for a reaction. If the man would just ask about him and Kaiti, Elias would tell the truth, but he hesitates to simply announce it.

Oddly, Roland seems less feverish than yesterday. Maybe because it's midnight? Or is this a bad sign, his body starting to cool toward shutdown?

"Can I get you more water? Help you out to the washroom?"

"No, *danke*, let me sleep. You, please . . . just return to your warm bed."

As Elias goes back to Kaiti, he reflects that he really might owe this marvellous new thing to Roland's illness. And why does it always work this way? *Mia hara, mia hara*. As if something must always sicken, or die, before a new thing comes to life.

The dawns are late and the mornings dark, and one morning Elias fails to rise and leave early enough. He startles at the sound of Lale's little sparrow voice as she wakes in the next room and sings to herself in Greek, that children's song about the noisy rooster. *Ko-ko-raiki!* His half-Greek mother used to sing it to him and he remembers the words clearly, though his mother's young face and voice are all but lost.

Aslan's bare feet come slapping up the hallway. "Kaiti," Elias says, kissing the side of her neck. "Ekaterini!"

"*Ti einai?*"

"*Ta pedhia!*"

Aslan pushes open the door, runs the few steps to the bed and vaults in. Elias tries to shift away from Kaiti but they're furled together on the far edge, nowhere to go. At night, overheating, he keeps easing away from her, but her small body pursues him, little by little, until she has forced him to the precipice. There is no space between them now, yet somehow Aslan wedges in. Soft flannel pyjamas, faint tang of urine. He kisses Elias on the cheek, then greets him cordially and casually, seemingly unsurprised to find him here. Then he says something longer, still in Turkish. Unlike his sister, he doesn't seem to grasp that Trif understands only simple Turkish—hello, thank you, and the word *baba*, which Aslan has just used.

"What did he say?" he asks Kaiti in English.

When she answers, her voice sounds as if she chain-smoked two packs of cigarettes last night. "I won't tell."

"I'm sorry, Kaiti. I slept too long."

"I feared that this will happen."

"Them finding me here?" he asks, as if she could mean anything else.

Lale, still singing, is running in through the door.

"No," she says in that same voice. "I speak of love."

Every lover in a Greek ballad goes forth with a sprig of fresh basil tucked behind his ear. A few days later, so does Elias. Sex and the euphoria of falling in love seem to have accelerated the healing process. He still wears an old compression wrap, but he can walk with no cane and only a slight hitch in his step.

Roland's condition, meanwhile, seems to have stabilized.

The lighter work of Sunday morning is done long before the sun noons. Today for the first time Elias has helped Stratis haul buckets of icy water from the well, three trips. Stratis quietly sings to himself and ignores Elias while they work. When they finish, the man squints cannily at him and says—either because Elias is healed or because he has become Kaiti's lover, as Stratis, the village security chief, must know by now—"So, he thinks he has God by the balls."

When he and Kaiti stop by the Tombazos' to drop off the twins, Stavroula envelops him in a bosomy hug, kissing him noisily on either cheek. "May your name-saint bless you!" It seems the whole village knows, and is delighted. Kaiti seems both amused and somewhat hurt—stymied—by this response and the pressure to stay that it implies. Elias knows better than to raise the matter. They walk south across the plaza, like honeymooners strolling across the living square of a European city. It's deserted, of course, yet she won't let him take her hand until they reach the far side. She wears jeans and a collarless black leather jacket that fits snugly, fetchingly, over her breasts. The jacket is both forty years old and brand new. "The one thing I'll miss is the shopping here," she says. "Everything free, and so much of it back in style."

Out of the evergreen sheathing on every wall, unseen songbirds sing in mass choirs, the living voice of the foliage. Unlike the towers along the beach, with their rotted facades and exposed viscera, the buildings south of the plaza are small and so overgrown that they hardly seem part of a decaying city at all, rather one that nature has already reclaimed. For millions of creatures thriving here, this is no dead zone. A hare appears and he notices, this time with joy, that while it resembles a large rabbit, it flees like a fawn, white-tailed, bounding off as if exempt from gravity.

They emerge into Varosha's arid hinterlands, which he hasn't seen since his first escape attempt last year. She's leading him along Stratis's snare line toward her favourite spot, a pretty valley, she says, not easy to find. He knows enough not to ask about her history of visits there; she must have gone in the past with Tansu.

They turn east and arrive not long after. Framed by two crags, on each of which an olive tree stands sentry, a meadow of high grasses and flowers. The ruins of a hut lie under the low crag on the east side. They find a place in the grasses among yellow anemones and he puts down a cotton blanket he brought in a pack, then brings out a wineskin and a canvas bag containing olives, strong cheese, fresh potato pancakes from Stavroula, green pistachios, a monstrous tomato, and a small pomegranate. They're ravenous, as usual, but first they strip down, Elias in seconds and Kaiti haltingly, methodically, half turned away, as if reconsidering—a shyness he is already used to but would never have foreseen. Naturally he watches, kneeling. Is she worried about the elusive Paris? Her feet and calves and forearms and face are honey-brown but the rest of her is pale, almost sallow in the noon sun. Beyond Varosha, in the world of the living she so misses, she'd be foolishly urged to lose a pound or two. She has that to look forward to as well, if and when she returns.

She lies back on the blanket in their bower of wildflowers and grasses, a few bees droning nearby. The sun shines full on her body, her chest rising and falling with her breath. The centre of the world. He's kneeling between her thighs. He can't seem to move. Her green eyes are slit against the noon light but her gaze is steady, frank, fatalistic, calmly offering itself while also claiming him. His face must be shadowed by the sun above and behind him, stalled for a moment at its peak. And he can't move. He doesn't dare. Time has snagged on something; but as soon as he budges, speaks, acts in any way—even breathes—it will start up again and sweep them on toward who knows what . . . most likely partings, endings. But it's desire that drives time and he can't stop what's happening to his body, she too moving now, pulling him down to her.

"Be careful," she tells him afterward, "please."

"I know." The condoms are historical but none has broken yet. He has been pulling out as well, though not today. She is on top now. Somehow when horizontal she stretches almost to his length, mouth to mouth, toe to toe.

"You love me," she says in Greek.

"You love me."

"Very much."

For some time they doze to the white noise of the bees' humming, then carefully he rolls her so he is back on top, licks sweat from the sea-salt creases under her breasts, and sucks her dark nipples until her legs open wide.

Later he takes a swig from the wineskin, locks his lips onto hers and passes the fluid through, a lover's Eucharist. He says, "Then again, you had no choice but me."

"There's the choice not to love. I don't need a man, except this way, now and then."

"This is what you call now and then?"

She misses the quip, forming her thoughts; or maybe the problem is his Greek. She says, "What I felt at first, I don't know—not love—but there was the right kind of hate."

Now it seems he has missed something. "*Ti?*"

"I hated to see you not eat, at that first meal! You seemed . . . strangled by something. You still won't say what happened in the war?"

He gives her more wine. "The exact opposite of this."

"It's true Roland is eating again?"

"Well," Elias stalls. "A little, I guess."

"If he gets better, we *will* go."

At first the "we" seems to include him; then the phrase settles into sense.

"Maybe I'll go with you."

"You can't. Not yet."

"Because I'd 'destroy Kaya and the village' if I reappeared? Then I won't reappear! I'll make up a new name. Leave Elias Trifannis at the bottom of the sea."

"You think you can live anywhere now in the eurozone without papers and money?"

"And what do you think *your* leaving will do to the village?"

"It existed before me, it will survive after."

"Without children?"

"Would you really place responsibility for its survival on two small children?"

"Kaiti, look, I don't even want to go—not yet. This place—it's restarted me." When he sleeps now he's asleep and when he wakes, every time it's like arriving happy, but he doesn't know where, and then it hits him. He sees her and it hits him. Out there, he thinks, everywhere is like a checkpoint in a war zone—you never rest, you just rearm and refuel. No such thing as being home. No simple belonging. He says, "You've been here too long to see what you've got here."

Out of the grasses into their bower prowls a scraggy orange cat. It teethes a morsel of cheese and steps daintily backward into the grass, its yellow eyes on Elias.

"Come here after I'm gone and think of me, Trif. Then, in a year, maybe sooner, maybe we'll find each other again."

"It doesn't work that way. You'll have moved on. Or you'll be with him again."

"With the father of my children? You make it sound like a tragedy!"

"You're right. I'm sorry." And he lies, "I give up."

Three more swigs of warm wine, the last of which he feeds to her, still beneath him, wrapped around him.

His nape and scalp prickle ice-cold. He pulls out of her, rises into a crouch, scans across the meadow. From behind the olive tree on the crag above the ruins, a face. *Paris*, he thinks at the same instant his eyes make out a caricature of Colonel Kaya—smaller, paler, a black scarf worn pirate-style on the head.

"*Ti einai*, Trif?"

"*Tipota!*" he says. *Nothing.*

He grabs his boxer shorts and walks his legs into them as he wades into the grass. The figure leaps from behind the tree and assumes a shooter's crouch, extending his arms, his hands gripping and aiming a pistol. Elias freezes. The pistol bucks twice as if firing, but there's no sound, and now the figure—a boy in adult-sized battle fatigues—scrambles away down the far side of the crag, out of sight.

Elias's heart is punching up against his palate. Kaya mentioned that his children would be visiting in the new year and now an after-image of the face above the pistol aligns itself with features he recalls from a portrait on the dresser in Kaya's room. The gun must be a toy. Stupid, stupid kid—this is a deadly game to play anywhere near Stratis's turf. He glances back, sees Kaiti's face peek up out of their bower. He guesses she saw nothing. He waves—"*Dhen peirazi!*"—then walks on toward the low crag, breathing himself calmer. He clambers up the side and looks east. The boy, apparently spooked, is fleeing straight back in the direction of the officers' club.

Below the crag Elias happens on a cross in the tall grass. For some minutes, until Kaiti calls him back, he examines it and the pathetic remains of what must have been Paris's abode.

As they eat, he says nothing to her about the boy or the cross. She leads him a few minutes farther south to a place where a seasonal stream trickles through a grotto enclosed by cedars, dwarf oaks, and rhododendron. A dozen turquoise butterflies—"flying flowers" in Greek—quiver on the rocks above a sinkpool: another Eden, cooler and damper, though for him paradise is now in penumbra, his nerves like wires ripped loose from a fixture, his eyes scanning. Still, there's her cry of elated pain as she lowers herself into the pool, his own shock of pleasure as he squeezes in beside her. It's no worse than a Canadian creek in late May. Soon her kisses, strokes, and more drastic intimacies restore him and he lifts and seats her up on the bank, kneels in the current on the stream's silty bed and buries his face between her cool thighs.

On their way home, with the sun setting behind the hill where Stratis and Argos captured him, he tells her about Paris's cross. She insists she has never seen it.

He pulls his hand free from hers. "But you knew he was dead?"

"Of course I knew! As you say, he died long ago, before I was born."

"So you all lied to me about him."

She looks at him as if at a child. "In English you have just one word for 'lie,' so I hear? Just as for 'love'? Sometimes your people seem young in all the wrong ways."

"Sometimes people here seem old in all the wrong ways."

"We brought him back from the dead," she says, "to help keep you here. We thought it might help. We didn't want to lock you in a room—we liked you—*I* liked you!—and we didn't know what might happen if Stratis had to chase you again. I've been wanting to tell you, *agapi*, but I wanted to talk to Roland first."

When she takes his hand again, he doesn't resist. Some cuffs he will happily wear.

Sundays the library is open late and now he hurries there to borrow a volume on the Crusaders in Cyprus that Roland has read before but has asked Elias to read him again, and a book of Seferis's love poems that he will read to Kaiti. It's dusk, the skylight dim, an oil lamp glowing on the circulation desk. In the cavernous shadows back among the shelves, Stratis is sweeping the floor, pointedly ignoring the late arrival like a weary waiter at closing time.

"Ah, here you are," Myrto says in the tart, officious Greek she defaults to whenever standing behind her desk. "We are ready to close. Stavroula brought the twins in earlier. Did you and Ekaterini have a pleasant walk?" Before he can reply, she offers to tour him through the shelves, which she is still reorganizing but which, she says, may well be approaching their final conformation. She holds the lamp high as she talks him through the twilit stacks. When they pass Stratis, he mutters something about closing shop and follows up with further blasphemies from his prodigious repertoire.

Twice Myrto slows, interrupting herself, and with hardly a glance plucks Elias's request from a shelf. Back at the desk she frowningly records the particulars of his withdrawal in the usual detail, then hands him the books with a professional, close-lipped smile. He exits through the side door, looking back with an obscure sense of misgiving. The desk is abandoned. From somewhere in the vortex of shelves, a hushed, murmuring exchange. It's good to get back outside into the relative brightness of dusk.

Neoklis and Roland sit under the pistachio tree playing chess, Neoklis in his gigantic parka, Roland in a vintage hotel bathrobe and slippers, a towel scarved around his neck, like a patient at a sanatorium in the Alps. Takkos sits with them, drinking raki.

Dusk is deep in the garden. A lamp hangs from a bough above them.

"Trif!" Roland exclaims.

"You're feeling better?" Elias asks in Greek. "So suddenly—that's wonderful."

"Yes, well. I think so. But alas, no improvement at chess." He looks down at the board, clumping his lips, then sighs and tips over his king—a replacement piece crudely carved out of soap. Neoklis seizes it, stuffs it into the parka and beams over his shoulder at Elias, while Takkos shakes his worry beads and cries, "Bravo!"

"To be fully honest, Trif"—he's encrypting his words in English now—"I've been feeling a bit better, oh, for some days."

"You don't mean you've been faking it?"

"Well . . . not as such. I really am not feeling my best, and I *was* very ill. But perhaps I have been . . . postponing my recovery somewhat."

"What? Why?"

"Where is she?"

"Kaiti?"

"Who else? Please—more quietly."

"At home," Elias says, "with the twins."

"When I realized the effect my illness was making on you two, I willed myself to do opposite things: first, not actually to die, and second, not to get well again too fast. I mean, not before the two of you, ah, fully . . ."

"Fell in love?" Elias realizes some part of his being must have sensed what Roland was up to, even played along, while keeping his conscious mind in the dark. He exhales through a half-smile, folds his arms across his chest. "Speaking of cover-ups, I finally came across your hermit."

"What?"

"I found his grave. His cross."

"I feared you might, *ja*. I saw it myself once, not long after I arrived. This one here"—nodding toward the oblivious Takkos—"he told me that he and the sergeant chose to bury him not in the cemetery but beside his little house, because the hermit always held himself apart and should remain as he wished."

Now Elias tells Roland about the mock ambush in the valley, speaking softy as if Takkos and his son, resetting the board together, could understand. He adds that Kaiti saw nothing and it's probably best that way. Roland nods pensively, then says, "I will send a message to the colonel, first thing tomorrow."

"You really are well again, aren't you?"

"Not fully, but . . . you will not have to read me the Crusader history."

Half-smiling again Elias says, "How will I be able to trust you from now on, Roland?"

"You will always be able to trust me. You simply might not know whether I'm telling the truth. Please don't inform Kaiti about my little delay, all right? Let me tell her, in due course."

"I'll think about it."

"When she arrived in the village, you know, she said that hatred had orphaned her, that her family were all dead to her. In due course she said that *I* must be father to her, and that the old ones"—another nod toward Takkos, who is mock-scolding Neoklis, who mimes contrition like a ham in a small-town theatrical—"they must be her grandparents. I always so much wanted a daughter, as they so wanted grandchildren! Trif, do you think there is hope that she might now remain in the village, with you?"

"I wish I could lie."

"If you must, then do it."

"There's always hope."

Roland's face twitches and his eyes brim over. Takkos regards him with astonishment, then looks at Elias as if to ask, Whatever have you said to the poor man?

"I told him," Elias lies in Greek, "that I feel a son's joy at seeing his dear father brought back from the edge of the grave."

Takkos Tombazo's voice trembles as he makes toast after toast over the Sunday meal: chicken in olive oil and lemon, stuffed with figs and dried apricots and halloumi; roasted rosemary potatoes, squash, carrots, eggplant, and onions; cookies made with powdered almonds and honey. There are toasts to Roland's health, of course, and toasts simply to love, involving many unsubtle glances at Kaiti and Elias, who can feel the villagers' communal will forcing them still closer together. "And may we continue to cherish a hope that our Kaiti and the children will stay with us longer. A drink to Kaiti and the village—no, no, to *Trif* and Kaiti and the village!" Even Stratis drains his glass, eyeing Elias with what seems a muted manly approval. Elias says into Kaiti's ear, "But today in the library I think he told me, 'May you be consumed by hepatitis.'"

"You're winning him over. He would never have said anything so mild to Tansu." She kisses his grin, as if nothing is ending. More toasts. Elias himself makes a toast to Myrto and Stratis (a rift has been widening lately between their chairs, though they still smoke their cigarettes in unison). Everyone clinks glasses, drinks. Another night stolen from sadness. But toward the end, Kaiti's face—which always televises her feelings instantly, vividly—looks stricken and he is shot through with shame, neck burning under his collar. "Why are we putting her through this?" he whispers to himself.

The next morning he and Roland are sitting on low stools in the courtyard, soaping dishes in a vat of lukewarm water. "Well, Trif . . . what say the stars?"

"She means to leave soon, but she won't name a day."

"I do hope you're making things as difficult as possible."

"Damn it," he says, "how could I fucking cut myself on a knife this dull?"

Roland tells him to wait and shuffles away into his room, emerging not with a bandage but with a manuscript. "Here, please, do this instead—you never properly clean the utensils anyway. It's the opening part of my chronicle. It starts on this coastline in prehistory, but by page twelve we reach 1974. I have written almost up to the point of your arrival. Please say if I need to correct the English."

"You're not going to try publishing it somehow, are you? I mean, if anything would compromise the village—and Kaya—"

"I leave him out of it. As for the village, it may well cease to exist at some point, perhaps not so long ahead. I want something to remain afterward. And now that you are fully, voluntarily a citizen, you should be privy to all the facts."

On the unlined rag paper the handwriting is so clear and tidy, the ranks of words so ruler-straight, it resembles a computerized cursive font. Even the infrequent ink blots are neatly spherical. Elias tries and fails not to leave a few bloody thumbprints. At random he starts reading about the arrival of Sergeant Stratis Kourakis—years before Roland himself—along with the death of Stratis's wounded comrade, and how Stratis avenged him "by killing a certain Turkish Lieutenant, who upon several occasions had entered the Dead Zone at night, as a Looter, and had already come close to the Village, which at that time comprised the Tombazos, Stratis himself, Paris (though he was seldomly seen), and the woman, Rita, who later became a kind of wife to Kourakis and died, with their infant, probably of Pneumonia, ~~back when the Village was entirely isolated with no outsider to assist in crisis~~." Roland decribes how Stratis smashed this looter's skull one night when he strayed into the outskirts of the village. With Paris's help he dumped the body just beyond the fence. The mystery must have been investigated but never solved; apparently it "created among the rural Turkish Conscripts a superstitious dread and Myth, thus putting an end to all looting and incursions."

He looks up from the page. Roland is humming as he washes the dishes and now Elias knows the tune, "Red River Valley," and hears the words of the chorus in his mind: *Sit here awhile ere you leave us . . . do not hasten to bid us adieu.*

THE EFFIGY

When Kaya returns from the airport after seeing off his children, Ali hands him a sealed envelope on which ALBAY KAYA is inscribed in Roland's precise hand. Kaya is eager to change back into his civvies. He starts upstairs to his room, opening the envelope as he goes and skimming the note's charmingly formal Turkish phrases. Then he stops on the landing, grips the railing, rereads. An adolescent male, probably Kaya's son, has been wandering around in the dead zone, playing with a pistol that may or may not be a toy. Naturally Roland is concerned, on the young man's behalf as much as the village's.

Kaya has been looking forward to having the club to himself again. He knew he would miss the children's presence, especially Hava's, but their departure is always a bit of a relief as well. Today, he thought, he could enjoy the silence and the restful snoring of the winter surf on the beach instead of the frantic sound effects of Yil's war-gaming—though, come to think of it, Yil was not at his computer much during the last few days but rather outside. Kaya figured the patrol had somehow aroused his appetite for the outdoors and assumed he was spending time on the beach. He'd instructed the boy never to enter the dead zone alone.

He flicks on the light in his walk-in closet, automatically glancing at himself in the full-length mirror. A preoccupied stranger broods back. He opens a drawer in his dresser and lifts out a stack of crisply folded pants. His small semi-automatic—a Beretta imitation of Turkish make—lies slumbering in its holster. He takes it out. The safety is off. He secures it, then releases an ammunition clip from the handle. He hasn't inserted one in years. He weighs the clip in his hand. Empty. He digs under the military slacks on the other side of the drawer and finds two full clips instead of three.

Could Ali have taken the pistol out to clean and oil it, and then, somehow . . . ? No. Ridiculous. Yil really must have loaded the thing and wandered around in the dead zone, shooting at God knows what. Now Kaya dimly remembers: Yil likened Varosha to the setting of a video game.

Pocketing the clip he frowns sympathetically at his own reflection, a fellow father commiserating. Most parents of withdrawn, morose teenagers would at least consider the possibility of attempted self-violence, but to Kaya the idea of suicide is unthinkable.

He writes a note of thanks and reassurance to Roland and gives it to Ali to take to the Jaguar gate. The note also asks Roland to inform the villagers—especially that erratic-looking ex-soldier, Stratis—that Kaya will need to enter Varosha tomorrow morning. He will not come anywhere near the village. Next, Kaya emails his son, fibbing that he has just apprehended a tourist couple who were exploring the restricted zone for several days and claimed to have noticed a young man answering to Yil's description. They thought he was a guard or commando! (Kaya hopes the boy will find this bit flattering.) Anyway, the matter is now taken care of and Kaya is willing to overlook Yil's failure to report these interlopers—not to mention his foolish escapade with Kaya's pistol, which must never, ever happen again—so long as he says *absolutely nothing to anyone else*, as a matter of national security.

Next morning, after breakfast and a shave, Kaya heads for the only nearby spot, behind the tennis court, where Yil could have entered the dead zone without shredding himself on the new barbed wire. At a few places inside the zone, the boy's hulking trainers have passed through rain-dampened concrete dust and left prints, roughly marking his route. Kaya spots plenty of animate creatures—feral cats, furtive rats and lizards, crows, fat rabbits, pigeons, snakes, a beautiful little owl—but none of the small corpses he keeps expecting to see or, by this point, smell. Instead he finds seemingly fresh bullet holes in lifeless things: a wooden gate, a stop sign, a tuxedoed mannequin on display in a menswear shop, and, propped against the wall of a taverna, a plywood silhouette-figure in a chef's hat. There's a divot in the wall beside the moustachioed grin, an umlaut of holes in the white-aproned paunch. Kaya ponders this pathetic effigy. Roland's note said nothing about audible shots, but that's not surprising—this place is a long way from the village, and the pop-gun reports would get lost in the deadening cover of vines and creepers, block after block. As for Kaya hearing nothing himself, the last week's onshore wind will have carried the sounds inland, away from the club.

How much happier Kaya would feel stumbling on a typical boys' hideout stocked with American sex magazines.

On the way back, he notices he can see right through one of the floors of a slender hotel on John F. Kennedy—the facade is long since collapsed, and so too is a chunk of the back wall. Through that jagged wound, a grey winter sky, a few white gulls. Time seems ever more intent on gutting things, laying them bare, stripping the world to its essences. *You are a lazy father*, a voice whispers, and the words are his ex-wife's but the voice is Kaya's. *You think everything always works out!* Yet by the time he gets back to the club, famished, the thought of lunch and the sports pages he has not yet had time to enjoy have silenced both her and himself.

THE MOON IN WAITING

The lovers walk through an orchard of small trees festooned with ripening apricots, or are they nectarines—no, mespilas. Under their bare feet the earth is sun-freckled, mossy, soft as a putting green. She wears an aproned peasant dress while he (looking down now) is naked, one leg palsied and purple, his cock shrivelled as if in fear, yet there is no fear, then the fear arrives: somewhere in this enormous grove they've forgotten the twins. With a snicking sound, leaves, twigs and fruit start falling around them. There's a hiss and sizzle of bullets soaring overhead and yet the actual gunfire is silent. How frantically he's trying to warn her—*Get down! Get down!*—but she, oblivious to the danger, is fiercely chiding him, *Coward, hurry, come help me!* Then she vanishes.

"Trif? *Agapi mou?*"

"Kaiti."

"*Ti eheis?*"

"You're here," he says.

"You were making sounds. Your heart is pounding."

"It's all right." His surging pulse is slowing now, beat by beat.

She keeps her ear to his heart for a few seconds, then kisses his nipple. Too dark to see her do it.

"More hair than on your head," she says fondly.

They fuck tenderly and slowly in the cold room, and the ache of it, the hollowed-out sorrow of early morning sex in the shadow of coming departure, sinks deep into his being. When he kisses her afterward, he tastes tears. They fall asleep, twined inseparably.

Sometime later it seems that a soft and furtive snow starts drifting down over Varosha, *for the first time ever in history!* a documentary-style baritone declares, and the roof and ceiling of her house are gone and snow is deepening on their blankets and he can't move or speak as it buries them.

He sits up, alone in the bed. The house feels empty. She is gone, she has left with the twins, they've left already, somehow they have gone back to Nicosia, she has fled secretly to avoid a scene, a painful parting. He fumbles to strike a match, light the small lamp on the table. The second lamp is gone. He upends a Coke bottle vase of winter orchids that the twins gathered yesterday. Under the shuttered window a carpet bag still sits, open, half filled. For days she has been packing, half-unpacking, repacking. There's a cloth bag containing the forty-year-old Kodachrome films she has amassed—photos of the twins since their arrival, mostly taken by Roland with a pocket camera from a dead-zone shop, though the film, he has told her, is likely too old. There are also canvas rucksacks for the twins, half-packed. Could they have left without taking anything? He pulls on his boxers and, lamp in hand, walks down the hallway to Lale's door. He hears her breathing before he sees her small shape cuddled under her *paploma*.

Back in Kaiti's room he dresses fast, seized by a hunch. For the first time it's cold enough that his breaths emerge as vapour. He goes out and jogs awkwardly toward the plaza, quickly overheating in a too-small pea jacket that once belonged to Tansu.

The sun is still below the horizon but its light is turning small clouds vermilion high above the church dome. The main door is ajar. He slips through the gap without pushing it wider. Smell of myrrh, beeswax, cold marble dust, the droppings of generations of mice. At the far end of the nave, by the weak light of an olive-oil lamp, a figure kneels at the communion rail. He might be glimpsing Kaiti as a *yiayia*, a little widow hunched in her shawls after a lifetime with Trif, or with some other man. Beyond her, dimly, the saints on the high screen of the *ikonostasis*.

He walks up the aisle, not knowing whether to mute his steps out of respect and discretion, or to step firmly to alert her.

"Ekaterini."

Still facing the rail she rises, crossing herself, then turns toward him.

"*Ksero,*" something in him says quickly, "*katalavaino!* I know, I understand—you can't stay here. It's all right. You'll go back, the three of you, and I'll come find you later." (Somehow; maybe.) Her face is dark, backlit by the lamp. She steps forward as if to embrace him, then her hands fist and she pounds his chest and lets her head sag against him.

"You picked the right time to say so," she says faintly.

"What do you mean?"

"Nothing!"

At a loss, he asks, "Were you praying just now?"

"What else would I be doing here?"

"But I thought you didn't—"

"I want clarity, Elia, what does it matter if it comes from God or somewhere in my mind?"

"Kaiti—"

"I can't stay, you're right—I and the children, we can't stay—but I can't leave you either. Not for one damned hour! It's . . ."

"It's what?"

"Even when you're near, with Stratis now, working—it's still too long."

"It's the same for me, Kaiti. Just the same."

"I damn you, I can't help it, but also . . ." She uses a mysterious phrase, something about the moon, *to fengari,* and a long wait. Trying to make sense of it, he pulls her close, her curly head under his chin. The glow of the lamp, the rich smell of her scalp. She says, "You didn't understand me, did you?"

"No," he says, but then—just as she uses the English word, cracking it into two syllables that echo in the dome five storeys up—he gets it. Pregnant.

"My moon never waits. Always on time."

"Oh," he says moronically, stalling, trying to contain his joy, afraid of seeming to celebrate a kind of victory over her will. But joy it is. His heart seems apt to fly apart with the emotion, this reaction he could never have foreseen.

"For now," she says in English, "it's our sacred."

"Secret. Our secret."

Enough light seeps in through the orient window over the door to show her face: perplexed. He kisses the skin between her eyebrows and the knot there eases.

"Different words," he says. "It doesn't matter. We'll say they're the same."

"I also *bless* you," she says in Greek, "not just damn you!"

He strips off his jacket and capes it over her shoulders. "If there were a priest here, Kaiti—I mean, if you'd let me—"

"I would let you. I can't help it."

Sunrise is ambering the outside of the dome as they walk across the plaza and into the streets winding toward the village, the same ones that she and Stratis marched him through, blindfolded, the night of his arrival. She begins to talk, in fact to babble in a way he has never heard before, explaining to him (and to herself, it seems) why staying in the village will be better for now, at least until autumn, or maybe the end of the year, yes, another year without bosses, bills, money fears, deadlines, constant time pressure and other, far worse things: traitorous friends and her own intolerant family, their ethnic hatreds, their obsession with the past.

"I wish Papa were alive now," he says. "He kept hoping I'd find a nice Greek girl."

"You still haven't."

The twins are waiting, photo-framed on the threshold of the open front door, Aslan with a snail of snot trailing from nose to mouth: he has woken with a cold. Elias scoops him up. He seems incredibly light. Elias's own large body feels so light. The boy's nostrils bubble and pop and he sneezes in Elias's face, then leans his hot brow on Elias's rough cheek. "I love you," the boy says in Greek. Lale attaches herself to him too—the twins have discovered how much heat his bearlike body gives off. The three sit in the day's first sunlight on the doorstep—for now, the warmest place in or around the house—while Kaiti goes inside to make Greek coffee and warm a little goat's milk for the twins.

Elias looks east in a stupor of happiness. Through his eyes, sunrise streams into his brain and fills it with heat and light.

THREE

But This Was My Village

I will not allow that I was moved by justice
rather than love, for justice also is a form of love.

—SUSAN SONTAG, *THE VOLCANO LOVER*

I was seeking you in heaven and I found you on earth.

—GREEK CYPRIOT SAYING

¡VIVA LA MUERTE!

It's April and the plum trees are in blossom in the valleys of the mountains of Kurdistan, that tragic almost-country that sprawls across a number of official borders, including the one between Turkey and Syria. Four A.M. At a base just inside Turkey the little officer whom his colleagues refer to as Napoleon—with a blend of mockery, wary respect, and profound bewilderment—is starting his day in a prefabricated shed crowded with exercise equipment: benches, mats, barbells, dumbbells, and a small plates-and-pulleys machine. Everything looks new except for the two shivering fluorescent tubes that light the shed, and the warped, splotchy mirrors. No matter. Polat rarely looks in the mirror.

Every morning without fail he trains in the shed from 0400 till 0600. A few enlisted men and the odd NCO sometimes squeeze in as well, but no other officers. They're all sleeping off last night's dinner and drinks at the officers' mess. Polat always dines with them, as protocol dictates, but he doesn't drink, he leaves for his quarters by 2000 hours, he is in bed by 2030, and till 2115, his personal curfew, he reads books of military history and strategy—Atatürk, von Clausewitz, Sun Tzu, Julius Caesar, Epaminondas,

Rommel, Patton, Wellington, and, yes, Napoleon Bonaparte. At present he's reading an old, sympathetic biography of the Spanish general and dictator Francisco Franco and has learned that the motto of Franco's elite *Legionarios*—men whose austere resolve he admires deeply and aspires to—was *¡Viva la muerte!* Thinks Polat: that spirit was the real key to their triumph. "Long live death!" they would chant as they swept into battle against the Marxists (like the partisans here!), the anarchists, the scholars, the political dreamers too attached to their lives, families, possessions, and utopian ideals to *fight*.

After he was posted here in the fall he began forcing himself out to the exercise shed in the pre-dawn darkness and cold. He was always alone for the first hour. Initially he could barely hoist the lightest bar and his bench presses seemed a true gamble in that cold, flickering shed: perhaps he would be found dead with the forty-kilogram barbell fallen across his throat. The prospect did not alarm him. Somehow it incited him to greater effort, greater risk. Impatiently but thoroughly reading the many instructional posters covering the shed walls, he set his will to work on his body, like a warden bent on imposing compliance on a resistant captive. By the new year, when he was promoted to major after leading a recon mission into Syria—three Turkish dead and nine wounded, but at least eight PYD killed and twenty captured—his strength was at least average for his weight, which was the same as before but more athletically distributed.

By now—the morning of 10 April—Polat has condensed himself into a stalwart little man, like a Greco-Roman wrestler, his waist neither thin nor fat but solid, legs strong from thousands of squats and dead lifts, shoulders still narrow and sloping but slabbed with muscle. His thickened neck twitches with sinew, his jaw is angular. Naturally his skull is the same size, but now it looks more or less proportional. Behind his spectacles (still held on with a strap) his Anatolian blue eyes are clear. Hair shorn close to the bone.

Moustache fuller, as if his training has triggered a second, more successful round of puberty.

The others who visit the shed steer as clear of him as the cramped space will permit. Some have switched to a different time of day. Polat doesn't know if this is because he's an officer or, more likely, because his body smells. He believes that even when his body is not sweating it exudes a heavy, bovine odour, one that all his soaping and scrubbing never quite expunges. But other men—and women—have smells of their own and seem not to know it, so he feels relieved to have the shed mostly to himself.

He has no family he cares to consider. His elderly parents already had two sons when he arrived a dozen years later: a slip, a mishap. They might be proud of him now, what with his latest promotion, but he will not accept their pride—that is, their fatuous gratification in taking credit for what he himself has achieved, by dint of will, without their assistance and without the roulette windfalls of good looks, wealth, natural prowess . . . How sweet it must be, he sometimes feels, to be born with a body! A deformee like Polat has no choice but to suffer, unless and until he invents a body for himself and, ramming it up against the world, forces the world to submit.

He knows how much he owes to that fraudulent idler Erkan Kaya. During Polat's trial by tennis, and afterward in the ruins of Varosha, he learned once and for all: will and integrity are not enough. The best general in the world is helpless without a body of troops to serve him; likewise, Polat's will requires the support of a strong physique. He has one now. Yet he hates this improved one almost as much as he hated the old. His will—the only part of himself he truly values—is elsewhere, up ahead, boldly advancing into a future of conquered goals. In the end, of course, the future also means death—at least to the body, fit or unfit—but where's the terror in that? Death is everyone's final achievement. What matters is achieving it well, with dignity, pride, and no fear.

He grunts through his final set of ninety-kilogram dead lifts, his favourite exercise, then checks his wristwatch and hurries out through the door just as a strapping private—eyes rounding, body recoiling as if Polat were a Kurd with a Kalashnikov—tries to enter.

The dawn is cacophonous with gibbering birdsong, the air thick and gravid with pollen. Blossoms on a kind of tree that Polat doesn't recognize whiten the hillsides around the base like a blight. It's 0520; Polat has had to abort his full routine so as to be showered, dressed, and fed before his new mission's departure at 0600.

By 0800 his company is inside Syria and by 0900 has relieved the troops who for a week now have been occupying a Kurdish village in a deep, forested valley. These troops have been absorbing periodic mortar attacks and sniper fire from the mountainside above the village. Polat's orders are to continue to hold the village, though the wording is sufficiently ambiguous (*by all means necessary, consistent with the preservation of the company under your command*) that an attack on the partisans on the mountain is not ruled out—and for two weeks he has been preparing for exactly that, poring over contour maps and photographs, neatly jotting and collating notes, sketching diagrams of all possible contingencies.

By 1300—as if the Kurds are getting back to business after lunch and a nap—the inaccurate mortar fire starts up again. It seems the partisans mean to assert themselves and harass the occupiers while causing as little damage as possible to the village. A sign of weakness, Polat decides, and he resolves to move on them at once—the last thing they will be expecting.

At 1410 he leads two platoons up a mountainside humming with heat. The slopes are wooded with well-spaced, high old pines that cast patches of louvred shade on the needle-thick ground. The heat worsens by the minute, but Polat's stamina is far better than it was. His two lieutenants, however, are soon suffering. When the group stops at his signal for a short rest and some water, both men urge a more cautious approach and advise Polat not to rush on ahead of the scouts—an invitation to waiting snipers. There will certainly be snipers ahead, sentries at least.

Polat squints through his spectacles at the lieutenants, the swollen veins at their temples, the sclera of their eyes very white against the overheating skin. In a strangled murmur he says, "The father of our nation believed—believed good luck is not given by God but made by the bold! As for cowards"—he's no longer sure whom he's quoting (maybe himself?), or addressing (maybe himself?)—"they don't die in bed but in chains." Yet even while this oratory still hangs in the air, something hits him. His officers are right. Having chafed through weeks of inactivity, he's now leading the group toward the enemy too fast: his habitual mix of plodding, meticulous preparation and then, at the end, blind tumbling recklessness. But he can't stand down now and accept their advice—not directly. Still, when he leads the platoons on up the mountain, he tries to rein in his pace a little, though he continues to precede even the scouts.

Just after 1450 the scout on his left, straining to keep up, whispers, "*Kaptan!*" while signalling the men, *Freeze, lie down*. Naturally Polat is the last to flatten himself. Moments later, through his binoculars, he spots the sentries. In a slight hollow between trees some sixty metres up the slope, a man and woman lie sleeping, as if drugged by the afternoon heat. The lenses bring the scene indecently close. Seen in profile, the man lies on top of her, between her bent knees. Her olive trousers are bunched at her ankles, his own pulled just halfway down his buttocks. She's still wearing her tunic, though it's unbuttoned, spread open over her chest. His torso is bare. Their rifles out of view.

On either side of him his lieutenants are using their own binoculars. The left one's ears scald redder than his sweat-glazed face. The right one moistens his lips and then, like a voyeur caught in the act, glances guiltily at Polat. As for Polat, he feels numb and queasy, he feels faint with fury, as if beholding the corpses of two murdered Turkish civilians.

"Send the scouts up to capture them, sir?" the blushing man whispers.

"No. They'll wake at any time. This is our chance. No shooting." Polat rises, signals. The scouts and lieutenants follow him up the silent, red-needled slope. The stink of resin bleeding from the trees is like that urine-coloured Greek wine that Kaya always drinks at lunch. Again Polat outstrips them all, his sidearm held straight out in front of him, pulse pummelling in his ears like covering fire. Seconds later his shadow falls across the couple. He looms over them. Their breathing is deep, synchronized. Their AK-47s lie coupled beside them. Her emaciated fingers clasp his shoulder blades, which look too prominent, like his ribs. His nape is sunburned. Her face is long, her nose thin, a shadow of hair above her parted lips. The canvas-belted waist of his pants covers the obscene juncture where their bodies, Polat knows, must be fused—fused forever.

By launching no raids or even recon on the mountain, the major who held the village before Polat has infected the usually alert Kurds with his complacency. So Polat guesses. There's a catch in her breathing. He looks back over his shoulder. *Hurry!* He holsters his sidearm, reaches urgently toward the nearing scout. The man hands him his M4 rifle. The nine-inch bayonet affixed to the muzzle is black, to reflect no light. Polat puts a hand over his own mouth, then points at the couple. He hefts the bayoneted rifle vertically. Feels the lieutenants and men behind him watching, not breathing. The scout—all expression swept from his face—kneels and claps a hand over the woman's mouth. Her eyes spring open. Polat brings the bayonet down.

EASTER

Songbirds flocking north from Africa appear over the dead zone in their millions, though something about the ruins unsettles them enough that only a handful alight to rest, where they're promptly netted by Stratis and Takkos, then served up by Stavroula as *ambellopoulia*, little grilled or pickled thrushes, warblers, wheateaters, and nightingales. (So beloved is this dish that only the most strenuous diplomacy on Roland's part has kept Stavroula from pickling the village's one resident nightingale.) On the fruit trees, engorged petals are propositioning the ecstatic bees and hummingbirds. Wherever there's soil enough for roots to clench, a fresh cohort of flowers is thrusting at the sun—the lewd blooms of the Cyprus sun rose and giant orchid and asphodel—while scarlet poppies are coming up in fields south of the ruins, where an ex-soldier lies dozing in the long grass with his pregnant lover.

Forget remembrance; let these be the poppies of sleep and forgetting.

On a seaside veranda a short walk to the east, the colonel inhabits April in his own way. He has passed the night with the belly dancer Filiz, who has been performing for the year's first tourists at the Palm Beach Hotel. Filiz has visited twice before during her gigs. This time she has stayed the night. So deeply was she sleeping, after her performance and then her visit with him, that Kaya couldn't bear to wake her and send her back with Ali—nor did he really want to rouse Ali, who over the winter for the first time has showed symptoms of old age. So Filiz and the colonel have slept in, then breakfasted together in the sun. Poached eggs and olives and dates and soft sheep's cheese and tomatoes and cucumber with salt, lemon, and cumin, and crusty white bread, and cups of syrupy coffee finished with a shot of licorice raki. It's been a long time since Kaya has shared breakfast with a woman. Is it spring that's making him crave and enjoy morning company?

Filiz must have gotten up quietly, before he awoke, to reapply her makeup: heavy eyeshadow in the seraglio style, blaring mulberry lipstick. She has a large, wide mouth—predatory-looking—yet her smile is shy and she keeps hugging her elbows, as if cold. A little lipstick on her teeth. She's pale and blinking, light-shy, like any nocturnal creature. She keeps flicking her head so that her hair sweeps over and curtains one eye, one side of her face. He invites her to stay for a swim (she's a smallish woman and can probably squeeze into one of Hava's bikinis) and then, perhaps, as he puts it with superfluous tact, a nap . . . ? Maybe even lunch. He knows she will be dancing again tonight; he has heard she's very good. Perhaps he'll come up to the hotel to watch.

"And let me ask Ali to find you a pair of sunglasses."

She listens, hugging her elbows, and accepts his invitation with that demure half-smile, though something else has surfaced in her eyes—a shrewd, dubious glint? Men must try to use her all the time. He's using her himself, in a way, he supposes, but maybe it's different, feels different to a woman, if a man can't help displaying true fondness? And if he can forget himself entirely in bed! Kaya discovered in his late twenties that sexual self-forgetting is the truest paradise, at least here on earth—and where else is there? Like any hedonist, he believes only in what his senses can grasp. Like any hedonist, he has no strong opinions, except when it comes to pleasure.

"I noticed the pictures of your children this morning," she says. "Beautiful."

"Well . . . the boy is a little awkward."

"Never say such a thing! I think you must miss them."

"They're coming to stay here again in August, the whole month," he says quickly, almost defensively, as if she's a moralizing imam instead of a belly dancer. But these days the truth keeps worming into his mind: he's barely lifting a hand to raise his children. This insight now strives to hold his attention, like a lone protester waving an earnest placard. A delicate tinkling sound interrupts: Filiz's ankle bracelets, her naked feet uncrossing under the table and nestling beside his own bare feet. "Perhaps, Colonel . . ."

"Erkan, call me Erkan."

". . . we could nap first and then swim?"

As if knowing that he and Filiz are about to retreat upstairs, Ali appears beside Kaya and leans down stiffly. "Sir, perhaps you would like to have your newspaper for a moment?"

"Oh, it can wait, thanks."

The old soldier's yellow eyes—sorrowful, stubborn—will not release Kaya.

"What *is* it, Ali? Can't it wait for an hour? Well, maybe two hours."

"There's news you will want to read, sir. From the Syrian border."

It's a front-page story. Two days ago Polat—pictured in uniform with a major's pips, his pared-down face unrecognizable but for those ludicrous little spectacles—led a small Turkish force to victory over a band of PYD fighters, surprising them on a mountainside, killing six, capturing a dozen, and seizing a large cache of weapons and ammunition. It seems that because of Polat's success, another Kurdish force that was preparing to infiltrate the sector has turned back. General Özel believes that for the PYD this setback, following others, might be enough to induce them to agree to a ceasefire. He calls Major Polat "a quiet hero in the fight against terrorism"—a fight that Özel dares to believe is almost over, on this front at least, after which the major will be able to fly back to Ankara and receive a decoration, a promotion to colonel, and a new posting of his choice.

"Colonel," Filiz says, "has something terrible happened?"

He looks up at her and fabricates a carefree smile.

Every year before midnight on Holy Saturday, under a one-week waning moon, the villagers walk to the sea, where the men and women separate and then, some hundred metres apart on the beach, strip and bathe. Not even Takkos or Stratis can recall how many years ago this tradition began. For Elias, of course, it's the first time.

The dog stays with the men. Leery of the sea, he will only dart into the shallows before streaking back up onto the beach to roll, breading his legs, back, and belly fur with sand, his mouth agape in a canine grin. After chasing him for a minute, Elias plows into the water—cool but not cold. A shallow dive and he strokes outward, pursued by anxious barking but untroubled by memories of his near-fatal swim, as if this is Lethe, not a sea saturated with memory and history.

As they towel themselves dry, Roland—very white but no longer skeletal—tells him that this year for the first time Aslan is on the men's side instead of with his mother. You can see how proud the boy is, inflating his little chest and crying "*Hayir!*

Ochi!" when Elias asks if he's cold and then spins him into a towel.

Neoklis has been eyeing the naked Elias but now seems more interested in what his father is up to, planted in the shallows facing out to sea, stocky and bandy-legged as a centaur. He lifts his arm slowly to point up the gleaming channel of moonlight tapering toward the coasts of Syria, Lebanon, Israel. When he turns back toward them, his expression is remote, his penis retracted into a froth of white pubic hair. "Something is coming to us from the east," he mutters.

"Ah, so now you all see dangers everywhere!" Stratis says with a hostile smirk, this particular rudeness surprising; usually he's more respectful of the village elder.

On the way home, once they cross John F. Kennedy and are back among the lanes, they light candles, forming a silent procession, and return to the village cleansed. Stavroula, who has not gone to the sea for some years now, greets them. They all dress up in their dated finery and drink a glass of wine, even the twins. Then to the church for midnight mass, Takkos serving, pompous as ever in his priestly robes, though unusually forgetful tonight. "*Hristos anesti,*" all chant at midnight, *Christ is risen*, and "*Alithos anesti,*" all reply, *He is risen indeed!* They return to the courtyard for the Resurrection Table: honeyed wine and stewed greens and a braided loaf studded with red-dyed eggs. There are other dyed eggs that they take and smack end to end, trying to crack the other person's egg, Christ hatching from the tomb. This year Kaiti's egg is the last unshattered, after Trif's succumbs to her expert peck, winning her a year's good luck and from him a hard kiss prolonged until finally she gives him a little shove away, her neck and cheeks inflamed, green eyes shining up at him.

You've done as much for me, he thinks. *Broken me open. Freed me.*

"Listen!" Takkos's face goes grey, all but his pitted red nose. "What was that?"

"I heard nothing," Roland says.

"No knock at the gate?" Takkos's glazed eyes search their faces as if he has just come to among strangers. These nights he always seems addled with wine—it takes just a little. Stratis is about to make some remark. Myrto stops him by butting out in his empty glass. Stavroula frets the cross over her bosom and regards her husband with a tender, resigned exasperation. Her arched eyebrows have been over-plucked by poor light, or maybe they've just stopped growing. "Let us go rest, Taki—we'll leave the young ones here to talk."

On a cool and perfumed morning in early May, Roland emerges from his room, clearing his throat. He has been listening to Greek Cypriot radio. The republic's economy, deeply exposed to that of Greece and staggering since the Greek economic debacle, has collapsed. In desperation the government is planning to expropriate ten percent of the value stored in private Cypriot bank accounts. It's not yet clear whether this means every account or only those of the wealthy. There's already a run on the banks, which will likely be out of cash by noon.

"Lucky we have a German here to bail us out," Elias says, sitting under the pistachio tree with the guitar and a Greek coffee.

"I will charge heavy interest, however," Roland says cheerfully.

Elias is waiting for Kaiti to arrive from the Tombazos' house, where the twins will stay for the morning. Then he and she will be going to fill bags—old hotel pillowcases—with the herbs and greens that flourish on the flanks of the main hill, not far from their bower and the seasonal spring, now barely flowing.

"They're also talking of confiscating disused and unclaimed accounts."

"Like Kaiti's?"

"And Myrto's, if she has one, and I believe she has," says Roland. "If one needed more reason not to leave the village, here it is. The situation might soon become chaotic."

"I'll have to let Kaiti know," Elias says.

She is now saying that she wants to return to the outside at some point after their child comes, maybe in the new year, and Elias has agreed. They haven't yet told Roland. By the new year, Elias might even feel ready to leave—but now he wonders if there will be no outside to return to, at least here on Cyprus.

"And you?" he asks Roland. "Do you have an account out there idling?"

"I keep my billions with the Swiss. Their criminality is of a more reliable kind."

After Elias and Kaiti return and while she rests—as she has to now every midday—he takes the twins to the library. They are less afraid of encountering Myrto the *magissa*, in her gloomy, echoing vault of books, if Elias accompanies them. He leads them in through the side door and lets them pick a path through the stacks—slightly, confusingly altered, as ever. No sign of Stratis. The surface of the main desk is uncharacteristically clear, the few remaining papers primly squared. Myrto rises from her stool and starts jabbering, using English as if to keep her meaning from the twins, though in fact she seems perfectly unaware of them, each clutching one of his hands.

"I recognize today that my work here is achieved," she says, pronouncing it *achieve-edd*. "My shelves have achieved their final, their ideal conformation."

"Great, we can celebrate tonight. We were just out gathering some of the fresh—"

"Of course," she snaps, "I smell them on you. Roland was here an hour ago and informed me of the news. I find it intolerable that an elected government should rob me of my savings, what remains of them, after my life in Nicosia was so . . . so entirely . . ." Her indignation all but asphyxiates her. Her chest heaves, her tiny nostrils flare.

He says, "Kaiti thinks it won't ever happen. It's a ruse, a way for the government to distract its creditors and buy time."

"I must leave the village," she insists, as if he hasn't spoken, "and return to reclaim what remains to me while I can. You see, so long as my savings remained, I had the conviction that I could return at a time of my own choosing, but now, you see, you see they try to steal from me also this free choice, and I . . ." She shifts into Greek as she always does when she wants to speak figuratively: It is time to gather the torn, scattered pages of her life, however many are left to collect, and bind them back together into some sort of order.

"And Stratis?" he asks, while the twins look up with wide, unblinking eyes.

The cords of her throat tauten. "I thought of asking him to accompany me"—this in English—"but I know he will not want to abandon his post. Nor will he want to leave the grave of his wife."

"Even for you?"

"To be honest, even if he would join me . . ."

"*Dhen peirazei*—you don't need to say anything."

"I need to say everything! Be patient, there is little enough, and there is no one else to hear it. Only you and Roland. Quite simply, I must leave Strati. He begins to frighten me. He doesn't want me to leave."

"Nobody wants you to leave, but—"

"He swears he won't permit me!"

Just as Elias had no idea the affair had begun, he has not realized it's over.

"So when would you go?"

"Tomorrow!"

"What?"

"When you and he are repairing the Tombazos' roof. You will please make this repair work last as long as plausible. Roland will assist me to carry my bag down to the end of the zone, where I can cross over discreetly. There is a village, a town on the other side. From there, a bus to Nicosia and my few relations. And so I will return to them from the dead."

THE FINAL PAGE

In late August, the very oven of the year, Polat returns to Varosha.

Kaya is on the tennis court with his daughter, Hava, while Yil, up in his room, plays some noisy new video game, an activity Kaya minds less now that Yil is also eager to venture outside late each afternoon and go "on patrol" with his father, just inside the perimeter of the dead zone. On these outings the boy's face betrays occasional signs of real pleasure. He also seems to like wearing Kaya's spare fatigues, laughably baggy though they are. He still sulks a little about Kaya's refusal to let him strap on the holster belt and carry the pistol, but that might just be a negotiating wile. After all, Kaya has already softened enough that he lets the boy fire off a few shots here and there, at old bottles and signs. Kaya uses these moments to show the boy how to handle the Yavuz-16 safely. On one outing he also invited Yil to pick off a hare or pheasant for Ömer to cook up. The boy reacted with such horror that Kaya has never brought up the idea again.

He knows Polat is due to arrive later today, but he has gently finessed the thought out of his mind, the way you might charm and conciliate a disruptive guest into leaving a party. He is relishing his daily set with Hava, who has improved steadily and now offers him a true challenge. Happily he praises her occasional aces, and between choppy breaths at the end of long rallies he calls to her, "Well done, my girl!" or "Wonderful volley!" or "Good try, Hava!" His heart swells. He wishes the children could be here all of the time. Well, more of the time. Half of the time, actually—that would be ideal.

Hava's eyelashes are so long that they look enhanced, but she tells him they're all hers. Come to think of it, she seems to groom herself less strenuously than he assumes most girls of her age do, but then, what does he know? He truly is in exile here, in his private club, on an island, supervising an enclave where the clock stopped almost forty years ago. He visits Istanbul only once a year and relies on articles in the back sections of the *Hürriyet* to keep up with the culture. Perhaps when Hava is back home, and out at night with friends, she's another girl completely, one he would hardly recognize? Yes, and yet he also knows that she's deeply comfortable and compatible with him in a way that he can't imagine himself and his brother ever having been with their father. Between them and Baba an invincible berm of decorum and formality loomed—perhaps also indifference, perhaps simply bewilderment. (Kaya sometimes forgets that the man is still alive, as he sometimes forgets that his mother is dead.)

Physically Hava takes after him, not his ex-wife, Pinar, who is taller than Hava and less daintily made. There's a lightness, a facility to the girl's speech and whole manner as she glides through a world that she fully expects will gratify all her desires—and why would the world ever think of refusing? Her wishes all seem so benign. But a child's character is a shifting frontier between the vying powers of the parents' souls, and when rare impediments crop up in Hava's road, she, like her mother, is given to panic and pessimism. "Of course," she will say, "I knew it!" "*Geçmis olsun,*" she will say, just like her mother. "May it pass quickly!"

He wonders, now and then, what became of his love for Pinar. A slow bleeding he could understand, but how could something so potent just vanish and leave not the slightest sign? Just ten years ago there were still nights when they swam in each other's sweat and with the same air panted each other's names. Now, if she should pass him lounging behind his sports pages at an Üsküdar café, her face rigorously made up and crimped in that frown of pained impatience (the world is a disappointment in ways she can't quite pin down), his body and soul would stay utterly unruffled, unreached.

"What can you really know of life," she once said. "You, who've never known a heartbreak?"

He sits sprawled near the baseline, inhaling the hot air and grinning as the clay sears the hairs on the backs of his legs. He has slipped while stretching for a hard, curving serve that might just have kissed the sideline. "Lovely shot, Hava!" Across the court, unmoving, head cocked to one side, Hava seems not to hear. She's peering beyond him. He looks over his shoulder. Polat is standing above him, two metres away, the toes of his gleaming boots just behind the baseline, as if it's a stripe on a parade square. The high sun is in Kaya's eyes but he sees that Polat—Colonel Polat—is dandied up in dress uniform, and not one that would have fit him last year. So, his face and shoulders in that *Hürriyet* photo were *not* digitally doctored for propaganda reasons. The change is stunning. He even seems taller. The lenses of his little spectacles aim down like field glasses. He salutes and says, "It's a pleasure to see you here, Colonel Kaya!"

"I did wonder if you might arrive hours early," Kaya lets out.

"I like to surprise people when I can." Polat's delivery, if less halting than before, is no less audible.

"You must be a little uncomfortable in that uniform?" Kaya says.

"Actually I find it an excellent fit."

"I do hope you remember how hot it can get here."

Polat's mouth tightens—a chilling little smile—and he puts out his hand as if offering to help Kaya to his feet. Instinctively Kaya accepts the offer, extending his own right hand by way of olive branch. After all, if Polat is going to be here for a while . . . Polat merely shakes the hand, first limply, then with suddenly intensifying force. At last he lets go. He stares down coldly. The hand that touched Kaya retreats behind his back.

Kaya springs up, cracks the knuckles of his smarting hand and—now looking down at Polat—says very softly, "Your timing is good, come to think of it. You may join me and my children for lunch, if you like—after my daughter and I finish our set."

"I was hoping we might meet alone," Polat says, loudly enough that Hava must overhear. "There are several matters that we . . . that I would like to discuss with you."

"Well, maybe after lunch—over coffee? We have plenty of time. We're honoured, of course, that you've asked to be posted back to Varosha, for now. Hava? Come here, my love, I'd like to introduce you."

She skims toward them, around the net, her toes barely touching the clay, a creature of air and light. At her approach, Polat's strident phrases begin to crowd up and jumble: "The main thing is—is the Restricted Zone. I feel, let me not waste your time, Colonel—I feel it remains imperative that, that—and now that I'm here, and we share the same rank, I believe—"

"Let me introduce my daughter, Hava. Hava, this is the decorated war hero I told you about at breakfast. He comes to us fresh from the Syrian front. I worry he'll find it too quiet here, again!" (Or too hot; one can only hope.) Kaya finally gets out the man's full title and name, "*Albay* Aydin Polat." *Albay* proves as difficult to say as some unpronounceable word in Greek. Hava is watching her father closely. He knows he doesn't sound like himself. She offers Polat her golden, glowing little hand. As Polat grabs it and squeezes, a sinew jumps in his jaw. The girl winces. In a swift motion that Polat must think imperceptible he wipes his palm on the side of his trousers. His boots remain planted behind the baseline. Does he think they might assault him with their racquets if he crosses it? (For a moment, Kaya pictures this assault.) "If my daughter and I might just finish our set," he goes on with Ottoman politesse, glad for his sunglasses, "after which we will take a short dip in the sea? Shall we meet you on the veranda at noon, *Albay*?"

"Very well, *Albay*."

"Welcome back, *Albay*," Kaya adds and thinks, *Geçmis olsun*.

Stroll through the village in late afternoon, late August, the hot air calm and expectant. Time hangs in the balance at the hinge of the day. A small breath of breeze arrives like an advance on a contract: another perfect evening is en route out of the west. Smells of coffee sift through the shutters of the Tombazos' kitchen window. Over the garden between their house and Kaiti's, sheets hang limp (Aslan has begun wetting the bed, as if anxious about something—the coming baby?). Kaiti's shutters swing open and out tumble noises of the twins' bickering, voices thick and cranky with sleep. Kaiti leans out the window in her white cotton slip, her elbows propped on the sill. She peers up and down the lane. Trif has woken early from the siesta—where can he have gone? Her whole being feels sodden, humid with sleep. Her breasts, bigger by the week, are plumped between her elbows. In this last trimester her nipples have darkened almost to black. She has told him it happened the first time too. He loves the change, he says, loves every change in her body, and he says he means it, and she calls him a liar. He sets his ear to her protruding navel. So silent are these afternoons, she almost believes him when he says he can hear the baby treading water in its landlocked little sea. But she adds, "No, it must be my stomach—hungry again." She is always hungry now but can't eat much without feeling stuffed. Suddenly she's weary of her condition, of her feet and lower back aching, and wary of having sex anywhere but in their bed, in certain careful ways.

Mornings before the breeze dies and the heat stupefies all birdlife, Varosha is a little less silent, yet the villagers have heard some distant shots. Kaya has sent a message. With their kind permission, he will be taking his visiting son shooting along the edge of the dead zone, mainly right along John F. Kennedy, at most a couple of streets in from the beach. *Please, not to worry.* Kaya's tactfully worded notice does not placate Stratis Kourakis, whose martial ardour blazes at the thought of two Turks violating Varosha's perimeter with a firearm, even if they are shooting at nothing but tin cans, which Stratis does not for a moment believe. They must be killing game as well—rabbits, hares, even wild goats. In other words, poaching. Then yesterday evening he returned from a recon to the southeast with proof, he said: he found a number of spent shells but no small corpses. "So they must be taking their catch home, for food. Our catch, our game!"

"But couldn't the lack of evidence just mean they haven't killed anything?" Elias offered.

"Why waste precious rounds shooting at walls and bottles?"

"The Turkish army has no shortage of bullets, Stratis," Roland said, and the man took the remark badly, seeming to interpret it as a warning that he, Sergeant Kourakis, with his limited munitions, should not think of confronting Kaya and the might of the Turkish army. Which naturally made Stratis even more eager. Since Myrto's departure in May he has seemed ever more pugnacious and suspicious, even paranoid, and Roland and Elias are bearing the brunt of it. His eyes again have an estranged, unfocused look. He sings rarely and, when he does, only battle songs.

When first he discovered her gone, he gripped the sunburned wrist of Elias, who'd worked beside him on the Tombazos' roof all day long, and demanded to know—was he aware that she meant to leave? Elias denied knowing anything. Who can avoid lying sometimes in a village? He can see that now. Stratis, of course, didn't fully believe him and never for a moment believed Roland, who he correctly thinks must have known Myrto meant to leave and must have helped her down to the Green Line. In fact, Stratis thinks the whole village—what's left of it, as he keeps saying—might well have been in league against him. In the evenings, when he drinks, this conviction boils over and he picks quarrels, once even shoving Roland to the ground before Elias stepped in. Eventually he subsides into his chair, grows maudlin, even weeps. His own neighbours have betrayed him, yes, despite his having stood guard over them for years. Still, even now he would fight and die to protect them from the ancestral enemy, and sooner or later—go ahead, smile if you will—the Turks will sweep down again from the north.

In the courtyard this early evening Roland is hunched over the row of tables in his reading glasses, working on the last pages of his history of the village, the full story up until now. Elias is peeling cucumbers. Takkos putters among the grapevines trellised behind the pistachio and lemon trees, clipping and culling, encouraging his plump, ruby clusters in an amorous murmur. Stratis and Neoklis are playing backgammon, a simpler game than chess but one at which Neoklis, oddly, is mediocre at best. As Stratis wins again, he drains his glass and stands, mumbling about checking the snare lines as he ought to have done earlier. He goes into his room and emerges in a clean shirt, his pants pockets showing the outlines of what appear to be both guns—his old service revolver and the Turkish one he captured last year. He stalks out through the gate with Argos at his heels. Roland and Elias exchange a glance and follow.

His route winds southward, as expected. Roland and Elias trail about a hundred metres back. Now he and the dog are crossing the emerald plaza, but instead of veering diagonally, toward the area behind the officers' club where Kaya and his son have been shooting, he proceeds directly south. In the shadow of the church he halts, turns toward the doors, crosses himself with the briskness of a military salute. Then he and the dog vanish into the ruins on the far side.

"This must be the way you and Myrto walked to the border?" Elias asks.

"As he would surely know, *ja*." Roland pauses to get his breath. "How quiet she was! Almost . . . ceremonial. She was dressed as if she expected a car to be waiting on the far side. She was not ever my favourite of the villagers, but as I walked back without her, I confess that I wept."

Ten minutes on, they pass a tumbledown cinema whose marquee still holds twenty or so slot-letters with a few gaps between. Sean Connery, it must be, in a film called, maybe, *Zardoz*. The edge of the ruins. An owl lifts out of a carob tree with a snake in its claws. Right ahead sprawls the ornate chaos of the necropolis, four black cypresses pluming its corners, though otherwise there are none of the trees or clipped greenery of cemeteries like the one where Elias's parents lie—no roomy plots, like mini suburban lawns. Instead, stone walls, slabs, crypts, crosses, marble statuary, all crammed up and impacted like the ruins of the vaster necropolis around it, Varosha.

Stratis is there, his back to them, standing before the wooden cross over the bones of his child and "wife," who, according to Roland's history, "fled Husband and Family in Paphos, for reasons that Kourakis chose not to tell, if indeed he ever knew them." From his pocket, Stratis draws a candle—probably the object Elias assumed was a gun barrel—and lights it with a match. He plants it at the foot of the cross among older offerings: dried flowers, candle stubs, other things Elias can't make out. The man's shoulders start to quake. Argos, beside him, looks around and sniffs the air, maybe realizing Roland and Elias are close by—lurking in a doorway some sixty metres from the necropolis wall. Both feel foolish and ashamed. Stratis crouches. In the ruff of the aging dog, whom he's usually more apt to kick and curse, he buries his face like a child.

That night Elias lies naked, propped up on pillows that smell musty and old despite their clean cases, a candle alight on the bedside table and Roland's manuscript by his hip. He has dipped into it here and there but now decides to read the last page, wondering how the man will have ended a book whose story is not yet finished. Kaiti is tucked fetally on her side, her eyes shut, her black curls matted with sweat against her temple and brow. Her small hand rests on his thigh, but there's space between their bodies. Neither can bear sleeping pressed together in this heat. Her pale belly, stretch-marked, sprawls, the life in there already advanced enough to survive out here, although to him that life still seems implausible, a figment with a pulse. When it doesn't seem implausible it seems overwhelming, so he has been setting his mind to practicalities—making domestic repairs, foraging for cloths and diapers in the stores along John F. Kennedy. He means to write Kaya and ask if they can trade something for a few small solar panels, for this house and the Tombazos', so they can run a fan in the hottest part of the night.

"Read to me," she murmurs in Greek. *Dhiavase mou.*

"You slept a little?"

"I was dreaming. I was in the womb, my own womb." Her eyes stay shut under the dark eyelids. "I don't like my dreams lately. What scares you most about going back out?"

After a silence: "Finding out nothing over here has changed me. Not the traumas, not the miracles. That it just seems I've changed because I'm in a refuge here, where there's . . . nothing to turn you against your better self. I couldn't bear that—knowing Elias Trifannis survived his death, and other deaths, real ones, and I'm him again, thirty-one years old and still not . . . still living a sort of coma. And you'd be disillusioned—you thought you were getting me, but you're getting him."

She pulls closer. "I think that stranger is truly dead, Trif. I'm a little sad I can never know him."

"We'll come back here to visit, though? Promise me."

"Of course, we'll find a way."

"What frightens you?"

"That the *world* won't have changed. And that once we get out there, you'll leave us. You'll think this was only possible in this little garden. This *phantasia*."

"Adam stayed with Eve after they left."

"They didn't leave, they were driven out."

He leans over to kiss her smile but before he can do it she says, "This tired, it's like I'm fifty years older. Just a month now. I can't wait. Read me Roland's story."

"Well, on the last page he says—"

"*Ochi*," she cries, "hasn't this place taught you any patience? Start on page one!"

And so he does, but before he can finish the long first paragraph, Roland's sombre, ponderous English takes effect and her breathing slows and thickens.

He turns back to the last page.

It is no easy thing to know what future awaits us. Barring the arrival of new refugees, deserters, or bankrupts, Folk who wish to hideaway from time and the World, the Village might well shrink to the way it began some 40 years ago, simply the Tombazos and their son, along with Stratis Kourakis, who I fear will more and more resemble one of those Japanese soldiers who at the end of the Pacific War, hid and would not [illegible word] *until they perished or went insane. And to think of Neoklis' parents dying, and leaving him alone here! It is a thought ~~that I~~ the author of these pages can not ~~permit my~~*

bear to consider. ~~*As for this author, if he considers the posibility of himself being the last Villager in this, his last Village, he is overcome by a terrible loneliness. But where else has he to go? It is not simply that he would be arrested and inprisoned were he to re-appear, but rather*~~ *But perhaps those soldiers stayed in hiding not so much out of fear, or in compliance with orders, but because the collapse of all they were defending allowed them to see: Civilization was simply the lies and rivalries of* [illegible] *dressed up as Princes, Prophets, Generals, Bankers,* [illegible], *Entertainers, etc; and lacking a normal, decent facility for self-delusion, they could not return to the ruins of Home.*

And at the bottom of the page, like a footnote added later, then reconsidered:

~~*"Perhaps my beautiful Homeland, it was a dream."*~~

VICTORY DAY

Colonel Kaya remains administrator of the Varosha Restricted Zone, and though Polat is now a colonel himself, he is also again Kaya's adjutant, and as such he reports to Kaya. So when Polat announces that he wants to accompany Kaya and his son on their next unofficial "patrol" in the ruins, Kaya knows he could simply refuse. But that would be a mistake. For one thing, Kaya has been violating regulations by taking Yil, a civilian, into the ruins, and Polat—if Kaya denies his request—will surely report him to General Hüseyin in Nicosia. It's odd, in fact, that Polat has not yet done so.

Polat discovered the transgression in a way so predictable that Kaya is, uncharacteristically, furious at himself. He should have seen it coming. On the afternoon of Polat's return, the man had told him that on the next day he would remain at his quarters in Famagusta for the morning, then meet Colonel Nurettin at lunch. It was a lie. The next morning Polat had driven a Land Rover down the beach and arrived at the club by 10 A.M., while Kaya and Yil were still out wandering and happily sniping at bottles a few blocks away. When they returned, by way of the tennis court, Polat was waiting for them, standing at the baseline, the maroon lips under his neat moustache compressed in a dangerous little smile.

Another thing. Polat is again pushing for a thorough armed reconnaissance of the dead zone, and Kaya is hoping to distract and delay the man until he can formulate some kind of scheme. He could of course accompany Polat on any recon mission and try to steer him away from the village, but what if Polat, *Colonel* Polat now, should insist on going, say, north instead of south at some key intersection? Kaya can only countermand him so many times without raising suspicion. As if Polat isn't suspicious enough.

Next morning, ahead of schedule, Polat arrives at the club for a tennis rematch. Kaya is laying out his court whites on the bed when a sound comes from outside: an urgent, seemingly coital snorting and puffing. In his silk undershorts Kaya walks out through the balcony door and looks down over the rail. Below him in the sand Polat is pumping out push-ups on a green exercise mat the size of a prayer rug. Sweat blots the back of his T-shirt. Desert-camouflage trousers, combat boots, fastidious gloves. Seen from up here, his bottom bobbing, it's like he's thrusting into an invisible someone. Another twenty or thirty times and he collapses, moaning (a gentleman, Kaya thinks, keeps his weight on his elbows), then starts to turn over, probably for sit-ups or whatever. Kaya withdraws from the rail and slips back inside.

As he approaches the court he notices his gut is untypically aquiver. Polat is a different man now, physically; what little authority Kaya still wields over him might not survive a defeat.

The man is already there on the court, grunting out practice serves. But if he's much stronger, quicker, and more durable than before, he turns out to be no more skilled. They start and he bludgeons forehand after forehand long or wide. His backhands bobble over the fence. The more he shoots out of bounds, the more frantic and clumsy his play becomes. When the score hits 4–0,

Kaya begins to ease off a little, and Polat, as if sensing this charity, grits his teeth and strains harder, gasping out rebukes to himself at every mistake: "Idiot, *IDIOT*!" "What are you *DOING*?" "Garbage!" "Stop, just stop it!" His T-shirt is sodden from neck to waist and appears to be not olive but almost black. The spectacle of his humiliation . . . by the end, it's almost sickening.

As Kaya reclines under his ceiling fan with a glass of mineral water, resting before his "patrol" with Yil and Polat, he hears a violent splashing from outside. It sounds like a wildebeest fighting off a crocodile at a waterhole. He goes back out onto the balcony. Polat is thrashing along in the shallows, parallel to the beach. If he's trying to cool down after their set, it can't be working. He's attacking the sea in a frenzy but generating little motion. A turtle hobbling along the waterline could keep pace. Kaya lights a cigarette, inhales deeply. The man's comic paroxysms make it possible to forget, for a moment, how dangerous he is and how grave this situation has become.

A half-hour later Kaya strolls downstairs into the atrium of the club. On the first-floor landing he meets Hava running up. She embraces him, kissing him lightly on either cheek; he keeps his right hip, where the Yavuz-16 is holstered, turned away from her.

"Baba, you're dressed like a soldier again! Are you and Yil playing soldiers again today?"

"We are, and I'm afraid Colonel Polat will be playing with us."

"Baba doesn't look happy," she says with a sympathetic pout. She loves to tease him and does it more and more now as she approaches adulthood. "*I* don't like that man, either. I think he scares me. My hand still hurts."

"That man scares *me*," Kaya says, only because he knows she'll never believe it. "By the way, I avenged your hand just now on the tennis court. Where were you? You said you wanted to watch."

"I was Skyping with Erdal." Her new boyfriend, in Istanbul. "I won't miss the next game, I promise."

"Unless," he says indulgently, "you're Skyping with Erdal. Where's Yil?"

"On the patio, all ready and waiting. And so happy! It's not like Yil."

"He loves these outings."

"He's excited about the scary man, too. Because he's a 'war hero.'" She cocks her head, exaggerates a frown. "Aren't there any height restrictions for war heroes?"

"Now, now, my love." Hava's exuberance sometimes brims over into mean-minded mockery, yet he can never bear to reprove her.

"Once we fly back," she says, "I won't be here to protect you from him." (She and Yil will be leaving after the Victory Day holiday at the end of the week.) Affecting a sad face she adds, "Well, may it pass quickly," and again it strikes Kaya how odd the antique phrase sounds in the voice of a teenager, especially one whose usual manner is cheerfully facetious.

Yil and the two colonels squeeze through a hidden gap in the barbed-top fencing behind the tennis court. Polat seems to have regained his self-control—or has he simply emptied himself, expending all his anger? He's quietly scanning the ruins. He bears a holstered pistol over his fatigues, like Kaya. As for Yil, Kaya has told him to wear street clothes today and the boy has complied, donning skinny black jeans and his huge trainers, though his choice of T-shirt may be a small act of defiance: it features a fancifully muscled commando and the English phrase SNIPER'S HONOUR.

"Really, Colonel"—Polat speaks softly, by his standards, as if the ruins might conceal enemy scouts—"there should be no—no breaches in the fence at all."

"But if any spot is secure, surely this one is, right behind the club?" Kaya says. "After all, I'm never far from my post. And with this shrub here . . ." He indicates the bush-like tamarisk that hides the opening from anyone on the beach or tennis court.

Polat says, "When you led Colonel Nurettin's men through Varosha—"

"This way, Colonel, please. That building there is dangerous. We can't have it collapsing on you."

"—did you enter right here?"

"What? Ah, no—it was the old U.N. checkpoint, on the north side. As I said, we explored for several hours, everywhere, and saw nothing." Kaya snaps a glance back at Yil. He has instructed the boy to say nothing of his, Yil's, presence on that recon—a more serious violation than these recent peripheral visits. Yil doesn't return Kaya's glance. He's planting his soles on the cracked asphalt with an absorbed, catlike care, as if fantasizing that the ground is mined. He's thrilled every time by this desolation: an organized adult world arrested and allowed to slip into decay.

"I hope you didn't bring your son along on that patrol."

"Of course not. May I suggest we go a little slower?" (Polat's face is cherry red under the brim of his forage cap.) "We did just play tennis, and this heat . . ."

Some minutes later they arrive at the back of the Hotel Aphrodite, one of the few structures along John F. Kennedy that Kaya will allow Yil to explore. Though the bomb-damaged facade has partly collapsed, everything else seems solid, especially at the back. There, a stuccoed arcade, shaded and breezy, ends at a wall some twenty metres off, where a niche must once have held mock-classical statuary or vases sprouting seasonal bouquets. Now it contains the jagged remnants of a mineral-water bottle and a tin can punctured by a couple of shots. The niche itself and the surrounding stucco are pocked with holes. Yil has brought along several more empty bottles in his knapsack.

"I've been teaching the boy how to handle a pistol safely," Kaya says. "Perhaps today I'll let him take a few shots."

"But, Baba, we've already—"

"Don't interrupt me," Kaya says. Yil looks at his father with amazement, as if a computer glitch has radically altered a character in one of his games: different voice, different personality. "I realize you may not approve, Colonel Polat, but I choose to exercise my discretion in this matter. In my view, if the boy is eventually to serve his country"—*good*, thinks Kaya, *very good*—"he should know how to handle a firearm."

"I understand," Polat says softly, his tone as surprising as his agreement.

"Yil, go set up a target," Kaya orders, then says, "No, wait!" He realizes how much he's longing to walk away from Polat, this little radiator of officious suspicion and rage, even for a few moments. He says, "I'll do it. Here, give me a bottle. Colonel Polat, feel free to question Yil about the care and loading of the Yavuz-16."

Strolling up the arcade to the niche, Kaya lights a cigarette in stride, relishing the breeze and the clarifying rush of nicotine. After clearing away the rusted can and the remains of the shattered bottle, he sets a new bottle in place. He takes his time centring it. Behind him, at the far end of the arcade, Yil and Polat can be heard talking. Kaya can't make out the words, which is odd; he expected Polat to be examining the boy loudly, drill-master style, even making him dismantle and rebuild the pistol.

Kaya turns around. He takes the cigarette from his lips and puts his hands up, stretching his mouth into a grin and calling, "Wait, shouldn't you offer me a blindfold first?" Silence. Yil has reverted to his old concave posture, looking down at the weapon that hangs limp in his hand. Polat—shorter than Yil, though with arms and thighs packed like sandbags into his fatigues—eyes Kaya through his strap-on glasses. What has just happened? *Things right themselves—they always do*. Yet now he can feel things tipping past the point of self-correction. Then the thought comes: What if there should be an accident, a little slip while somebody reloads? A shot fired inadvertently while Polat sets up a new target? If only, he thinks, that could just *occur*, no real decision on his part, no deliberate action.

He rejoins Yil and Polat and instructs the boy to fire at will. Yil lacks his usual eagerness and his aim is awful, worse even than on his first day. His hand and arm tremble. He won't meet Kaya's eyes when he hands over the hot gun. Kaya's grip, too, turns out to be less steady than usual, his sharp eyesight little compensation. Several of his shots miss the niche altogether before his second-last one smashes the top half of the bottle.

Polat says, "You must have performed better than this in training, Colonel?"

"I performed better than this yesterday," he says coldly. In truth, he never was much of a marksman, but he was so well liked in officer training that no one really considered failing him at anything. "Would you care to reset our target, Colonel Polat?"

Behind his glasses Polat's eyes are red and tiny, as if the glare on the tennis court has shrivelled them. "Perhaps your son could do it."

"Very well." More gently, a little worried by Yil's withdrawal, Kaya asks, "Yil? Are you all right?"

Unconvincingly the boy nods at his shoes.

Polat's aim is impressive for a man with glasses and whose speech is often uneven, faltering, surging ahead. By the time he has emptied the clip—his left hand expertly bracing his right—he has reduced the target to splinters.

They return to the club in silence and Yil dashes up the stairs to his room. Kaya hasn't seen him run that way in a long time. Timur Ali, uniformed as always, emerges from his own room beside the kitchen. He will not so much as glance at Polat. He addresses Kaya with greater deference and formality than usual, as if to remind Polat of the colonel's status in this jurisdiction. "Is there anything the *albay* requires?" Playing along, Kaya answers gruffly, "*Hayir!*" and signals Ali to leave them alone. The man salutes and withdraws. He will be listening, of course, from behind the door.

Kaya turns to Polat. "What did you say to my son back there?"

"No, it's what he said to me—that's why he's so—so—"

"What are you talking about?"

"I asked if the two of you noted any signs of intruders, or—or occupants, in the Restricted Zone. I told him I had suspicions. He was very respectful. He was eager to please, in fact, and he told me, 'Sir, you should have no suspicions!' He confessed he did go in there once, alone, and he saw something—two people—he thinks Greek—but they were only tourists, trespassers—or so you told him, after you'd 'caught and arrested them.' Then he was silent, your son. As if he had said things you told him not to say."

"Yes," Kaya scrambles, "because he shouldn't have gone in there alone. I didn't want him to get in trouble for that. Just for going in. After all, he—"

"Him in trouble, or you in trouble, Colonel?"

"Keep your voice down."

"You, Colonel Kaya—you are in trouble here."

"I am in *command* here, Colonel!"

"Yes, for now. And so, I request to look over your record, your commander's record, of capturing these, these 'tourists.' Photographs, copies of passports, the transcript of their interrogation. You—I assume you did interrogate them?"

"Naturally, yes. Then I had them tortured to death and their bodies flung in the sea." Kaya's voice is shaking. "Isn't that the protocol that men like you favour?"

"The opposite—that would be chaos! I'm on the side of order. I perceive that you are not serious. I assure you that I am serious."

"There's no order like the order of death, Colonel. Life is chaos."

"I believe—no—I *know* there are people in there, living people!"

"What is it about the idea of 'living people' that so offends you?"

Polat's eyelids are flickering. "I see it clearly now—you're on the side of our enemies."

"Enemies like the Kurds? God forgive me, if I were on their side I would never have arranged for you to go kill them in droves."

"Ah, now—now you imply that I'm in your debt—that I owe you my rank!"

"Debt would entail a connection between us. There is none."

"I will return to the base now, and—"

"Do it and stay there. That's an order. And I order you, as my adjutant, not to go into the Restricted Zone. You understand?"

"—I will be speaking to the general about leading . . . leading forces into Varosha. I will also inform him that you—that you have been—"

"General Hüseyin will have started his holiday by now," Kaya bluffs, hoping with little hope. "You'll have to wait. You might never take a holiday, but the rest of us . . ." Victory Day: as defeat and disaster heave into view, the irony sweeps over him. "Meanwhile, stay out of Varosha! And do not speak to my son again or go near him for any reason."

"Very well."

"What?" Kaya says, surprised.

"Very well, *sir*!" cries Polat, saluting and clicking his heels—apparently some grotesque stab at humour. His face, pink and sheened with sweat, whitens, showing the old acne pits. His pupils have sunk into irises of cold Anatolian blue. Kaya's own face has never felt so naked, as if the skin there has been flayed and peeled down over his throat, or ripped clear off, the courtly mask gone forever. The feeling is awful in almost every sense, yet in some rogue corner of his soul Kaya is thrilled.

Two armed men who hate each other stand a metre apart, conspicuously averting their hands from their holsters—Kaya by crossing his arms over his chest, Polat by tucking his right hand behind him.

As soon as Polat drives away up the beach, Kaya scrawls a note in Turkish and asks Ali to take it in to the Jaguar gate. "Right away, *efendi*." Ali's saggy eyes look especially doleful, his moustache so droopy it appears to be melting.

A quarter-hour later, while Kaya sits sternly talking to his son in the boy's room, he hears a faint honking, as if a car alarm is going off in a living city. Yil, poor boy, is crying and doesn't notice.

> *A problem has come up. I fear it is serious. Until further notice, all villagers, for their own safety, should please remain in the village, going no farther north than the well and no farther south than the main church. No, please avoid the church. Stay right out of the plaza. I will send more news as soon as possible. May this trouble pass quickly.*
>
> *Kaya*

* * *

Some years ago, when patrols along the perimeter fence were a little more frequent, one of Nurettin's sergeants had driven down the beach to report a curious find. Stuck on the fence not a hundred metres from the bar entrance of the Palm Beach Hotel was a piece of white boxboard on which Greek words had been written by hand. The sergeant presented this item to Kaya. The colonel knew little Greek but recognized one word, MOY, and seemed to recall that it was the Greek equivalent of the English "my." A tall, bold exclamation mark ended the inscription. The puzzle intrigued Kaya, so after the sergeant drove away, he took a glass of beer up to his room and sat down at his computer by the open balcony door. Character by character he keyed the words into a Greek–Turkish translation program.

The result popped onto the screen almost audibly, a howl of grief that seemed aimed directly at Kaya: I LEFT MY SOUL IN THERE, OPEN UP! Mostly it had been easy to forget that at one time twenty thousand people had resided, laboured and loved in the ruins that were now his little sultanate. Easy to forget, too, that an ever-dwindling number still dreamed of returning to reclaim their homes or rebuild businesses. For the most part these exiles spoke collectively, impersonally, in litigious or diplomatic jargon, through lawyers or government bodies or the E.U. But the simple words of this inscription—they pierced him like a deathbed plea. The writing looked shaky, as if rushed, written in the dark, maybe on impulse, probably in a state of fear. For Greek Cypriots back then, getting into the north took real effort and paperwork. Kaya has wondered from time to time who this daring individual might have been.

The sign troubled him enough that he thought of burning or shredding it. He couldn't bring himself to do it. He left the thing in the back of his closet, behind his dressing mirror, along with a framed photograph of Pinar, himself and the children. He guesses he will have to destroy it now. The thought of the military police arriving to search the club, finding it in his closet, deeming it further evidence of treacherous sympathies . . . In his optimistic soul he finds such a scenario fantastical, yet another part of him realizes that he has to consider it. He has tried to reach General Hüseyin, of course, but the general actually *has* gone away on holiday. Surely Polat will not act, really act, without the general's consent? He may be a hothead, but surely he's also too dutiful to violate specific orders without permission. Still, Kaya wonders whether he ought to send Hava and Yil back to Istanbul early.

He needs to get some idea of what Polat is up to but knows that he can't trust or confide in Colonel Nurettin now: Polat will already have spoken to the ever-cautious colonel, probably threatening him, and Nurettin will do anything to stay out of trouble. So Kaya calls his doctor, also in Famagusta. After speeding through the usual pleasantries, he asks Dr. Günsel to keep an eye on Polat, for Polat's own sake. The heat is extreme; Polat's behaviour was erratic when he reported here to the club; and as the doctor will recall, Polat collapsed and had to be hospitalized last November. Kaya adds that he has ordered Polat to return to his quarters and stay there for a few days. Would Günsel please make discreet inquiries and let Kaya know if his orders are being obeyed—and if not, what Polat might be doing instead? Kaya then suggests a few other helpful measures. The doctor responds that he's always happy to be of service but doesn't feel he can go so far as to have Polat—now a ranking officer and decorated war hero—"confined to hospital for the weekend on suspicion of illness." Calmly and reasonably, smiling into the handset, Kaya says he understands.

As he rings off, he feels another tremor of elation at the thought of having an actual enemy. Something his father told him years ago returns to mind: "It's a pitiful man whose actions produce only friends." He dismissed the idea at the time. He thought it obvious that with a bit of effort it was possible and desirable to get along with everyone . . . with the possible exception of one's own father! Nice irony. But maybe a young man's father was his natural adversary—a necessary one—while Polat is the kind that simply means to destroy you.

On August 28, two days before Victory Day, Kaya receives a call from Dr. Günsel. The doctor has learned through Colonel Nurettin's adjutant that yesterday Polat visited Nurettin's quarters. This adjutant could hear Polat addressing Nurettin loudly and angrily, though he couldn't make out the words. A quieter, more civil-sounding exchange followed. Then, this morning, Nurettin ordered his adjutant to make two platoons available to

Polat for whenever he should need them. Dr. Günsel adds, dryly, that according to his source Polat looks to be in excellent health and quite unbothered by the heat.

Kaya decides he will send the children back to Istanbul early, as a precaution. It turns out to be impossible. All flights for the next few days—summer's-end holidays—are sold out. For some minutes he feels vexed and anxious, then decides that the impossibility of early departure is really a sign that it's not necessary and he should stop worrying. Polat means to enter Varosha, certainly, but not just yet. There's still time to find a solution or let one suggest itself.

The night before Victory Day, Kaya sends another note to the villagers, asking them to continue to lie low. If the situation changes in any way, he will notify them at once. Later that evening—Ali having retired to his prayers and the rough campaign-cot he insists on, Hava and Yil in their rooms at their computers—he chauffeurs himself up the shore to the Palm Beach Hotel, where Filiz, back from Izmir, will be belly-dancing for the holidays. A kilometre south of the hotel he stops under a palm tree by the perimeter fence. The moon, a few days beyond full, is blistering up out of the sea. From under the driver's seat he takes that boxboard love letter to the ruins and wrists it hard over the fence, beyond a heap of cinder blocks and other refuse.

He watches Filiz perform her last set while sipping two Keo beers. It's good to be away from the club, the seat of his worries. Her body, almost chubby, yet supple and sleek and seething with vigour, stiffens his cock, while her artistry makes his eyes sting and his throat swell up. No. It's mastery. Mastery of any kind is moving. This huddle of sunburned Russians and English don't see it; they whistle crudely, expecting her to strip naked. They didn't realize she would only be dancing. But such dancing! It occurs to Kaya that he has never mastered anything in his life—he has skimmed glibly and cheerfully over the surface of his days. This thought tugs at him for a good three or four seconds, then he reverts to his pleasure, his escape from worry.

At midnight he drives her back down the beach under the rising moon, she with her eyes closed and head thrown back to drink in the night.

At 0600 hours Colonel Aydin Polat leads two platoons in full battle gear toward the old U.N. checkpoint on the north side of Varosha. By an ill-maintained guard hut, before the rusty gate in the perimeter fence, he calls a halt and addresses the men. It's an auspicious moment to launch such a mission, he explains: sunrise on Victory Day, the ninetieth anniversary of the Nationalist Army's crushing defeat of the Greek invaders at Dumlupinar, "After which, as you know, Mustafa Kemal founded our republic and later became—as you know—became Atatürk—the father of our nation . . ." Addressing a group is no easier for Polat than it ever was, even if he is a hero now. But for once his delivery is not too loud. He's subduing his voice almost to a whisper because of the way his speech is echoing, the echoes overlapping, mounting in volume. Forty-two slack faces gape at him from under helmet rims. He explains again that they will be searching out and uprooting "probable intruders—probably armed," yet the men look as if they think he's still pretending, this mission a training exercise or war game. Their lieutenant—weary face, greying moustache, an unnaturally fleshy rump packed into combat trousers he probably hasn't donned in years—seems unable to hide his reluctance. Last night he told Polat, "There is no sign of life in that awful place, sir, believe me! The *albay* Kaya, he led us on a thorough search."

"I'm sure he led you very carefully," Polat said.

He'd tried and failed to reach the holidaying General Hüseyin but decided his plan could not wait; he must act before Kaya thought up some way to thwart him, charm others, or spirit away the intruders. This mission's results will more than justify ignoring his orders. Polat's soul recoils at disobedience, but he reasons that Kaya's commands are invalid because he is not a real colonel of the Turkish army. He is a charlatan and will very soon be exposed. Atatürk himself defied timid orders in Libya in 1913, fighting the Italians, a mere captain then, as Polat was on that mountainside in Kurdistan.

He leads the men south into Varosha, where the dense enveloping quiet begins to affect them, block by block, making them crouch lower, plant their boots with more care, bear their M4s more attentively. Very good. He wants them as ready as such inexperienced troops can be. They are soft, complacent. Nurettin and Kaya have made no demands on them at all. Among them are the four who drunkenly botched that confrontation with the Greek and the journalist on the beach.

Polat has no doubt that he will be seeing this Greek before the sun is high.

He halts them beside a gutted restaurant—you would think a terrorist bomb had blown out the plate glass facade and atomized the interior—and consults an old street map, along with an internet printout of a satellite view. These streets, weedy and shattered yet walkable, should show up better on the printout, but the effect is of a catastrophic blurring, as if someone took a bird's-eye image of a city and all but erased its grid, all linearity, all civic order. Several blocks do look less fuzzy, but who can say what that indicates? A cluster of more durable buildings? A cobblestone square that has held up better than asphalt? A patient man might petition the army to create a high-resolution satellite image to reveal clear signs of habitation, but not Polat. Polat smells blood—mainly Kaya's. He expects he will find the intruders living in the small wilderness south of Varosha, near the zone's only hill, or perhaps in an area just north of the main church and square—an area that he and the men are now approaching.

They enter a minor square not unlike the one where he collapsed last autumn. He pulls back the slide on his Yavuz to cock it. The snap echoes and a flight of pigeons erupts off the mottled dome of a chapel. A monster cat, something writhing in its jaws, darts into an alley. The scouts are at ten o'clock and two o'clock; they glance at Polat; he waves them forward. Even the waddling lieutenant looks uneasy, although he still hasn't drawn his pistol.

The long shadows of dawn lie stretched over the cobbles. High up, the alarmed pigeons swirl in tight, frantic patterns, round and round, and he curses them in his heart. Lit violet by the sun they're as conspicuous as a warning flare. Faster now he leads his men around a prehistoric-looking tower of pear cactus and down a high-walled lane that appears to open into another square a hundred metres ahead. He pauses, consults his map, nods firmly and notices—as he noticed on that pine mountainside in April—that the pulse pumping in his ears is not speeding up as he approaches the crisis but rather slowing down. *You were born for this, like the young Kemal in Libya. The captain they idiotically discounted. You will overcome them all.*

With a scout at either shoulder, his pistol poised, he leads the men out into an open area, a wide roundabout that must have been one of the hubs of the living city. And he sees it, he knew it, this is a living place still! There is order here. Ahead on the large traffic island, a lush little grove flooded by sunrise, blobs of colour among the leaves, oranges or some other fruit. On the northeast side, a large-pillared neoclassical structure that might once have been a museum, its facade clean, its front steps free of debris.

"*Albay*," the lieutenant whispers, drawing his pistol, "where are we? I've never seen this place!" And a scout: "Sir? I think I just saw a man and a dog!"

"Of course," Polat says hoarsely, signalling everyone down

and squinting across at the grove and beyond it, his heart full, tears prickling his eyes. "Of course you did."

Kaya wakes to four knocks on the door, each sharper than the last. "*Ne, ne*—what is it?" he mumbles. Then he recalls. Filiz lies beside him. Ali was to summon her at 8:00 A.M., well before the children emerged from their rooms, and drive her back to the hotel. But it seems earlier than 8:00, the band of light above the curtains soft yellow. He gets up, crosses the Persian carpet and opens the door, naked. Ali was about to knock again—his arm and fist are upraised. In the hallway's gloom his cascading grey moustache glows dimly, but the rest of his face is shadowed.

"Forgive me, *efendi*, it's early."

A mere moment passes but already Kaya's eyes have adjusted enough to read the features of this man he has known for so long. "Oh, no," he says.

"Shots are being fired, *efendi*. Many shots."

"From the direction of the village?" Kaya asks, as if he doesn't know the answer.

"I am at your disposal, sir, as always. Shall I get my pistol?"

Kaya tries to unjumble his thoughts. In the pit of his stomach a hummingbird flitters. He has had maybe three hours' sleep after a night of dedicated lovemaking and many shared glasses of retsina. His mouth tastes like turpentine.

He steps out into the hallway and pulls the door softly to. "All right, listen. What we'll do is . . . What I'll do is wake her, *Bayan* Filiz. You'll take her up to the hotel, then return here. I'll have the children ready to go. You'll drive them back up the beach and . . . No. Wait. Take her and the children at the same time. Yes. It doesn't matter now if they meet. There's no time for two trips. I'll give you a thousand—no—two thousand lira. Drop Filiz at the hotel, then drive on to the airport. Get the children onto a flight today. The flights are full but there might be cancellations. If not, offer a bribe—three hundred or so. It might work. If not, get them a room in the airport hotel, get one for yourself, and stay there with them until their flight goes on the 1st. By then, it should be all right for you to come back. I'm the one in trouble, I'm the one responsible—the note I leave will make that clear."

"The note, *efendi?*" Ali's mouth, usually hidden by his moustache, hangs open.

"Ah, no, not that kind of note!" Ali's concern touches Kaya to the roots of his being. "Don't worry, my friend! Death is nothing I would ever choose. Death will have to hunt me down." Kaya has never before addressed Ali as "friend," *arkadash,* and he wonders if the old soldier will see it as a breach of decorum, but Ali's expression of concern and affectionate loyalty remains fixed.

"*Efendi,* what will you do?"

"I really don't know."

"You have made no plan?"

"Plan?" Kaya repeats with a helpless grin. Then he takes a deep breath: "All right. Wake the children now. No, wait. I'll do it. I need to tell them goodbye."

He slips back into the room, opens the curtains and the balcony door. The sun is low over a sea as placid as a pond. In his head, a voice he doesn't recognize murmurs, *This could be your last sunrise, look well.* Filiz's eyes open. She smiles in her shy-seeming way and stretches her arms out toward him, bracelets jingling. He would like nothing better now than to fall onto the bed and slide in between those plump arms and sturdy thighs, but he says, "Forgive me. Something has happened. I have to go wake up the children. You need to get up too."

"Really? What time is it? Can't it wait a few minutes?"

Seeing her gloriously nude and illuminated by the sunrise he feels his blood diverting even now. He makes for the bed, that muddle of sheets and pillows and pillowy flesh, his prick filling.

Then he hears through the balcony door an unmistakable sound.

"What's that?" she asks. "Not holiday fireworks, so early?"

"No." He leans over the bed, grazing her lips with his, kissing her cheekbone where the heavy kohl has smudged. "Forgive me. Get up now and dress."

In his silk robe he hurries up the hallway and wakes each child with a kiss—Hava on the sunburned scalp where her hair parts, the scent there like honey and walnuts, the way her scalp smelled in infancy. Is he imagining it?

"You have to get up, my love."

"Is something wrong, Baba? You smell funny."

"Hurry, Hava. And remember, girl, I love you very much."

Yil he kisses on the boy's pimpled cheeks and brow, just under the close-cut widow's peak, the skin dewed with the sweat of deep slumber. To wake him he has to jostle him. The dark eyes open but they're blank, unseeing. Now they fall closed. He's snoring again. Ali will have to re-wake him, more decisively than Kaya can bear to. He calls Ali up, gives him a bundle of banknotes and a few last instructions, then rises onto his toes to kiss the dry hollows of the man's cheeks.

In his room, Filiz is sitting at the foot of the bed, dressed, her nightbag in her lap, her scrubbed face pale and—without its stage makeup—somehow vague, unfocused. She looks bewildered and hurt, as if he's rejecting her. Oh, he thinks, nothing could be further from the fact.

"Are those gunshots? What's happening, Colonel?"

"I'm Erkan. If ever I was a colonel, I'm not now. Please go downstairs and wait for Ali. He'll take you back to the hotel. For your own safety, please. I can't explain now."

"What do you mean? What about you?"

"Don't worry about me. And to be honest, you won't—you won't want to—not after what you'll be hearing soon."

"If you're in trouble, let me help!"

"And it'll be best for you if you tell nobody that you've spent these nights here."

Her face goes to stone. "You're ashamed because I'm a dancer!"

"No—not at all! I fear you're the one who will feel ashamed. Listen, there's no time now. You have to go back. Just know at least that there was nothing false in . . . in what you and I . . ." He pulls her to her feet, kisses her one last time. "Forgive me."

In his closet he freezes again, his hand in the pants drawer, clutching a pair of army-issue camouflage trousers. He looks left at the tall mirror, as if the man reflected there could advise him. He seems to be developing a slight paunch. Bad time for that. He drops the uniform and from the civvies side of the drawer takes a pair of dark slacks. From his shirt rack he picks a crisp, brilliant white shirt he has never worn and a lightweight black blazer so he'll have an inside pocket for the pistol. Italian leather shoes, wristwatch, wallet with passport, aviator sunglasses, cigarettes and lighter.

He sits at the table by the balcony door, flips open his laptop, two-fingers a brief note addressed to whoever will be arriving here to arrest him, probably this afternoon, maybe sooner. He hears the Jeep starting up and growling away up the beach. Then more of those popping shots. The officers' club accounts are kept in several large files and he deletes them, along with all of his emails, though he gathers that such things can be retrieved by experts. Well, so be it. He returns to the first screen and rereads his note. It's awkwardly phrased and spiked with typos, but at the same time devoid of hypocritical apologies or protestations of shame and regret.

At a quick jog he crosses his beloved tennis court and slips through the hidden gap in the fence. He allows himself no last look behind. Now here is that broad, apocalyptic avenue, John F. Kennedy, and Kaya is running up the middle, as if back on the football pitches of his boyhood. He's dodging the oxidized carcasses of cars, unruly tamarisks, ramparts of prickly pear. Adrenalin should be aiding him more than it is—his legs feel bloodless and weighted and he's panting through his parched mouth.

He cuts northwest along a side street, toward the Jaguar gate and the village. If he didn't know the way, he could just follow the rattling of the gunfire. The weapon in his breast pocket jounces awkwardly, so he takes it out and grips it. A window of the Cyprus Popular Bank is intact and though it's dusty, grimy, the sunlight is direct enough that for a flash a man appears there, clean-jawed, smartly dressed, holding a pistol as he runs. Absurd. It's the British film character James Bond. If only Kaya felt now as 007 always seems to feel, the way Kaya himself has usually felt: vigorous, cool, and unkillable.

Elias comes to on a beach at sunrise among wandering turtles and realizes it was a dream, all a dream. The soldiers from the bar attacked him and Eylül and they shot her (the reports still hammer in his ears) and they beat him savagely and left him for dead, and in the course of one short night he has dreamed all of the past year: his escape, his time in the village, Roland, Kaiti Matsakis and the twins, everything.

There is no Kaiti Matsakis, no child in the womb.

He wakes, reaches, feels in the dark. The very pregnant Kaiti lies beside him, breathing. Shots are ringing in his ears—no, not ringing, the shots are faint, but for him clear enough to have triggered a nightmare and then ripped him out of it. He leaps up in his boxer shorts, his heart hurtling. He stumbles out the bedroom door into the hallway, opens the front door. Shots are coming from the direction of the well. He runs back into the bedroom and pulls on blue jeans and an undershirt. No time for shoes, laces.

"Kaiti? Get up."

"*Ti einai, agapi?*"

"Finish packing the bags. Stay inside till I come back. Ten minutes."

His feet sinking into the Tombazos' vegetable patch, he pounds a fist on their bedroom shutters and calls, "*Ksypniste tora, tora!*" He runs around the corner. The gate of the inn swings open and Roland staggers out into the sunrise, red-eyed, his hair on end, one side of his face more creased than the other. He's trying to tuck in his faded blue U.N. shirt.

Elias says, "Stratis, up at the well?"

"It must be, *ja*, it was his watch. Argos must be with him. Listen—the guns have stopped!" But a moment later they start up again. Elias sets out running toward the well and the library, Roland plodding and panting behind him. The shots are from assault rifles—he knows that heavy thudding, *fump fump fump*—punctuated now and then by a handgun's slighter report. His sight and hearing have gone hyperacute and yet his body feels numb, as if he's about to faint, as if he half wants to. Because of Kaya's note, he was on watch until 2:00 A.M., Roland from 2:00 until 4:00, Stratis after that.

They approach the well and hear shouting and barking along with the gunfire, and from above the alley where they run, the buzzing flight of shots fired much too high. No way to know why soldiers might have come in here, but it's obvious that they're green, or just scared. Elias knows the feeling. Maybe it's not too late to stop this. From the mouth of the alley, he and Roland peer out across the very wide traffic circle. Library on the northeast side. In the centre, the old traffic island where the well is tucked into that dense little orchard. Somewhere in there Stratis's pistol cracks and Argos barks in support, or imitation. The rifles return fire from the far side of the traffic circle, from behind scrapyard cars and taxis, from the mouths of alleys, from behind the pillars of the library.

On the library steps a figure lies and Elias's sight is telescopic: the helmet tipped forward over the face, blood pooling and running down the steps, the uniformed body slack and abandoned. So it is too late to stop this. Other helmeted men flit along the edge of the circle, from one car to the next, moving to surround Stratis. He must realize it's happening—the pincers spreading open. Maybe he doesn't care. "Strati!" Elias calls and the name leaps out of him, shockingly loud. "They're surrounding you—come back!"

Argos emerges between two trees on the near side of the traffic island. He stops, glances back into the grove, looks across again toward Elias and Roland. He sniffs the air, wags his tail, barks frantically. It's maybe twenty metres across the ring road to them.

"Hurry, come now!" Elias yells. "Argo—Strati!"

"I understand none of this," Roland says in a small, shattered voice. "Something has happened to poor Kaya, I fear."

A bullet slices through the leaves and fells a branch glinting with cherries. Argos canters out from under the boughs and makes for Elias and Roland. On the far side of the traffic circle the Turks continue spreading in both directions, their arc now over ninety degrees, and on the west side an officer stands, no camouflage, no helmet, disdaining to crouch or dart for cover like his men—barely moving at all. He looks short and gym-fit and wears a peaked cap and (it's hard to be sure from here) sunglasses or spectacles that reflect the low sun. Something familiar about him.

Argos reaches the mouth of the alley and stops there, wriggling his backside with joy and relief, though in fact still exposed to the shooting. Roland merely pets Argos's trembling head—Elias has to seize the dog's scruff and haul him into the alley. Bullets fizz overhead, each sounding like a match struck into flame. One hits the corner of the wall and concrete chips shower down onto Roland's hair. He doesn't notice.

"Roland, are you all right?"

The man looks at him blankly, as if the crisis has aged him into dementia in minutes.

Stratis appears between the cherry trees, revolver in one hand and semi-automatic in the other. He wears his beret and his torn, mended paratroop gear, combat boots, all of it from the time of the first Turkish invasion. So this is fate for him, full circle. He lopes out into the road and then, halfway across, where he's no longer sheltered by the grove but exposed to the rifles at either end of the firing line, he turns and walks backward, holding his pistols out to northwest and northeast, though not firing. Is he out of bullets? The soldiers have taken cover but the officer remains in the open, maybe eighty metres off, pointing at Stratis, snapping orders. The rifle fire increases but seems no more accurate, until a round strikes sparks from the paving stones behind Stratis's heels.

He backs into the alley. Without looking at either of them he says, with a kind of ferocious glee, "Did I not tell you two *poustes* they would come! Now hurry back, take everyone under, into the tombs."

"Tombs? What are you talking about?"

"Catacombs," Roland says vaguely. "Under the church. I never told you."

"I will hold them off here. Go now. I'll give you time, maybe twenty minutes. I've reloaded and have four extra rounds. In the Turkish gun are maybe seven rounds—here, one of you take it to protect the others."

"I will not shoot a man," Roland says flatly, seeming to snap awake at last.

"Maybe you could shoot your handsome catamite, Kaya! You see in the end how he betrays us!"

"No," Elias and Roland say together, Elias adding, "Come back with us, Strati. It's hopeless here. We'll run south and cross over the Green Line, down where—"

"Down where Roland took Myrto across?"

"Look, this isn't the time to—"

"You think the old ones can even walk so far? And Neokli? You think the Turks won't overtake them, and all of you?"

"You can't hold them off here, not this many."

"I have hit three, maybe four!" He bares his teeth, his hairy nostrils flare, the whites of his eyes shine. "And here is the one place where they can be held!" Leaning his head and shoulder out of the alley he aims the semi-automatic but holds his fire. "That Turk we found, all but dead of the heat? He is here, that's him now!" (Ah, of course.) "He won't hide himself. Yet I keep missing, even with his own weapon." Stratis has raptor-sharp eyes, a non-reader's eyes, but it's too far for an aimed pistol shot. He fires, then spits explosively. "*Ghamise to, moreh!* I told you we shouldn't save him!"

"But you're happy now that we did," Elias blurts in English.

"*Ti?*"

"*Tipota.*" Nothing.

Stratis shoves the semi-automatic at him, very new, black and burnished. Elias watches his own hand grip the barrel, burning hot, no pain.

"*Pai!*" Stratis says. *Go!*

"All right, but in a few minutes you should back down this alley and find a new spot to—"

"You and the devil can write it on my ass! I've planned fighting retreats through these streets a thousand times, a thousand different paths. I am ready. Now hurry to the tombs—there are supplies, a plan, Roland will tell you!" They start out and he roars after them, as if cursing them, "*Katevodhio!*"—*God speed you*—and then his high, ecstatic chanting pursues them down the alley, an old Cretan war song he used to quaver while working, *God gives us this hour to kill, to die, to live on in the songs of those we love.*

The two men and the dog retrace a path marked by a few bloody footprints and Elias sees they're from his own bare feet, his body anaesthetized by shock. Back through the labyrinth of lanes, the battle sounds muffled. Stratis is right: the Tombazos can't flee, would never reach the Green Line ahead of the soldiers. And Kaiti, eight months pregnant, and the twins? As he and Roland stop at the courtyard gate, he says, "Maybe it's best—safest—just to surrender?"

"*Ja,* but for one problem."

"What? I mean, they can't just shoot us all." He frowns down at the gun he holds. "And you're a German citizen, I'm Canadian."

Too winded for words, Roland stares intently, urging him to understand.

"Right. I'm not thinking. We're already dead."

"Just so."

"We don't exist, so they can do what they want with us—I mean, if they—"

"If they choose. And Kaya did say there was a grave problem. I fear he must mean this officer—he has returned for us."

"Maybe Stratis was right. We should have left him."

"Why speak of what was never a choice, not of your nature nor mine?"

As Elias runs around the corner, he shoves the pistol into the back of his jeans. In his panic, magical thinking overtakes him. He never deserved these last eight months. He always knew it. The gate of the Tombazos' small courtyard is open and he can hear the old couple arguing, Neoklis sobbing. He crashes in through the door of Kaiti's house, his house now too, and calls, "*Prepei na pame!* We have to go!" In the bedroom Kaiti sits on the edge of the made bed with the long-haired twins on either side, their feet in their Sunday shoes not reaching the floor. Rucksacks on their backs, the button-eyed face of a stuffed lamb sticking out of Lale's. They peer up at him, their mouths loose. Under Kaiti's huge green eyes, dark crescents. Her belly bulges inside a tan cotton frock made forty years ago for a woman of ampler build.

"This all started with my arrival," he says.

She raises her hand, juts her chin. "Not another word. Must we go now? Are Stratis and Roland . . . ?"

He explains what is happening in simple English, over the

twins' indignant protests, *Tell us, tell us in Greek!* While he speaks, he pulls socks onto his torn-up feet, jams them into running shoes, puts on a shirt. He can feel the pulse even in his eyes. She closes the shutters and gets the twins out into the hallway. He picks up the heavy carpet bag and sees Roland's manuscript on the bedside table, a glob of candle wax adhering to the top page like a seal. He opens the bag and stuffs it in.

Roland and the dog are outside waiting as Kaiti, the twins, and Elias emerge. Roland holds a lantern. No luggage. Funeral face. The Tombazos stand at the gate of their courtyard, arguing in Cypriot dialect. Elias gets the gist of it; Kaiti sends the twins back into the house for more candles so they won't hear. Stavroula is urging that the family flee and hide from the Turks under the church, while Takkos is refusing to abandon the house that he built with his own sweat and blood and spit. He refused back in '74 and he refuses again now. Let the Turks kill and bury me here if they will, why should I leave after standing my ground for so long? Why should you? Let us stay here together! The others will take Neokli down into the *katacombi*. We can't leave our chickens, our doves, the bees . . .

Stavroula cuts in, "No use arguing with a fool. Stay if you insist, an old man with a few blunt kitchen knives against the Turkish army!"

The fighting, heard from out here in the open, sounds louder, and seems to be approaching, as if Stratis is now in retreat, down to his final shots. Kaiti runs back into the house and comes out dragging the twins by their hands. A few more candles. Elias thrusts them into the bag. He keeps his body angled face-on to Kaiti so she doesn't see the gun. Now Stavroula and the tearful Neoklis join them—he lurching along with his tiptoe gait, his chessboard folded under his arm and shirt pockets bulging with pieces—and the group sets out for the plaza, ten minutes to the south. Nobody says a word about Takkos. Stavroula carries only a small nightbag. Her paisley headscarf is dark with sweat and her breath comes heavy and ragged. She holds Neoklis's hand. She wears her slippers and, over her housedress, an apron.

"Why didn't you tell me about the catacombs?" Elias asks Kaiti in English. He's walking at the back, switching the heavy carpet bag from hand to hand. Kaiti carries a smaller bag and the sack of film. The sun-brown ovals of her calves flex like an athlete's, though her sandalled feet are swollen, a much older woman's.

"Because I hate underground," she says. "Places like a cave. I hate the—how do you call it—*nikhteridha*, night-winger?"

"Bats."

"I didn't like to think of going. Roland agrees, it is not safe."

The plaza is visible ahead, at the end of the street. From behind them, echoing, a slap of shoes on the paving stones. He grips the handle of the pistol at the small of his back and looks behind. It's Takkos, advancing at a bow-legged jog, cradling a fat pigeon and holding a chicken upside down by the feet. He wears dark slacks, a black shirt with no lapels, his porkpie hat. The fugitives stop while he catches up and Neoklis embraces him in his distinctive way, bent low, grappling him around the waist like a wrestler and pressing the side of his face against his chest, next to the pigeon, while the old man holds the flapping chicken clear.

"You will want someone who can perform the mass down there," Takkos announces, kissing the bald patch on the head of his son, not meeting anyone's eyes. "It's not very far from the house," he adds. "We are not abandoning the house."

"Of course not," Stavroula says.

They enter the sun-filled plaza. The dead topiary tree is vibrating, chittering with starlings. As they head for the church, three crows lift hawing off the dome and Stavroula makes the sign of the cross . . . Quickly now into the cool and dim interior, where Roland urges everyone toward the back, but Elias halts in the doorway and looks outward, listening. The shooting has stopped. Is Stratis dead, then? Now comes another sound—running steps. The villagers' murmuring recedes behind him into the depths of the church as he squints out across the plaza, the sun in his eyes. And a man appears, dashing into the plaza from a side street—white shirt, blazer, sunglasses, like a bodyguard running beside a motorcade limousine. It can only be Kaya—yet he isn't coming from the direction of the officers' club, more the direction of the village. For a second Elias wonders if he *could* be involved in this invasion and is actually pursuing the villagers (he has a pistol in hand, it's now clear). No, impossible. Now Elias notices motion in the next lane over, parallel to the one Kaya is emerging from. It's Stratis, he too running into the plaza. The lane is narrow—a good choice to delay pursuers. The Turkish troops are still out of sight, but just before Stratis enters the plaza he pivots to face backward, holding his revolver out with both hands. Nothing. He turns to lope forward again. He's going to spill out into the plaza just seconds after Kaya. Elias is paralyzed in the church doorway. He glances behind him into the gloom but his eyes, after facing the sun, can see nothing. He turns back, opens his mouth to shout a warning to Kaya, feels pressure at the base of his spine—the pistol. He spins back around.

"Kaiti! Jesus Christ, I thought—"

"You didn't tell me about the gun."

"It's Kaya," he whispers.

"What about him? Don't hide these things from me, Trif, I've been here longer than . . . what, is that *him*?"

"Kaya!" he gets out, just as the two men with their handguns, the Greek in his old uniform and the Turk in his civvies, see each other. Having heard Elias's shout, Kaya looks over. Stratis too sees Elias and Kaiti in the church doorway, then looks back at Kaya. The two men stand about thirty paces apart. Kaya points his gun down at the pavestones, raises an open hand, utters words in a soothing tone. Unfortunately they must be in Turkish. Kaiti's fingernails dig into Elias's wrist. She too must be imagining Stratis's thoughts: it's the colonel, he's running from the direction of the village, maybe to head me off, maybe to catch the villagers, and he's hiding in a coward's uniform, the civilian garb of a spy. Raising his pistol like an executioner he strides toward Kaya. "*Stamata!*" Kaiti screams and the scream echoes, "Strati, *ochi!*" Elias can't make a sound now, afraid he might startle Stratis, who halts a few steps short of Kaya and aims point-blank at his forehead. Kaya—hand still raised, pistol pointed down—continues to blather, as if the Turkish words might somehow get through. The Greek's revolver twitches. Kaya flinches and stumbles backward but no gunshot comes, just a faint click. Stratis curses, rolls his head, aims again, *click click click*. He flings the revolver down and throws himself at Kaya, hands stretched out as if to throttle him. Kaya shuffles backward. He raises his own pistol but is still showing that placatory palm, still talking, louder now, trying English, "Okay, please, please not, okay!"

Elias jerks his arm free of Kaiti's grip and runs out into the plaza, drawing the Turkish pistol out of his belt. This adrenal spike feels like a heart attack, or a dream of one. He glances straight up the lane Stratis just came down. There's movement, figures nearing, though still some way off and not running, it seems, maybe creeping along, fearing ambush. Elias can't tell if the little officer is there. Maybe Stratis finally got him.

He stops in front of the two men. Kaya—his pistol trained on Stratis—gives Elias a desperate look. His sunglasses are gone. Sweat gleams on his forehead and drips off his chin. "Trif, please to say him in Greek," he starts but can't seem to find the English words. Stratis says in Greek, "Now give me back that pistol and I will kill him! A Turkish pistol—God's justice. Now do you see that he's our Judas?"

"Come into the church," Elias says. "Kaya too. The Turks are almost here."

"The Turks *are* here and this is their leader!"

"You're wrong."

Kaya looks back and forth between them. Stratis holds out his hand to Elias, steps toward him, his boot crunching Kaya's sunglasses. Elias backs up and aims at Stratis, though the pistol is still uncocked, the safety on.

"What in the devil's ass . . . give it to me now!" Stratis says.

A shot echoes out of the lane where the soldiers are. "*Elia!*" Kaiti calls from the church doorway, "*grigora!*"

"Come now or I'll shoot you," Elias lies.

"*Ghamisou!* You're too scared to shoot the Turk and now you would shoot me?"

Elias slips the safety, racks the slide and fires into the air. Starlings erupt out of the dead tree with an incendiary whoosh.

"Idiot! Stop it!"

"Now, or I'll waste every round." He aims upward again.

"All right, all right!" Stratis cries, hands raised in horror, then turns and stamps away toward the church.

"You come too," Elias tells Kaya in English. "You're in trouble, right?"

"Pardon? Oh, yes—I am in trouble."

Stratis and then Elias and Kaya cross the plaza to the church doorway, where Kaiti stands beckoning and pointing toward Stratis's lane: here comes the little officer, walking calmly up the middle. Men are clumped behind him to either side, crouched low as they follow, guns pointed, bayonets fixed. "*Pai, pai!*" Elias yells. Right ahead of him Stratis is glaring off toward the enemy, his bloodshot eye in profile seeming to bulge out of the socket. His shoulder twists round, his right hand sweeps back as if to strike Elias but instead seizes the barrel of the pistol and rips it free. He grips the handle with his left and fires point-blank into Kaya's chest, then turns to face the soldiers and advances straight toward them. Elias grabs the sagging Kaya by the elbow and pulls him into the doorway of the church, shoving Kaiti inward while a crackling salvo funnels out of the lane. A last look: Sergeant Stratis Kourakis is pacing evenly into that focused hail, holding the pistol out in front of him. He might be singing as he fires, in the pure ecstasy of his hatred, though nothing can be heard over the shooting.

By the glow of a candle-lantern and a flashlight, they study the wallet that Elias has taken from a breast pocket of Kaya's removed blazer. Kaya sits on the stone floor of the underground gallery where they've stopped to rest. Shirt open to the navel, he's prodding a darkening spot on his hairless chest just above his right nipple. His small Turkish semi-automatic—the group's only weapon now—is tucked into his belt.

The fat wallet is neatly perforated, as are most of its contents: credit cards, a driver's license, military ID, a wad of Turkish banknotes, and the maroon passport that the wallet was folded around. It looks like an expired passport officially voided with a hole-punch. Elias extracts a misshapen wad of lead from the coin pouch—the part of the wallet that was nearest to Kaya's skin. Most of the coins are bent. One looks slightly melted.

He reinserts the black wallet into the jacket pocket and reaches a hand down to Kaya. "Can you walk on now?"

"Can I . . . ? Ah, of course."

Elias pulls him upright and gives him his jacket. "You were very lucky."

"I was . . . pardon?" A brilliant grin spills across Kaya's face. "Ah—lucky!"

Holding his lamp up like Charon, Roland leads them down the gallery. The walls and the low, rounded ceiling are of mortared stone. The gallery is not straight like a mine shaft but slightly winding; there are side chambers too dark to see into and, along the walls, niches packed tight with human skulls and bones. It's cool and dry. No moss or any growth on the walls or on the bones.

No cobwebs. Clearly Argos is coming along only out of fear of being left behind; his trembling tail all but brushes the floor. To Elias's surprise Neoklis and the twins seem less frightened than fascinated.

"But where is Uncle Stratis?" Neoklis asks again and the twins look behind them as if expecting to see him following. "You said he comes soon?"

"Still talking with the Turks," Stavroula says quickly, before anyone else can reply. "It might take a bit longer, my child. Their Greek is very poor."

For the first few centuries of its existence, the church was part of a Byzantine monastery—that much Elias already knew. Now Takkos explains that these *katacombi* hold the bones of thousands of monks but were also used, during the Ottoman occupation, as a place to take refuge from the Turks. When Takkos brought the five-year-old Neoklis down here in the early '70s, with a tour group from Athens, he could never have believed that the place might once again conceal fugitives from a Turkish attack, and that he and his family would be among them.

"You all right, my love?" Elias whispers to Kaiti.

"*Mia hara*," she says dryly, her lips hardly moving, her face set.

"No bats down here, I think," he says. "Nothing alive down here at all."

"And you, *agapi . . . endaksi*?"

"*Endaksi*," he says, maintaining a steadfast facade, like her, though in the wake of the violence he is numb at the knees, swept with tremors, his mouth dry.

The gallery opens into a wide, high, circular chamber, like a beehive tomb. Faint indirect daylight filters down through a hole in the summit of the dome. Elias shines a flashlight upward. Faded frescoes cover the dissolving plaster, the faces of saints and patriarchs mostly reduced to featureless ovals. Let into the walls of the domed chamber are doorless rooms in which he glimpses further niches crowded with bones and skulls. In the centre of the chamber's stone floor, a dangerous-looking hole that must be a well or cistern. On the other side, the gallery continues into darkness. Over its threshold an inscription in what might be black felt pen: ALICE & NIGELS HONEYMOON, LAST DAY THEN HOME 4/73.

Roland enters one of the side rooms and starts dragging out what must be supplies. Elias—seeing him pause, put a hand to his chest, struggle to cough—rushes to help him. They bring out bundles of sticks, two large plastic water containers, a loaded burlap sack, a heap of wool blankets, and a few unlabelled bottles—olive oil and wine. Takkos's pigeon settles into a less crowded ossuary niche. Stavroula rolls up her sleeves and bears the fussing chicken into one of the dark side rooms.

The hope is that the soldiers, after searching the church and not finding the catacombs' entrance—the stone lid of what looks like a bishop's sarcophagus—will assume the villagers must have fled through the small vestry door, suggestively left open. It will seem they must be hiding in the ruins or have fled southward. If the villagers stay down here long enough, the Turks should give up looking. Then they can emerge by way of the catacombs' other entrance in the cemetery, a kilometre south of the church.

By lamplight Kaiti and the twins create a nest of blankets in one of the side rooms. The ossuary niches are at chest level, and on the ledge of one of them Kaiti sets a candle and a roll of toilet paper, having pushed the skulls and bones farther back—no easy task with these niches so crammed. But she and Elias manage to fix things so that no skulls will actually be grinning down at the twins when they're trying to fall asleep.

The forehead of each yellow skull is inked with a sepia inscription. Elias shines a flashlight on one of them: a paragraph of some twenty crabbed lines. He is too shaken and weary to try making out the tiny Cyrillic. Roland and Kaiti are at his shoulders now,

Roland whispering in Greek, "Takkos says that they wrote every monk's story on his brow, so that even in death you would have to live with what you'd done."

"I wonder if some monks settled scores that way?" Kaiti asks.

"Monks especially, I should think. Trif, I realize that my history—my manuscript—it's probably not . . ."

"No, I brought it. It's safe."

"Safe is a relative term, I suppose."

Aslan and Lale are peering up. They want to hold the skull. "You have to share," Elias says absently, absurdly, handing it down to them. "Elia!" Kaiti scolds him, and in fact the twins are already squabbling over it, four hands gripping, tugging. The quarrel turns abruptly, tearfully ferocious. "*Sout!*" Kaiti says. "Not a sound! Give it back to me now!" At the same moment Elias, trying to help, hands down a second skull. Lale takes and holds this other skull, gazing earnestly into the eyeholes, while Aslan turns the first one in his hands like a schoolroom globe. Kaiti now shrugs and looks away, the twins' distracted silence too much of a relief to disrupt.

Hours later, after the light in the hole in the summit of the dome has weakened and vanished, Elias and Kaiti light a small fire in the ancient firepit beside the well and begin roasting the spitted chicken. Roland lies on his back on a blanket as if peacefully asleep, though his hands are both fisted on his belly, his brow clenched. The Tombazos have been asleep for several hours, like the twins, but now the smell of the fire and the roasting meat brings Stavroula barging out of one of the bone rooms in her apron, ready to take over.

Kaya is on watch, sitting on a folded blanket at the entrance of the domed atrium, facing back toward the church. He has the pistol. He offered it first to Roland, who said, "Must I continually refuse these things? I do not want it!" Then he tried Elias, who said unhappily, "Why don't we share it, on our watches?" Now as Elias pulls the rag stopper from a bottle of wine, Kaya—on some hedonist intuition, as if a cork has popped loudly—glances back, stubs his cigarette on the floor, gets up and strolls over. He squats beside the coals. The prospect of food and drink seems to be coaxing colour back into his face. He nods to everyone; to Kaiti he also lifts one corner of his mouth, the ghost of a roguish leer. When Roland sits up and asks him something in Turkish, pointing to his chest, Kaya winces theatrically and then grins as if saying, There is pain, to be sure, but I will survive it!

Elias fills five small juice glasses with the wine. It's good to have something to do and others to do it for. He grips the bottle hard to disguise his hand's trembling. The others seem too benumbed for a toast, but he calls out "*Stin zoi!*", then translates the words into English, for Kaya's sake: "To life!" "To Strati," Stavroula says, "for holding the Turks at bay once again." She adds, "Forgive me, Colonel," as if he can understand her Greek. The five drink to Stratis. Stavroula turns the chicken, drizzling it with oil, the coals beneath it snapping into flame. As if talking to himself Roland mutters, "I suppose any army would wish its troops to consist all of men who have just been spurned by their women. Farewell, my difficult friend!" Tears fill his eyes as he drains his glass.

A blood-congealing scream comes from the candlelit recess where the twins are sleeping. Kaiti claps a hand to her chest and leaps up, crying, "Lale *mou!*" Elias is already on the move. He and Kaiti together gather the shaking child into their arms as she looks around, sputtering. Aslan sobbing too. Elias lifts him into his lap. Kaiti kisses the girl with frantic tenderness, then asks Elias, "*Mia nikhteridha?*"

"No, I think just a dream—a night terror. I know them."

"She never has dreams like this! It's because you let them play with the bones!"

"*Ochi!*" he snaps back, the first time ever he has really lost his temper with her. "It was the day, obviously—the shooting, the fleeing. It's not dead people they need to fear—children know that better than anyone."

"Never assume you know my children better than I!"

"Stop at once!" Aslan commands in the tone of an adult whose patience is finally spent.

"We must be quiet," Takkos calls, emerging from the far recess, while behind him Neoklis in a possessed-sounding whisper echoes, "Must be quiet!"

The fugitives gather around the firepit and all of them, the twins included, sip the vile wine ("cellared for five years," Roland says, "and all the worse for it"). Kaya, his good teeth edged with sediment, gallantly praises the wine, but even he can find nothing kind to say about the water from the receptacles, which tastes of kerosene. Roland says it's actually preferable to the well water, which is a last resort. They devour the tender, smoky chicken, far too little for the group, and handfuls of almonds, raisins and sun-dried mespila. Each of them receives a rusk, an item that looks and feels like a hunk of dried sponge. Takkos loses a tooth to his rusk and gives up, tossing the rest to Argos, who even while devouring it goes on trembling as he has since coming underground.

Everyone goes to sleep except Roland, who says his rest has done him good and he wishes to take the first watch. Elias thinks he looks ghastly but says nothing, too exhausted to argue. He and Kaiti climb under a thin wool blanket with the twins. He spoons behind her, kisses her nape and whispers in English, "Sorry, beautiful."

"I am more sorry."

"More beautiful," he mumbles.

"Ti?"

"Nothing," he exhales, barely able to form the word. "Sleep."

In seconds he plummets into a state of utter cessation from which he emerges only when the dream begins, as he knew it would, his shade staggering through a maze that leads down into a sort of stadium lit up by floodlights, and here again is the olive grove, here again the "firefight" stuck on replay, the stench of opened bodies, and one in particular—Eylül Şahin beneath him now and shrinking fast, while a medic stands watching and says, "Chest compressions never really work, they just give bystanders something to do . . ." Elias shakes himself awake and gets up. Orients himself by the embers of the fire. Wrenches a candle stub off the lip of the niche, lights it with a match and slips out into the central chamber.

There in the spot where Kaya kept watch sits Roland, in his lap a pile of papers—his manuscript. He holds a skull close to the candle-lantern on the floor beside him and squints down through his reading glasses, a pencil in his other hand. Elias approaches. "Ah, Trif," he says without looking up. "I keep myself awake, you see. I have almost finished this one. Dimitrios returned to Christ at fifty-two, in 1834. He was an orphan and found a loving family here in the monastery. He knew Hebrew as well as Greek. He was well liked, except for his habit of provoking fights on his name-day, when he would take too much wine and become sad. He is missed by all, even his antagonists." He taps his wrist with the pencil, as if indicating a watch. "Go back to sleep, Trif. That was hardly an hour."

"I'm done for now. You go rest. Take care of that cough."

Surprisingly, Roland agrees right away.

Kaya takes the third watch. He is in pain, a rib cracked, he guesses, quite considerable pain when he breathes deeply, so he doesn't, but then every little while a hunger for air forces him to yawn and inhale. Still, these dagger jabs, along with the chill, help keep him alert. Maybe young Trifannis is also in pain? He seemed very alert when Kaya relieved him. Really this Trif, despite what he says about never wanting to fight again, seems quite soldier-like in some ways—or, maybe, like a man unknowingly, helplessly imitating a soldier. Kaya was not surprised to learn that his late father was in the military. Or was he a policeman? Kaya always has trouble recalling the details of other people's lives, though during the conversations when he hears those details he's the most interested listener in the world. His ex-wife was always shocked when somehow his forgetfulness was exposed; *but you seemed so interested when I told you!* Yes, and that interest had not been feigned . . . He wonders what poor Pinar will think when this story breaks. He hopes that the media won't bother her too much. *Erkan? Erkan Kaya is dead to me and has been since our divorce.*

His blazer is caped over his shoulders and he wraps it tighter around himself. How he dislikes this dark and chilly cellar, this glorified mass grave. He asked Roland, in Turkish, if this place had been a sort of dungeon—if delinquent priests were sent down here as punishment and left to rot. No, Roland said, they all lived above in the monastery. When they died, they were buried in shrouds so that the earth could eat their flesh, and a year later the bones would be exhumed and moved down here.

Though Kaya likes the Greeks well enough, he can't understand the horror-film quality of the Orthodox faith, which seems so unlike them: their places of worship gloomy inside, their icons depicting prophets who look more or less suicidal, and at the centre of it all an emaciated torture victim on a vertical rack, the blood gushing. Islam bewilders him too—the murderous hatred of rival sects, the inclination of fanatics to self-detonate in public places—but Islam's aesthetic is airy, spacious and bright, celestial instead of cavelike, bespeaking life and pleasure, not death. How he misses his seaside club already! As the day's adrenalin seeps away he can feel the encroaching heaviness of a future filled with, of all things, regret and nostalgia. Of course, to have a future you must first survive. He has almost died twice today, and third time decides the case, as the saying goes. May there be no third time! (Like most men, he would describe himself as unsuperstitious; like most men, he is superstitious.)

He seems to hear a sound from far up the gallery. He listens closely. Nothing. He butts out his second-last cigarette, then shrugs the blazer off his back and gets up, stifling a groan. He holds the Yavuz-16 in his right hand and in his left the old aluminum flashlight that Roland gave him. He leaves the candle-lantern on the floor. He starts up the gallery, walking softly, seeing his way by the increasingly dim candlelight from behind him. Now the gallery veers to the left and he's walking into the kind of darkness where shutting your eyes makes no difference. He flicks on the flashlight, casts the beam around. The gallery and intermittent bone chambers seem like sudden creations of the light itself, hallucinations that will cease to exist as soon as he thumbs off the switch, or the batteries die. A face leers out at him from the wall and he startles: a jovial-looking skull in its own private nook. On its brow a dense paragraph—a warning of some kind? It hits him that this place must be just how death actually does look and feel, if in fact one sees or feels anything. Silent, sunless, fleshless, wineless. Cremation is permitted in Turkey, unlike in stricter Muslim countries, and that's what he would prefer—to have his body burned and the ashes scattered on the beach at noon. But now his children spring back to mind; there must be no thoughts of death or dying, whatever the coming days might hold.

He wonders how much farther it can be to where the gallery ends, at the stone stairway they all climbed down, earlier, out of the church. Seems he has been walking for a long time, sweeping the flashlight from side to side, and he's starting to frighten himself, wondering if somehow he has erred into a secondary tunnel and won't find his way back. He cocks the Yavuz. Now the flashlight picks out the steep stairs, not twenty metres ahead. He aims the light slowly upward: each ancient step worn down, polished smooth in the centre. Above the top step, the light passes through a gap, up into the church. He stands staring. The stone lid that he and Trifannis slid closed has been dragged back open.

A short figure steps out of a recess in the gallery wall between Kaya and the stairway. Kaya gasps, then cries out in pain—his rib. The light beam glares off Aydin Polat's strap-on spectacles under his peaked cap. Polat holds his own pistol loosely at hip level, aimed at Kaya in an insouciant, almost playful manner, not like him at all. "Colonel Kaya! I suppose you must be fleeing your Greek captors?" His speech is unlike him too—relaxed, amused, almost suave. "Or do you have some better tale?"

Kaya's own phrase returns to him: *Death will have to hunt me down*.

"Lower the gun, Colonel Polat," Kaya says with little hope.

Polat's trimmed moustache widens slightly. Then, to Kaya's astonishment, the man does lower his gun, setting it down on the floor in front of his boots and saying, "There. Now we can discuss things. You won't feel so frightened."

"Frightened!" Kaya scoffs, as if Polat doesn't actually terrify him. "I've already been shot a number of times today."

"Well, it need not happen again," Polat says. "By the way, I recovered my stolen pistol"—he nods downward—"from the Greek soldier we killed outside the church. A brave old man. He will receive proper honours. There need be no more such violence."

Kaya nods, badly wanting to believe that all the violence is over. His pampered body is unaccustomed to pain, to such extreme weariness.

"We'll start by you putting *your* gun down," Polat says. "Or, better, handing it to me. And your flashlight."

"That would be premature," Kaya says. "Where are your men?"

"Some are waiting up in the church, some guarding the other exit from this, this . . ." He nods toward the recess he just stepped out of. "An underground cemetery, I suppose? So crowded! You'd think the Greeks would show their dead more respect. I was waiting in the dark there. You'd think it would be unpleasant, but it was actually quite peaceful."

"You must be getting used to the presence of the dead," Kaya says. "How many men did you lose today?"

Polat crosses his arms over his puffed-out chest but his voice remains steady, quiet: "Three killed, five wounded—two only slightly—all in the line of duty and in the course of a fully successful mission. Well, almost fully. Only one thing remains."

"I don't believe your men are blocking the other exit. You'd never find it in these ruins, and . . ." *Now I've admitted there's another exit,* Kaya sees. He is not thinking clearly. He is not thinking.

"I did careful research before launching this mission," Polat says.

"I don't believe it."

"I see you're in pain. Have you actually been shot?"

"Yes and no."

"I can help you. *We* can help you. This situation . . . certainly you won't go entirely unpunished, but if you help me—help me now—I'll see that you survive it. More than survive it! I can do that much and I will. Who knows? You might even be able to return to the officers' club, after some time."

"What do you want from me?"

"Just them. That's all." He steps forward. His boots now straddle the pistol on the floor. "Just lead me to them quietly."

"Stay where you are."

"You're not the sort of man to shoot someone, Colonel."

"*Evet,*" Kaya hears himself admit. *Yes.*

"We won't . . . they won't be hurt, these, these—these people you've been hiding—these Greeks, and the foreigner." Polat's speech is lapsing into its old patterns, jagged and jerky, a polygraph line warning *liar.*

"But how can I be sure you mean it?"

"I am a colonel of the Turkish army and a man of my word! For me, truth is a simple matter—not like for you."

"Truth 'a simple matter'?" Kaya can't keep the derision out of his laugh, but then he moans and brings the hand holding the flashlight to his cracked rib, so for a second the light shines straight up into his eyes. In a panic he aims the light back at Polat. The man's posture is identical, yet he seems to be a step closer.

"Give me the weapon," Polat says. "Lead me to them and I promise, you will not be destroyed."

Little lenses filled with light, pale eyes barely visible . . . Kaya scours Polat's face for any reason to believe him.

"Colonel Kaya, I know you. You're a gentle man—lazy—you enjoy life! I see no reason why that gentle, lazy life shouldn't continue—in due course. Simply do as I—"

"How could we possibly know each other? We're completely different!"

"I never said you knew me," Polat whispers excitedly. "You don't! Your kind doesn't know anyone. You don't have to—happy people don't have to—they—they—they live within themselves, happily! It's the others, it's men like . . . *we* understand *you*. We watch you—God, how we watch you!—we know you—and in the end, if we choose, we can . . . overcome you." He draws in a deep, ragged breath. "But it needn't happen."

Kaya's pain, ever worse, is blurring his vision in waves. Maybe he really has been hurt badly.

"You say I could actually return to the club, maybe?"

"I do have influence now. I will have even more, after this victory."

Some victory, Kaya thinks, while another zone of his mind pictures himself back on his tennis court, or lazing up on the rooftop with a litre of retsina in a bucket of shaved ice and maybe somebody beside him, yes, Filiz.

"And my children?"

"I would ensure that they'd be able to visit you, in the short term, and—and in due course, well, you'd be free to do as you wish. Colonel, you sound very weak. I think you need to sit down. Shall I call the medic?"

"I don't know what to do," Kaya hears someone murmur. It's himself. "Maybe it would be best for the villagers? They could be hurt down here. Or hurt if they flee. Or killed! A young woman is pregnant, one couple is old, and their son, he's—"

"I didn't want to mention such things, but, yes, I can't ensure their safety, not without your help. The foreigner is known to be a danger, and after today—my men are inclined to shoot first."

"And if I can't help—I mean, if I refuse?"

"Then we come in from both sides and—as I say—I can't promise . . ."

After what seems a full minute's silence Kaya, sickened, says, "Will you want to call a few of your men now, or . . . ?"

"No, no—it's fine—I'll come alone! No use scaring these trapped people. By the way—there are no more weapons down here, are there? I saw the old soldier seize the foreigner's pistol . . ."

"This is the only one now."

"Which you will now give to me?"

"You can pick up your own. I'll keep this one until I see that you mean to keep your word. And no pointing of guns at any of the villagers, you understand?"

The words are commanding but Kaya's voice has a pleading thinness, nothing beneath it. Polat says quietly, reasonably, "As you wish, Colonel."

His heart burdened, almost broken, Kaya guides Polat back up the gallery. Polat has turned on a flashlight of his own. To a sentry—if there were one—the approaching lights might resemble the two eyes of one creature, a single mind. Horrible thought. Then again, maybe Polat is not what he was before, maybe he has changed just a little, just enough, an aggrieved zealot made a little more human by success? It seems plausible. It has to, now. A muffled screech comes down the gallery and Polat jumps in his tracks. "One of the children," Kaya whispers. "She's been having bad dreams all night." *But I'm doing my best to keep her and all of them safe.*

He and Polat round a gradual turn in the passage. Ahead, a lamp glimmers at the entrance to the central chamber. Beyond it, the faint embers of a fire.

"We should turn off the flashlights," Kaya says. "So we don't startle them."

"Very well."

Darkness but for the weak glowing ahead. Then, for a second, something eclipses that glow. Something has entered the gallery. It seems to be sticking close to the wall. The dog? Kaya isn't sure if Polat has seen. But whatever is there must see him and Polat, since the two of them are approaching the light source. He hears somebody draw breath. Polat turns on his flashlight. It's the young Cypriote. She averts her face and hurries a hand to her eyes, squinting through her fingers. Her other hand covers her very pregnant belly. On some instinct, Kaya addresses her in English, though her Turkish is perfectly adequate (and her accent a delight). "Madam—why are you here?" The question has a guilty sound.

"The girl wakes me again. You were not in your place. I came to find you. Who is this? I can't see. Is it . . . ?"

"Lower the light," Kaya snaps at Polat in Turkish, "have you no manners?"

"Watch your tone," Polat says but complies.

". . . their officer, yes. I thought so. But—why do you bring him?"

"I am so sorry. His men are here. There must be no more dead." It's agony for Kaya not to explain himself fully in Turkish. He can feel the Cypriote's dawning comprehension and anger, and he hates being the object of bad feeling, especially on the part of a woman, yet some intuition still urges him, *No Turkish—don't let on that she knows Turkish!*

"So sorry," he repeats. "I wished to help. To save us all."

"Your*self* to save!" she hisses, stepping forward and swatting his face. The blow is far louder than their words. Polat whispers, "Tell this cunt to shut up and to keep her hands off you—you are a Turkish officer until you're officially drummed out!"

The Cypriote, understanding, turns to Polat and opens her mouth to speak, but Kaya cuts in: "Watch your tongue, *Albay*. I won't let you insult this woman."

"Ah, so that's *your* child in there? Or is it the foreigner's? Do you even know? Does *she* even know? "

"That's enough!"

"Take me to them now." Polat draws his Yavuz and aims it from the hip, more or less at Kaya's groin. "And give me your pistol." He keeps the flashlight fixed on Kaya. The woman and her belly hover in the penumbra alongside. "And let me add something—because the truth *is* simple, and I won't conceal it from you. I can protect you and the others, but not the foreigner. His fate is out of my hands." (Kaya can feel the Cypriote listening hard.) "He's already considered dead, and it will only cause injury to the Turkish republic and the army if we should . . . bring him back to life. I won't let that happen. Do you understand?"

"Then I won't help you."

"It's too late."

"*Anlıyorum!*" the woman says, *I understand!* Her hand darts out of the shadow toward Kaya. Seeing what she means to do, Kaya grabs the barrel of Polat's gun and twists it downward. She pulls Kaya's pistol from his belt, turns to Polat. She's bathed in light, as if Polat, struggling, is trying to fend her off with the only thing he has left, the flashlight. For a moment there's only this woman in a ring of radiance, her shaking hands holding a small pistol above her huge belly. Polat's pistol, held down by Kaya, fires. Pain pierces Kaya's foot like a driven stake. Maybe the crashing report shocks her into squeezing the trigger—she lets out a gasping cry—or maybe she does it on purpose. The muzzle flare blinds Kaya. He hears the clatter of the flashlight as it hits the floor, then the thump of Polat's body.

Kaya has survived a third attempt on his life. In the toe of his right shoe is a neat little hole. Around it, the Italian leather is already stiffening with blood. The bullet passed between the bones of his first and second toes, bruising both without breaking either. The searing pain intensifies by the minute. Still, when no soldiers come charging out of the darkness from the direction of the church after the thunderous shots, he accompanies Trifannis back along the gallery to the end, where they creep up the ladder-like stairway and peer out into the church: dark and silent, the front doors closed. So Polat was lying. His men must be asleep. He must have returned alone to the church to search further, or to follow some hunch.

Kaya and Trifannis shift the stone lid—not quite as thick or heavy as it appears from above—back into place.

They return and haul Polat's body into one of the bone chambers, where the spirits of the dead monks will haunt him forever (Roland tells Kaya that this is what the old woman is saying as she crosses herself yet again). By lamplight, Kaya can see that as Polat's face cools and pales, the faint old acne scars are showing clearer. Death is aging him backward into youth and boyhood. Before shrouding the corpse with a blanket, Kaya unstraps the blood-spattered glasses and slips them into a breast pocket of the tunic, where he finds a notice of decoration—Polat was to receive the Medal of Honour, first grade, at a ceremony in Ankara next month—and a photograph, mounted on a precisely cut square of stiff cardboard. "His wife and children?" Trifannis asks, barely audible. Kaya says that he had no wife, no children. He, Trifannis and Roland look closer in the weak light. The villagers' dog stands on the threshold of the chamber, growling from his gut. The

Cypriote can be heard nearby, soothing her children in a stricken voice broken by occasional sobs.

The image seems discoloured, as if tea-stained, a portrait of a head-scarved mother with a large nose, a blanched and pale-eyed father dressed like an extra in a historical film, two handsome lads with identical rakish smirks, and a small boy who must be Polat—that large head, the too-small glasses, yet grinning for all he's worth. Kaya shakes his head and whispers, "Like that, he never smiles." And Roland, nodding wearily toward a nook full of skulls: "He will again."

Time to get out and across the border. The mission was Polat's initiative, according to Kaya, and with him gone, it's unlikely the soldiers will know what to do. At the same time, as soon as they find out that he's missing, they will start searching, and by mid-morning, noon at the latest, the ruins and the church will be aswarm with troops. They might well find their way down into the catacombs. Even Takkos seems to understand there's no longer any choice. ("But maybe we can go back to the house before long?" he asks, in the way a child might, not wanting the truth but a postponement of the truth. And Stavroula indulges him.)

They enter the gallery on the south side of the domed chamber. They pass a dozen more recesses stocked with bones, after which the gallery narrows to a tunnel, the arched ceiling lowering and flattening until Elias, if not the others, has to stoop. Soon the way is so narrow that he can't hold the luggage out beside his knee but must cradle it high and close with one arm, carrying Aslan with the other. Kaya has taken Lale from Roland and is singing to her, a Turkish lullaby, his hushed voice thick with emotion. Aslan has wet himself. He's dozing, softly head-butting Elias over and over as he nods. Argos keeps scooting underfoot, as if terrified of being anywhere except among the villagers' knees. Elias has never kicked an animal in his life but now, tripped again, he does. At last

Kaiti with the flashlight picks out white stone steps, ladder-steep, where the tunnel ends. "*Dhoksa to Theo, i skala!*" she whispers.

They climb into an ungated crypt in the cemetery, beside the section used by the villagers over the years. As they emerge, Takkos's pigeon flees him on panicky wings. The moon is down but the Milky Way is so densely luminous it seems to cast shadows. Argos trots over to a cross in a raked mound of earth and sniffs. At the foot of the cross, the stub of the beeswax candle Stratis left here a few days ago. Elias picks a flat stone off the ground and sets it on the middle crosspiece. As if the grave is Stratis's own, and Elias a believer, he murmurs, "*Katevodhio*"—Godspeed.

By dawn a small band of refugees and a dog are nearing the fences of the Green Line. Neoklis's spasmodic gait no longer stands out, not amid this straggle of limpers and sloggers, even the supple Kaya hobbling in his perforated shoe. Nobody says a word. Not a breath to spare among them. A blood-and-yolk sunrise colours the crest of the one hill like a desert mesa and drips slowly down its flank. Far behind them, over the ruins, a tiny aircraft is circling—a helicopter, it seems, easier to hear than to see at this distance.

Elias has never felt more weary in his life. Yet no one, not even old Takkos, seems as gutted as Roland. His complexion is Gothic despite the dawn's colours; the cross-hatched lines in his brow seem deepened, redoubled. The sun appears now over the sea and the last few skeletal hotels a kilometre to the east, the southern limit of the beachfront strip. They're crossing a rocky plain of cropped grasses, gorse, broom, a few olive trees. And then Roland is gone. Elias looks behind. The man sits slumped against one of the trees, his head fallen back, mouth open, arms limp. Elias drops the carpet bag and runs back to him, not alerting Kaiti or the others—he wants them to hurry on, they're almost there, maybe ten minutes farther.

"Roland? Look at me! We're almost there. Roland, wake up!"

The left eye opens. Sunlight transects it from the side. The iris no longer seems blue but translucent, the pupil a flooded tunnel.

Elias is gazing down to the murky bottom in search of someone he now loves, but there's no one, nothing there, just a cavern beneath all identities and concepts, no Roland, no Kaiti, no Elias, no Cyprus or Turkey, no tribes or borders or histories, just matter, stripped clean of human tragedy, just molecules fleetingly organized.

Roland's faint voice retrieves him. "Ah, Trif . . . I dreamed I was back in Mexico." The eye re-closes.

"Roland!" Then, to keep him talking: "When were you in Mexico?"

"*Es war ein Traum* . . . a dream. Yet this dream . . . it seemed many years. I had a wife, children, much joy. Please, let me return. I can't make a step more."

"I'll carry you."

"Such nonsense! Do you hear a fly?"

Elias squints into the distance. He can't make out the chopper but he can hear it, a faint, steady drone. Soon there will be others, some flying in this direction. He grips Roland's wrist, first step for a fireman's carry. The skin is corpse-cold. He tries to find a radial pulse. Roland is murmuring, "Cold sweat . . . chest pain . . . nausea . . . numbness of arm. These clues I know. For some days, in fact. But now, worse. Many in my family—"

"There'll be doctors, Roland, just on the other side. Roland!"

"*Bitte*, you must hurry."

"We're not going to leave you. She couldn't bear it. And I . . ."

"*Ja*. I feel the same."

"I couldn't bear it."

"But this is my village . . . Tell Kaiti . . ." He says something in German that sounds like poetry. And in Greek: "*Martis mou o Theos . . . poso tis agapisa*." God alone knows how I loved her. Then, wrinkling his nose, lifting his hand: "*Bitte*, please kill me that fly!"

To sling Roland over his back and get upright is by now much harder than any toy test in a weight room, on a sports field, on a hockey rink. Games in the end just prepare you for games. *So what has prepared you for this?* Burying parents. Not wanting to bury another, a last one. *Stay . . . stay here . . .* That's it, the old song he likes you to sing, the cowboy tune, *Stay here awhile ere you leave us*. God, Germans and their Wild West fixation! *Do not hasten to bid us adieu . . .* Trif hasn't the strength or the breath to sing a word. Roland's own breaths shorten to toilsome gasps. Then nothing, not even a rattle.

He feels the last tension pass from the body and now, with the will and spirit gone, it seems heavier. He carries it step by slowing step. Ahead, Kaiti is beckoning, no voice left, while also glancing over her shoulder at the others, who are wobbling onward. She holds the carpet bag and her other hand protects her belly. She walks back a few steps to meet him, her brow already tightened in grief and her lower lip quivering, though she looks totally unsurprised. Maybe Roland told her about his heart. Maybe no further death could surprise her.

"Kaiti, I can't—I'm sorry—I can't carry him anymore."

She helps him lower the body and drag it under the boughs of a younger olive tree. They sit him up against the trunk, facing back toward the village. When she stoops to kiss his brow, her tears trickle down into his beard and glint there as if they were his.

They stumble into the main square of Deryneia at eight in the morning. It's a farm town but seems a deafening metropolis—buses, scooters, trucks and cars, all shockingly functional, revving and braking and beeping horns. Awestruck strangers approach them. In minutes a crowd gathers, uniformed schoolchildren pointing, *yiayias* with shopping baskets, men blurting into cellphones or snapping pictures, two soldiers with Uzis, an old doctor identifying himself and asking *Boro na sas voithiso?*, the ring of faces mostly pale, overfed, jabbering questions like a media mob, kettling them like riot cops, someone offering a banana, a can of Red Bull, *Stop, give them room now, let them breathe, I'm a doctor!* Neoklis squawks and clings to his mother, who is tearfully laughing. Kaya rakes back his hair and shakes hands like a homecoming celebrity, though his bloodshot eyes dart around. Elias is so weak that only the crowd holds him upright. Then his and Kaiti's hands, though locked together ever tighter, are wrenched apart. He looks around and for a moment can't find her, find the twins, find the villagers, too many strangers are crushing in, their faces eclipsing the faces he knows, his people, his family, his little nation, as if they have ceased to exist or never did.

PARIS, SEPTEMBER

A week before Eylül's thirty-fifth birthday, her sister, Meltem, reads her a piece of astonishing news. Meltem is excited too, and in her hurry she stumbles more than usual over the English *v* and *th* sounds. Eylül's post-concussion symptoms are still serious enough that she has to spend much of her time alone in a darkened room, but every morning—if it's not a setback day, and recently such days are rare—Meltem comes in with hot tea and a chilled plum, opens the curtains, kisses Eylül's olive-grey cheeks, and reads to her. Eylül lies fully dressed on the made bed with her eyes closed, strenuously listening. First Meltem reads any messages that have come in from the handful of family and colleagues who know Eylül is alive. Next, having chosen the material in advance, she will read a few items from the *Hürriyet*, then from the pro-government *Sabah*, then from the website of *The Guardian*. Lately, she also reads a few pages from a novel—just translated into Turkish—by one of Eylül's heroes, the American writer Susan Sontag. Every word that Eylül's healing brain has to process wearies it, cutting into her slim daily quota of concentration, so she desperately wants to avoid trivialities. Hard as she tries, she often fails not to scold Meltem when the girl reads things Eylül deems to be less than vital.

For half an hour each afternoon, Meltem takes dictation. Lately, along with brief replies to messages, Eylül has been dictating sentences, a few per day, exhausting, exasperating: the opening of a long article about how she came to be here in hiding, in a small but pretty flat in Paris's 10th arrondissement. It belongs to an international NGO that assists and protects journalists and other writers in danger. Eylül, Meltem, and a private nurse are also supported by the *Hürriyet*, which secretly helped get her out of Cyprus.

To think that her little sister was the first hero of the operation! Of course, crises can do more than traumatize and shatter—they can be the making of someone. But Meltem? Maybe one always underestimates a younger sibling. Yet during the hour in which the girl saw her father and older sister get run down outside a hospital, then rushed back inside by paramedics—who failed to revive her father—Meltem aged a decade, from frivolous and chattery to quietly focused, patiently determined. Realizing what must have happened, saying nothing to the distraught-seeming Kaya (who after all was with the army, his motives unknowable), she used Eylül's new cellphone to reach Eylül's main editor in Istanbul. He acted at once, no doubt backed by one of the journal's anonymous liberal benefactors. Arrangements were made with the hospital. By noon, Eylül's death was being reported along with that of her father. By the end of the day, two of her editors had arrived from Istanbul to deliver certain pledged sums in lira banknotes. The next afternoon they had her flown out covertly, at real risk to themselves and also to Eylül, who at that point was barely stabilized, back in a coma with a midbrain concussion and other significant injuries.

The editors still hope to break her story as an exclusive when the time is right, then release it as a book through their publishing arm, though increasingly the plan looks unfeasible, not so much because Eylül can barely dictate a paragraph a day but because of deepening media repression in Turkey. Maybe in two years, maybe in five. Maybe an English or French version can appear somewhere sooner.

This morning the news—news the *Hürriyet* will not be able to run, at least not yet or this frankly—comes from *The Guardian*. Greek Cypriot authorities are reporting that a group of fugitives has escaped across the Green Line, apparently after hiding for some time in the sealed ruins of Varosha. Cypriot border guards heard shooting and assumed the Turkish army was conducting exercises in the ruins. In fact, these fugitives, or refugees—some of whom claim to have survived in Varosha for years—were evicted after a Turkish assault in which at least one of them, along with several Turkish soldiers, died. It's all unclear, the reports conflicting. What is certain is that one member of the group is Elias Trifannis, a Canadian soldier missing and assumed dead since an incident last October involving Turkish troops and the "radical journalist Eylül Şahin," who was "killed just two months later in a traffic accident widely viewed as suspicious."

Meltem stops to say there are links here to previous stories about both incidents. "And here"—she turns the laptop toward Eylül, who sits up and puts on her glasses—"this must be him?" A poor-quality shot of a large but lean, dirty, beleaguered-looking man, street-mobbed by people who might be either determined fans or rabid attackers. If not for the context, Eylül wouldn't know him. Meltem watches her face but makes no comment.

Over the next few weeks, as the story simmers and then dies out, Meltem follows up for Eylül on the internet. For now, Elias is in a small town called Agios Giorgios, about as far as you can get in Greek Cyprus from the Green Line and the Turkish army. The Canadian media and authorities want to talk to him, but he has declined their overtures and ignored their threats. He refuses to give any interviews in Cyprus, either, saying that he hopes to make arrangements to publish "a fellow villager's full history of that secret place," preferring the story to emerge in that way. He is said to be living with a woman who, like him, disappeared, though several years earlier. There's also an old couple and their disabled son, who were all assumed killed back in 1974. They, however—or at least the father—seem *eager* to talk to journalists, even to badger them for more attention. The man has launched spirited if slightly incoherent attacks on those who refuse to believe that anyone could have survived in Varosha for so long. Finally, there's a Turkish army colonel who has "defected" to the Republic of Cyprus. Although he too is declining to give interviews, the Greek Cypriot media already seem very fond of him, referring to him as a hero for having "aided and protected the refugees" who were "hiding in the occupied zone."

As Meltem pauses and shakes her head, saying, "Maybe I should have trusted that man," Eylül remembers again how Kaya's face appeared above hers as she lay on the pavement, his hands open, fingers splayed out as if he meant to finish her off, while his naked eyes begged her to believe him innocent. She does finally believe. Like her American hero, she's a skeptic and a pessimist, but this latest reprieve is forcing her to reconsider a few things. Maybe not everyone who sings has her throat cut.

A month later, October, she starts to emerge from the tomb. She'll have to emerge sooner or later. Few know that she's alive, but every story breaks eventually. A spell of cool, wet weather, low cloud, sombre light, the glare not too much for her eyes and brain. It's like January in Istanbul. Overruling both Meltem and the nurse she goes out for a walk alone, nameless and unnoticed, along the Canal St-Martin—lipstick, eyeliner, a headscarf, grey raincoat over a sweater and decent jeans and black loafers. She doesn't go far. Every step depletes her and yet her heart grows lighter every step, across the arc of a small steel bridge and then back simply for the joy of crossing a bridge and returning—no metaphor, just pulsing physical fact, the joy of her mind and body's free choosing, step by step, in resurgent delight.

LOST COUNTRIES

For almost a year now Kaya has been working for the Greek Cypriot government and living in Nicosia a few blocks south of the Green Line, which runs through the centre of the city, but his Greek is still deplorable and his English little improved. *Arkadash, it is no problem!* What with his charisma and the bewitched affection of his colleagues, the language barrier simply collapses: they so want to understand him, and be understood by him, that it all works. His new friends include diplomats, journalists, executives, recording artists, local football stars, and politicians both male and female. They hardly seem to regard him as Turkish at all. Really you are one of us, they all tell him, and Kaya, only half understanding, will affably agree.

He is said to be in touch with Elias Trifannis and Ekaterini Matsakis, and rumour has it that he plans to visit them this summer on the island's far coast, but when asked about them—whether by journalists or by colleagues—he politely offers no comment, out of respect, he says, for their wish for privacy. In fact, he and they often correspond, in Turkish, via Kaiti. Just last week she sent him another family picture. Adjusting to the outside has not been easy, she writes, especially for the half-Turkish twins, but lately they've started to make friends and talk less and less about the village. In time they might barely remember it at all, except as a kind of dream, which is probably for the best, if sad in some ways. Rolande is the baby's name and she remains an excellent sleeper, a bit surprising after all she has gone through. As for Kaiti, she's looking forward to working again part time once the tourists come, leading groups to the Avakas Gorge and the Baths of Aphrodite. Trif is doing better—he's finally off the anti-anxiety drugs and working out daily, something Kaiti doesn't understand but which does seem to help him. Working on their house helps too. It's a traditional Cypriot farmhouse, long abandoned, which they're struggling to repair and re-inhabit, room by room. While arranging to have Roland's story published, Trif is also trying to write his own, although he finds the writing painful—not just the hours of sitting but also the need to remember things. Often he will take Rolande and the dog and walk down to the sea through the abandoned olive grove behind the house. For a while Kaiti and he were attempting to tend the old, orphaned trees, but they soon realized how little they knew about olive farming. Now they've apprenticed themselves to a local expert. Meanwhile (Kaiti writes) Trif has been trying to adopt the twins and secure a work permit. Various bureaucracies are making difficulties (difficulties that Kaya is now taking discreet steps to remove).

Kaya is wanted by the Turkish government for desertion, corruption, fraud, embezzlement, misappropriation of funds, dereliction of duty, insubordination, aiding and abetting the enemy, espionage, harbouring fugitives, obstructing justice, and suspicion of murdering a Turkish war hero. There can be no question of his returning to the north, or to Istanbul and his children. But his losses—of family, of home, of country—don't seem to affect him all that much. Or so his new colleagues believe. He will admit to a certain nostalgia for daily swims in the sea, but after all, the beaches of Agia Napa are only an hour's drive away. Here in Old Nicosia he belongs to a tennis club and likes to frequent the many rooftop bars and sit out with new friends, drinking aperitifs and watching the evening's first dancers while the sun sets stupendously over the Mesaoria.

One morning not long ago he returned to Deryneia. A hill town, it's the best spot from which to observe Varosha. Kaya was accompanying a dozen Greek Cypriot government and military officials who, scanning the ruins through high-powered binoculars, resembled men plotting a re-conquest. He answered their simple questions, chiefly about the condition of major buildings and roads, and he made helpful references to a large-scale map on which an NCO took notes and marked corrections. In due course, the discussion touched on his former residence, the officers' club. Through binoculars it was visible, just, between the hulks of two hotels, a dash of glittering white with the turquoise sea beyond it. Suddenly he wanted to tell them how he used to play there in the shallows with his children when they were younger, and how in the evening little Yil and Hava liked to watch the small owls in the tangerine trees, but he struggled to find the words in Greek and heard himself lapse into his beautiful mother tongue, then trail off without finishing.

People never notice when a charmer is overcome. They're too busy performing for him, auditioning for his approval, while taking at face value the exterior he's always staging—polished, winsome, witty, gracious, constantly shifting but somehow solid. Who can say what ruins lie behind it?

PLEASE

I LEFT MY SOUL IN THERE

OPEN UP

ACKNOWLEDGMENTS

I want to thank the following people for various kinds of support: actual editing, helpful conversations, encouraging words or notes, and other generous acts and gestures. Cheryl Cohen, Bernard Covo, Michael Holmes, Helen Humphreys, Smaro Kamboureli, Alice Kuipers, Maureen Lascelles, Alvin Lee, Amanda Lewis, Ginger Pharand, Anne McDermid, David McDonald, Stephen Myers, Scott Richardson, Sandra Ridley, David Ross, Alexander Scala, Helen Smith, Janice Weaver, Martha Webb, Christina Yianni, Janice Zawerbny, Irene Zouros, and Eleftherios Zouros.

Mary Huggard. Elena Heighton. Liam Fenton. John & Christina Heighton. Pelly Heighton. Esme & Alita Varvis.

I'm also thankful for the support of both the Canada Council for the Arts and the Ontario Arts Council.

Finally, inevitably, I want to thank my editor and publisher, Nicole Winstanley, for her keen insight, energy, patience, fierce belief, and advocacy on behalf of her lucky writers, now including me.